Desert Sailors series Book 4

Sea Duty

K. J. Frolander

Special Thanks

Thank you to all my dear friends and fans of Wakefield and Rivers who have encouraged me to continue writing their story. Your questions and enthusiasm keep motivating me to roll out of bed on those early mornings to write. Hopefully you won't have to wait as long for the next installment of the Desert Sailors' adventures!

Series order:

Desert Sailors
Azure Tiger
Grecian Vendetta
Sea Duty
Baghdad Green Zone
Intel Leak

CHAPTER ONE

The phone's jingle derailed Lieutenant Commander Judah Wakefield's worn trench of thought. Her core jolted at the interrupted silence that had fallen over the office. The U.S. naval officer looked up at the empty bullpen. When had everybody gone home? The security lights and her desk lamp illuminated the scribbled notes she had re-traced with blue, black, and red ink and then in an orange highlighter sometime since lunch.

A second ring. Who would be calling this late? "What time is it anyway?" Wakefield pushed her first knuckle into the corner of her right eye to relieve the building pressure. How many hours had gone into building this profile? She glanced at her watch and back to the paper with the heading Hamid Rafiq. A reference textbook lay open three-quarters of the way through with a pastel rainbow of sticky notes jutting out from previous pages.

The officer reached for the black, standard-naval-issue office telephone. It rang the third time under her hand. "Wakefield," she spoke efficiently.

"Not for long." A voice laughed on the other end of the line.

Wakefield dropped her pen and stretched far back in her office chair. "Only 13 days and 16 hours," she sighed. "David Rivers, why are you calling now? I'm meeting you for dinner in—"

Wakefield broke off as the time she had just looked at registered in her mind. "An hour ago. Oh, I'm sorry. I got caught up here."

"I hoped so." Rivers said softly. It was the voice Wakefield had come to recognize as his I'm-worried-about-my-fiancée voice.

"So, did you eat yet?" Wakefield picked up her pen again and twirled it through her fingers.

"The caterer had another showing at 1930 in Alexandria. He's really good. I chose my favorite three. You can set up another appointment and choose when you get a chance. The offer for dinner is still good though."

Judah massaged her right shoulder and sucked in her breath as she found a knot and pressed. "It'd better be, if you're still going to make me paint the new den after the day I've had."

"Mmm," Rivers purred low. "Want to talk instead?"

"Love to, but it is super-secret—need to know." Wakefield cut her eyes wryly to the side to study Rivers' picture on the left corner of her desk. Her mom had taken the snapshot two months ago just before Christmas, on the one-year anniversary of the day she and Rivers had met. Rivers' broad shoulders showed on either side of Judah as he draped his arms around her. Their pink-from-the-cold cheeks pressed together as they stood next to an eight-foot snowdrift at Judah's Minnesota childhood home. Judah's sea blue eyes sparkled with mischief and her blond hair hung in wet locks, covering the knife scar on her cheek that had brought them together. Judah remembered that as soon as the camera had flashed, she had shoved a handful of snow into Rivers' collar, and the chase was on. She had let him catch her. It had been a pleasant weekend.

"And I don't need to know." Rivers sighed as he repeated his part of the conversation they had at least twice a week.

"Not yet." Judah ran her tongue over her front teeth and glanced at her clear blue water bottle. Not even a drop left in the bottom. "Your SEAL team will probably be briefed in the next couple days. Captain Clasden won't send you off this close to the wedding, will he?"

"Probably not. I can prepare the guys from here. But if we get the go—"

"I know," Judah reached for the picture and tilted back in her chair, "we have the church for two weeks later."

"That's not what I was going to say. I still have time to go and get back if we get the call in the next four days."

"Maybe," Judah was unconvinced. "But you'd would be cutting it awfully close. My dad is catching a COD back from the carrier that Saturday morning. He can't fly in from the *Reprisal* in the Arabian Sea twice, and I want things to be just perfect. And they'd be perfect on March eighth in the Rose Garden, like we have planned. But we will do whatever we need to do."

"Where do you want to meet for food?" Rivers asked.

She could hear his engine rev as he moved with the traffic.

"I'm really more tired than hungry. Would you mind terribly if I just go back to my apartment tonight? Can we do dinner and painting tomorrow instead?"

"Of course. I'll go ahead and start taping the living room and kitchen."

"Thank you." Judah sighed heavily. These profiles weighed on her. "Tomorrow should be easier."

"Ha. In my line of work we say, 'the only easy day was yesterday'."

"God, I hope not."

Baghdad, Iraq
Presidential Republican Palace
South Dining Room
11:12 PM local time

Homer Asheed pulled the chemical analysis report he had compiled from his robe with a flourish. "I've done it." He unfolded it and passed the three-page document down the table to his dinner host.

The mustachioed Iraqi king smiled before the papers reached his hands. "So you can reproduce Arafeh Filasek's results?"

"I have a test batch that has proved successful." Asheed grinned. It had taken him three months with four separate teams of chemical engineers from different parts of the world to narrow down the process to produce an efficient eliminator. The world's newest weapon of mass destruction, WMD, as the American media liked to call them. The Husseini royal family of the male persuasion just liked to call them efficient. "In testing, day before yesterday, by the time the bomb sniffers detected that the chemical arrangement was deadly, the operators were dead." Asheed informed King Hussein.

"Excellent." Hussein clipped. The man's thick fingers shuffled the stapled papers. Asheed was certain he could have brought in a toxicology report for bleach and Hussein wouldn't have known the difference. While the king was a brilliant soldier and cruel taskmaster, he had no brain for the intricacies involved in chemical engineering. "Let's get production up and running. I want enough to cover the globe in the next two months."

Asheed practically choked back his laugh. "It will take that long to make enough for your own country." He pushed up his glasses by the rim. "It is an extended and delicate process, sir."

"Then get more people on it."

Exactly the words he wanted to hear. Asheed smiled. "I will recruit immediately, but I need funds."

"Everything I have is at your disposal." Hussein shot a darting glance at his oldest son who sat at his right hand in between them, silent until now.

"I want to take a sample to the north. We have a little border dispute on tomorrow's schedule." Qusay curled his lips to the left.

"You may take what I have on hand now," Asheed told the prince, "if, of course, you have no objection," Asheed quickly cut his eyes to check with the king. It would not do to cross him now. His temper rolled before him like a mighty army. "Qusay could begin testing the most efficient distribution for his application, such as using wind currents or a containment room."

The elder Hussein nodded once. "Design mobile labs to create this substance. Store inventory in the tunnel chambers until there is enough to distribute to the entire border at once. I want this weapon to act as an invisible shield. If the Americans dare come knocking on our door, they will run into it and die in heaps marking our boundaries."

Asheed nodded. He would figure out the details later, he just wanted access to the treasury. He could easily fold his personal expenses into the raw chemical purchases or the cost of personnel he had just received permission to hire. He smiled, he could now buy a way out for his family to escape this nation before the inevitable war began.

"And mark my words," Hussein went on in a gruff but experienced voice, "the Americans are already mounting an army to annihilate us. They desire to spread their unclean, Infidel ways to the pureness of our holy land. They are determined to teach us a lesson." The president's laugh just then scared Asheed a bit, but at least Asheed knew he was not living in denial. Saddam's cruel mouth turned up. "But we will remind them who the child is. Allah be praised."

"Allah be praised," the crew around the table echoed as expected.

Asheed began to re-think the prospect of a chemical compound of this strength in the hands of men such as those around the table. He would eke this process out until his family was settled and the production teams were in place; he would not release the final step in the process until he himself had joined his family. Away. Anywhere but here.

The general of Saddam's Special Republican Guard entered through the main double doors, inlaid with silver from Egypt. "General Mafias, excellent timing. Join us." Hussein raised his glass to the highly-decorated career soldier in his 60s. Asheed had seen pictures of what this man had done in the name of allegiance to his king, but he had never met him in person.

"Sir." Mafias clicked his heels, shut the door behind himself and strode confidently to sit on the far side of the table.

Asheed stirred his soup in a mechanical, counter-clockwise circle while he listened. He focused on the fruit basket centerpiece, hoping to be invisible while he gathered clues to exploit the others. It was what he did best.

The grapes and apples glistened as if a servant had misted them with a fine atomizer. A drop of moisture rolled seductively along the deep red skin of an apple. Asheed slowed his stir and reached to catch it before it splatted on the tablecloth. A stinging slap removed further thought.

Asheed jerked his head to the source at his left. Qusay eyes him harshly. "Later." Qusay growled. He jutted his black goatee toward the soup as if Asheed had been grabbing the fruit to eat.

Asheed shrank under the unveiled hatred in the younger man's fudge-colored eyes. Qusay's cruelty was the stuff of whispered nightmare legends in al Qaeda camps. Asheed had made the rounds of those camps teaching on the uses of chemical weapons several times. He'd heard a myriad of those whispers. His concentration drifted back to the conversation eddying around him.

General Mafias spoke in nervous, but reverent tones to King Hussein about several upcoming incursions.

"But is the next attack beyond outline form?" Saddam Hussein leaned into the table. The silver spoon in his callused hand looked as if he could squeeze it into liquid if he did not receive an affirmative answer.

Mafias' eyes squeezed shut and blinked back open. "Yes, sir. Yes, sir. My team in the so-called Zionist State has been begging for a new assignment. Bin Laden approved the plan, as proposed the second time. We have a tentative date chosen."

Saddam's eyebrows lowered and Asheed could barely distinguish his slanted eyes underneath the thick hair. "By all that praises Allah, speak clearly, man. Give me the details, or should I hook you up to battery power?" Hussein's fist rattled the wooden table. Condensation droplets sprayed from the fruit centerpiece, spreading in dark splotches on the red tablecloth.

Asheed smiled as he heard Mafias swallow from across the table. He was glad he was not in the king's crosshairs at the moment. He wouldn't be surprised if the cleaning crew found a puddle where Mafias sat.

"Yes, sir. I mean no, sir. Ugh." Hamid Mafias, greatest soldier in Iraq, squeezed out another nervous blink. His eyes flited among the men, not able to stop on any single face for more than a second. Maybe Asheed should re-think his double cross. "Bin Laden has a man prepared to fly into Tel Aviv at two hours' notice. He will lead the operation. We have 18 fully-trained operatives imbedded in al Quds (Jerusalem) who await only supplies and a plan."

Hamid seemed to gain confidence at Hussein's sly smile.

"The plan is to affix explosive material to prayer papers and slide them into the Jewish dogs' wall in the Old City. When our men are away, we will remotely detonate the blasting caps. Their Purim holiday is approaching next month. Distribution shouldn't be difficult because of the crowds, and costuming is hardly necessary. If the platform of *Qubbat al-Ṣakhrah,* the Dome of the Rock, is opened that day to the filthy Zionists, as is planned by the weak-minded Palestinian Authority, then we have a few volunteers who will plant the same explosive material strategically." Mafias was in his element by then. "We will have a high body count, lots of blood, and very little damage to the Dome or the *al Aksa* mosque. It will ignite and unify passions across the Islamic world. No matter how quickly the Israelis respond, it will not be fast enough. They will have to choose between us and their own people. Either way they choose, the chaos and death will be blamed on those black-hat Hassidic crazies, because it is happening on the Temple Mount." Mafias shrugged and it seemed to Asheed as if the old soldier thought it was the simplest plan in the world.

Saddam exhaled with a slight wheeze as he leaned against the back of his chair. The cavernous eating space dared echo his sigh only after the corner of his mouth turned up in the slightest arc. "A few Islamic tourists we can spare, and as many of those Palestinian pawns as necessary." He was nodding now. Asheed's stomach turned. He wasn't sure why he was still surprised at the family's depravity when it came to taking lives, the faithful or the Infidel.

"The detonation can take place early, if you would care to increase the body count. The men are committed to Islam's greatness."

"General," Saddam turned to pin Mafias, "Can we get an American military man under our control? If we convince the Zionists that an American is involved in the planning, even a rogue soldier, we will gain world-sympathy to our cause, dividing the forces against us. If Islam can lure even a few European countries to our side, it will throw the rest of the world into chaos as the Americans draw their line in the sand. They are preoccupied with keeping face. It is to our advantage. The Israelis will draw back from their relationship with the U.S. in fear of deception. It has been their pattern for years."

"Yes," General Mafias said as a contemplative smile grew under his steel mustache. Saddam leaned forward to compel the focus of his audience. "It will be an excellent strike on all fronts."

Qusay tapped the pads of his fingertips on the tabletop. The slash of a smile widened his bushy-bearded cheeks. "You know where their holiday we chose came from of course?" he asked. "On the first Purim, the Persian leader Haman the Agagite was tricked, and his plan to demolish the Jews from the whole of Persia was turned around by an infiltrator Jewish-dog Queen. Now Ishmael's descendants will take back what rightfully belongs to us as the firstborn son of the covenant with Allah. The holy city of Al Quds."

Saddam lifted his glass. The others hurried to follow his example.

"May I live in this body long enough to see our lands united as far as the northern shore of the Caspian Sea, and may my firstborn son sit on his throne to rule a United Middle East from the Holy City of Mecca, with the jewel of al Quds in our pocket."

"Here! Here!" Qusay's smile was more like a snarl, Asheed thought. *God help the world if that ever happens.* Germany's Hitler would be written in the history books as a playful bear cub compared to the evil that resided in Qusay Hussein.

CHAPTER TWO

"You'll pick up my gown from the cleaner's, Melia?" Judah fought to open her coat closet door over the super plush carpet in her apartment.

"Of course. I already put the receipt from the table in my diaper bag." Melia smiled sleepily. "Jack and I are going to find a park this morning." She jostled the baby on her lap to rouse the drowsy boy as she nursed him. "We'll have everything done in time to make dinner for the three of us this evening. Then I can go over the last minute checklist and rotational airport duty schedule with both of you together."

Judah buttoned her black service coat's last brass button and stared at the contented picture her younger sister and newest nephew made. Someday life would slow down and she'd stay home to nurse a young Rivers while David left for work. "Thank you for coming, Melia." Judah crossed the room with quick strides. "I couldn't have pulled this off without you." She leaned down and touched Melia's shoulder while she pecked her on the top of the head. "I'll call and confirm the block of hotel reservations, too. Grandma and Grandpa arrive on the last flight in from Tampa tonight." Judah said.

14

"Just get through your last day of work, Lieutenant Commander Wakefield." Melia shoed her toward the door. "Leave everything to me," Melia grinned. "Now go on before you're late."

Judah shrugged, "I've never been late yet." Judah dead-bolted the door behind her.

ADM Tamburillo's Office
Naval Intelligence, Suitland, VA
0910 hours

Admiral Tamburillo slammed the receiver into the phone cradle on his desk. "Three days' notice, yeah, it's considerate all right!" He squashed back the expletive that surged behind his teeth. "New Sec-Navs," he growled. Tamburillo ignored the bite of his short fingernails into the palm of his hand and pounded his polished wood desk that had been issued with the office when they appointed him Commanding Officer (C.O.) of Naval Intelligence.

"Washington Weenies wouldn't know a stupid decision if it bit them on the six and introduced itself." Tamburillo pressed the intercom button to summon his yeoman in the outer office. "Get me Commander Wakefield, A-sap."

The intercom crackled in and out with garbled words. Tamburillo sighed. It was going to be like one of God's days today— lasting a thousand years. "Doesn't anything in the Navy work anymore but her war cannons?" he mumbled and wiped his brow. When did he start sweating in March? He rolled his eyes. "About the time of the appointment of the new Secretary of the Navy whose only battlefield experience is letting his limo driver fight Beltway traffic." He answered his own rhetorical question.

The intercom broke intermittently again. Pulling in a deep breath Tamburillo bellowed, "Greenberg! Get in here."

The office door cracked open and Petty Officer Greenberg stuck his head through. "Sir?" His voice wavered. The young man was as

15

skinny as a zipper; his beak-like nose masquerading as the zipper pull. But Greenberg was as sharp as they came.

"Intercom's on the blink again. Get maintenance in here before noon." Tamburillo willed himself to a military poker face. "Grab some coffee for Wakefield and get her in here immediately. I want to see Huntingdon as soon as I'm through with the commander. Dismissed."

Greenberg stepped fully into the room, pushing the door to behind him instead of leaving. "Sir, the commander isn't here yet." The kid's voice dropped tentatively. "You're sure she was coming in today?" With her wedding this weekend, I thought—"

"Yes, I'm sure," Tamburillo snapped and threw the petty officer a dark look. He kept track of 547 naval personnel, 204 world-wide intelligence-gathering operations, a multi-million dollar budget, 2 ex-wives, and 3 kids every day. "I did not give her the day off. Where is she?"

"According to the morning traffic report, there was an accident en route from her residence, sir. I've tried her cell. No answer, sir." Greenberg shrugged and his black eyebrows puckered together.

"You don't think she was hurt?" Tamburillo felt his gut lurch.

"You wanted to see me, Admiral?" the alto-feminine voice of his query sounded behind Greenberg. Wakefield stepped around the enlisted man still in her winter coat and carrying her briefcase.

"Where have you been, Commander? You are 75 minutes late." Tamburillo thundered. "This is not a drop-in daycare center."

A smile played at her lips and it irritated him. She always managed to stay level-headed when he yelled. It probably meant she had a good excuse, just like the only other time she'd been MIA from the office. The CIA had shanghaied her TAD to Italy without telling him.

"Traffic, sir. There was an accident on my way in." She stiffly awaited his response.

"You've never heard of a traffic report?"

Still staring at the wall behind his head, the small smirk had not dissipated. She probably didn't even know it was there. She was, after all, getting married in three days. Her cover tucked under her arm, Wakefield's blond hair was pulled into that braid she wore that looked like a seahorse spine. "It wouldn't have done any good, sir. The accident happened immediately in front of me. I had to give a police report."

"You've never heard of a cell phone?"

"Dead battery, Admiral. I used the phone in the police cruiser and left a voicemail, sir. Eighty-five minutes ago."

Tamburillo stared and she didn't flinch. She never did. "Don't let it happen again."

She broke protocol to jerk her eyes in a quarter-second glance at his face. "Aye-aye, sir. I will strive to prevent all Beltway accidents in the future, sir."

P.O. Greenberg stared openly at the two of them, as he stood behind her. Tamburillo snorted. Sometimes it was good to keep his command guessing. He shuffled three pages on his desk, just to hear the sound.

"At ease, Wakefield," he told her. "Greenberg, take her coat and hop to that coffee. Dismissed." The kid grandly helped the officer shed her covering and closed the door without a sound. If Greenberg had not been so timid, his silent feet would have made him great as an operator in their field.

Wakefield's smile came on radiantly. "Sorry, I had you worried, sir." Her blue eyes looked into him. She had a sixth sense about people that he had never been able to duplicate in himself. "I always enjoy our little tete-a-tetes for the enlisted people. You've never quite grasped that this crew doesn't need to fear you to follow orders. They comply because they admire you, sir."

Tamburillo looked at the commander. "Have a seat, Judah." He threw his hand toward the two barrel-back chairs across from his desk. Theirs had been a relaxed relationship since she had introduced him to Jesus three years earlier. "You may not have the same opinion as the staff when I finish."

"What is it, Admiral?" She chose the seat closest to him. He felt a coward, but kept his seat behind the desk in order to have something between them.

"I just got off the phone with SecNav." Tamburillo laced his fingers. "Your orders came through this morning." She showed no reaction. "You are being transferred to the USS *Theodore Roosevelt*, mid-deployment. It's a six-month assignment, and it's renewable. Your flight was to leave in the morning."

Wakefield's skin paled and her left eyebrow twitched, but she did not recoil. Tamburillo continued. "I was able to explain about your impending nuptials, and SecNav agreed to compassionate leave until Saturday—only because you're on the President's calendar of events. You're on the 1500 flight from Andrews AFB on the eighth."

Her chin trembled and her knuckles whitened at the grip she held on the carved arms of his chair. The muscle in her jaw flexed.

"Judah?" Tamburillo prompted. No response. "Lieutenant Commander Wakefield?" he said, upping his volume. Where was Greenberg with that coffee?

She cleared her throat as if there had been no long silence. "My wedding is at 1330, sir. I can't change the time. My father can't be here until 1100 that morning."

Tamburillo watched his most-collected junior officer struggle for control. "Why don't you and Rivers go before a judge tomorrow? Shoot, I can marry you even." Wakefield's back stiffened and she met his eyes again. "Then you can have your ceremony when your father arrives. You can have at least a few days together to remember at sea."

Wakefield's head shook back and forth in a tiny movement. "Thank you though, sir. We're going to do this the right way, sir. The way I've planned. One of my fathers will be present at my wedding, and we are *not* moving the ceremony to Arlington."

Tamburillo cut his eyes to the door. How long did two cups of coffee take? Wakefield had hit the wall of her father's death one more time. As long as Tamburillo had known her, he'd watched her fight against his ghost. It was the catalyst to her perfectionism, the thing that made her a good leader and excellent linguist and analyst. But wasn't 23 years a long enough fight? She needed to bury him.

Tamburillo tapped his feet under the desk. Today was not the day to mention it. He swallowed hard. He would miss her. It was unlikely that he would still be stationed at Suitland, Maryland if she happened to be transferred back to headquarters at the end of her tour. There was too much shaking going on across all branches of the military these days.

"Go ahead and pack up your office. Transfer your cases to Huntingdon. He can redistribute among those whom the SecNav has not yet transferred out." Tamburillo pushed his chair back from the desk with his hands. "Take the rest of the morning to say your good-byes and go rearrange your wedding. Please." He stood, and she followed on what appeared to be automatic pilot. "We'll all see you at the ceremony."

Her body looked weighted on the right as she stood holding her briefcase.

"Dismissed, Commander."

USS *Reprisal*
Arabian Sea
1726 hours local

Admiral Isaac Graham closed his Bible and blew out his breath until his lungs ached. The man responsible for the front lines of the War on Terrorism looked at his watch. Nineteen minutes before the appointed hour. "God, it's a heavy load. But you have promised to bear my burdens. So, I cast them on you and expect that you will fulfill your word." The book thunked with a metallic echo on the desk in Graham's small but well-appointed at-sea cabin. He stood, smoothed his khaki work uniform and watched the final sliver of orange disappear on the western horizon of a region in turmoil.

"God, give me your wisdom." He gripped the window frame with chilly fingertips. "Sending in this wave of elite tier-one operators as scouts is needed to set the groundwork for the campaign to free these oppressed people. I know that setting captives free is what you do. And this feels right, yet I hate the cost to families of their husbands, brothers, sons, and fathers. Father, I trust you to give me the specifics on how to set the Iraqis' hands free while you work on setting their hearts free."

A phrase from the scripture he had just been reading tumbled through his mind. "…the wise men came from the East…the wise men came from the East."

Graham gasped and turned from the window, stretching for the telephone at the same time. "It's brilliant!" he mumbled. He released the phone from its protective hanging box. "Why didn't we think of it before? CIC (Combat Information Center)." Graham ordered into the phone.

"Jonsey? Admiral Graham here." Graham smacked his lips. "Have you tried to configure this infiltration from east of Baghdad instead of south?"

"No, sir," the disembodied voice drawled in his ear. "We have a contingency plan for the northwest."

Graham could almost hear the tick of the colonel's brain as he considered the possibilities, the terrain, the air support capabilities, the retreat options. It was one of the perks of admirality, as he liked to call his rank; even the off-the-crib-wall ideas were given respectful consideration because of the stars on his shoulders. Nobody just says "no" to an admiral.

"The rock mountain region will be tough on ankles and equipment, but sir," Lt Col Jonsey paused and his voice lightened, "They'd never see us comin'." Jonsey gave a jolly laugh.

Graham turned toward a rapping sound at the metal hatch of his cabin. "Take an extra hour, Jonsey. Confer with the Team leader. I have every confidence that your SEALs and Rangers will be safer and will be ready for anything you throw at them."

The knock came a second time. "Admiral?" a far-away and unfamiliar voice called.

"That is all, Colonel." Graham pushed the phone away. His spirit felt light. "Thank you, Lord," he whispered. Quickly glancing over his desktop for classified material lying out, he called, "Enter."

A dungaree-clad Master Chief shut the hatch behind himself. Graham tried to place him. His wide face boasted the wrinkles of a full lifetime at sea. "Master Chief Logan, sir." Graham read the man's insignia as the ship's master-at-arms. "Sorry for the intrusion, sir. I wasn't sure when you were leaving for the wedding."

M.C. Logan carried flat in his arms a five-inch deep 16- by 20-inch green leather case that had seen better days. Graham could smell the old must from eight feet away. The metal hinges and clasps were black-tarnished silver.

Graham chuckled. "How'd you know about my daughter's wedding, Master Chief?"

Logan's face spread in a grin that looked too youthful for his wrinkles. "You're kidding, sir. She's breaking 4,000 men's hearts on this ship. About 300 of us enlisted men were around August before last when she investigated the serial murders on board. We all went in on a gift for her, for clearing us and all." Logan held out the old green box.

Graham eyed one of the oldest men serving on the carrier and took the gift. He remembered Judah telling the story of the August investigation just before September 11. Naval Intel had pointed to the *Reprisal* as being a murderous vessel. Four sailors had gone missing in three ports in a row. The crew had been at each other's throats and morale was low until Judah had spent a month on board profiling the murderer and winning a shoot-out contest on the fantail every weekend, beating even Captain Ellsworth, a former top-gun naval aviator, turned sniper, turned ship's captain, with a couple of other stops in between.

"Boy, that is a month I'll never forget," M.C. Logan said. With a twinkle in his green eyes, he gestured to the box. "It's a pair of dueling pistols for the newlyweds." He chuckled. "Antiques from Rota, Spain."

Graham felt himself lean forward. Surely he had misunderstood. There was the master chief's raspy guffaw again. "Dueling pistols?" he asked, flipping the left clasp open first. He had heard correctly.

"We wanted to make sure Commander Rivers has a fighting chance, sir."

Graham glanced up with raised eyebrows. "You've seen his designator? He's a SEAL."

M.C. Logan clamped his wrinkled lips closed in a smile. "I know, sir."

CHAPTER THREE

David Rivers sat in a black short-sleeved T-shirt on the front porch swing of the new house he had purchased for his bride. The swing creaked comfortingly under his planted feet like the one at his grandmother's house in California. "God, I need answers. And fast." His tiny movements did not even shadow the painted plank floor. The sun had set almost two hours earlier. When he had sat down for a moment at dusk, he had not thought to turn on the porch lamp.

"Is this just pre-wedding jitters or are you warning me that I shouldn't marry Judah?" A single tear dropped to his goose-flesh forearm. It was the first utterance of the words that had plagued his last six nights. "I mean, it's not too late." Even as he said it, Rivers felt a giant hole open up in his heart, as if his blood and flesh had swirled down a bathtub drain.

In their new yard, Rivers watched in the dim light of the rising moon, a pair of birds land on a narrow, naked bough of the giant Scarlet Oak that took up most of the front lawn. They squawked at each other in black silhouette and one flew away.

"What are you guys doing back up here? Shouldn't you be back in Florida with the rest of the snow birds?" David wondered aloud.

Rivers' Bible lay beside him on the long swing. He didn't need to open it to remember the words he had just read. Matthew 19:11. "…and some choose not to marry for the sake of the Kingdom of Heaven. Let anyone who can, accept this statement." Jesus' very own words. *…and some choose not…for the sake of the Kingdom. The sake of the Kingdom.*

David Rivers picked up the closed paperback words of God. The cold cover felt slick with freezing humidity. "I," he had to stop and clear his throat. But he did not fool himself. It was more a pause to gather courage which scattered in every direction away from him. "I will do whatever you ask of me, Father."

He pressed the book into his chest and held on.

"If loving Judah as my wife would cause me to turn away from you, or even to love you one ounce less, then I don't want it."

As he stared at the silhouette of the grand oak without seeing it, the second bird rose on silent wings. One gentle swoop before soaring into the blackness out of view in the direction of the first bird.

The empty branch wiggled up and down. The only movement in the darkness.

A pair of low-slung headlights turned into the cul-de-sac. The deep growl of the engine, a Mustang's powerful V-8, slowed. Rivers vaguely remembered various neighbors pulling into their garages, the lights inside homes coming on. They were probably sitting down to take-out dinners or eating leftovers from Styrofoam boxes. The neighborhood was made up of all young, two-income families. The few children he knew about were day-care age.

The Mustang pulled into the driveway, quite naturally, he thought. Yet it was not natural. It was the first time they had been alone together at their new house. Real estate agents, friends, and sisters were all missing.

Judah slammed the car door and her heels clicked fast on the walk. She hadn't tucked her keys in her purse; they jingled a familiar sound in her hand. She didn't even slow through the cracked and sloped, second-to-last section of sidewalk. That was Judah Wakefield, charge straight ahead, tackle consequences later, if they dared to rear their heads.

One foot planted on the lowest wooden step, the other hanging, she stopped her assault on the front door. She'd just seen him.

"Hi." Rivers couldn't find strength in his SEAL-toned body for more.

"David?" Judah touched the roof support next to the stairs as she squinted in his direction. Her voice sounded as nasal and congested as his. "I've been calling for hours. Are you all right?" Her fingers drifted down the painted wood support, and she finished her step.

"I don't know." He blinked long. She had covered half the distance to him on silent feet when he opened his eyes again.

Her figure was lovely, even under a winter coat. Now just an arm's length away, David longed to touch her, but the weight of his hands seemed too heavy to bear. Black wells dipped beneath her eyes. *She knows?*

Judah stopped as her quads hit the swing. She stood between his planted feet, one warm finger followed the tear track on his face. "So you already know then?" she asked.

God give me your strength, Rivers pleaded silently. He nodded. Her face blurred as water gathered in his eyes, seeking freedom.

She sank to her knees in front of him, one arm sliding to the outside of each of his legs. "I am so sorry, David. It's going to be so hard on both of us. I know though, that we'll both come out on the other side better and stronger than ever."

He looked into her black-rimmed eyes. "You think so? It sure doesn't feel like it now." He traced the white scar on her cheek. He still felt like he could have prevented it, but the guilt was just a memory. "What about the wedding plans? It's only three days out."

"I called my sister this morning and rearranged the reception and the ceremony. She's been calling everyone on the guest list today."

"You called this morning?" He stiffened. "Without talking to me first?"

Her eyebrows raised into peaks. "I told you I've been trying to get a hold of you since Admiral Tamburillo gave me my orders."

The 29-degree warm spell the Greater D.C. area had been experiencing suddenly felt chiseled from a North Atlantic iceberg. "What orders?" Rivers asked. They were obviously not on the same page. Maybe in completely different books, in different languages.

"I thought you said you already knew."

Rivers swallowed. "What orders?" he parroted.

Confusion wrinkled Judah's forehead as she stared up at him. He could feel the muscles in her arms tense through his jeans. "I'm to report to Andrews Air Force Base for the 1500-hours flight on Saturday. I'm being deployed to the Arabian Sea for six months of sea duty." She shook her blond head slowly as her brow hooded her eyes. "What were *you* talking about?"

The silence lasted too long, but he could not wrap his mind around any words, much less the right ones.

"David, you're scaring me. Why have you been crying? Why are you sitting on the porch, in the dark, in short sleeves in the dead of winter?" Her neck seemed to stretch toward him swan-like.

"I'm not sure this is the right thing."

"What—sitting out here? Being alone here at the house? What?"

"Getting married," he whispered. Would the quiet words make them more palatable? He heard her breath leave her. No.

The tendons in her throat tightened and released. "Now or ever?" He felt her arms quiver where she lay draped over him. Please say *now*, her eyes begged him. "I don't think I can live through another broken engagement." Judah confessed. Slowly she slid away from him until they were no longer touching.

With her dress-uniformed knees curled under her, Judah dropped to her side until she was sitting flat on the porch. Her feet moved around to the front and she folded them Indian style. She scooted away from him twice and then met his eyes.

"You don't love me?" she asked. "Please help me understand. When did you start thinking this way?"

Judah seemed remarkably calm. He didn't know what he had been expecting, but this certainly wasn't it. Rational talking he could deal with. "Last Thursday, I had to do some research on Stockholm syndrome. It got me thinking about that first mission we shared."

Judah squinted her black-rimmed stormy eyes. "Stockholm, as in when people are held captive they begin to bond in somewhat unnatural or unhealthy ways because of shared experiences?"

"Simplified, yes." Rivers nodded. Of course she would be familiar with it. She was a psychological profiler. "I wonder if that is what happened to us. We began bonding as Filasek's hostages and followed the pattern of male-female relationships until here we sit."

Her face was a mask while she processed. "It was traumatic," she nodded. "But I don't think Stockholm syndrome applies. First, we were not hostages. We could leave at any time. And we did, as God directed."

Her eyes felt like lasers as they searched his heart. "What else?" she asked.

Rivers flexed his fingers. Their relationship had already changed. Now he knew why Judah Wakefield was good at her job. She had an ability to compartmentalize personal feelings during an interrogation.

"Do you love me?" she prompted.

"That may be the source of my problem." Rivers looked away, not able to stand the knowledge that he had caused the pain etched in her eyes.

"Did you ever love me?"

David shook his head. He had misspoken. For a man who valued words as much as he did, he had made a muddy mess tonight. "I love you, Judah. I think I may love you too much."

"You're afraid you've misplaced your priorities?"

Rivers shivered. If only it were just that. "I think that you are the price for which I might betray God. I think I must give you up for the sake of the Kingdom."

Judah inhaled deeply. The smallest smile turned up her lips. The lipstick was gone, only the outline remained. "I think you just have a Christianized version of cold feet."

He opened his mouth to deny it. Judah's raised hand stopped him from breaking in.

"You are free to go," she said. "If you need to. Your well-being and relationship with God are what is most important to me. If you will move closer to His love without me or with someone else, then go." That drew his full attention. "I love you, David Rivers. The preciousness of the treasure you are on the inside has called this love out of me. I love you with a love that will always belong to you, because it exists only because you do."

Judah's lips disappeared inside her mouth, showing an impression of her braces-straightened teeth. "You can have both, you know." She tilted her head to the side. "That is part of a wife's job: to help her husband love God first-most."

Rivers looked at her fully. He had never seen this woman before.

Judah rubbed her shin, covered only in black slacks. She must be freezing. "Do you want to come in?" he asked.

"I'm going to my apartment now." She stood gracefully. "Please pray tonight and we'll take action in the morning. You know how I feel, but you are the head of the household. We'll do whatever you decide."

Baghdad, Iraq
Republican Palace
2:18 AM

Qusay Hussein turned from the private liquor cabinet in a rage. "How did that horrid little imp create this formula?" He cursed, knocking back his fifth bourbon in three hours. "Filasek was a paranoid freak who did not deserve the intelligence Allah bestowed on a frog." Qusay hated unworthy people, especially dead ones, to receive his father's praise.

The elder prince of Iraq clenched his fist, surrounded by rich woods and fine fabrics in his salon, and shook his head. Like a great grizzly bear, he gargled a roar of rage that had begun turning in his belly since 28 hours earlier at the dinner meeting. "I got relieved of the imp, now the gnat, Asheed, buzzes around my head."

Filling his shot glass with another two fingers of amber fire, Qusay stomped heavily to the lounging sofa in front of the stone fireplace. He threw himself into its plush pillows, sloshing his drink

"What is it with these men who try to usurp my place?" he muttered. "I will crush that sneaky gnat. He will not betray us like Filasek did to the Americans." His language slurred even though he spoke with care.

A woman slithered sleepily through the doorway. Qusay caught her movement out of the corner of his eye. As he turned on his elbow where he lounged, she leaned into the doorframe and slid her fingers suggestively up its length. "Come back to bed, Love," she intoned in formal Persian. Jarrah, from Iran, did not speak the Arabic he preferred.

The churning resumed in his stomach. He tightened his fingers around the smooth glass. The woman had been living in the palace for 11 months. Why could she not honor him enough to learn a few phrases in his language?

Jarrah thrust her lower lip out. It was still painted red from their dinner together. "Come now, Qusay. I am cold without you."

"Try putting on some clothes, woman," he spat. "Or fastening your robe." A familiar tickling began at the dip in his collarbone. The prince scratched through his shirt at the spot. His nails tore at the fabric to relieve the itch. "Get out!" his anger boiled over.

She stood still as if she had not heard him. "I said, get out!" Qusay screeched. Leaning fully into the couch on his right elbow, he drew back his left arm and hurled the glass at her head.

It shattered against the wall a half-meter from his target. Liquid spattered and dripped.

Qusay cursed. Jarrah blanched. "Ask my first wife about women who order me about like a dog and do not obey me." Qusay's voice dropped low as he sat up.

His head spun as he tried to remember where he put his weapon through the haze of alcohol. It had been pushing into his waist earlier. Where had he been standing when he took it off? "Cursed alcohol."

When he looked up from his standing position, Jarrah still rooted to the Persian carpet, was splattered with shards of sparkling glass and bourbon. A drop of red had appeared on the side of her chin. By her drawn brow and wrinkled nose, Qusay assumed she had not noticed it yet.

"I thought you said your first wife had died," she babbled.

Rage exploded. He flew toward her with his fingers curving into claws. *Her neck. Get to that thin neck and she will quiet,* something inside him screamed.

She back-pedaled into the hall. "I'm sorry. I'm sorry." She held her hands up defensively. "Please don't hurt me," she whimpered in Persian. Her chin quivered and the drop of blood rolled, gravity pulling it to the floor.

Her skin felt cool under his hot hands. The snap had a pleasant higher pitch than usual.

Her body thudded to the floor. The quiet was blissful.

Qusay slammed the door to his salon. With a flat palm, he smeared the bourbon into the wall where the stain dripped toward the carpet

CHAPTER FOUR

Yorkshire Apartments, Washington, DC
Judah Wakefield's Residence
7 March 2003
0504 hours

J udah Wakefield turned over for perhaps the fifty-fourth time
since midnight. Between her spinning mind and baby Jack waking
up every two hours, sleep had never settled over her. Drowsily,
she pushed her hair out of her face and reached for the alarm clock.
She brought it close to her face to read. "Zero five hundred," she
groaned, "I didn't think you'd ever get here."

In the predawn grey that filtered into her bedroom, Judah's
wedding dress hung ghost-like on her open closet door. Turning
away, she pulled wrinkled running clothes out of the laundry basket,
and sucked in a deep breath. "Not my will, but yours be done."
Judah leaned into the strength of the words Jesus had uttered at
Gethsemane before walking to his death. But she couldn't tell if she
was really at peace or stuck in denial.

The soft, grey Marine T-shirt with its tattered collar and faded
letters went over her head first. It had been her biological father's
and she needed the familiar comfort it provided.

She grabbed a Navy sweatshirt to throw over it, after coffee. She
plunked down on the unmade bed to lace up her Adidas runners.
She could taste the velvet smoothness of her first cup of coffee

already. Two creams, two blue sweeteners. Her mouth watered for that comforting morning ritual. Pressing her fists into swollen eyes, she stood, "And I need it this morning."

"More than you need me?" The quiet question of her Lord washed through her mind.

"Of course not," she whispered.

"Let me fulfill that comfort need this morning, Judah."

Her mouth watered in defiance.

"I trust you to do it. I'll drink water until you tell me otherwise." Judah pushed open her door, hoping not to disturb her sister or baby Jack who were asleep again in her guest room.

A soft intake of breath sounded in the living room. She made herself small at the corner between her door and the open room. She categorized it as male from the pitch. Coming from the direction of the recliner by the window. Having heard no commotion of a break-in while she was awake all night, she relaxed her instinct of hiddenness prone to all sniper-trained officers, and she moved into the room. Her eyes adjusted to the darkness of the west-facing room.

Rivers had let himself in. She had woken him by walking into the room. Judah chuckled. "Always a SEAL on alert." Her voice sounded raspy.

"Hmm. You too." The back of the chair came upright, and he resettled himself. "How far you running this morning?"

"Probably do an hour." She shrugged. He always asked for mileage. She always answered in time.

"You up for company?" He stood, and she moved into the kitchen.

Flipping on the light, she asked, "How long have you been here?"

He followed her to the cupboard. "Since zero-three-thirty." He was dressed in running clothes, too. She filled her glass from the gallon of spring water next to the fridge and saw that her sister had wrapped up the dinner she'd not been able to stomach the night before.

Eyeing Rivers over the rim as she gulped the water down, she winked at him. Setting the empty glass on the counter, Judah wiped a trickle from the corner of her mouth. "You can come if you want to. Just don't slow me down."

Rivers snorted. "Just try to keep up." He reached for her car keys while she grabbed her purse.

On the trail near the parking lot at Annandale Park, Wakefield stretched while her breath froze in white puffs in front of her face. She sneaked a peak at Rivers' face. He looked at peace. He had his answer, but she could not work out what he knew. He would be at peace just being obedient to the Lord, whether it included her or not.

Curiosity nagged her, but she was determined to let him wait until he was ready to speak. A surprising number of joggers braved the chill. A woman dressed entirely in pink spandex looked hungrily at Rivers as he lunged to stretch his calves against a bare pine. The blonde shot her a slanted eye and a curled lip. Rivers missed the entire exchange.

Wakefield rolled her eyes and looked at David with fresh eyes. His normal #2 razor cut had grown out longer than usual at her request for the wedding pictures. The coarse lightest brown thatch was perhaps two-thirds of an inch now, almost long enough to lie flat without coaxing.

His toned body bulged in the blue Navy sweat suit that proclaimed in gold lettering his status as a SEAL. His shoulders formed a platform for his thick, corded neck. His lips, pink from the cold, turned up as she studied them, remembered them. She jerked her gaze to his blue-green eyes. They were laughing with silent pleasure.

"I like it when you look at me like that," he said.

Judah swallowed to compose her voice. "Will I ever be allowed to again?"

"I'm sorry," he cooed, pulling her into his arms. He buried his face in her hair at her neck. "I was going to go through the process I went through last night while we ran."

"That's fine. I just want to read the last page of the book first." She pulled away to look at his eyes for some clue.

Rivers dug in his pocket and removed a scrap of fabric. He handed it to her. A yellow ribbon. "Yes, you can look," Rivers said. "Yes—yes to everything. Just make sure you come back to me safely."

Wakefield's world tilted right-side-up again. Her fingers curled around the silky half-inch wide strand of ribbon. Reaching for his face, she touched the dimple in his unshaved cheek. "I'm glad." She smiled. "Let's run and you can tell me of your grapple with the Angel of the Lord, Jacob." Judah grinned and swatted his chest.

The adrenaline flowed freely at mile six. She led their pace while he concentrated on talking. They had sped up to pass the woman in pink and her dog miles earlier.

Rivers had been quiet until they were out of her ear-shot. Maybe he'd seen her after all.

"So," he spoke on the four-beat exhale rhythm. "I had been praying and reading for hours, looking for something to calm my spirit. Then you pulled up with your transfer announcement. I thought it was God's answer."

Rivers shrugged. Judah was glad she knew the outcome. Or she'd not be able to process this information with any sense of order.

"I gave you up completely, right after you left. I was sure it was over. I was just going to wait until this morning to let you know. I cried, I mean really cried and fell asleep. At two, I woke up from a dream.

"God allowed me to experience the entire Abraham/Isaac story from his perspective. It was so real, Judah, down to the smell of fear. Isaac was really sweating it."

"So was I." Judah admitted. "I gave my fear to God 26 times. And that was just on the drive back to my apartment.

Rivers chuckled. "I know what you mean." He paused as they passed an older couple holding hands while they fed a half-dozen pigeons from a green park bench. "I feel like God has given you back to me." Rivers breathed in for four paces. "I will cherish you now more than ever because of it. Plus, I know that God is in the right place in my heart."

The cold air slapped Wakefield's open-mouth grin, hurting her teeth. "That's worth every bit of last night's heartache to me. Him first, is what I need from you."

"Keep reminding me?" he requested.

"You got it," Judah smirked. *Probably often more than you want*, she added to herself.

Rivers pointed across the street from the running trail to a grouping of pastel shops. "Want to stop for coffee?"

She felt the Lord smile. "Yes. I'd like that very much."

CHAPTER FIVE

1183 Whitby Lane, Richmond, VA
The Rivers' Residence
8 March 2003
1125 hours

Judah Wakefield-soon-to-be-Rivers, spun like a princess in her long, white wedding gown in the living room of their new house. Ella Fitzgerald sang of love on the CD player. David Rivers caught her at the apex of her twist away and reeled her back in. Laughing in gulps, Judah couldn't remember a morning when she'd had more fun. The crowd of 49 guests buzzed with excitement.

"Last call for cake or punch." Melia announced from the island in the kitchen. Judah could barely see a sliver of the frosty grape bridesmaid's gowns she'd chosen for her sisters to wear.

Ella repeated the last line and a saxophone faded into quiet. "Count me in for cake to-go and a dance with the bride," a voice boomed from the front entrance as an eddy of cool air slurried around Judah's bare arms.

Judah's smile grew. "Daddy made it," she whispered and patted the service ribbons and heavy medallions that clanked on Rivers' mess dress uniform. Stretching up to peck his cheek, a camera flash went off, again. If annoying, the photographer was at least thorough. "I'll be right back."

Judah Wakefield could not squash the grin in her cheeks as she maneuvered in the crowded space and Tony Bennet crooned about flying to the moon with love. But then there was no reason to try to mask her excitement. Admiral Isaac Graham had already set his bag down at the door. He wedged his cover under his arm and Judah walked into his outstretched arms. "I didn't think you were going to make it." She squeezed his shoulders tight. "We leave for the White House in about eight minutes." The flash went off behind her again. The foyer mirror reflected the blinding light into her eyes.

"Corporal Stanley said there was a plan change and brought me here. What's going on? I thought cake comes after the kiss."

Judah saw her mother approach in the mirror and backed out of the admiral's arms so her mother could greet her sea-faring husband properly. The yellow satin-and-lace mother-of-the-bride dress wrinkled at her waist with Graham's snug grip. "I'm so glad you made it." Judah's mother sighed and received his kiss.

"That seems to be the theme for the day." Graham's questioning look caught Judah's eye over her mother's shoulder.

"I'm shipping out at 1500, today, to join the Carrier Strike Group you're leading. But I'll be aboard the *Theodore Roosevelt*."

"Ahh. The *Big Stick*."

"And I needed you to be at my wedding." Judah felt Rivers' arm curl around her waist.

"So I get to see my bride all dressed up before the wedding," Rivers said. Judah leaned into him, grateful for his positive attitude. His wedding gift to her, she knew.

"Here's your cake, Pop." Judah's second sister's husband joined the growing group at the front door. He held a squirmy three-year-old Emma in a flower girl dress in his left arm and passed the purple and white cake on a paper plate with his other hand.

Graham winked as he accepted the cake just as Melia called out, "It's 11:35 people! Let's get the caravan rolling." The music cut off abruptly. "Directions to parking for the Rose Garden are on the credenza by the door. Pick up one per family on your way out."

Graham winked again as Melia stuck her head in the doorway to check on the stack of directions. "When did my quiet one learn to do all this?"

Melia chuckled and hugged him. "Hi, Daddy. I'm so glad you made it." She twisted in his embrace to look at Judah. "Judah's been bossing me around since I was born; I learned from the best."

The family with five different last names guffawed at the truth of it. "Hey! You're supposed to be nice to me today." Judah chuckled.

"I was," Melia sent the group into further degeneration as she threw the parting words over her shoulder to expedite things elsewhere.

The group milled toward the bedroom that would one day be the nursery, to stuff themselves into their winter armor. Several guests still crammed in last bites of cake on their way out. Judah's nephew, Justin, burst in, weaving through the group, chasing David's seven-year-old niece, Lauren.

"Honey," Graham looked at Judah, "Have you talked to the SecNav about getting an extension?"

Judah's smile fell as she remembered again that she would be spending her honeymoon with 5,000 other sailors instead of the one sailor she wanted. "SecNav's orders," she replied softly. "He already gave me three days."

"What about Secretary of Defense Shulman? The President even?"

Judah sighed. He was only speaking things she'd already considered, but it was such a temptation. "I don't want any special treatment, Daddy. It is my duty to go. What kind of officer would I be to shirk my duty for self-indulgence? Not one worthy of this man, that's for sure." She patted David's hand at her waist and threaded her fingers over his.

The cake plate was still in Graham's hand at the too-high-to-be-comfortable height at which he'd accepted it. "You saved the President's life last year, surely that is worth something."

Judah smiled and guided the group from the path to the door. "It's his Rose Garden I'm using for the ceremony."

A slow, sad smile appeared on the admiral's lips. His eyes softened at the same rate at which his shoulders dropped into a relaxed pose. "I'm proud of you, Judah Wakefield. You've been a good daughter, a good officer, and will make David here," he paused to clap David on the shoulder, "a good wife."

"People!" Melia burst in, "what are you doing still standing around?" She had her coat on and carried Jack in a baby seat in her right hand, toting Judah's white fur stole in her left. "Get your coats and get out."

Graham chuckled, "She would've made a good officer too."

As Rivers placed the thick fur around her shoulders, Judah reflected on her father's blessing. It was kind, and much of her ability reflected his fathering more than any effort on her part. It just didn't feel quite right. She grimaced as she made the connection: The words sounded more like a funeral benediction than a wedding blessing.

Rivers kissed her cheek, careful of her make up. "Let's go."

White House Lawn
1420 hours

"Sweetheart," Rivers squeezed his bride's hand as the last of the well-wishers in the line moved away. "You're going to miss your flight. We've got to get on the road." Not that he wanted her to go. But he knew the fallout of missing a movement.

Judah pressed herself into his chest. "Dear, sweet husband," she grinned. "I love calling you that." Her blue eyes sparkled like sunlight on whitecaps of the sea. "President Bush is on his way to Andrews too. He offered me a ride just now. Is it okay that I go with him?"

Rivers heard a chop-chop whirring of a helo warming its engines. "It'll give us a few more minutes here."

The engine noise grew. "That wouldn't be your ride now, would it?"

Judah grinned wide, all of her teeth showing. "Well it's not exactly Cinderella's pumpkin coach, but it'll do."

Rivers threw back his head and laughed loud. He was going to miss her. "Only you would finagle a ride to your next duty station in *Marine One.*"

"Pretty cool, huh?" Judah giggled.

River kissed his wife fully. "It is very cool," he whispered into her hair. "I'll make sure that annoying photographer your sister hired gets a couple of shots of you leaving."

"She's your sister now, too." Judah laughed.

"I didn't say your sister was annoying, just the photographer." Rivers hurried to correct.

Judah's smile crackled mischievously. "That's because you don't know her well enough yet. Wait until she comes over to clean up the reception mess this afternoon."

A pair of men in black suits, ties, and sunglasses strolled purposefully over the England-green winter carpet of lawn. "Where do secret service men shop, a Hollywood backlot?" he asked.

"Your duffle, ma'am?" the slightly shorter of the two bulky men asked. His mustache gave him the appearance of a boy playing dress up.

"It's still in the limo." Judah pointed to the driveway where the sleek black car waited.

"I'll get it." Rivers straightened away from her.

"They can get it, right?" his wife turned to Mr. Mustache.

"Let me. You still have to say good bye to your folks." Rivers smiled. Sadness threatened to overwhelm him. "Let me serve you in this way." How could the happiest day of his life also be the saddest?

He pecked her lips once more and pinned his clanking medals with his left hand, as he jogged to the car. Rivers patted the trunk twice with his white-gloved hand and the driver popped it open from the front seat.

Untying the duffle's cord closure left-handed, Rivers reached inside his breast pocket where he had kept Judah's wedding and engagement rings all morning. "Where is it?" he wiggled his fingers further inside until he felt the silk of a ribbon.

He pulled out an eight-inch length of new yellow ribbon. Knotting it into a loop with two tails, he tucked it into the Army-green duffle bag with LT CDR Wakefield stenciled lengthwise.

He slung the bag over his shoulder and trotted back across the bright grass.

Rivers watched his bride move from her mother's neck to sweep her step-father in to a tight embrace. His gold admiral's bars glinted in the impotent winter sunshine.

Judah glanced up as if she'd felt his gaze. She whispered something to Graham while not taking her eyes from his. The ribbons of her bridal bouquet streamed down the admiral's back.

The steady chop chop increased until the noise and wind were nearly intolerable. The engines whined and the giant bird appeared over the tree line. The rails settled like a feather on the grass. The press, the Secret Service boys, and the president descended from the White House like a mob toward *Marine One*.

Judah broke away from her family and burrowed under his arm. "I already miss you," she shouted over the racket.

Rivers blinked slowly, reveling in the soft curve of her jaw. He missed her too. Taking her hand in his, he walked toward the wind tunnel of *Marine One*. Rivers pushed her green sea bag through the opening in the side and turned to kiss his bride good-bye. He tried to memorize her softness and her taste.

The wedding party had circled around them when Rivers finally broke his starved gaze. Press flashbulbs snapped a dozen photos every four seconds while the president boarded.

"Gotta go," she mouthed. Rivers released all but her hands and she climbed the stairs, standing, bent over to hold on to him in the open hatch. He followed her eyes as they flickered down to her hands. She was still holding her bouquet. A wide grin lit her face and she motioned the crowd to stand back.

Even the six Secret Service members that were left behind complied. The president's face appeared in the window. Judah turned her back to everyone outside and tossed the bouquet over her shoulder.

The Secret Serviceman who had talked to her before stood just inside the hatch and said something to Judah that Rivers couldn't understand over the wind, and she laughed. She shook her head and then turned back to face him.

Judah pointed to just above her knee and then pointed at him, then tapped her slim silver watch twice. Her left eye closed in a sexy wink he'd never seen from her before. Oh-ho! She was keeping her garter until he could take it off of her. *Lord, have mercy,* Rivers prayed as he swallowed hard.

Judah blew him a kiss and disappeared inside. A hefty marine with a black thatch of hair just on the crown of his head pushed the hatch into place with a crash of metal that Rivers felt inside himself more than hearing it over the wind.

In the window, Judah's face replaced the president's smiling one and she waved good-bye.

The helo lifted and her fingers pawed at the glass. She shrank smaller and smaller until he couldn't distinguish the window anymore. The two decoy helicopters joined in then, immediately flying crisscross maneuvers, until even Rivers' practiced eye was unsure which bird carried his bride. The sound faded until *Marine One* was just one more black speck in the sky. She was gone.

Reporters scrambled over themselves like puppies trying to get to their mother's teat as they converged on him.

"Who was that?" "Where is she from?" "Where are you from?"

Rivers sighed. The story would be Sunday's front-page news all over the country as soon as pictures of a bride tossing her bouquet for a weapon of war were developed.

"Come on, David." It was Melia pulling on his elbow. She pressed the bouquet back into his hands. It was still warm from Judah's morning-long grip. "The girl who caught it donated it back to you." She explained. "We have a mess to clean up at your house," she said and turned him back toward the party.

Rivers chuckled. "Judah warned me about you," he said.

"Well, she ought to know." Melia jostled a fussy baby Jack.

CHAPTER SIX

Asheed's Baghdad Residence Apartment
9 March 2003
5 AM

The muzzin blasted long in calling the Muslim world to their knees facing Mecca, Saudi Arabia. Asheed lay in bed, guilt needling him as if he lay on a grass mat instead of the plushest mattress money could buy. He yawned wide and his ears popped. In the fog of morning, he remembered his clock striking three as he shut down his laptop.

Asheed smiled. It couldn't have been a more productive night's work. His plan was fully in place. "It's foolproof. Absolutely undetectable." He sighed with pleasure. "Not even Allah could stop me now."

The call to the ritual morning worship faded from the wind. Asheed rolled to face the wall and went back to sleep.

1183 Whitby Lane, Richmond, VA
Rivers' Residence
9 March 2003
0540 hours EST

David Rivers pushed back the covers, his only wedding-night company. He blew out his breath like a blubbering horse. The west-

45

facing room was still black, save the digital red numbers announcing the arrival of morning. True dawn was still an hour away. He clicked on the bedside lamp as he stood.

"I hope my wife's night went better than mine." He lifted the top white T-shirt, folded in thirds, from his second dresser drawer. Next to the undershirts lay two even stacks of folded, not balled, socks. He withdrew the top pair.

Rivers paused in the middle of double knotting his left running shoe. The tail of a pale ribbon lay on the floor next to Judah's empty dresser. It ran up the side of the dresser next to the right-side drawer pulls and disappeared into a bundle of bows at the base of Judah's white wedding roses.

He pushed off the bed, his right shoe still lying sideways with laces strewn on the carpet. Fingering the yellow fabric ribbon, David held it to his lips, wishing for one more scent of her. The bird he had watched fly away three days earlier flashed in his memory. "Bring her back to me safely, Father," David whispered.

Sliding his foot into the second shoe, but not bothering to tie it, the SEAL grabbed the flowers with their trailing ribbons and walked through the dark house toward the front door.

Two homes in their cul-de-sac already had lights burning in their windows. Rivers pulled the door closed behind him. Walking on crunchy ice-coated grass, he circled the massive ancient oak on his lawn in order to wrap the tails of the ribbons completely around it.

The striations in the bark would have held the silk in place, had Rivers' knots been inefficient. He smoothed the ribbon flat against the curve of the trunk. Stepping back to critique his work, Rivers nodded once, satisfied. The bouquet was still tied in the ribbon where he could view it from the front porch. A curl of yellow ribbons announced street-side that he waited for his beloved to return from war.

Slapping his hand against his thigh to verify keys in his pocket, Rivers finally bent to tie his right shoe and moved toward the sidewalk. The sky lightened from dove gray to silver before he began to jog at the corner of Ketchem Street and Blandon.

USS *Theodore Roosevelt*
9 March 2003
1915 hours local

LCDR Wakefield braced herself for the standard whiplashing of landing on an aircraft carrier deck. Her uniform felt too tight from the swelling of 18 hours of travel dehydration.

The wheels touched down heavily and the reverse thrusters screamed as the Carrier Onboard Delivery (COD) C-2 aircraft went from an airspeed of 180 to 0 in under two seconds. Her head bounced against the headrest and the harness cut into her shoulders and bladder.

As she unbuckled, the side door opened from the outside. "Welcome aboard the *TR*, ma'am, sir." As Judah's eyes adjusted to the light, she noted the petty officer's crow on the young man's blue sleeve. She'd almost forgotten she had shared the flight with a nearly silent computer tech rep who looked like he had just stepped off a high school campus.

The petty officer lifted a hand to help her hop to the deck. The familiar sea gales ruffled the collar of her wrinkled khaki uniform. Thankfully, she'd managed to secure her hair under the white skull helmet en route from Naples, Italy.

The kid thudded to the deck next to her. She couldn't see his eyes because of the goggles everyone on the flight deck was required to wear, but his lips stood out bright orange against pale freckled skin. His chin twitched every few seconds as he looked around.

"The captain requests you come to his quarters, immediately," the petty officer yelled over the wind.

"His quarters?" Wakefield turned on her heel. How unusual.

"Not you, ma'am. Sorry." The petty officer sniffed. "He wants to see you on the bridge, 2000 hours, after you've cleaned up." He nodded toward the glass encased bridge that towered 12 stories above the waves. "Skipper wants to see Mr. Robinson about his computer now."

Wakefield found her quarters in female officer's row with simple directions from the enlisted man in birthing. Reading the bulls-eyes' IDs overhead on the bulkhead as she passed each frame as she walked, "Two deck, is no problem," she said. "Now frame 97, 98, and yep, now 99." Wakefield let her sea bag fall from her shoulder to her forearm as she stepped over the final kneeknocker. She slowed as she counted hatches on the starboard side, "One, three. This is me: 2-99-3-L for the duration." She whispered it aloud once more as she pictured it in her mind to burn it into her brain forever. It wouldn't do to have to ask for her compartment number again in birthing. There had been an officer aboard her first deployment who had done that when Judah was still enlisted, and oh the jokes that circulated the mess hall for weeks! Judah shook her head with the memory and slung her sea bag upright to the deck. The hatch to her room opened as she was straightening up. A hipless woman with her face bent to the floor and ball cap concealing her features scurried by her.

"Hello." Judah smiled and tried to catch the woman's attention. Might as well meet the roommate sooner than later. She wore lieutenant's bars on her shoulder. But the officer did not acknowledge her presence except to increase her heavy-stepping pace, away.

Wakefield followed the woman's progress with her eyes until she disappeared around the corner. Judah raised an eyebrow and shook her head. "I'll bet she doesn't have any trouble with the fraternization regs." She pitied the shy lieutenant.

The nameplate next to hatch 3 called her LT Melissa Garvey. "At least she got a feminine name," Judah said before opening the hatch.

In the light that shown from the private head, a tall figure stood in the left corner of the room swathed in a sheet.

Judah knew she did not have two roommates. "Lieutenant Garvey?" She asked softly, taking a single step inside the darkened room.

The tall statue came to life. Spinning away from a poster fastened to the wall, her thick red curls flounced at her shoulders. "Ma'am!"

Her cheeks glistened in tracks of tears in the dim light. "I heard I was getting a roommate on the evening COD." Garvey sniffled slightly. "Welcome aboard, ma'am." Her voice trilled overly bright.

Judah felt heat creep up her neck. The strap from her sea bag cut into her palm. "Thanks," she mumbled. She yanked the bag inside. It thudded dully on the floor.

"I work nights in CIC. Com officer." The redhead pulled the sheet higher on her chest. "I was just about to step into the shower, then I'll be out of your way, ma'am."

Judah dropped the strap of her sea bag and leaned down to pick up a discarded uniform from the floor. Folding the trousers, she choked out, "You should really take better care of your uniforms, Lieutenant." Wakefield handed her the square of khaki material and looked into her sad green eyes. "Are you all right?" she asked.

Garvey wouldn't hold her gaze. She looked at the wall, then the ceiling. She blinked back more tears. "I just," she whispered, "just really miss my family today."

Judah left it to hang in the air for a moment as the woman clutched the uniform to her heart. Her thin fingers clawed into the fabric. Judah touched the slightly younger woman's freckled forearm tentatively. "I assume the man who just walked out of here was not your husband."

Melissa threw back her shoulders as she returned her gaze to the wall. "I don't know what you mean, ma'am."

Judah's spirit cringed. This was going to be an interesting cruise. "I can handle any truth you tell me, Melissa, but I hate being lied to."

Garvey's eyes tightened briefly and relaxed.

"Take your shower." Judah backed to the door. "I've got an appointment with the skipper."

Fear shadowed LT Garvey's eyes. "You're not going to tell him, are you?"

Judah tilted her head to the side as she held on to the bulkhead. "Tell him that his night com officer is lonely, missing her family, and is accepting a cheap knock-off of love because she doesn't know where to find the real thing?" Judah felt her heart soften with compassion. Compassion for Melissa, but hurt for herself. "No. Instead I'm going to tell you about a lover you've never known. One who sees your shame and loves you thoroughly. One who will not abuse your weakness."

The woman trembled visibly and another trickle started down her cheek.

Judah moved back into the passageway, and shut the hatch firmly behind her. She scooted her feet out 25 inches from the bulkhead and pressed each vertebrae individually into its firmness. "God, I can't deal with this right now."

Judah pressed the heels of her hands into exhausted eyes. How long since she'd lain flat to sleep? Before the wedding. Just yesterday, but now, on the other side of the planet, it was three days later. *Or something like that,* she rolled her eyes.

Come away with me. The calmest of voices resounded in her spirit.

She absorbed its strength in her soul a moment, but had to swallow a disrespectful snort before it got away from her. "I'm on a carrier with 5,000 sailors and marines. Where do you propose we go?" Tears of exhaustion built and she touched her eyelids with cool fingertips to quell the tingling at the bridge of her nose.

A picture of the hangar deck, full of aircraft undergoing maintenance and readiness tests flashed through her mind. There was no way it was quiet, but Judah pushed away from her prop, compelled to follow the prompting. She'd learned years earlier that her Lord worked mysteriously, and it was better to link up with his plan early on, through obedience.

Her steps echoed hollowly as she trudged through corridors, turned sideways to pass people, and climbed the ladders of the mammoth floating city. She wondered if she looked like a bear on the prowl. Every time she turned around, she was given the right-of-way. So different from the last full-length deployment she served. As an enlisted corpsman at 21 years old, she had gotten grunt work and clean-up duty more than interacting with people. Now, she had to pop off a salute every minute and a half.

Only asking directions once, Judah opened a door onto a catwalk twenty feet above the buzzing aircraft hangar. A pair of enlisted women in sweats jogged in tandem toward her. The metal of the catwalk clashed rhythmically with their steps. Judah closed the hatch and sidestepped with her back against the bulkhead to let them pass.

Her hand behind her back, Wakefield felt the seam of another door. "What in the world?" she turned to find an unlabeled hatch. It was unsecured and she pushed the metal door open.

A single high-watt bulb lit a storage room. Odd airplane parts lined industrial metal shelving. The scent of used engine oil permeated the air. Brooms and two mops in a bucket tangled like matchsticks in the corner closest to her. A fabric sling chair like a movie director might use sat open and inviting in the middle of the room. "Hello?" she asked, though the room was obviously empty. She could see all the walls through the metal shelves.

She breathed deeply and plopped into the chair, not bothering to test its worthiness first. "How could I doubt you, beautiful Savior? You set a place for me, not exactly in the midst of my *enemies*, but in a place where I needed rest. Your goodness and mercy overtake me. Please help me adjust my attitude. I love the Navy, but I am starting to resent her coming on my honeymoon with me. This was supposed to be my special time with David." She paused to push back tears. She couldn't go before the captain with swollen eyes. What kind of intelligence officer would that present?

"Instead I am sharing a room with a woman who has circumvented the rules that I desperately worked to keep. I'm whining, I'm sorry. It's just that it was finally my turn. I feel that you allowed my time with David to be stolen by the enemy." That nagging doubt finally voiced itself.

"Did I ask you to keep your original date?"

"You knew I needed my dad at my wedding." Judah puckered her brow.

"When will I truly be enough for you, Judah?"

Questions by the Almighty cut deepest into the soulish realms. Judah squirmed in the director's chair. Thirst sucked her tongue dry. "I thought—" she hesitated. "I pray it will be soon," she whispered. Her shoulders slumped forward. "I need you to heal me, that you will be more than enough to satisfy my needs, Lord. Let it be so."

Her eyes fell to her watch. Just enough time to change into an unwrinkled uniform before 2000 hours.

"Thank you, Father of all, for your continuous love and dedication to work on me." Judah trekked back to her stateroom "Two-niner-niner-three-L," she repeated once more for good measure. She felt lighter than when she'd left. LT Garvey was gone.

"Help me set aside time for us, Lord. I know I won't make it through this deployment without you."

Up the ladders again, LCDR Wakefield stood at the door to the bridge, next to the sailor standing watch. "Lieutenant Commander Wakefield reporting as ordered, sir." Judah held her stiff salute, watching the skipper hiss instructions at his Executive Officer (X.O.).

Twelve seconds passed. Then twenty slipped by.

"At ease, Commander. You're early."

Wakefield stepped shoulder width apart in her fresh khaki uniform, and she folded her hands into the curve of her lower back. She squinted at his comment. *Two minutes is too early*? "Sorry, sir."

Eight other men on the bridge worked quietly at their stations, whispering only as necessary.

"I want you to know up front, Commander," the captain looked out to the black sea, "I didn't want you on my ship."

Judah swallowed to loosen the constricting of her throat. The captain smoothed the front of his immaculate uniform. "The SecNav insisted on a new intel officer. My old one was fine." The man's short hair had traces of gray lacing through the russet curls at either temple. "Then he insisted that it be you." His rigid posture pulled his body tighter than a dancer's. "I don't know what this is about, Wakefield, but I know who you are." He paused, finally turning in a quick about-face on his heel and toe.

Captain MacSod stared her down as if she were a smudge on a Navy brass bell. "Do not expect to get away with the tom-foolery you have in the past. Not on my ship. I'll see to it that your next billet is Iceland, no matter who your father is."

Judah flexed her thigh and jaw muscles simultaneously. "I don't know what you've heard, sir, but while under your command, I will do my level best to abide by every statute of the UCMJ. I will stay off your radar, sir." Wakefield barked evenly like a good recruit.

"I don't need a smart mouth, Commander. Your scar will get no sympathy in war. Begin your duties at 0500 sharp. That is all." MacSod turned his back to her.

"Aye, aye, sir." Judah saluted and retreated to the corridor. Slinking back to her room, she whispered, "What was that all about?" She pressed a hand to her stomach. It pained her as if she had physically been kicked.

Stripping off her fresh uniform, she hung it in her locker. The pocket lay funny, so she reached in to flatten it. A scrap of fabric curled around her finger. Curious as to how she had missed it when pressing the uniform, Wakefield wiggled it out. A yellow ribbon marred by black ink.

Holding it to the light, Judah could make out words in the smudges of a felt tipped pen. "I am my beloved's, and she is mine," she read aloud.

Squeezing the ribbon into her fist, Judah wasn't sure if the message was from her husband or her Maker. Fighting tears, she whispered, "Probably both."

Judah Wakefield-Rivers climbed into her top bunk and switched out the light, not even bothering to unpack her sleep clothes. "Married life is changing me already." She forced a chuckle. It sounded more like a snort as it echoed in the tiny stateroom.

CHAPTER SEVEN

David Rivers hung his eighth starched and pressed uniform in the master bedroom closet. Traipsing back downstairs to the laundry room, he placed the hot iron on top of the dryer to cool. "That's it," he said circling the kitchen. The entire house was clean. Even the gunk in the fabric softener hole of the washing machine was gone.

Wandering back through the just-vacuumed living room, Rivers sat heavily on the sofa. "Now what?" There was no maintenance to be done. The previous homeowners had been fastidious about upkeep.

He kicked his left foot up across his right knee. Two minutes later he squirmed. "I stink at liberty," he huffed.

Come away with me, the soft words of invitation sluiced through his mind. A picture of his plane ticket to Grand Cayman Island flew across his mind's eye.

"Oh, no. There's no way I'm going on my honeymoon alone." Rivers said. "I'd never hear the end of it from my Team."

"You'll regret it if you don't go."

David Rivers caught his breath at a warning he'd never heard from the Father before. There were fewer than a handful of things he regretted in life. "I'll pack now," he said aloud as he stood. He glanced at his watch. "Four hours to flight time."

With the car loaded, Rivers sat down at the computer.

Dear Wife,

How that word fills me with joy today. And anguish. I missed you last night, and more this morning.

He paused, tapping lightly on the space bar, more to hear its loose clack than enter a space in his letter. Rivers copied a picture of their newly adorned oak and told her God had asked him to go on their trip alone. He rolled his eyes. "She's never going to believe that."

I feel He is preparing me for something big, a hard work ahead. God bless you and protect you while I cannot.

Yours,

D.

Maneuvering the mouse, Rivers clicked, and the electronic message disappeared into cyber space.

Baghdad, Iraq
Abdullah Residence
11 March 2003
6:45 PM local time

Mohammad Abdullah's wife slid the first full plate in front of him from over his shoulder. "You are a good woman!" Delight rumbled his belly. He caught her fingers and kissed them before she could sneak back to the cupboard.

"Eew." Abdullah's 11-year-old son, Ramsey, turned his nose up.

"Not at the table, ugh," Takita, his 15-year-old daughter rolled her eyes and looked away, a blush tingeing her cheeks.

Mohammad touched his small skull cap and chuckled at his children's typical reaction. "It is my table." He released Mecca's hand. "I don't believe these ungrateful children deserve lamb this evening, wife." He forced his lips into a frown, but it was hard to push down his jubilant heart. "Just add their portions to my plate."

Takita's slim shoulders bunched up as she turned back to the table. Her light hazel-brown eyes filled with tears as she lowered her gaze. Mohammad rejoiced that Allah had not cursed this wee one with her mother's blue eyes. That her eyes were light was enough to deal with. The girl had the most tender spirit he'd ever encountered. The teasing she would have endured, would surely have broken her.

"How is the greatest scientist the world has ever known supposed to think, father," Ramsey asked, "without food to sustain my synapses process?" He tapped the table with his spoon handle between his first two fingers.

"Hmm," Mohammad pretended to consider the appeal while studying his son's deep-toned face. It was like looking in a mirror 30 years before. "Mecca, I suppose the boy has a valid point. I will need him to support us in our old age." Ramsey giggled and increased the speed of his table tapping. "You may bring the children their food." Mohammad couldn't keep the twinkle out of his eyes. He couldn't wait to share his and Mecca's secret with the children.

His wife had long ago determined his teasing voice and had the plates dished already. Ramsey dug in as soon as the plate touched the table. Around a mouthful of peppered rice, he announced, "I am going to be the one who defeats the Great Satan, America."

Mohammad froze and stared at his son who had glanced up with a proud smile for approval. The boy's teeth still gapped where baby molars were missing, and already he spoke of killing. Americans. It was time they had a talk, man to man.

"You did not hear those words in this house. Where did you learn to speak that way?" Mohammad swallowed the burning bile that rose in his throat.

Mecca slipped gracefully into the seat beside him. Her warm fingers brushed his under the table.

Ramsey shoveled another spoonful of rice and vegetables into his mouth and shrugged. Takita stared into her untouched food. "At school," Ramsey lifted his black eyebrows as he swallowed and reloaded his spoon. "The princes were there today. Both of them. Qusay spoke to me himself. He was the one who told me that I could work for King Hussein as soon as I finish my schooling." The proud smile on his son's face turned Mohammad's stomach.

"He is the *president*, son." Mohammad corrected.

Ramsay shrugged and shoveled anther over-sized bite into his mouth. "Prince Qusay said he was the king."

Exactly the trouble in this country. Mohammad looked at his daughter. "Did either of them speak to you, Takita?" Suddenly he remembered the man from their family grocery on the ground floor beneath their flat who had been watching his daughter two hours earlier.

The top of her head glistened with sweat as she studied her plate. "No, Papa."

"But the elder prince," Ramsey interrupted and shoved a chunk of lamb into his cheek, "he seemed to really like her. He was staring at her like he knew her already."

Mohammad Abdullah picked up his knife and began to saw his meat. "Cut your meat, son." The first strip of grey-brown broiled lamb had no fat. He snipped it into eight miniscule tastes. "So, Qusay Hussein, you say?" He pushed the squares of lamb into a line with the tip of his knife.

Had the royal palace put together his trips to Bahrain 17 years ago with his wife's and daughter's light skin and eyes? It wouldn't be unheard of.

"Takita?" Mohammad questioned her.

"I didn't say a word, Papa." Her hazel brown eyes finally released the plate under her nose. They begged him to believe her.

Mecca touched his hand gently once more, out of the children's view. "Let's move on to our pleasant news, shall we, dearest?"

He noted that Mecca had not touched her food either. He cleared his throat and wished he could clear his nagging doubts as easily. "Children," Mohammad caught Mecca's gaze, "we are expanding our flat to the third floor this summer, so the two of you can move upstairs." Ramsey and Takita looked up, delight written on their features. "It seems we need to turn one of your bedrooms into a nursery again."

Takita jumped to her feet, her chair hit the floor with a crash. It almost sounded like breaking glass. Mohammad checked the window behind her and the cups on the table as Takita threw her arms around Mecca's neck. Everything seemed in order.

"When will the baby arrive?" Takita asked brightly.

The tinkling crash came again. From the grocery beneath them.

Mecca stiffened even as she held their firstborn. She'd heard it too. "In October, Tiki. The beginning of October." Mecca's eyes searched his at the sound of heavy treads on the stairs.

Prince Qusay Hussein held his shoulders erect as he climbed the rickety stairs behind his thundering guards. Everything they did was loud. But, he supposed, the noise did help to strike fear in the souls of the enemies he sought, if they did, in fact, possess souls.

The eight Special Republican Guardsmen that preceded his advance waited in lines on either side of the narrow stairwell, flat against the walls, as flat as men fully outfitted for quelling an insurrection could be.

Qusay gave a slight nod to his captain. Captain Zeref enjoyed the crack of breaking doorframes, so Qusay did his best to accommodate the man three or four days a week. More often in a productive week.

Captain Zeref had worked in Qusay's contingent guard for twelve years. The prince stood back from the splintering wood and the eight guards rushed through the opening. He took his time with the final steps.

The Abdullah family sat white faced in silence around a meal as the newest member of the guard held his rifle on the father at shoulder height.

"Good evening." Qusay greeted them to no reply. Qusay took inventory. The two women wore the hijab but no headdress. What was the man thinking, allowing his women to dress like Western Infidels? Qusay touched the rough wood of the open door. "Why was the door locked?" he asked, pursing his lips until he could feel the whiskers of his stiff mustache.

The man, named Mohammad, if he remembered correctly, like 3 million other followers of Islam, looked around for an answer. His eyes bulged like a fish in a round bowl.

"Uh, we, were not expecting any visitors this evening, your highness." The man's voice brayed like a wild donkey.

"Am I not welcome?" Qusay loved this game. Pity it always ended so soon.

"Of course you are welcome, your highness." It was the woman who dared speak this time. Her voice was full of arrogance, confirming his suspicion that she was not of pure blood. "May I prepare tea and cakes for you and your men?" She started to rise. "It is so kind of you to bless us with your presence, unexpected though it is."

"Sit down, woman!" Qusay spat the words the husband seemed to be trying to convey through telepathy and hand gestures. "Your Arabic is quite good. Hardly a Western accent at all. You have been practicing for years, no doubt."

The woman's eyes tightened at the corners. The girl he had tried to entice into speaking at the school gasped and clapped a hand over her mouth. She knew. They all knew. And they had all tried to hide. Qusay touched the bridge of his nose.

Takita felt her little brother's feet swing-kicking under the table. He could never keep his feet still when he was excited. She cut her eyes away to take in his boyishly round face, still too young to realize they probably wouldn't live through their second encounter with Prince Hussein the elder. And if they did, they'd wish they hadn't.

Since becoming a woman three years earlier, Takita's school friends had started including her in their whispers of the princes, their likes and preferences in a woman. It was all speculation, she knew. None of the Husseins' women ever left the confines of the palace to indulge the curiosity of young girls.

Ramsey began to wiggle more obviously in his seat. She tried to catch his eye to still him, but her brother grinned foolishly at the future king.

"Sir, sir!" the kid finally burst out. Takita wished she could reach her leg far enough under the table to kick him, then perhaps, he'd shut his mouth. "Have you come to take me up to the research labs of the palace already? I can pack a bag and be ready in four minutes, sir." Ramsey's face fairly glowed. "I told you, Poppa."

Takita shrank in her chair, hoping to become invisible. No matter what the girls at school said, she didn't want that palace life. A simple life with a husband poppa chose.

Ramsey broke the silent staring contest between Poppa and the prince. "I'll just go pack now." He rose from his seat at the table. The crashing thuds of the guards ransacking the rest of the flat made Takita's insides quake as each sound registered on her mind, but she refused to let the prince see her fear. For only the third time in her life, Takita wished for the veil.

Qusay did not order Ramsey to sit as she expected. Her brother skipped toward the powerful man on his way to the hall.

As quick as summer lightening, Qusay Hussein reached for his waist. He drew a glittering silver blade.

Ramsey was one step past the prince when his right hand jerked forward and then back again, just as quickly.

Momma choked back a gasp. Ramsey took another step and his knees buckled. His body lurched face-forward toward the Persian rug Takita had cleaned by hand the day before.

What's wrong with the kid? Takita reflexively jerked toward him in her seat to help. Then she remembered Qusay. She put her hand to her hair and pushed it back from her face to cover her movement.

Qusay looked right at her. Her whole body jolted and began to heat like the electric water boiler.

Ramsey gurgled from the floor. It was the same sound he had made as a newborn.

Momma whimpered deep in her chest. Her eyes flooded. "Keep your Infidel woman quiet." Qusay's harsh words edged into Takita's mind.

"It's okay, Mecca." Poppa shushed her.

Qusay stepped closer to the table, lifting his knees high, to step over Ramsey. The large man's chest and stomach strained his button line. His right arm maneuvered at a strange angle behind him. When it reappeared, he held a revolver with a funny criss-cross pattern on the plastic handle.

Qusay's fingernail on his trigger finger was torn or chewed, she couldn't decide, down to the quick. The skin was dry and cracked. The pull he gave the trigger angled a wrinkle into his wrist. The shot was loud.

Takita felt it in her chest. She jerked her eyes to Qusay's face and saw his lips moving. The smoke that wafted from the muzzle covered her brain with a fog she couldn't hear through.

Finally Takita forced her neck to turn. Momma sat upright in her chair. Balanced as perfectly as always. A black hole centered in her forehead. Redder-than-crimson blood flowed downward for two inches to the bridge of momma's nose and then split into two streams that ran down her cheeks.

Dear, sweet momma.

Takita blinked. The wee baby was gone too.

"Poppa!" Takita screamed. But she didn't feel her vocal chords move in response. She could barely break the magnetism of momma to look at poppa.

Poppa was staring at her though. Such sorrow in his eyes. "*Salaam Alikium*, peace be unto you." His words of blessing broke through the fog that strangled her brain.

"I'll care for her in your place. Do not fear." A snort of laughter followed the prince's words.

Poppa's head flung sideways into momma. He threw off her perfect balance. The discharging gun muted all sound again.

Turn that sweet stick of relief on my horror next, Takita begged. Her lips would not release the plea.

The floor rocked under her feet.

She waited, looking at the refrigerator that had been hidden by her poppa's tall form, seconds earlier, or was it minutes? *Where is my metal sleeping pill?* It didn't seem to hurt; none of the others had cried out.

Warm liquid crept under her toes, the arch of her foot, to her heel. Her foot was identical to her mother's.

She jumped. Qusay's fingers wrapped around the upper section of her arm. He bellowed out orders that she couldn't formulate into individual words. He wrenched her to her feet. Eight men appeared from the hall and filed downstairs.

Takita stubbed her left pinky toe on the table leg. She wanted to hold it and press out the pain, but some hurts were deeper than others. She stumbled. Ramsey's legs lay in her path. *Pick up your feet*, she commanded herself. The fabric of the black trousers he had been forced to wear that morning touched the sole of her warm foot.

Fifteen steps down. Careful, Tiki, don't forget to breathe. In and out. Simple. The ground-floor grocer's glass windows lay as broken as her family on the not-so-clean Persian rug.

CHAPTER EIGHT

USS *Theodore Roosevelt*
10 March 2003
1100 hours

L CDR Wakefield clicked her mouse to close down the computer she'd been working on during her entire six-hour shift. She stretched her long legs under the metal Navy-issue desk. She assumed it was a security feature that she faced the inside of the room and door, and her screen faced the wall behind her.

The droning of the nuclear powered engines facilitated a pounding headache in the back of her skull and an unhealthy heap of irritability.

Standing, Wakefield dispensed a squirt of unscented lotion from her newly-organized desk drawer. Rubbing her hands to replace the moisture lost from the dry air in the bowels of the ship, Wakefield studied her new office. She had gone straight to work at 0500, almost expecting Captain MacSod to check on her at 0502 hours. Instead, her assistants, PO Gates and Ensign Juarez, were not slated until 0730. Even then, Gates tottered in 13 minutes late with a spot of scrambled egg grease on his trousers. After sending Gates to change, he got down to business at 0810 on the dot, apologizing all the while. Juarez just rolled his eyes.

What a first shift.

She rubbed the moisturizer into her cuticles, puzzling over her predecessor's taste in dispelling the institutional white of the walls. The wall behind her was made of wood panels. Framed pictures and unframed magazine tear-outs of exclusively U.S. Navy aircraft adorned every wall. Commander Wallace was either a former aviator or a wanna-be.

Wakefield peeled back one of the slick magazine pages. Wallace had adhered it with green ticky-tack that strung away from the wall. "A nightmare for another day," she sighed and smoothed the picture back in place. The large black-framed photo on the wall behind her desk looked to be an enlarged personal picture of an F/A-18 Hornet after take-off, taken from the cockpit of another. The bird had a trail of white exhaust showing his curving climb away from an aircraft carrier on a crystal blue day. Maybe that one could stay.

"What I don't understand," she said aloud in the empty office as she ran a finger over the frame to dust the hornet picture, "is why the powers that be always think that intelligence officers want to work near the brig." She stretched with both palms on her lower back. "I'd rather put some space between my work and my interrogation subjects."

The ship rocked. Wakefield had to shuffle step to steady herself. She hadn't quite gotten her sea legs back. "I'd prefer at least as much space as the length of the carrier, maybe at much as the width of the Atlantic." She blew out her breath. It was time for lunch.

"Are you unhappy here already, Lieutenant Commander?" a gruff voice asked from behind her at the door.

She closed her eyes as she recognized the voice.

About facing crisply, Wakefield stood at attention. "Captain. What a surprise."

"I'll come and go as I please. This is my ship." MacSod scowled. Then his stance softened. It was barely detectible, but she was trained to see such things. "Chow time, Commander. I do allow breaks."

"Breaks, sir?" Wakefield dared slide her eyes to briefly catch the skipper's gaze. He was studying the picture behind her.

"Chief Cochran reports that you missed morning chow."

Wakefield started. A strange tingling shivered up her spine. Five thousand souls aboard and the skipper gets reports on who shows up for breakfast. Didn't he have better things to do? "I have a little trouble digesting before sun up." She countered.

"Well, it's up now." MacSod said. "Dismissed."

Wakefield glanced at the screen, glad she'd already changed passwords. Something was weird with the skipper. Though she was under his authority on the ship, she knew her security clearance was probably two levels higher than his, just because of her job description.

"Aye, sir." She touched the mouse to put her computer into sleep mode, and left by the only door in the office.

USS *Theodore Roosevelt*
1900 hours

A surge of joy shot through Judah's abdomen as she typed her personal email password. R-I-V-E-R-S-3-8-0-3. It was now her name, as well as his. Maybe not aboard ship, but certainly in her heart. She understood the necessity of keeping "Wakefield" as her professional name. It was too confusing to have two Lieutenant Commander Riverses in one household.

"Two hundred and six emails?" Judah's jaw hung lax. "I've only been off-line four days." She eliminated 40 as spam, and dove into her husband's letter first. She'd counted 17 personal notes from friends and family, all dated yesterday. Maybe being deployed would *help* her stay up-to-date with her relationships. "It's not like there is a lot of other options for entertainment."

67

Judah had noted that wherever she went, people tended to shy away from intel personnel, thinking that they knew all their dirty secrets. It wasn't entirely true.

"Ohh," she trilled at the picture that she downloaded. It clarified, line by line and she recognized the oak from her new front yard about the time the yellow ribbon on the trunk appeared. "Is that my wedding bouquet?" She leaned toward the screen, wishing for a higher resolution. "It is." She giggled. "For a SEAL, he turned out to be much more romantic than I figured." She shook her head, "Except that part about going on our honeymoon alone. I could have gotten our money refunded because of my deployment, even without insurance." She let her mind wander to David Rivers in his swim trunks.

"Whatever," she printed the email and clicked on the one from her mom's address, "I hope he has a wonderful time."

Baghdad, Iraq
Republican Palace
12 March 2003
3:45 PM

"King Hussein." The page at the door bowed low in the office doorway wearing blue flowing robes. "The Grand Mufti seeks audience today."

Hussein held his finger on his place in the letter delivered three days earlier from the U.N. delegate. The United Nations had considerably sent the Frenchman again. "Tell him my door is always open for the Mufti," he said. He looked back to the fine linen stationary on his official desk until the door clicked shut. The list of world leaders that ran down the extreme left margin took two pages to list everyone with their pompous titles. "I wonder if they have an official stationary collator that makes sure the paper goes to print on opposite pages."

Returning to his place in the letter, Hussein rubbed his thumb over the ruby signet ring on his first finger and chuckled. They were all fools. "Destroy your chemical and biological weapons or face dire consequences. The world will turn our backs on you," he read again aloud. The committee had not changed the phraseology from last year's letter. "If *only* you would turn away." The king frowned. With his left hand he reached for his left eyebrow and began plucking out the loose hairs between his fingers. "We don't seek to dominate the world as you do," he folded the paper in half, "but to set her free from her vile nature that has seeped in from the West."

Hussein folded the stationary in quarters. "Who do they think they are?" He filed the letter in the same location as the others: the circular file next to his desk.

"We are an enthusiastic nation, but we are small next to the Great Satan. It is necessary to arm ourselves with efficient weapons for our protection from the armies of the West." Hussein snorted. "Bring on your inspectors. We will offer guided tours of our factories."

A tap sounded at his door and the page reverently swept it open. "Your highness, the Grand Mufti and his second are here to see you."

The black-robed cleric in his seventies swirled into the office like a sandstorm at midnight, followed by his perpetual shadow, the younger man being groomed to take the scholar-leader's place when he passed to the heavens.

Grey tresses escaped the mufti's square headdress and curled with sweat around the religious leader's chubby red face. The devout man's sole overindulgence was rich food.

Saddam Hussein stood as respect dictated while the mufti seated himself without invitation. Hussein had hoped it to be a short in-and-out, but the wide man settled himself comfortably back in the leather chair. The second, Nephtali, a learned mufti as well, stood stone faced, to the left and behind the chair. The Grand Mufti of Iraq, Ali Zuzchen, was never intimated by his stare, but they considered it an unspoken game, 26 years in the making, of trying to stare the other down.

This religious leader held the heart of the nation in his sweaty palm, while Hussein held their heads and purse strings. Avoiding a peasant uprising was the only reason the softening Islamic mufti was still around. If the people of Iraq rose against their king, Saddam knew he would have to neutralize them. Then what kingdom would be left to rule?

Zuzchen blinked first. "I have some concerns, your majesty. I am hoping you can clear up some things for me."

Hussein heard the 33-year-old apprentice stifle a choke. Hussein's thigh muscles tensed under his desk. Nephtali he had hand-picked for his radical nature. He would have made a wonderful jihadist, giving his life to further Islam, but Nephtali would be an even more successful national religious leader. His strict interpretation of the Holy Quran would encourage more young men to give their lives to the jihad.

Hussein wrinkled his forehead innocently, but he didn't ask what had concerned Ali Zuzchen this time.

The mufti rubbed his palms against each other with fat misshapen fingers. Stilling them in his lap, his tongue snaked out between his lips to wet them. "We are encouraged by Allah through Muhammad's revelation to wage jihad on the Infidel disbelievers." The old man's head nodded as he spoke like a plastic bobble-head doll, "But I wonder if it would be wise to comply with the U.N.'s requests at this time to preserve our way of life and the lives of all Iraqis. Just for a time. It is perfectly acceptable according to the Quran's authority on these things."

Hussein's throat began to close up. Nephtali had been put in place to discourage this kind of thought in the older man. Was the head of religion in Iraq actually in his office suggesting that they roll over for the Great Satan's threats?

Zuzchen held up one hand with wide-spread fingers. "Just a little while, so we can regroup. You need not give up all your weapons, just some would satisfy their need to save face."

"Saving face is not what motivates the Cowboy President." King Hussein rubbed his eyebrows again. "That is an Eastern weakness. He is moved by idealism, with a powerful military on whose back he can ride as a conquering Christ.

"No, he is coming." Hussein continued. "You can count on it. Our only hope is to discourage the hearts of his army. Sow discord among the individuals, and cause the bright-eyed Americans to lose trust in their leader."

"Excuse me, your majesty." The young man's voice startled him from his plan. Hussein shifted his focus to the well-groomed Nephtali. "Why not find a woman to seduce him?"

His visitors faded before him as an idea formed in Hussein's mind. It had not worked with the last American President, but the political support for this man lay in Christian fundamentalists who would not re-elect an immoral man. Hussein felt excitement stir his insides. This kid would go far.

"You are permitted to lie," Grand Mufti Zuzchen nodded slowly. "The Quran permits lying in three instances, and for purposes of Jihad, it is for the Infidel's own good."

Hussein nodded his agreement. Not only would a woman be able to take down the lauded integrity of the Cowboy President, but letting the mufti think it was his idea would buy equity with the feisty old man until he could do something about him. Sooner than later he would need to move the Iraqi People's affections onto Nephtali for the ultimate goal to be attained. The goal he had never even spoken aloud yet. "Zuzchen is correct, Nephtali, and your idea has great merit. We will find a woman willing to seduce him. It will defile him and his reputation. It should not be hard in America, no?"

The three men shared a chuckle. "They must be caught in the act. Like the woman in their Bible. He will be destroyed in his weakest exposed moment. He will spend 2003 and 2004 covering his back side, and in January of 2005, a complacent man will assume the White House throne. "And if we cannot find a woman who can prove he is just like every other Infidel on the planet, we will find a woman to *claim* he seduced her. And that will bring his head down." Sadaam rubbed his fingertips together in anticipation.

"Less than two years," the religious leader's fat cheeks, still pink from his walk, bunched into gladness. "Then the sleeping giant will return to his slumber," he said.

"At which time, we will prick his heart with the needle of death," Saddam added. The silence of the office gave him hope. He had some grand ideas taking shape. Things he could do with the chemical compound Asheed had reproduced that would make the death toll of bin Laden's World Trade Center attacks look like child's play. And there would be less rubble to clear afterward too. Saddam rolled his jaw to the left in pleasure.

CHAPTER NINE

LCDR Judah Wakefield smiled as she stepped over the final kneeknocker before reaching home. She was ready to get out of her uniform and start daydreaming while staring at the picture of the oak tree in her front yard. *What is Rivers doing right now?* she wondered. With the time difference, she decided he was probably eating lunch.

The hatch opened without sticking. "Good. Maintenance has been here," she mumbled under her breath in the dark room. The smell assaulted her before she was fully inside. Alcohol. Forbidden while underway.

A sniffle came from the lower bunk *I suppose we'd better deal with this now.* Judah pushed aside thoughts of Rivers.

"Melissa, get up and get dressed. We need to talk." Judah said gently. She shut the hatch to douse the solitary source of light and offer her bunkmate privacy.

Melissa sniffled again and hiccupped. Evidently she'd been crying hard. How could someone do this to herself? Why?

"I can't. I need to get some sleep before I'm on mid-watch tonight."

Wakefield sighed and raised her voice. "Lieutenant Garvey, out of that bunk. We are talking and that's an order."

A choking whimper came from Garvey's bunk. "Yes, ma'am." The sheets rustled and Judah looked away, even in the blackness. She had hoped that she'd be able to conduct the conversation as Judah and Melissa instead of a senior officer to a junior one.

The head door closed and Judah flipped on the overhead light switch. She was giving the woman exactly two-and-a-half minutes.

Melissa appeared in a T-shirt and cut off sweatpants at a minute-forty-five.

Melissa's pretty blue eyes were swollen and her sculpted cheeks mottled. A truer daughter of Erin, Judah had never seen. The woman's red hair was a glorious riot of color and curl. Judah pointed to the chair across from her. With military precision posture, the junior officer took her seat.

"Why are you doing this to yourself, Melissa?" Judah jumped right in. "I can see it is killing you on the inside."

Garvey sat up straighter if it was possible. Her arms crossed over her breasts. "It doesn't hurt me."

"Right. That is why I found you crying, twice, after you've been with this man. And this room smells like a distillery." Wakefield poked.

Melissa closed one eye as she shook her head and glanced at the ceiling. "It's just how I deal." She shrugged. "It's how I come down, you know. Don't worry about it."

"You're lying. Those are tears of regret." Judah paused, not ready to go on. "I recognize them," she inhaled, "because I've cried them."

"Think what you want." Melissa shrugged in her wrinkled T-shirt. "I miss my family and the—um, he is a good man." Melissa had almost revealed the man's rank. "He makes me feel good about me, you know, as a woman, not just another uniform to get the job done." Melissa shifted at the revealing comment.

Wakefield smoothed her hands over her khaki pant legs. "I figured you to be a smart woman. You finished in the top third of your class. I assume you did all right in your Military Justice courses." Wakefield took the reins from her softer Judah personality. "Let me be clear. You are smack in the middle of the fraternization chapter. Do you want to get shipped home for a court martial and then hauled to the brig because you can't figure out how to separate sex from your view of your worth?"

Melissa's eyes widened and she hugged herself tighter. "I'm not hurting anybody, besides, you said…"

"I'm giving you space to change, Melissa. I thought I'd try to help you, but your attitude stinks. Being a military officer is not about not getting caught breaking the rules. It is following the rules to a T when no one is around to know that you did. It is setting aside your own desires for the greater good. Integrity. And now you have contraband alcohol hidden somewhere in our room. I don't know how you got it, but it is going over the side in the next 12 hours."

"Mm," Melissa Garvey grunted.

How had Garvey gotten as far as she had in the Navy with her attitude? "Look," Judah leaned toward her roommate as the Lord placed a picture in her mind. "Melissa, God is not like your Father was. He will not throw you around like a rag doll. He will not stomp on your seventh grade Planets Project. He will not call you a whore to your boyfriends." Judah swallowed, grateful for the loving environment of her own youth.

"God is loving and kind. He wants to heal those broken places in your heart." Judah said slowly.

Melissa caught and held her breath in her chest. Her white grip on her own forearm loosened.

Please soften her heart to your words, Lord, Judah prayed silently. "Jesus loves you, Melissa. Your past matters to him."

The girl moved her hand to rest over her heart while her face leaned into Judah's words.

"God is a Father to the fatherless and wants you to crawl up in his lap to receive his comfort."

Melissa leaned slowly back in her chair and swept her thick hair back into a ponytail and dropped it behind her shoulders. "That is the biggest bunch of hokey I've ever heard. What are you, some kind of freaking mind reader? I'm not a whore. Greater good—ha," she choked high in her throat, "I'm living only for me."

Judah's stomach clenched. She'd never seen a word so clearly rejected before. She knew it was right too. "You'll change your mind, when you've been tormented enough," Judah said. She rose and went to her closet, unbuttoning her uniform blouse. "I'll be praying that God allows torment to be loosed. You don't realize how needy you are."

Judah watched Melissa's jaw fall open in her tiny locker mirror. She rolled stormy eyes. "I can't believe you! I'm so outta here." Melissa grabbed her ID and charged out the hatch. It crashed in her wake.

"So maybe that was a little strong." Wakefield bit the inside of her cheek.

**Hyatt Regency Resort
Grand Cayman, Cayman Islands
11 March 2003
7PM**

David Rivers propped the two suitcases just inside the door in of one of the Hyatt Regency's third-floor suites. One held clothes, the other SCUBA gear. The open sliding glass balcony door invited sweet sea breezes to eddy into the white tone-on-tone room. Gauzy drapes on the mahogany canopy bed wafted in the cross breeze before Rivers shut the door behind him.

Picking up a gray cordless phone, he drifted outside to take in the view of Seven Mile Beach. The sand and water lay in shades of gray with palm trees silhouetted in black against them. He dialed the perky native islander at the front desk. "This is David Rivers in 314. I need to confirm my dive time for tomorrow." He nodded as he listened. "Yes, it is a tragedy that she couldn't make it." Rivers shook his head as Mela at the front desk repeated the soft clicking disapproval under her breath of a groom that went on his honeymoon alone.

Rivers sighed as she put him on hold. "Even in paradise," he shook his head and pushed against the iron balcony rail to test its strength. Finally she came back. "Two o'clock is perfect," he said. "In the lobby. Thanks, Mela." Rivers hung up before she could reiterate her concern for his future.

He returned the telephone to its cradle. "I wonder what Judah's up to now. Probably just greeting her day." Staring at the suitcases at the door, he prayed, "God, give my wife discernment in her work tomorrow. Cloak her with your wisdom, insight, and discernment. Please, keep her safe. Bring us together in your perfect timing. Show me how to treasure her and care for her always."

A deep timpani drum began to pound out a steady rhythm. Rivers stepped out onto the high balcony again and watched a line of flickering dots wend through the darkness of the manicured palm trees.

"The Hawaiian luau," Rivers slapped his hand down on the rail in front of him. Another drum joined the first at a higher pitch. It touched every beat twice.

The lonely wail of a conch shell sounded on the wind. As it faded, the frenzy of excitement in drums, talk, and rattles tripled in time.

"Talk to me, Lord. Teach me who you are, and who I am."
Rivers turned inside the room and kicked off his travel tennis shoes
in favor of flip-flops for the sand of the luau cove.

CHAPTER TEN

L CDR Judah Wakefield flicked her pen back and forth while her interviewee slurped at his mug of water. For the ninth time. Meticulously, he pressed the paper napkin to his mustache. Twice.

"Mustafah," Wakefield tried again to capture the man's attention. "Tell me something else about the attack." She softened her voice as if it would be an intimate secret between the two of them. *Yeah, me, you, and the entire U.S. intel community*, she thought.

"I'm out of water," Mustafah said in Arabic.

Since his wrists were manacled to his waist with only 12 inches of mobility, Wakefield rose and smoothed her uniform blouse as she reached across the wide interview table to refill his glazed stoneware mug.

"My accommodations and food were better in the detainment camp," Mustafah whispered as she leaned near him.

Wakefield glanced at the mirrored window. Did the video camera on the other side pick up his lip movement? "You have complaints?" She raised an eyebrow in question as she reclaimed her seat.

"I want to go back to my family. I need to take care of them."

"See that they have fresh water and bread?" Wakefield asked.

Mustafah's eyes narrowed. "The refugee camp in Jordan has not seen fresh bread, ever, ma'am."

"But the detainment camp gets it every third day," she countered. "I visited one for a week, not three months ago."

"Yes," Mustafah's jaw hardened. "The U.S. Zoo Tours. I remember them well." He threw his shoulders back. His lips pressed into a thin seam.

"Tell me about your family."

Mustafah sighed. "You know them now as well as I, Commander. When will you realize I am innocent and let me return?"

"Your mother?" Wakefield pushed. She had been over Mustafah's story of escape from Afghanistan to Jordan four times straight through. She couldn't count the number of threads she had picked apart to question him about.

Like Commander Wallace, her predecessor, Wakefield knew Mustafah was more than a new refugee caring for his mother after months in a detainment camp. He carried a confidence about him that undermined his sob story of a gutted father and raped mother and sisters who needed him 'back home.' Yet she'd not been able to catch a discrepancy in his story.

"My mother, Nadia is 42. She lived with the Bedouin, wandering through the desert until she married my father when she was 16. My father used to say she was like coming into the sea in the middle of the dusty desert."

This was new information. Wakefield stilled her fingers on the clip of her pen. "That's beautiful. Why did he say that about her?"

Mustafah looked left into his past. "She had eyes as green as the sea."

Wakefield smiled. "Where did a Bedouin come across green eyes?"

Mustafah's voice picked up a hard edge. "The man who fathered her was a white man. A Russian." His black-brown eyes chilled. Wakefield knew that this was his real story. And it wasn't a love story.

"So your grandmother was raped by a man in the Russian Army when they came through Afghanistan in…when, 1961?" Wakefield prompted. "I'm sorry."

"Yes, well." Mustafah suddenly looked younger than the 21 years he claimed. Defiance sliced through his eyes as he looked up at her. "Not sorry enough to keep your miserable army from raping our country." Mustafah sneered and white dots of spittle formed in the corners of his mouth

Wakefield felt pressure build behind her jaw. Her teeth clenched together painfully. *Ungrateful little punk*, the thought flew through her brain without asking permission. *Cool it, Wakefield*, she cautioned herself. *We're finally getting past his mask.*

Mustafah must have sensed the nerve he touched for he leaned forward, the links of metal at his waist rattling. "I'll bet you've even done some of it yourself," he goaded. "You've killed the innocent and stolen their inheritance, haven't you, Commander?"

Wakefield's core shook as she remembered Filasek's seven-year-old son, Nasser. He was dead because of her. So was his mother. Their beautiful home was also destroyed in the same missile attack. *I never knew her name.*

"I can see I was right. No need to confess." Mustafah smiled slow and lazy. Then there was a single beat as she watched his countenance shift as his chin dropped. He looked up at her through thick eyelashes.

If Wakefield didn't know better, she might have even classified the young prisoner's grin as flirtatious.

"We are alike, you and I." Mustafah's voice dropped low to match his new approached.

Take control of this meeting, Wakefield, she commanded herself. She cleared her throat. Sweat rolled down the bulging belly of the plastic water pitcher between them. "No, Mustafah, we are not. You kill for revenge, for some misplaced notion of Jihad. I have had to kill to set people free."

"Did you kill the one who scared your face to set others free, ma'am?" Mustafah touched his own cheek in a caress that followed the pattern she had often traced on her right cheek.

Judah clenched her jaw tightly closed.

"We're through here." She tucked her pen in her pocket and slid her notebook off the table as she stood in one smooth motion.

"Are you afraid of me, ma'am?" Mustafah's smooth voice was back in full force. His cuffs clinked again as he held an open hand toward her.

Wakefield smacked one hand down on the table for the effect of the noise that echoed in the interrogation room, then she slowly leaned into the table coming inches from his nose. "I can't fear an impotent momma's water boy. You have come to the Americans for help. You can't even take care of yourself." She straightened and turned her back to him. She hoped to cut into his ego if his story of family in Jordan were true, or force his pride to undercut his lie and confess to the manly things he had accomplished.

"Then why not dismiss the soldier?" Mustafah referred to the private first class (PFC) marine who was unlocking the hatch to let her out. "Then we can talk fully, soldier to soldier."

Gotcha! Wakefield forced her face into a blank mask instead of the grin that lit her heart, before turning to look him in the eye. "He's here for your protection, Mustafah, not mine." She put her back to him and walked through the open door.

As soon as the private re-locked the door, Wakefield breathed deeply, expelling the personal issues Mustafah had stirred. Wakefield stepped into the observation room next door to stop the tape. She watched her prisoner sit alone in the room for a moment.

He had finally slipped. She hit rewind on the camera. Had he noted his words, "soldier to soldier" yet? He just sat, still and staring, at the mirror.

Having been through intense interrogations herself, mock and otherwise, Wakefield knew the young man must be replaying their conversation over and over in his mind. Committing them to memory and searching for mistakes.

Hyatt Regency Resort
Grand Cayman, Cayman Islands
13 March 2003
1:45 PM

David Rivers strolled through the long marble Hyatt lobby wheeling his black diving suitcase behind him. His black flip-flops slapped the bottom of his foot with each step. He admired again the quality of the establishment. "Judah sure can pick 'em."

Rivers glanced at the reception desk. Mela was on duty again. Her long black hair hung over one shoulder, the way Judah wore hers after it was freshly washed. Mela stopped typing on the keyboard in front of her and stared at him. Wiggling her fingers in a decidedly feminine manner, Mela pointed toward a group gathered in a seating area across from her desk. There were six people chattering in the awkward stop and starts between strangers. Rivers nodded his thanks.

Rivers could feel Mela watching his progress. In his peripheral vision he watched her lean over and nudge the woman working the check-in spot next to hers. The second woman shook her head as

Mela whispered to her. Rivers could almost hear their clacking tongues across the lobby.

Rivers rolled his eyes and turned to observe the group. *Lord, I'm ready to learn whatever it is you want to reveal to me. Then, can I please go home? Everybody on Seven Mile Beach is talking about the poor man who came on his honeymoon alone.*

Rivers popped his neck from side to side. *Shake it off,* he told himself, *who cares.*

Standing behind a turquoise and pink striped wingback that was thrift-store tacky anywhere but the islands, Rivers jutted out his chin in greeting to the three couples. *Talk about a sore thumb.* "This the outfit going out to Devil's Throat?" he asked.

A skinny kid in his early twenties looked up with a lazy grin. "Yeah. You joining us?" His face still had pillow wrinkles and his hair stuck up on one side. Perched on the arm of his chair, Rivers assumed, was the long-legged reason why the kid still looked half asleep.

"Yep." Rivers set his wheeled case upright, lowered the retractable handle, and assessed the strengths and weaknesses of his team. *Not "team." This is a group,* he reminded himself.

"Tommy Balin." The kid waved at him. He was already dressed in his shorty wetsuit. Tommy squeezed the knee of the girl sitting on his chair arm. "And this beautiful creature is my wife," Tommy beamed, "Chloe Jacks, I mean Chloe Balin."

Rivers chuckled with all the others as Chloe, who didn't look old enough to be out of high school, patted Tommy's head.

"David Rivers," he said. "Nice to meet you." The girl would be a liability. She held onto her husband's dive computer like it was a foreign currency calculator. A definite newbie. Why would anyone put someone he loved at risk with an overhead-environment dive like Devil's Throat?

A sunburned couple in their forties occupied either end of the couch with a full cushion separating them. "We're the Kaliffs from Akron, Johanna and Ron." The woman spoke for them both. The way she drew out every vowel into two syllables, Rivers knew she was not originally from Ohio, more like the Bayou.

"Ron here is the new president of ChemTech." Johanna stretched her neck high, obviously waiting for some recognition. Rivers shook his head, he'd never heard of it. Ron stared out the window at a woman sunbathing on the patio. "It's only the largest chemical company in the Midwest. Well, for technical use anyway—Ron!" she broke off to bark at her husband.

Her husband snapped his eyes back to the conversation. *He may be newly in charge of his company, but I know who's in control at home*, Rivers thought.

Rivers only exchanged names with a brother and sister pair, Jenea and Dan. Both had well-worn bags of scuba equipment at their feet and deep tans. Rivers felt confident in their abilities.

"Hey, y'all waiting for the McKinley Dive Operation?" A loud male voice hailed them from the direction of the elevator bank that Rivers had used. The twenty-something's boisterous voice echoed over the quietude of the lobby.

"Jace," an impossibly thin blonde on his arm slapped at his chest, "shh." She looked like she had poured herself into the scraps of her white bikini, and she didn't bother with one of those cover dress thingies that Judah had searched all over Washington to find in February, and now it was at home in her bottom drawer.

"Yowzers!" Apparently, the young woman's admonishment didn't faze Macho-man at all. "This dive is going to rock!" He threw his free fist in the air. "Yeah!" he shouted again.

The girl giggled, a shade of embarrassment colored her much softer tone as they approached. "He loves diving." She smiled and leaned in to smooth a suggestive manicured fingernail over her boyfriend's tight six-pack abdomen.

They stopped, standing too close and crowding Rivers. He stood his ground.

"Any of y'all been on many dives?" Macho-man Jace postured himself like a strutting rooster. "What about you, big man?" He shoved a fist in Rivers' direction.

"David," he said controlling his urge to laugh at the young man's cockiness. "Yeah, I've been on a few." River's unshaven jaw twitched with amusement.

"Jace's been down 18 times." The kitten on his arm purred. "One time he even out-smarted a shark by diving down to 300 feet in complete darkness."

"Really?" Rivers lifted a single eyebrow and glanced at Jace's face. It was impossible for the human body to survive that depth on regular air without going into decompression. Rivers remembered well trying to breathe at a depth of 205 feet in the South Atlantic while he planted mines on a druglord's loot-exchange-location without using the proper Nitrox mixed gas. No way had a kid who'd dived 18 times survived 300 feet.

"Interesting." Rivers added when he saw that Jace knew that he knew he had lied.

Jace cleared his throat and touched the front of his spiky bleached hair. He mumbled something and tightened a playful hold on the woman. "I told you not to call me that down here. Y'all can call me Smitty." His arrogance didn't suffer at all.

"Well great, Smitty," A new voice came from the entrance door behind Rivers. "I'm Marta McKinley of McKinley Dive Operation. I'll be your dive master and driver today. Glad to see you're all getting acquainted. On this advanced dive it's important to buddy up."

Rivers turned to find a woman of no more than five-foot-one with close-cropped brown hair. Even in cut offs and a ragged tank top, she appeared competent. "This is an advanced dive, you need to be able to anticipate each other's needs. How many of you are diving?" she asked. "I have seven reservations and nine bodies." Marta double checked her clip board.

"I'd like to go and just snorkel a bit." Chloe Balin stood up from the arm of the chair, "If that's all right." She lowered her brow.

"Wait," Tommy stood up next to her. "You got your certification. I thought you wanted to do this." He turned his bride around to look at him.

"Tommy, that was in a lake," she pleaded. "This is different. I just don't think I can do it for real."

"So you only made one reservation? When did you plan to tell me?" he hissed. Quieting his voice didn't hide anything in the echoing lobby.

"You can snorkel if you want," Marta put in. She motioned for those with equipment of their own to gather it. "But there is not much to see from sea level where we are going. And you still have to pay full price."

"Okay." Chloe said, red-faced and avoiding her husband's glances. "Can you just charge it to our same card?"

"Sure." Marta gave a quick nod. And made a note on her clipboard.

"I'm not planning to get in at all." Smitty's kitten tossed her platinum locks. The water would ruin my suit."

Rivers snorted in the back of his throat. What a group.

Marta led the way and they scrambled for the van. Except Smitty. He pulled Rivers back.

"Hey, big man." Smitty's eyes flashed and he shoved his girl on ahead. "Wait for me at the door," he told her and smacked her nearly-bare behind. "The two of us have some man business."

Curious, Rivers watched the bikini-clad girl saunter in the direction of the others, then he turned back to Smitty. "Can I help you with something?"

"I seen you eye-ballin' my woman." Smitty hauled himself up to his full height, which was still two inches shy of Rivers' six-three. "I feel I gotta warn you, I'll take any man to the mat over that piece of flesh." Smitty narrowed his eyes boyishly at Rivers.

Rivers leaned down toward Smitty's ear. "Your arrogance, Smitty, has reached comical proportions. I've only known you four and a half minutes." Rivers stepped closer to the young man, challenging him the way he would an errant man training during Hell Week at Coronado's BUD/S training, "That's four minutes too long in my opinion." Smitty stood stock still at the unexpected counter attack. "Start treating that woman with a little respect, and get her some decent clothes, or you're headed for trouble, and not from me." Rivers pulled back.

Smitty re-inflated his chest. "What are you talking about, big man? She dresses herself."

"Uh-huh." Rivers made sure Smitty knew his answer was wanting.

The kid squirmed. "Just keep your hands and your eyes to yourself, big man. Or you'll be sorry. Besides," Smitty tossed his head to the left, "what kind of female respect are you claiming to know? Wedding ring on that finger and you're down here in the islands ogling taken women." Smitty's lips curled away from his teeth like a cat that had trapped a rat. He pointed his first and middle fingers into River's chest. "Where's your poor wife? At home taking care of the kids while you mess around in the tropics. Bet you're even writing this off as a business trip."

Rivers fixed the man with a stare. "My wife, of four days, is deployed to the Middle East to hunt terrorists. Maybe someone should tell her about you."

Smitty's eyes registered a moment of shock but he recovered his persona quickly and snorted. "You let your woman do your fighting for you? Just watch your back on this dive down Devil's Throat, big man. You never can tell when he'll try to swallow you whole."

"Boys!" Marta's voice strained from the doorway next to the McKinley van. "We're leaving with or without you. You can argue over whose is bigger on the boat."

The hotel clerks giggled.

"But—" Rivers rolled his eyes. "Aye, aye, ma'am," he said densely, as only a career sailor can. Unlocking the handle of his pull-along gear-case, he marched toward the auto-sliding glass door.

Smitty stormed past him, leaving his girlfriend in his tailwind, too. She stood on the door sensor keeping it open and waited for Rivers. The air conditioning rushed to escape. "I heard what he said to you." The girl spoke as he got to the door. Rivers motioned her on ahead of him, "And what you said to him. Despite what Jace thinks, he doesn't own me. And I bet you *miss* your wife," she said with mournful eyes, heavy with make-up. "You can look at me if you want. I don't mind," she offered with a twitch of her painted lips.

Poor mixed-up kid. Rivers stopped in the doorway. Lifting his T-shirt by the back of its collar, he pulled it over his head. When he looked her in the eye, a haunted little girl looked back through her woman's eyes. "Put that on." He tossed her his shirt and walked to the 15-passenger van scrawled with tropical pink, green, and orange lettering.

CHAPTER ELEVEN

Warehouse, 609 East Risken Blvd
Baghdad, Iraq
13 March 2003
10:02 PM

Homer Asheed signed the docking slip and showed the hired driver back to the warehouse door. Asheed shuffled his feet as he locked the door from the inside. Six blocks west was the main entrance to the palace, he was connected to it at least five different ways by his count, through an underground labyrinth of passageways. He leaned against the locked door, smiling at the stacks that had arrived.

Another installment on his coming riches. "One stack for you, one stack for me." He mumbled aloud. He paper-clipped two purchase orders for nine hundred blocks of Semtex to the back of two invoices for nine hundred blocks of Semtex.

Sending the invoices to the palace accounting office would satisfy the Russians who would be eager for their payment on the invoices. However, the palace's inventory record would reflect only one invoice entry. The other would go into his own private and growing stash. When the Russians brought attention to the discrepancy at 120 days past due, he would be long gone. If audited before then, the second paid invoice number he would claim as a shipping error if the goods were still around. And, if they'd been sold for profit already, "Well, those dirty Russians," he practiced the indignity in his head, "everyone knows they cheat and wouldn't bother to return an invoice paid twice." Asheed chuckled at his own cleverness and unlocked a side door.

Three Afghani Taliban refugees working off the cost of their rescue and housing, waited with hand trucks to deliver the 18 boxes to their respective storage-homes in the labyrinth. He motioned the men through the short alleyway.

The Israel Purim attack would have to come out of Hussein's batch of Semtex, and would ship immediately, first to Syria, then Lebanon and over the border by sea. Asheed had a buyer lined up for his portion already too.

"Hurry up," Asheed snapped at the lanky, grey former Afghani government leader. They'd have to make three trips each to transport the explosives a quarter-mile through gas-lamp-lit corridors to the storage room Asheed had secured for Hussein's purchases.

The olive-skinned man pushed a dusty-sandaled foot against the bottom of the loader on his hand truck, but stared outside through the barred glass door next to the rolling warehouse door where Asheed could hear the driver pulling away. The man looked down and shoved. The shelf hit the side of the box once more. "Not like that, you imbecile!" Asheed cursed. The other two were already loaded and turned around ready to descend underground.

Asheed cursed. "Be careful! You're going to blow us all away."

The old man glanced up at the outside again. He seemed unconcerned. Asheed would have to see that the old man became concerned. Lock-up would be appropriate. *After* he finished the assignment, of course.

"Down you go," Asheed hit the button to lower the new freight elevator. "See that you hurry, and I can probably scrounge up an extra portion at dinner," he promised, never intending to do so.

As soon as the door closed, Asheed auto dialed his contact. "You can pull around now. Have your men ready to load fast while I count the cash." Asheed snapped the cell phone closed and turned off the power. He was not going to be tracked and traced like a fox by Hussein's hounds.

Asheed rolled up the loading door, his thoughts returning to the old man. He had seen a longing in his eyes. Why were those who sought refuge with Hussein never satisfied just to be alive? They seemed to think that they should not work off their debts. A few years of service to the king was certainly better than the alternative: death or imprisonment by the Infidels who had taken over Afghanistan's government and country.

Asheed shrugged. He understood the debt just fine. He would not expect to rise to the top in his next nation. He would buy his place. And his freedom and respect.

The dirty white lorry squealed to a stop in front of the doorway.

**Open Water
Cayman Islands
3 PM**

"Okay people, listen up." Marta stood on the metal grate off the stern of the 24-foot pontoon boat. She tossed the red and white dive flag on a plastic float into the calm water beside the boat.

The pilot turned off the engine, and threw an anchor overboard with a splash. Smitty's girlfriend still covered to mid-thigh in Rivers' T-shirt, squeaked as the turquoise water splashed her.

The crowd of ten settled to quiet for final instructions before the dive. "Most important is this," Marta hardly had to raise her voice over the sea breezes. The sun shone golden and hot on the million diamonds sparkling on the water. "Do not panic. If you run into trouble, stop, breathe, think, and act. I'll repeat that as often as I need to." She gave Chloe a hard look. "I'm still not comfortable with your change of heart. I want you and Tommy immediately behind me."

Chloe gave a small affirmative jerk of her head. Her fingers were twisted with her husband's and lying in her lap.

"That's the current you want to catch, the darker blue stripe about 20 feet south." Marta pointed. "We are three-quarters of a mile from Devil's Throat. When you get into the water, catch the current. We'll drift dive over. Don't overshoot. Save some energy to swim back outside the current. The opening is at 80 feet. A hole about eight feet across in the rock formation at the ocean floor.

"There are several twists and turns and it gets tight. Stick close together, people. We'll come out at a depth of 120 feet. If you start feeling nark'ed ascend some. Take your time coming back up. We have a beautiful sea today, 90- to 100-foot visibility. Take advantage of it, but do not, I repeat, do *not* hot dog around with your air supply. I charge overtime if I have to come rescue your butts."

A nervous tittle raced over the deck.

"However," Marta continued, "for everyone who avoids getting nark'ed at this depth or out at the wreck on the second tank, there is all the rum punch you can hold in that cooler over there for the ride home."

A cheer went up. Rivers laughed. Island vacationers were all alike.

"Just remember that's 'all you can *hold*.' I charge extra for cleaning up puke, too," Marta warned them with a comical scowl. Everybody laughed.

"Test your air flow." Marta directed, not allowing the group to get side tracked as she tucked her regulator into her mouth. Nine staggered breaths in and out swooshed in the air.

"Hey, Marta," Smitty took the regulator out of his mouth, "I've got 18 dives behind me," he tossed his head to the left, his spiky hair didn't move. He pounded his fist into his chest twice and flashed her a peace sign. "I've got the back end of the line for you."

Marta raised an eyebrow. "Actually, I've already asked David to do that." She smiled with closed lips. "He's got a few more dives under his weight belt."

Rivers looked over in time to see Smitty's snarl return, but went back to spreading liquid Sea Gold around the inside of his mask to keep the lenses from fogging up.

Smitty took up his mask as one by one the group disappeared with a splat off the stern's metal grate. Smitty spit hard into his goggles. "A real man uses his own spit." He spit into the other eye hole and began to spread it around with his forefinger.

"How many real men have used that rental equipment before you, do you think?" Rivers screwed the cap back on his bottle and tossed it into his black mesh at-sea bag on the deck. It only distracted the pompous twenty-something for a moment.

Dan went over the side, followed by Ron Kaliff. "How many dives you been on, big man? Twenty? Thirty?" Smitty pestered like a fly as Rivers rose and walked to the stern platform carrying his split fins. Top of the line, and fully worth the extra expense, he deemed, having previously dived for twelve years in regular web-fins for the military.

Rivers slid one black foam bootie into a fin and snapped the clip of the rubber heel grip on the inside of his ankle. He considered ignoring Macho-man, but decided it probably wouldn't do any good. Rivers stood and pulled the legs of his shorty wetsuit down toward his knees. "Two thousand four hundred thirty-eight logged dives," he said. "Twenty-four-forty by the end of today."

Rivers popped his regulator into his mouth, covered it and his mask and regulator with one hand while holding his octopus lines with his other and took a giant step with his left foot. The water smoothly closed in over his head. Much warmer than the Pacific where he had trained SEALs in the surf for the past six years before transferring to Little Creek.

Ah, the silence. Bubbles gurgled past his ears. His inhale hissed loud. Silence was relative underwater. Rivers pressed the inflator button to add a touch of air to his buoyancy compensation (BC) vest to maintain positive buoyancy back on the surface as he checked his equipment. After signaling "ok" with a quick fist to the top of his head, the 15-year SEAL walked himself through the double check of each piece of equipment while on the water's surface. A recreational dive on plain, compressed air to 120 feet was a walk in the park.

Dive computer, calculating. Lead weight, he touched the Velcro pouches on his vest where love handles would form if he discontinued his rigorous workout routine, secure. Regulator, obviously functional. Octopus, an extra air regulator for his buddy in an emergency, Rivers popped it into his mouth and sucked air into his lungs, all good. He secured the octopus in a clip on his BC and returned to his primary regulator for his next breath.

Smitty splashed down beside him in only swim trunks and his BC. He seemed to be a macho idiot through and through, insisting to Marta that a member of a college Polar Bear Club couldn't possibly use a wetsuit in the tropics.

Rivers touched the folded lump of his knife in the Velcro waist pocket on his right. His flashlight with fresh batteries, was secured to the latch outside.

Smitty shot Rivers a perfunctory scowl before descending past him. Jenea tossed her well-worn fins onto the grate. She had finally finished braiding her hair out of her face, and she slid her feet in with practiced ease. She smiled out from under long dark bangs at Rivers. "He doesn't like you much, does he?" she asked in a pleasantly deep voice.

Rivers pushed his mask against his face while inhaling to create a seal against the water. As his depth increased, he would exhale some through his nose to add air to the space inside his mask when the pressure compressed the air molecules together. "I don't think he likes anybody but himself." Rivers replied. "You ready?"

Jenea plopped easily into the sea. Signaling OK, Rivers watched as she ran expert hands over her equipment. "Let's join the others." She popped the regulator into her mouth and upended herself to dive.

The current pushed Rivers along at a steady five miles per hour. At 18 feet, Rivers popped his ears against the water pressure, and again every few feet. The only work was to continue downward. And that could hardly be considered work.

As the beauty of life at 30 feet below sea level floated beside him and beneath him, Rivers began to pray. The steady swoosh-in, bubble-out flow comforted him. There was some majestic connection with the Creator in places so few others accessed. The sea was a personal sanctuary. Except that when the water was black instead of blue, the sea was generally a job instead of recreation. A place to kill instead of worship.

"I am overwhelmed by the beauty and diversity of life you've made, Lord." An orange and white striped clown fish horned his way through a school of several dozen hovering yellow angelfish whose fins looked as if they'd been dipped in neon blue paint.

"The colors seem comical in their extremes, but when thrown together in a single palate, they not only over-stimulate the human senses, but they scream out of your deeply passionate soul." Rivers sighed. Master painters of old taught to associate pastel, airy colors, pinks, lavenders, mints, yellows, soft blues, with romance. Rivers hovered three feet over the coral at a depth of 45 feet. A tall, spindly, lime green and hot pink anemone seemed to dance to the current's rhythm.

"Is this what you wanted to teach me?" Rivers asked. "The color of your love for me is not some sissy pink, but hot and deep. I love the love with which you love me." Rivers smiled, keeping his lips tight around his regulator. Three and a half minutes into the dive, he recognized the salt already tightening the skin around his mouth. Swoosh-in, bubble-out, light kick, kick from the hip.

"No," the answer came simply into Rivers' heart.

"Hmm?" he grunted pulling out his dive computer. The digital display read 58 feet. "Well, I enjoyed the realization anyway," Rivers commented with a shrug.

An indention in the floor held what looked like a field of kelp south of the current. Rivers ducked out of the current a minute to examine the red and purple spiny ball-shaped sea urchins that lived in the blue-green plants. Returning to his dive plan, Rivers found the drifting current and watched a flowery anemone catch an unsuspecting parrotfish in its deadly tentacles. Rivers passed over blood star fish and red algae, barnacled conch shells with delicate pink insides. A crab scurried into a crack in a rock wall. An entire swarm of tiny yellow Adaman butterflyfish darted as one, first left then right to avoid him.

Ahead, Rivers saw what had held the others' attention. A huge coral reef grew into the underwater hills of the ocean floor. It looked at least six layers deep. Most layers were the soft spiky coral that branched out in every color. Even as the spectrum of color diminished into shades of blue, the left side of the reef from his approach seemed to glow golden in the shape of a fifteen-foot high petrified tree of coral. Its branch tips were pink fire. Unmatched beauty. "God, you've outdone yourself here." Rivers breathed as he soaked in the creativity of the Father. A spotted moray eel slithered to safety in the reef away from the human interlopers.

Rivers glanced at the ragged line of divers forward of him. Smitty's bare beefy arms caught his eye. "God, please forgive my arrogance," Rivers prayed. "I see myself in part of him. I know I'm dependent on you for my every breath, and I'm nothing on my own."

He glided over a long silvery tarpon fish nosing a clump of seaweed. Swoosh-in, bubble-out. The bubbles tickled his ears as they rushed toward the surface. "Today, more than other days, I depend on you to sustain my life." Rivers thought of the air strapped to his back.

"Yes, you do." The stark answer he heard echo in his spirit surprised Rivers in its intensity.

He released more air from the top buoyancy pouch in his vest and descended as the ocean floor fell away in a cliff beneath him. He passed 67 feet.

The group waited for Jenea and him next to an eight-foot jagged hole in a barnacle encrusted rock mound eighty feet to his left, out of the current.

Marta flicked her flashlight on full beam and dove head-first through the opening. From the angle her fins disappeared, Rivers determined that they would have to swim down at an angle. Chloe and Tommy dove immediately behind her. Jenea's brother, Dan disappeared inside. Ron Kaliff moved for the opening next. In an explosion of bubbles, Mrs. Kaliff tugged her husband's fin back and pushed herself in front of him.

Even under 80 feet of water Rivers identified the Smitty's deep grunt as he followed them. Water actually conducted sound more efficiently than air. Rivers had heard the mournful whale song when on Pacific exercises hundreds of miles from reports of whale sightings. Smitty smoothly slid through the opening. His hair had come unglued and waved around his head like a fan.

Rivers reached for his dive computer again as Jenea positioned herself to enter. Eight minutes into the dive with 2550 PSI of air left. "So far, so good."

Jenea's fins disappeared into the black hole in a sea of blue, and Rivers maneuvered to follow her. The entrance dropped at a 30-degree down angle. He hung at the entrance as if he were a prize mouse about to be dropped down the gullet of an angry barnyard tomcat. Barnacles and seaweed added the illusion of fangs.

The circle of light ahead was the size of a doughnut. He switched on his flashlight and gave a mighty kick to catch up. He crashed into a tangle of arms and legs, stopping abruptly.

Millions of tiny bubbles assaulted his face in a mass of white lights. Rivers felt a thick arm shove him backward and into the wall. His BC hung on something sharp on the cave wall. He was hit again in the lungs with clawing hands, but he couldn't move out of the way. His breath was pushed out with a grunt and huge glub-lub of a bubble.

Chapter Twelve

Illuminated from behind, Rivers jerked himself free before Smitty came into him blindly again.

Rivers inverted, avoiding another encounter with the sharp wall. A single kick propelled him a full six feet back into open water.

Smitty barreled out behind him, turning wildly. His eyes flashed with panic behind his mask. His chest heaved. Jenea swam out behind him, holding onto her knee. Smitty grabbed like a wild man for his buoyancy hose to inflate his vest that would shoot him to the surface.

Rivers clutched the back of the young man's BC and lightly applied pressure to his neck. He didn't want Smitty to get decompression sickness from ascending too fast, neither did he want to render him unconscious underwater.

Rivers slowed his own breathing in hopes that Smitty would calm and follow his example. The kid squirmed to get loose, but Rivers held fast. He jerked Smitty around to face him and grabbed the front of his vest with two vice-grip handfuls of the thick material. Rivers shook him, once.

Then Rivers saw it. When Smitty stilled, the water clouded red around his head. He pulled the man closer to him to examine the damage. A nasty gash cut into his forehead above the mask and back into his hairline on his right temple. It didn't take corpsman experience to determine that he needed stitches—a lot of them.

Smitty began to heave and squirm for his free-floating buoyancy inflator button again. Jenea swam over and placed her hands on top of Smitty's head away from the wound. His breathing began to calm, but his eyes still twitched back and forth like a hunted rabbit.

A brief satisfaction floated over Rivers at the justice of it all. The saltwater, he knew, stung viciously. The scar on Rivers' right shin proved it.

Jenea pointed to her knee and Rivers saw that she was bleeding too. She jerked her thumb toward the surface, pantomiming that she would haul Smitty up top with her, and that Rivers should rejoin the group in the Devil's Throat.

Rivers nodded. Jenea seemed calm and competent enough to handle Smitty. He tapped his wrist where his watch would have normally been and held up four fingers. Under 80 feet of water the pressure was more than three times that of the surface atmosphere. To avoid "deco" they needed to make the topside trip last at least four minutes. Eight would be better.

Jenea nodded. She knew procedure. She snapped a line from her vest to Smitty's to tether them together and waved goodbye to Rivers.

Rivers reentered the tube-like cave, kicking powerfully. He continued between 20- and 30-degrees as he moved through the cave.

Four yards inside the tunnel was a second entrance to his left, smaller than the eight-foot hole his group had used. The cave closed in smaller as it curved to the right, away from the second opening.

"Only a single passageway" that was what Marta had told them on the boat. Rivers maintained his pace. There they were, just ahead.

The light wavered at four o'clock in his field of vision. Fifteen yards. He kicked with simple straight-legged strokes.

The throat closed smaller. If he reached out, he could put his shoulder on one wall and touch the other side with a flat hand. Peering under his arm, Rivers looked behind him. The darkness was complete. He had dropped his flashlight at the entrance when Smitty barreled into him.

Returning his gaze ahead again, Rivers searched for his guide mark. Where did it go? He scanned, turning only his head and eyes to keep his body position from changing his mental perspective, based on his last known position.

He made a slow knee kick.

"Find the light," Rivers grunted to himself in his best command voice.

It was simply not there.

Keeping one hand extended in front of his face in the dark, Rivers felt down his vest for his redundant light. His fingers found the plastic latch. The bottom of the enclosed hook was sheared off. His back-up flashlight was gone.

The deep blackness pressed into his pores. "Look for the light. Find the light, Rivers."

What a way for a SEAL to go! a voice in his head mocked. *Swallowed by the Devil's Throat on a recreational dive.*

"Find the light! Do it now," his bones cried out. His eyes ached for even a pin prick in the ink.

Rivers stopped, breathed, and considered. Pressure tightened his abdomen. "Do not panic," he ordered himself. "Just keep swimming and keep breathing."

Rivers raised his forearms directly in front of his face, it wasn't as if he was blocking his view. He kicked tentatively at first. Then he grew in confidence and kicked from his hip. "Look for the light." He repeated it like a mantra. "Find the light."

How long has it been? Strange that we have trouble judging time when there is not light or shadow to guide us. Rivers felt the wall in front of him with his hands before he crashed into it fully. He walked his hands over it until he felt it curve back to the left. The angle of his bubbles over his ears told him he was still heading down. He felt as though he were crawling through the bowels of the earth itself.

"Look for the light."

The contrast of the bright color just minutes earlier made the black all the blacker.

"God, are you still there?" Rivers regulator swooshed as he inhaled and bubbled as he exhaled.

"Yes," came the warm and immediate reply. "There is no depth where I cannot reach you." Rivers had not noted the temperature change until then. Not only the absence of light but his slowed movements chilled his insides. "Well, could you reach down and turn the lights back on?" Rivers joked.

"I could."

"But you won't," Rivers sighed.

"You'll live." It almost sounded sarcastic, and yet His words held promise at the same time.

Find the light. Find the light. His eye muscles screamed at him with fatigue. Had it been 25 seconds or 15 minutes? It couldn't have been longer than that, could it?

The decompression alarm on his dive computer had not gone off yet. That would mean too much nitrogen in his blood. It could cause joint pain, dizziness, tingling, headache, extreme fatigue, hallucinations, unconsciousness. It was as if he could read the words from his textbook in relief against the blackness. Definitely not a positive effect under millions of gallons of water. "Of course," his own mental voice echoed around his skull, "I *am* talking to myself, and slowly."

Rivers shifted his eyes back left again, 10 degrees further. A small light registered on his brain. He searched the black blanket for the fuzzy lint of light. Had he made it up in desperation?

Swoosh-in, bubble-out. Swoosh-in, bubble-out. "Find the light." Each slow, practiced breath took him closer to the bottom of his tank. There it was again.

Not even second guessing, Rivers began to kick, twisting side to side with the effort as he poured 15 years of SEAL strength training into it.

It was gone. Did he just imagine it?

His arms crumbled beneath him, but protected his head as Rivers found another tight turn in the cave. The sphere of light flickered enticingly ahead. Closer now. Rivers yanked on his ear, feeling the pain immediately. It could be a mirage, but his brain was still functioning on a fast response time.

The flickering had to be the bodies of other divers blocking the path of the light, he deduced. He hoped.

One more angled turn to the right and a jagged disk of blue appeared ahead, small and fuzzy. Kick, kick, kick, KICK. He swooshed out the opening and was struck in the face by a great wall of bright blue sea.

Rivers squinted as the brilliance stabbed into the back of his eyeballs. Yet even with his eyes closed the blackness was not as complete as it had been inside the belly of the beast.

His left hand grasped for his dive computer. Seven minutes. The longest seven minutes of his life.

Like being aware of being born, he equated. Not something a man should have to experience twice. More intense than combat, more frightful than torture. Under the sea there was no back door, no appeal. The adrenaline surged through his body.

He touched the broken plastic latch that had held his flashlight. "Never again without double redundant lights." Rivers vowed.

When he took inventory of his group, Marta was counting on her fingers as she swam toward Rivers. He held up two fingers and jerked his thumb toward the top.

Eighty minutes later, on his second tank of air, Rivers felt his adrenaline let down at the wreck they explored. Sure, the ship was full of majestic beauty, and sleek lines, but she was dead. She would never fulfill her purpose ever again. Now she was just a heap of metal covered with sediment for humans to poke around in her innards.

He strayed from the others' playfulness. Even Mrs. Kaliff seemed more jovial toward her husband. Barely propelling himself, Rivers floated inches above a bed of colorful coral that teemed with life.

Rivers surfaced with 14 minutes left in his tank. He was ready to go back to the hotel. Macho Smitty lay on the deck with his head in his girlfriend's lap. He had insisted that the group take their second tanks down despite his head gash.

Speeding toward shore less than an hour later, Rivers listened to the party start rolling. Chloe chattered about wanting to go down again the very next day.

Rivers peeled off the top of his wetsuit and left it flapping around his waist as he took his plastic party glass to the quieter stern. He plopped down with one leg on either side of the ready-benches. Leaning back, he folded his vest under his head. Smitty competed with Chloe for the most outrageous story. Rivers chuckled to himself as, even under the influence of a quart of rum punch, Jenea wouldn't allow the large sea bass at her and Smitty's solo deco stop to be told as a shark.

Find the light, the mantra still boiled in his brain. "Just like in the Kingdom," Rivers mumbled, searching the dusky blue heavens from under the boat's awning. "Even in the darkest hour, there is light somewhere. Seek and ye shall find." Rivers planted one foot up on the bench to balance his body through the pilot's way-point turn toward shore.

"I'm guessing that's what you wanted to teach me, Lord." Rivers felt the Lord's smile as the sky deepened in hue. Somehow, he had a feeling that this was just part A of the lesson. "Whatever it costs, Lord, I want to know you more," Rivers whispered into the wind.

CHAPTER THIRTEEN

USS *Theodore Roosevelt*
14 March 2003
0442 hours

Lieutenant Commander Wakefield stepped into her crisp uniform pants and zipped up. She almost liked the early morning hours she had to keep now. Melissa Garvey ate morning chow and had a workout before returning to their stateroom. The tension between them wasn't so bad when they never saw each other.

Spreading blue paste across her toothbrush, Judah thought of Rivers. She touched the yellow ribbon in her left breast pocket where she put it every morning in a new uniform. The silk slid between her fingers. "God, please guide my husband. Continue holding him safe in your palm, that he would come to know you more intimately every day. Give David assurance of his ultimate security in your presence."

Forty minutes later, Wakefield focused the lens of the video camera on Mustafah's face behind the one-way glass of Interrogation Room A. Pressing the "on" button, Wakefield exited and rapped twice on the hollow metal hatch for the Marine to let her inside the interrogation room.

ADM Tamburillo from Intel Headquarters had emailed every intelligence officer at 0230 zulu. Someone inside had leaked information on a possible holiday attack.

The email actually raised more questions than it answered. Someone inside where? A *possible* attack—what kind—missile, chemical, biological, nuclear? Attack in which city? Which holiday? Every day is a holiday somewhere. Wakefield sighed as she laid her pen and paper on the table, facing Mustafah.

"Good morning," she told the prisoner. The 21-year-old's jaw-line beard and mustache were starting to look scruffy from seven days aboard ship without a razor to clean it up.

Her predecessor's notes said that he considered Mustafah suicidal and had ordered that all threat objects be removed from his vicinity. *Could be a bargaining chip*, she decided. "Let's talk about some people you might know today." Wakefield started in a conversational tone. "Any friends or acquaintances that might have a grudge against anyone?"

Mustafah chuckled in spite of his floating-prison circumstances.

"What's funny?" Judah asked in English. In the four days she had been interviewing him, they had switched among Arabic, Farsi and English. Mustafah was certainly a native Farsi speaker, but his command of the other two languages was more than adequate.

"Ma'am," Mustafah inclined his head. "Every person I know resents someone. Be it tribal warfare, the Russians, the Americans, the Zionists." He shook his head, a knowing smirk still played at his mouth.

Wakefield snorted and tapped her pen against the closed notebook in front of her. "I'll admit," she allowed a small smile as she looked at his chocolate eyes, "the question was a bit naïve. Who, among your circle of friends, might have means and opportunity to produce an attack based out of Iraq?"

"Not many, ma'am." Mustafah sounded respectful, but then he clammed up. He shifted his eyes to the floor at the right of the table, indicating to Wakefield as a profiler, that he was remembering something.

Mustafah was such a strange character, as terrorists go. He fit the general age description, but he did not speak from the Quran in scripture quotes as fanatical terrorists generally did. He harbored anger, but, like he said, every one of his countrymen had reason to resent someone.

"Let me be more convincing. You are a young man. One who has many years ahead of him. Those can be years of plenty or years of misery. Your old life is gone. There is a new government coming to power that will change the Middle Eastern region. The sooner you get on board, the better you will do for yourself." As an afterthought she added, "And your family."

Mustafah shifted forward and glanced sideways over his shoulder at the one-way glass. He leaned his chest over the table between them. "What can you do for me, Commander?" he whispered.

Wakefield saw green rise in his dark eyes. The interrogation table often became a negotiating table for her. And why not? Most of the men marked as terrorists that she had interviewed since September 11th, had been regular family men, more concerned with getting by as foreigners in a foreign land than exacting a sting against the U.S. military or mainland. Most of them.

"What are your plans for five years from now?" Wakefield pulled back from the prisoner.

A look of confusion settled on his features. She wasn't sure he was going to answer. Mustafah finally leaned against his seatback and the chains in his lap rattled. The Marine on security detail visibly relaxed his tense stance at the door behind the detainee. "In five years, I'd like to be reunited with my family, of course." Mustafah's glance darted to her face, "And go to school to learn welding, start my own shop, repair things that are broken and build new things to sell."

Wakefield felt her eyebrows shoot up in surprise. Mustafah saw the disbelief and looked down. His shoulders slumped enough for her to decide she had crushed his dream.

Well, it wasn't her job to encourage dreams. "So you're not likely to commit suicide?"

Mustafah's eyes narrowed slightly in a short flash of confusion at the subject change. "No way." He shook his head emphatically. "Those men who go through training camps, they're out of their heads, you know. They're crazy, talking about how they'd rather die to kill than live and let live. I'm not crazy."

"What camp?"

She heard Mustafah cross his ankles under the table. "Oh, you know, ma'am. I've seen it on CNN, when we could get it. The rebel training camps."

Wakefield honed in on his dark eyes that stared toward the wood-grain veneer of the tabletop. "But you were talking about a specific camp and specific people who are crazy like that."

Mustafah moved; Wakefield heard him breathing. The Marine's blacked boots squeaked as he shifted his weight. The clock mounted in the wall above Mustafah's head ticked away 14 seconds, 15 seconds.

"If they are out of their heads crazy, your family will be safer when we take them into custody. You want your mother and sisters to be safe, right?" she prodded.

He was exactly where she wanted him. To support his own thorough cover story, now Mustafah would have to reveal names.

He shrugged. "It's nobody important. Just some fanatical guys I went to school with when I was young."

"These guys have names?" Wakefield opened her notebook. She raised her pencil, though she knew these names wouldn't be significant. It was the second batch she was after. Judah felt a flush of shame wash over her as she thought of revealing names to her torturer some months before.

"There was Ja-hal and Kin-Jallah They were always trying to one-up each other with their plans." Mustafah shook his head and scratched his thigh through the blue jump suit he wore. He was due for a fresh one tomorrow. She could smell the jumper's ripeness over the table.

"Saliel was always a loner, a real freak." Mustafah said. "He used to write arrogant obituaries for writing assignments in school. There was also this posse of four guys who were a couple years ahead of me. Dahlan and Mohammad bin Sava were brothers and then there was Karviel and Rahim al Qhateb. Rumors floated around that Jamal bin Selah joined up with the hometown boys in camp."

"How long ago was this?" Wakefield asked, recording bin Selah's name on her list.

"Um," Mustafah looked up at the metal ceiling. Wakefield couldn't help following his gaze to the freshly painted white ducts and water pipes mounted to the ceiling. "Would have been before the '01 Jihad. Mohammad bin Sava and Dahlan died after camp in that attack. So it must have been '99 or 2000."

Something in the way Mustafah intoned "after camp" led Judah to believe he'd been there too. "So how would someone decide if he wanted to go to one of these camps?"

Mustafah stared at her; Wakefield blinked several times and cocked her head to the side. "Probably the same way you were recruited, ma'am." Mustafah finally spoke. "Al Qaeda, Muslim Brotherhood in Egypt, Hamas or Hezballah in Syria and Palestine, even the Iraqi Republican Guard, send videos into schools and small community centers. Twice a year from the time we are ten, men come ask boys if they want to be men. They ask if we will give up our education for Allah."

"Who came to your school?"

"A man named Asheed."

Wakefield scrawled his name into her paper. "How young are boys accepted?" she asked. Her voice sounded gravelly as it echoed in the room.

"Fifteen for camp. But occasionally the brightest ones," Mustafah paused, "or most depraved ones, depending on your perspective, ma'am, as young as twelve."

"What if they go and don't like it or want out? They're so young."

"They don't. When a man goes into a sect, he never comes out. He completes his assignment and moves forward or is dead. The disloyal are taught to hate more fiercely. Each man is thoroughly groomed for an assignment, a target based on his personal resentment.

Wakefield tucked her chin toward her. "For example?" She let her voice trail. It was a major breakthrough, *but why*? She couldn't help asking herself.

Mustafah pursed his lips. "Saliel, for example." He smiled tightly. "I would bet that he has been planted in Israel."

"There is an attack planned for Israel?"

"There's always an attack planned for Israel." Mustafah smiled.

Seven Mile Beach
Grand Cayman, Cayman Islands
14 March 2003

David Rivers squinted against the reflection of the noon sun on the powder sand strip in front of his hotel. A pair of young brothers were building a sandcastle with a green, pre-shaped bucket eight yards from his lounge chair and umbrella, nearer the lake-like ripples of the sea. The smaller boy reminded him of his younger brother, Sam. He followed the orders of his older brother, the castle foreman, just as well.

"Not like that, dummy." The older boy snatched the bucket the five-year-old had turned over. "Now I have to fill it up again. You never do anything right, Connor."

Connor's chin began to quiver and Rivers looked for a parent. A thin woman in big sunglasses slumped in a chair in the light surf. A book lay open in her lap and her head rested against the chair back.

"See if you can get some water without spilling it," the castle foreman ordered.

"Aiden, I don't want to," said Conner softly. He crossed his arms and lowered his head.

"You'll do as I say, or you won't play." Aiden threw the words at the younger boy without even glancing up. He tossed the bucket at Connor's sand-covered knees.

"Mister Rivers. Mister David Rivers." An island-slow drawl called from behind him. Slowly, so as not to attract attention, Rivers looked over his shoulder. A hotel employee, dressed in white, waved a black cellular phone over his head as he threaded among the chairs planted in the sand. "Mister David Rivers?" he called out again.

Only the U.S. government would track him down on the beach in another country while he was supposed to be honeymooning. Rivers lifted his right hand and waved it at the hotel employee with a groan. "Over here."

The tall black man broke into a white-toothed grin. "I am sorry, Mister Rivers, to disturb your peace."

Rivers shrugged and reached for the receiver as the man's walkie talkie crackled at his waist, "Mister Rivers is not in any of the restaurants."

Rivers' eyebrows shot up. "Been looking long?" he asked the man.

"Twenty-three minutes." Rivers now recognized the concierge from the lobby. "I wouldn't have bothered you at all, but the man," he pointed to the phone, "insisted he would land a chopper on my beach and find you himself if I couldn't put you on the line."

Rivers snorted. "He probably would, too."

The concierge's thin eyebrows peaked like rockets. "Just press star, three. Then off to end the call." He straightened up after releasing the phone. "We transferred the call to my personal phone. You may return it at your convenience."

"Thanks." Rivers toggled the phone. "Go ahead and start checking me out. I'm going to have to head back to the States in the next couple hours."

"Very good, sir." The tall man nodded once and took a long glance at the boys whose disagreement had escalated to shoving, before he walked away.

"No. Not 'very good'." Rivers muttered. He pressed the buttons to pick up the call. "Lieutenant Commander Rivers," he sighed into the speaker. "This had better be good."

"Please hold for Admiral Collins" a tinny voice spoke.

Rivers blubbered his lips, "Government efficiency at its best."

"Yes, it is Commander," Rivers' new commanding officer's tenor came on the line. "The little people keep me from spending my day on hold." He grunted, "Except with the Chief of Naval Operations."

"What can I do for you, sir?" Rivers asked. He moved a leg to either side of his lounge chair and dug his toes into the cooler sand below.

"You can get your six on the next mass transport back to Little Creek. PT exercises started this morning for the Teams. Your active duty status is about to get a whole lot more active. You're shipping out with the SEALs to the Middle East. Soon as you get your Team back in order. A massive team is being called out on this one."

Rivers caught his breath. "Sir, this channel is unsecured."

"Secure, unsecure. Doesn't matter. The whole world knows were going. Don't you watch the news?"

Rivers stood and tossed his empty water bottle to the dent in his chair. "How many men do you know that watch the news on their honeymoon?"

"How many men go on their honeymoon without their wife?"

"Touché." Rivers shook out his towel one-handed. The sand sprayed back against his shins.

"ASAP, Commander. Not island time. We need all our desert warfare experts in the sand, yesterday."

"Aye, aye, sir." Rivers pushed the off button.

Connor stood behind the curved spine of his older brother and slowly lifted the bucket to chest height with a squinty-eyed smile.

"Hold it right there, mister."

The youngster whipped his head around. Rivers looked the five-year-old directly in the eye. He froze, just like the SEALs-in-training under his command did. Rivers took a few steps toward them as Aiden noticed his brother's shadow and turned around.

Connor lowered the bucket, but Aiden looked up defiantly.

"Can I tell you a secret, Aiden?" Rivers asked.

"How'd you know my name?"

"I'm a SEAL in the U.S. Navy. We know everything." Rivers squatted next to Aiden.

The child's blue eyes went round. "Really?"

Rivers nodded. "I've commanded whole SEAL Teams on secret missions and in battle before."

Connor tipped the bucket and a stream of water trickled harmlessly into the sand. His eyes were fixed on Rivers' face.

"Do you want to know a secret I learned?" Aiden leaned forward and jerked his head up and down without a word. "People always listen better when you ask them instead of ordering them around." Rivers jutted his chin toward Connor. "You understand what I'm saying, don't you, Sailor?"

Aiden looked over his shoulder again at his little brother and turned back to Rivers. "I sure do, sir."

"Then the proper sailor would respond, "Aye, aye, sir."

Aiden popped to his feet, bumping into the closest wall of his castle which promptly dissolved around his ankles. With a stiff little body, he saluted. "Aye, aye, sir!"

Rivers returned his salute and about faced in the sand with a grin. Before he had taken five steps, he heard Aiden yell, "Daddy! Daddy, guess what just happened."

USS *Theodore Roosevelt*
15 March 2003
1426 hours

LCDR Wakefield leaned forward and pressed rewind on the VCR in her office, marking the eighth time she had studied the entire two-hour interrogation in two days. ADM Tamburillo had commended her efforts three hours after she had uploaded the transcript. But, she stretched her long legs with a groan, she still felt troubled by Mustafah's quote, "They complete their assignment and move forward or are dead."

He had said it without a flinch, without regret or remorse. She was convinced he had been in a camp. He knew too many details.

"What is *your* assignment, Mustafah?" she asked the office wall of Navy jets.

The drums of war beat louder each day. The sorties flown from above decks grew closer together. Even now, in the belly of the city-sized carrier, Wakefield felt the slam of the catapult. And again, as another pair of aircraft were hurled into airspace above Saudi Arabia and Kuwait and headed toward the border of Iraq.

The *Big Stick*, a nickname sailors used to refer to the USS *Theodore Roosevelt*, would steam from the Indian Ocean, along with the rest of the double-carrier Strike Force and all its many support ships, into the Arabian Sea, round the Arabian Peninsula at Oman and the UAE to enter the Gulf of Oman. They would shoot through the Strait of Hormuz and settle off the coast of Iraq in the Persian Gulf. Of course the long coast of Iran would be to their east, and keep the CIC busy with constant vigilance for threats originating from an additional sinister nation. But, for the time being, Iran, under the scholar and reformist leadership of President Mohammad Khatami, was in a calming phase. However, Iraq, under President Saddam Hussein was just gearing up into a manic phase.

The pilots Wakefield had breakfasted near that morning were down to choosing hours in a betting pool about when they would stop drilling holes in the sky and start drilling holes in the sands of Iraq. Specifically Baghdad.

That they were headed to the heart of the rebellious nation's capital was no longer a question in the mind of anyone in uniform.

Chapter Fourteen

Jerusalem, Israel
8 AM

Lazloni clung to the blue metal bar fixed to the ceiling and floor of the city bus as it turned left on the alley-sized Jerusalem street. He had called the Holy City home for the last six years. Squealing breaks indicated that the public transport was stopping before Lazloni could feel the momentum change. He shifted his weight to distribute it evenly.

Three-deep in a Sunday-morning work- and tourist-crowd, the young man twisted around to view his partner, Shevka. A wave of diesel fumes wafted over him as the bus gunned its engines to look for speed. With Shevka's dark braids and red backpack she looked like any one of the thousands of international students that packed into Israel's universities each term.

As he watched, Shevka lowered her chin to fix her eyes on the floor. The old ways were engraved on her soul. No amount coaxing or admonishing had freed her to blend into her surroundings as a Western Infidel woman.

She shifted the backpack and slid a finger under the black Nylon straps.

Lazloni's phone rang in his trouser pocket.

Holding it to his ear in the jostling crowd, he heard the hissing words, "Abort, abort. The Mossad brought soldiers and they are sweeping the entire Wall! They've cleared the entire area."

Lazloni maintained his loose posture. He recognized 16-year-old Feru's high tenor by the time he finished screeching his second word.

"Calm now, boy." Lazloni spoke in his second language, Hebrew. It matched his kippa-covered head and the prayer cloth costume that hung beneath his shirt. The bus rumbled forward to the next stop. Only two stops to go. He looked at his watch.

"Did anyone get picked up?" He searched for Shevka again in the crowd. Where did she hide?

"No, no." Feru's breathing slowed to normal—a fast, annoying wheeze. "The others, the teams, are away. But the soldiers found the material and are taking every scrap of paper from the crevices of the Wall."

"Do they appear to know what they are looking for?"

"Yeah. Somebody talked." The kid's phone crackled.

"This whole operation has stunk since—um, the second party got involved." Lazloni didn't want to use Hussein's name on the phone or in public. All calls were monitored. "We will change our own plans. Good-bye."

"Good-bye?"

Lazloni heard the questioning tone, but had already moved his finger over the END key. Shevka was staring at him, her brown eyes wide. He would miss those eyes. Maybe she'd be one of his 72 virgins in Paradise.

The bus rumbled to a stop and an elderly woman hobbled off in front of him. Lazloni settled into her seat and motioned Shevka to join him.

"Change of plans," he whispered. "We are no longer going to make it to the Platform. Let me into the pack." He motioned for her to turn around. Unzipping the top, Lazloni glanced around. "Sheep without a shepherd—their Scriptures are correct," he mumbled. Everyone on the bus was wrapped in his or her own thoughts. The papers he and Shevka spent four days gumming with C-4 felt smooth and tidy in their two-column stack.

It wasn't planned, but better to take out the crowd of 70 people on the bus, than let the day pass with no statement. Purim. The Israelis would not escape their due today.

Lazloni unwrapped a blasting cap inside his coat pocket with his left hand. He'd always been more dexterous with his left. He shoved it into the top of the C-4 and leaned over Shevka. "Everything worthwhile costs us something," he whispered at the back of her bare neck so she alone could hear him over the din of the motor, the chattering of the children, and the honking of the traffic.

Her smooth skin bumped into gooseflesh.

Lazloni timed his ignition with the next left turn. The momentum would render the Mamilla intersection useless for the day and destroy buildings on all five corners.

SHLOMO HA MELEKH/HA' EMEQ the sign pointed. "King Solomon Street and Emeq Street" Lazloni exhaled slowly in English.

Lazloni sucked in his final breath and loosed the hatred he had let fester and bottled in his belly for this moment. "Allu Akbar!" he screamed and pressed the detonator before anyone could stop him.

USS *Theodore Roosevelt* Bridge
16 March 2003

Wakefield stepped over the kneeknocker in the hatchway at the entrance to the bridge. An efficient hum of duty filled the air. "Bring her about. Two-six-zero degrees." Captain MacSod ordered. "Catch that tailwind and give those boys as much lift as possible on their way home.

The X.O. repeated the order to the helmsman who began twisting knobs to turn the behemoth ship 70 degrees to starboard.

Wakefield assumed a couple of planes were coming in low on fuel. She snapped to attention when the movement died down. "Lieutenant Commander Wakefield reporting as ordered, Captain," she called out.

The skipper adjusted his ball cap over his short hair as he turned from the giant windscreen. His eyes flashed wildly. "What took you so long, Lieutenant Commander?"

That was certainly not an invitation to stand easy. "I was in the middle of an interrogation, sir." She tried to phrase her statement with humility to keep from further riling his anger. "Did I wrongly assume that you'd want the prisoner secured first?"

"When are you going to finish with that kid?"

"He's cracking, sir. Revealing more information every day."

"He's been here 18 days. What's he planning to do—take over the ship? You have one day. Twenty-four hours and I want that terrorist off my ship!"

"Aye, aye sir." Wakefield straightened her backbone. *What is up with the skipper?*

"If he's not on the COD tomorrow, you'll be on your way to Gitmo with him. Is that clear?"

"Crystal, sir." Wakefield grunted with as much respect as she could fake.

"Dismissed. And don't bother to say good bye tomorrow."

Wakefield about faced and the duty guard released her. The hatch slammed with a metallic clatter behind her.

Her thighs had not yet recovered from the 16 ladders up from the lower decks and she was headed back down. "Well, Mustafah, it looks like your wish will be granted tomorrow afternoon." Mustafah had been asking for two days what the prison at Guantanamo Bay was like, bargaining with information at a chance to be sent to minimum security.

Back in her office, Wakefield logged into the secure portion of the Naval Intelligence site. "How should I phrase this," she mumbled. If she was wrong—would it damage her career more, or his?

Maybe CAPT Huntingdon would be a better choice. She changed the address of the email to her former immediate supervisor instead of her former C.O.

Could you do some discreet inquires for me, personally? I am concerned about the command here. The skipper in particular. See if there is something in his background to suggest mental—

Wakefield paused—should she type *mental illness?* She back spaced and typed *drug use.* That might be worse. Backspacing again, she settled on *anything unusual.*

She hit send and would deal with the consequences later.

Suitland, VA
March 16, 2003
2345 hours EST

ADM Tamburillo stood facing the bank of six televisions along the right wall of the empty war room on the third floor of his building. He clasped his hands by rote at the small of his back. Twenty-four hours a day the screen figures clamored mutely, until something happened. They say a picture is worth a thousand words, but Tamburillo's mouth was speechless as his eyes flicked between CNN and the secure channel beamed to all the national security agencies and military intelligence.

The blackened hull of a city bus protruded like a cigarette butt from the front doors of a white stone and glass building. Flames devoured a nursery school at the Mamilla pedestrian shopping mall junction on King Solomon Street in Jerusalem, early on a holiday morning. The man reading the script kept using the street name over and over. Probably because it was finally a foreign name that the young anchor could pronounce. Tamburillo shook his head.

"Wait a minute," Tamburillo mumbled. "Where are the screaming mommas? The crazed kids? Why take out a school on a holiday? Where's the damage?" Something had gone wrong; this was not the primary target. It was plain as day. Pulling in a deep breath, Tamburillo bellowed, "Somebody get me some sound!"

No answer. He stomped back to the door in the room lit only by the blue and red lights of the screens. "Where is the officer on duty in here?"

"Right here, sir." A female voice spoke from his left at the second entrance to the war room.

Tamburillo whirled like a momma bear and stalked toward the petite brunette. "Where have you been?"

"In the head, sir." She looked startled out of her skin. "Sorry, sir. Coffee got to me."

"Ensign—" Tamburillo leaned toward her to read her name plate in the flickering shadows, "Bowery—"

"Sir, yes sir." She interrupted.

"Get everyone back here by 0100 hours."

"Are we in crisis mode, sir?" The tiny officer peered around him at the television monitors.

"The crisis is over, Ensign." Tamburillo said. She snapped back to attention. "We missed it. This is damage control."

"Right away, sir."

"Dismissed."

Bowery about faced and disappeared through the entryway where she had just appeared. Tamburillo seated himself in the theatre-like arrangement to absorb as much as he could from the broadcast. No need for sound. CNN wouldn't have more than old, repetitious information yet.

The images flicked through his brain. A woman staring at the commotion as she stood motionless on the sidewalk. An onscreen blurb interview with a man who apparently called himself a rabbi, but who looked as if he might have been sleeping on a street corner next door to the attack. A pair of toddler-aged brothers trying to ride tricycles over ash–covered cobblestone. A grey-faced woman with two beige tracks on her cheeks beating her chest with her fist next to a hulk of charred wood that looked to have been a flower kiosk. A somber Muslim cleric with a black-bearded jaw that twitched back and forth as he spoke to the off-screen reporter with fire trucks spraying out the flames behind him. A squinty-eyed young man yelling at something off-camera with a mouth too wide for his face.

"What was your real target?" Tamburillo chewed as the camera man closed in on the butt of the charred bus. "I'll figure you out before the morning news hits the air waves," he vowed. Tamburillo ran a thick hand over his tight-spiral hair.

CHAPTER FIFTEEN

USS *Theodore Roosevelt*
Tuesday, March 17, 2003
1145 hours

L CDR Wakefield plunked down her third empty coffee cup and tucked the telephone closer under her bent neck. "I heard a couple hours ago, sir. We have satellite TV aboard, remember?" she said to CAPT Huntingdon. She glanced at the clock. "Got called in, huh?" It was the wee hours of Tuesday morning for him. Wakefield chuckled lightly. "I don't miss that part at all."

Huntingdon groaned then laughed. She could picture him smoothing his thin thatch of hair over his ever-widening bald spot like he always did when he spoke on the phone. "I don't miss spaghetti and bug juice twice a week," he said.

Wakefield rolled her eyes. "Only once a week, so far," she informed him. "So, Mustafah was telling the truth about the holiday attack. Last night at sundown began Purim in Israel."

"If they don't quit bombing each other nobody will want the leftover wreckage of Jerusalem." Huntingdon sounded fed up with the situation.

"It is the Promised Land, sir. It will always be desired. Have you had time to research my other little matter?"

Huntingdon hesitated. Was it the subject change or the new topic? "I have," he said finally. "Captain MacSod's wife Martha was diagnosed with a stomach condition about six months ago that the doctors believe was due to ingesting poison over a period of months."

Wakefield gasped. "That's unbelievable."

She grabbed a pen from her desk top and took notes.

"The poison had built up in her system, but Dr. Johns, her treating physician at Naval Medical Center San Diego, thought they'd caught it in time to purge her body of the toxins."

Wakefield blew out the breath she'd been holding. Had MacSod been poisoning his own wife? He had the intelligence and temperament for a calculated murder, from what she had seen so far.

Huntingdon went on, "Two weeks after she began the regimen, Martha MacSod ended up back on the good doctor's exam table. Only this time she was dead."

Judah's spirit jolted in her chest. The pen dropped from her fingers. Dead? She chased the pen as it rolled toward the edge of her desk.

"Her neck snapped in half after she was hit from behind on Torrey Pines Road. Her car nose-dived 110 feet into a wooded ravine." Huntingdon cleared his throat.

"When did she die?" Wakefield poised her pen to record the details.

"I already cross-referenced MacSod's duty record. He was at sea. Three weeks into a five-week shakedown cruise at the time of her accident. The *TR* had just come out of a nine-month dry dock for maintenance and repairs."

"So he was deployed when she discovered the poison in her system and began treatment. If she told him over the phone, do you think he could have hired someone to run her off the road since the poison had been discovered?" Wakefield glanced at the closed office door, almost expecting the skipper to burst in on her the way he did the first day.

"The investigating San Diego County Sheriff's deputy cleared him via skype in the JAG office. Lieutenant Commander Wallace, your predecessor aboard the *Theodore Roosevelt*, also noted personality problems with MacSod. Wallace was aboard during the shakedown cruise and said the oddities started after his wife's death."

"Could be guilt." Wakefield doodled a circle within a circle.

"Or grief."

"Maybe." Wakefield was skeptical. She'd never seen grief manifest as the captain was behaving. He seemed almost paranoid.

"I already talked to Admiral Tamburillo, he said he wants you to observe MacSod over the next couple days and determine if he needs to be relieved of his command."

"During a time of war?" Wakefield swiveled her chair to gaze at the F-18 Hornet on her wall. She knew what being relieved would do to the skipper's career.

"More certainly now than if we were at peace. The Navy can't have a carrier captain in an underway Carrier Strike Group who is not in top form."

The door creaked open as two raps sounded. Heart in her throat, she spun her chair to identify the intruder. Just Juarez. She motioned him inside. "I, uh, I'll see what I can do, sir." Juarez held the prisoner transfer papers in a file for her to sign and seal for the marine gunnery sergeant who would escort Mustafah to Gitmo. "Ensign." She held out her hand for Mustafah's file as she hung up with Huntingdon. "Let's get this show on the road."

On the flight deck, Wakefield zipped her mandatory white flak jacket—a life preserver if she got knocked overboard. The wind whipped blond strands that had worked loose from her French braid into her face. The COD that would transport her prisoner to Ramstein Air Force Base, Germany, sat impatiently on the blacktop.

The pilot had already claimed his seat and Wakefield could see him in the tiny cockpit window completing his pre-flight checklist as the engine spooled up.

A pair of Marines under arms brought Mustafah topside. They stopped in front of her. The now orange-jumpsuited prisoner carried a worn paperback Quran between his cuffed hands. His suit looked crisp, but Wakefield knew from 12 years of traveling with the service that by the time he reached his tropical destination, Mustafah would look and feel like somebody's leftover ragdoll.

"Where am I going, ma'am?" Mustafah shifted from one foot to the other and looked up from the deck to meet her eyes.

"Guantanamo Bay, Cuba." He knew that.

"How long until I can go back to my family? You know I have nothing to do with your war. This imprisonment is unfair. Un-American." He lowered his chin and Wakefield got the impression he was disappointed with her. Or acting like he was in order to gain sympathy.

"You will be held until the Middle East is secured, then shipped out with all the other EPOWs."

"That will be years, Commander. Can't you do something?"

Wakefield transferred Mustafah's folder to her right hand and the sea wind flapped it open. She tightened her grip before the contents fouled the deck. "Gunny," she turned to Gunnery Sergeant Balfour, "This prisoner is now in your custody."

The man in his mid-thirties jerked his chin down in a gruff affirmative gesture. "Yes, ma'am," he said with Marine enthusiasm.

"There must be something you can do," Mustafah came as close to pleading as he ever had. "I have to get home."

"I've recommended minimum security once you get inside, Mustafah." No harm in telling him up front. It would give him something to daydream about on the 29-hour trip.

A brief glimmer twitched the corners of his eyes. His face softened. "Thank you. Peace be unto you. *Salaam alikium.*" He switched languages.

"*Alikim a'Salaam,*" Judah repeated. "Don't disappoint me, Mustafah," she warned in his native tongue.

The pilot stuck his head out the door. You boys waiting for an engraved invitation? Hop on; this bird is flying the coop."

Wakefield turned to Ensign Juarez as the green shirt on deck shut the COD's cabin door. "Get me the commanding officer at Gitmo on the line A-sap. I didn't like the look in his eye when Mustafah got the news."

CHAPTER SIXTEEN

Fourteen-year-old Takita Abdullah awoke to silence. Qusay Hussain's upper respiratory snoring was not something the girls at school ever mentioned. Takita listened for tell-tale noise from the private marble bathroom off the prince's opulent bedroom. Not a sound.

She rolled to her right side. Her pillow was damp against her cheek.

Fear bit into her bare stomach. "Not again," she moaned under her breath. Takita's shallow breath came faster as the prince's threat resounded in her mind. If she woke him with her crying again he would send her to the labyrinth prison.

He had promised she could keep the silk gowns no matter what, but—she swallowed and placed a hand on her heart to keep its beating in her chest—the underground prison was wet. And cold. And smelled of something she was afraid to identify.

The prince of Iraq had taken her there on her first day in the palace. Silk would warm her as much as cellophane in that horrible place. "Allah, if only I could disappear from this place." Tiki whispered.

Heavy tread sounded in the hall, coming closer with each step.

130

Takita clenched her jaw and snapped her eyes closed against the darkness. "My father's Allah has done nothing for me." She whispered. "God of my mother," Tiki squeezed her eyes until the pain numbed. She had never addressed Jesus before. "Come and save me from—" *What exactly?* she wondered.

The heavy steps stopped in front of the double doors of the prince's chambers. Her eyes snapped open at the silence. "Jesus, save me from this man," she pushed the tiny words out in a rush as a crack of light broke into the darkness.

She snapped her eyes closed again and willed her body to relax. He would never believe she was asleep lying as stiff as a 16-hour-old corpse in his sheets.

She pinched her waist to make herself relax. The track of light from the crack in the doors moved across her closed eyes.

Behind her eyelids the red light flashed off a moment as a body obstructed the path from the door. The shoes clicked three steps against the marble tile floor and softened as they hit the thick Persian carpet.

"Tiki," a low female voice whispered. "Little one, wake up quickly." Jocina, the heavyset ladies' maid in her sixties shook her arm. "He will return any minute."

"I'm awake," Takita pushed against the mattress to sit up. "Have you come to help me run away?"

Jocina chuckled low and deep. "There is no running away from the palace, child."

"But, I prayed." Takita's stomach sank. Something in the old maid's tone unsettled her further. "Why are you here then?" She tried to keep her chin from trembling, but the constant companion of nerves was manifesting in her thighs again.

"The crying." Jocina said as she propelled Takita into the bathroom. "The prince ordered me to leave you in the West Prison with the other women."

Jocina opened one of the drawers in the prince's bathroom bureau and pulled out a gleaming pair of silver sheers. Takita's eyes, not fully adjusted to the light, caught the scissors, and she stepped back, bumping into the wall.

"Come now," Jocina said. "I'm going to hide you in the East Prison. It's better there and the West guards won't bother you."

It was then that Takita noticed the dusty boy's trousers, robes and cap folded on the countertop. She stepped forward.

The metal sheers felt cold against her neck and the air stung as her hair disappeared in fistfuls. Scurrying through the lengthy halls, Takita couldn't stop touching the blunt ends of her hair.

"Hurry now, and don't speak to anyone." They stopped at the oak door at the bottom of a stairwell Takita had never seen before. "God be with you, Little Tiki, I've done my best."

Jocina pounded a meaty fist on the thick door. "To the East Side with this boy! Elder Prince's orders," she barked at the skinny uniform who opened the door.

The guard's fingers closed around Takita's upper arm. "What'd you do little boy? Burn his breakfast?" He laughed.

USS *Theodore Roosevelt*
16 March 2003
1816 hours ship's time

Lieutenant Commander Judah Wakefield signed the last copy of her Mustafah report and pushed back her chair. "That's about as thorough as anybody will ever read." She tossed her pen to the desktop. She had included every detail on the video, down to every school chum's name. Even her thoughts on his personality and vocal tones and nuances under questioning being rehearsed. "Twenty-one-year-olds don't naturally flirt with interrogators unless they have practiced holding up under interrogation," she assessed for whomever would read the report in future days. Maybe with the right database, headquarters could cross-reference and find the discrepancy. She stared at the F-18 Hornet pictures. "I know I missed something with him."

Still slumped in her chair, Judah spun to reach for her computer mouse. The files she'd requested on CAPT MacSod were available to download. She glanced at her watch. She could afford a few more minutes to browse his personnel file before the chow line closed.

As the downloading file progress-indicator line widened, Wakefield stepped over and opened the office door. Ensign Juarez stared blankly at his screen, all eight fingers immobile on the keyboard. Gates' desk was cleared and so was his chair.

Her eyebrow jerked up in surprise. But it wasn't so surprising really. "Juarez, I'm going to stay around a few minutes, but your shift is over. Get some chow."

He glanced around slowly as if trying to identify some strange sound after coming out of a deep sleep.

"Can I get you anything, ma'am?" He said when he finally saw her standing in the hatchway. He palmed the desk surface four times searching for a pen as he rose to a stoop.

"You're dismissed, Ensign." She smirked and tapped her ear to show him where his elusive pen was hiding.

Juarez reached up and touched the pen and the left half of his face rose in an embarrassed smile. "Aye, aye, ma'am." He straightened his back as she returned to the office and closed the door behind her.

Easing herself back into her chair, Judah's eyes flicked to the bottom of the open file. "Eighteen pages," her eyes bugged. "Who has an 18-page service record?" Certainly none of the Navy men she had investigated before.

MacSod's dark eyes stared her down from the two-by-three-inch service picture he'd had taken when he made captain, six years earlier. The wrinkles at his eyes were deeper now, as was the dark baggage under his eyes. His somber expression turned his lips inward. MacSod had shaved the steel-grey mustache sometime since the photo was taken.

The first entry past the names and numbers of his commanding officers stated that MacSod had been passed over a second time for an admiral's star. Cross-referencing the date, she breathed, "Just six days before his wife's death. What a week! He probably found out about the Admiral's board results the same day. And at sea to boot. Double whammy!" Wakefield winced, "Even if I don't like the guy."

"Even if you don't like what guy?" a deep voice growled from the doorway.

"Skipper!" Judah gulped, hoping to steady her voice. Wakefield jumped to stand in the senior officer's presence. "What can I do for you?" *How long have you been standing there?* her mind reeled trying to recall what she'd said aloud.

"Who were you talking about just now?" CAPT MacSod strolled completely into the room and pushed the door shut with his weight. The click was just what she needed.

Wakefield leaned into her desk and clicked the X to close the document.

Do you want to save document? the pop-up screen asked. She clicked YES. "It's a man I've been profiling for the last couple of days," she reverted her gaze to MacSod.

MacSod took two steps toward her and stopped, rocking from heel to toe with his hands behind his back. "You have an aversion to all Arabs or just that young Mustafah fellow?" MacSod asked. His voice held no contempt, and based on what she had just skimmed in his record, she couldn't decide on the best way to answer.

"I don't trust him, sir." she finally said, deeply grateful he had misunderstood who they were talking about. "I sent my uneasiness to Gitmo. I'm sure they'll get to the bottom of it, sir."

She stood still under his inspection while he continued rocking heel toe, heel toe.

The clicking of his soles in the silence was too much. "What can I help you with, Captain?"

"I just came to be sure my intel officer didn't miss another meal, Commander. Grab your cover. We'll eat together."

Judah's stomach churned. The screen asked her to name the file. Leaning down she pressed the B key and then enter. Finally the incriminating document was closed away into the depths of her computer universe.

"It would be an honor, sir." She straightened back up, heart pounding. *And a chance to continue my profiling,* she added to herself.

"Yes, it is, Commander Wakefield." MacSod's mouth turned up, but his eyes did not participate in the smile.

Little Creek Naval Base, VA
Wednesday, 18 March, 2003
0848 hours EST

LCDR David Rivers switched his coffee mug to his left hand and pushed open the briefing auditorium door. It would squeak, he knew, from past briefings he had held for Teams here. Invariably, one SEAL was late. Today, it was him. A lot of firsts recently, he thought as all the bald-to-#2 razored heads turned at his interruption.

"Mister Rivers, good of you to join us," ADM Collins said jabbing his metal pointer at him from the lectern, "finally," he added with a grin.

Does everybody know about the botched honeymoon? Rivers wondered. He saw far too many grins on his fellow warriors' faces for there not to have been an announcement. Rivers tossed a grin back at his C.O. and slid into a theater-style seat.

"As I was saying," ADM Collins picked back up easily, "Team Two will remain ready on the West Coast. Team Three, here on the East. All others are deploying to the Middle East. Team Six that usually responds to that area is dividing up and will mingle with the rest of you. Each team leader—that's LT Locklin on Four, CDR Jackson with Five, LCDR Rivers with Six, LT Howard with Seven, and LCDR Chassey with Eight—make sure you have at least two pair of the Desert Warfare specialists with you."

Rivers shifted in his seat and looked at the back of all the shaved heads around him. All the men would make it back to the States, he knew that much. They were SEALs. And SEALs never left a man behind. But how many of these men would return to American soil in body bags? That was the question.

"This is desert warfare, but it is also urban warfare," ADM Collins tapped the map with his pointer. "I know it will be different for some of you who've excelled in Jungle or Underwater Demolition specialties. Not a ton of water in Iraq. Just those famous rivers." A chuckle waved through the men. "Just do what you do, gentlemen."

"Ooh-rah," the warrior grunt resounded from deep within more than three hundred SEALs.

What Collins said was true, but it was the first time Rivers had heard Iraq mentioned specifically. "So, old Saddam is finally being de-throned," Rivers whispered as more ooh-rahs echoed.

"When do we start exercises, sir?" a young petty officer third class called out from the front row. The room quieted instantly. The question had apparently been on everyone's minds.

"Fourteen hundred hours," the admiral bellowed. Rivers couldn't distinguish any of the comments that stirred in the room. "Those of you with families stationed here at Little Creek have until 1200 hours to go home and back your bags, kiss your wives and babies, and report back to this room. This deployment will be on lock down after noon. Any other questions?"

A hand went up to the left and three rows in front of Rivers. "Masterson?"

The wide man stood and haltingly asked, "What about me, sir?"

Collins paused. His face blank. "Masterson is without a partner. He and Bear were together."

"Until three weeks ago," a voice spoke up, barely under his breath. Bitterness dripped and Rivers wasn't completely sure the speaker didn't *mean* for everyone to hear.

"Who wants him?" The admiral asked, pretending to ignore the comment. Rivers had seen the tell-tale jaw muscle tightening though.

"Has he been cleared?" a second voice asked.

Before Collins could reply, Rivers shot to his feet. "I'll take him, sir. Put him down as my partner for Team Six, or wherever we end up."

Masterson twisted around to find the volunteer. "If that's all right with you, Chief." Rivers challenged the younger man with a hard look.

The crowd of SEALs stirred once more. Rivers knew from experience they were speculating to their neighbors on Masterson's dereliction of duty charges. Chief Petty Officer Masterson nodded once and sat back down.

"Anything else?" ADM Collins asked. Everyone looked around. "Dismissed."

Rivers had dropped his SCUBA gear at the house and picked up his sea bag on his way to the base, so he headed back to the coffee maker in the hall while more than a hundred men reached for their cell phones and jogged for the parking lot.

"Commander."

Rivers identified Masterson's baritone behind him. He slurped up a mouthful of black java and swallowed before it had time to burn his tongue. "Funny thing about coffee," Rivers said turning toward his new partner. "Everybody likes it different. Some like sludge, some as sweet as dessert, some when it looks more like tea. But I never saw a SEAL turn it down, and I never saw it fail to pick me up."

Rivers paused. He reached for a second stoneware mug off the double-stacked pile. He held it out. "Have a cup, Masterson."

The chief petty officer nodded. He understood. They would be partners, and they would never speak of his dead buddy, at least not in any accusing manner.

"I believe I will, sir." He held out a meaty hand. "James Masterson. Call me Mass."

"Mass." Rivers tried it on. "Can't imagine how you got that handle," he said taking in the chief's girth.

CHAPTER SEVENTEEN

Wakefield followed MacSod's lead and rose from the captain's table, leaving most of her plate full. The stares and the captain's inane conversation had made swallowing difficult and tasting impossible.

The mostly congenial X.O. had joined them half-way through the meal. Bradshaw, a handsome man with Italian good looks and charm had a charisma about him that would cause men to follow him as a captain. Someday soon, according to her assessment. He did have a tendency toward arrogant speech, but Wakefield couldn't determine whether it was a put on or if it came naturally to him.

CAPT MacSod had given as much friction to the X.O. as he usually did to her, so maybe that was just his personality post-wife's-passing.

The long walk back to female country gave her time to think. First about Melissa Garvey then about CAPT MacSod. Something was definitely not right about him. She just couldn't quite make it fit into a consciousness-slot in her mind.

Wakefield rapped twice on her own hatch. She felt her jaw muscle flex as she reached for the handle, despising that she had knocked, but even less wanting to walk in on something she would never be able to un-see.

Twisting the knob, no sound or light came from the shared space. Judah breathed a sigh of relief. She hated living this way.

Opening her locker, Judah stared at her running shoes for a full seven seconds before the tiredness won out. "It's gonna be an early night instead." Her mouth scrunched to the left as a bit of guilt snuck in. She had worked out exactly once in over ten days. "Tomorrow," she promised as she reached for a nightshirt instead.

She propped herself up in the upper bunk, even though the lower one was hers by seniority rights. She couldn't stomach taking it from Garvey. Judah opened her Bible, with the intent to read herself to sleep rather than study.

Twenty minutes later she found herself staring into space, still thinking about the captain. She refocused on the black letters scanning for her place. What had sent her spinning off into thought who-knows-how-long ago?

"Acts 27:42," she found it again and read aloud. "And the soldiers' plan was to kill the prisoners, lest any of them should swim away." It was in the story of Paul's shipwreck at Malta. Probably not the best reading material aboard a ship that is underway, but what made her think of MacSod? "'Kill the prisoners'?" Wakefield repeated. "Which prisoners? Lord, are you warning me about Mustafah? I already called Gitmo." She shook her head. It didn't feel right.

She ran her first finger lightly up and down her nose as she thought and rethought. "Did MacSod hire someone to kill his wife? What motive would he have? Inheritance, Insurance? Revenge for some wrong she had committed against him?" Her eyes bore a hole in the line where the ceiling met the bulkhead at the end of her bunk. Was there any other motive for a man of the captain's rank and clout? Murder always came down to love, money, or revenge.

Wakefield let her Bible fall forward on her chest as she reviewed MacSod's service record in her mind. She'd always been able to recall minute details as if she was reading them in front of her face again.

Up to the time he was passed over for an Admiral's star, MacSod's record was exemplary. Every rank had several commendations and pleasant remarks about his proficiency and leadership. The file was a little short after becoming captain though. There was a nice recent letter to the Admiralty Board from X.O. Bradshaw saying how pleasant he was to work for. But that was all for the entire previous year. That was outside of normal for MacSod, according to his service record. It wasn't that there was anything bad, just nothing besides the adequate service check-marked by his superior officers. No comments, no commendations, no stories of great leadership. Like maybe his file was expunged.

"Do they do that?" Wakefield whispered. What could he have done that would have left his record so squeaky clean? Or *not* done that had left it so empty? She flashed over to think about some of the missions Dietz had sent her on for the CIA over the previous five years. None of that—good or bad—had made it to her service record. *Has MacSod has been moonlighting for the CIA?* she wondered.

"And yet, the man still has 5,000 men and women under his command and an aircraft carrier to steer. The CIA I know is a bit more understated than that."

She shook her head. Even though her mind was spinning, her eyelids were dropping. MacSod was one mystery that would not be solved tonight.

Judah closed the leather-bound book and shoved it under her pillow with one hand, as she twisted the switch and extinguished the light with the other.

Her eyes were already closed against the blackness in the room, and she felt herself sinking into the slightly-softer-than-a-board mattress when she heard it. It wasn't the catapults slamming or other normal shipboard life sounds of living with 5,000 other people. It was a still voice. It was a feeling, and it was words, yet it was not words exactly. The knowledge she now had was "Something big is coming, and I will be there with you."

Her eyelids flew open against the blackness and she inhaled deeply. Her mind raced again wondering what circumstances were ahead and whether she would have what it would take to survive it. But surviving was not enough. Judah wanted to be sure she came through well. "All right, Lord. We will go through together."

And Judah went to sleep.

Little Creek Naval Base, VA
Wednesday, 18 March, 2003
1350 hours

SEAL Team Six had already dispersed themselves among the other Teams and Rivers' was now leading Team Seven. Rivers' last man shoved his gear under the bus and slid his hand up the handrails at the entrance. In two large steps where there were three stairs, SEAL Team Seven was all aboard a charter bus.

Having stored his pack with CPO Masterson right after they'd finished their coffee, Rivers mounted the stairs himself, and leaned outward as he grasped the handrails. He glanced up and down the line of busses to be sure everyone else was loading in a timely manner. He saw bus 4 slowly pulling away from the curb in a pouf of thick exhaust; it turned in a tight maneuver around the rest of the bus line.

Ten minutes early and only a dozen or so men still milled around waiting to board their team busses, Rivers felt good about the assignment. He had exchanged handshakes with men from nearly every BUD/S class he had ever taught.

"We're good to go." Rivers nodded at the driver and turned his attention to his men. Forty men leaving, forty men he would bring home. However long the campaign lasted.

The door swooshed closed behind him as his foot hit the top tread, and Rivers completed his transition from civilian bridegroom to battle commander of one of the most elite teams on earth. The familiar rush pulsed through his bloodstream. He discarded his flip phone into the shoebox at the entryway with more than 50 other phones and PDAs. They would be phone-free for the duration.

"Good to have you aboard, men." Rivers grasped the vertical bracing bar with his left hand as the driver pulled away from the curb. "Let's go earn our Tridents all over again."

As one, even the new guys joining Team Seven, grunted, "Ooh-rah!"

Rivers gave a single nod of agreement and strode back to sit in the empty seat next to Mass. The men all sat in their pairs, leaving several empty seat rows without being told. These fighting machines were honed and needed no pep talk on their way to The Facility where they would hash out battle plans.

As the men unloaded their gear into the multi-room barracks on the southern end of Little Creek Base, immediately next door to The Facility where they would begin planning their raids according to their assignments, all the Team Leaders, and their seconds-in-command (2IC) flowed directly to the Facility.

Rivers filed in with the others and saw that the Chief of Naval Operations (CNO) James Abbot himself was on-line in the secure uplink room waiting for them. His four admiral's stars glinted on his golden shoulder boards under the fluorescent lights of his office.

The room darkened slightly as the last person closed the door at the top of the stairs behind himself. The CNO began speaking and each leader in the room stiffened to attention.

"I want to thank each of you personally for the service you are about to perform for the U.S. Navy and for the world." Abbot was not a political appointee but one who had climbed through the officers' rankings through blood, sweat, and tears. Rivers hadn't seen his record personally but had heard the rumors that Abbot had attempted BUD/S as a lieutenant, but had to wash out in the second-to-last week because of a broken collar bone; Rivers could hear the genuine respect the CNO held for the men who surrounded him.

"I have every confidence in you."

"Thank you, sir," someone in the front said.

"Your assignment is critical in the growing tensions in the Middle East. As you know we are deploying boots-on-the-ground in Iraq soon. I'm sure each of you have friends in theater or headed there now.

"We need to cut off the head of the snake that is destroying his own people for the sake of his ego. Sadaam Hussein. From what our profilers are reporting, we have a textbook narcissist on our hands. He is doing everything he can to strengthen his position and not lose power. And his sons are worse than he is, if that is possible. We want the three of them to stand trial at Peace Palace in The Hague. ASAP.

"However we don't particularly expect him to come willingly, so if plan A of arresting them does not appear to be working, you may want to watch for any attempt to take as many of us with them into death as possible.

"Your budget, is not unlimited." The CNO's eyebrows furrowed as he dipped his chin, "But, I'll see that you have access to all the funding you need. The Husseins have deep pockets lined with oil profits working against us. This will be a chess match between masters, gentlemen, not a game of checkers, and we know you will plan accordingly."

After fielding only a couple of questions, Abbot signed off with a nod. "Happy plotting." Then the giant screen displayed the test-color stripes.

USS *Theodore Roosevelt*
Wednesday, March 18, 2003
0606 hours

The catapult had begun sometime during the early hours of the day, and had continued for hours. When Wakefield had risen at 0400 to prepare for the office at 0500, the constant barrage of sound and motion had made showering—even a Navy-style, wet-soap-rinse shower—difficult to accomplish without the support of a hand on the bulkhead at all times.

In the passageway, the flight deck crew in their red, green, or blue shirts coming off watch had been excited, chattering like schoolgirls about a crush.

Something big was in the works.

In the office, Wakefield had no prisoners to interrogate in her rotation and by 0630 was caught up on all her paperwork.

She glanced at the closed door and then signed into the Naval Intelligence Community Database and grabbed a few files with headlines that looked like they could relate to what she was experiencing aboard ship for analysis.

"Hmm." She read the screen and she stirred her coffee. The chatter was that Saddam Hussein was in Baghdad and the Coalition Forces, with the Americans in the lead, were going after him. "That explains all the noise."

For two long days the limited bombing in Baghdad had continued, and Wakefield read about it via Naval Intel Community headlines. Reading between the lines Judah could see the American strategy seemed to be softening up the target area by painting the military and transportation lines. She drank coffee, dusted the office, read stories, and ruminated about MacSod and the late-night word from the Father about something big coming. The whole ship was living at-the-ready, and Wakefield could feel the tension even in the bowels of the ship between the two sailors in her front office.

Maybe Huntingdon had more info on MacSod than he had given her. She picked up her phone by habit and then replaced the receiver in the cradle. It would not do to be overheard by any of the coms crew asking more questions about the captain. And besides, Huntingdon should be at home with his family right now anyway.

Email. Next best thing. Unfortunately that would leave a paper trail. Well, she shrugged knowing she would not be able to let it rest, if it went to the point of an official investigation at some point in the future, at least she could secure the information flying through the ether by classifying the conversation, including the questions she was going to ask Huntingdon.

Eight o'clock came and went while she still composed and reframed the questions for Huntingdon. So many, maybe she should just get him to fax or scan and email all the evidence from the cops' investigation into Martha MacSod's unfortunate demise.

Her outer office rattled at 8:22 ship's time, and she looked up expectantly at her closed office door. MacSod would not surprise her this time.

Nothing. Not even any voices in the reception office where Juarez and Gates helped anyone who came by and prioritized any access people needed to her.

She needed a stretch anyway, so she got up and grabbed her empty cup.

As she entered the office the front hatch was just closing behind someone. "Who was that?" She asked Ensign Juarez who was also up and headed toward the coffee pot.

"A buddy of Gates, ma'am."

Wakefield eyed Gates' empty desk. "And where is the illustrious Mr. Gates?"

"I don't know, ma'am that's what I told the other guy too."

"Aren't you guys buddies? How long have you been working together? Is he always late?"

The ensign's eyes widened like a doe.

Judah stifled a sigh. "Just answer one at a time." How did this guy ever get assigned to work in Naval Intelligence? Both of the sailors assigned to her office were subpar in her book. What had Wallace let them get away with while he was assigned to the *Theodore Roosevelt*? Judah had met Wallace once and he seemed like an officer that had his head in the game. She shook her head. Just one more mystery floating around this big ship.

Gates came wandering in just then. He froze just for a moment in the doorway as he saw the two officers staring at his entry. Then he continued on to his desk and scooted around to the seat on the backside that faced the middle of the room, much like Wakefield's did, for securing information on the screen from prying eyes.

"Are you kidding me?" Wakefield asked. She felt like her eyebrows were above her hairline. "Not even an excuse or explanation?" She asked. She turned around to set her coffee cup down for safekeeping.

"Report. Front and cenTER!" she called out. Her Army-drill-sergeant impersonation voice echoed off the walls, even intimidating her a bit. Both Gates and Juarez jumped, but Ensign Juarez stiffened to attention at least twice as fast as his enlisted shipmate.

Wakefield waited, somewhat impatiently, somewhat curiously, to see how many seconds it would actually take for Gates to get himself squared away.

She went toe-to-toe with him. The top of his head only came up to her nose, so she was yelling directly into his eyes. "What time do you think we start the day around here?"

Gates lifted half his face in a shrug.

"Use your words." Wakefield knew she was being a bit degrading, but this man's posture and attitude was all wrong.

"I don't know. Wallace said he didn't care what time I came in."

"I don't believe you, sailor. Shall we call him and have him tell me that he just let you show up any ol' time you felt like sashaying through the door?"

"But it's true ma'am. The day I was transferred over here at two in the afternoon, Wallace told me, 'I don't care what time you get here tomorrow'."

Wakefield blinked at him and turned to Juarez. "What time do you think we start around here?" Her voice was still sharp but a lot lower in volume.

"Ma'am, I've been shooting for 0730, ma'am." The young officer replied formally. "I know I was late that one day and had to change my uniform, and I am sorry about that. My first day was the day you arrived on board, so when I showed up my first morning the office was empty, no C.O. The second morning, you were already here working away. Um," Juarez finally took a breath. "What time do you want us here, ma'am?"

That was a good question. She liked the peace and quiet of 0500 to herself, and there was no reason they should have to be inconvenienced just because the captain had ordered her into the office at such an hour. "Zero seven hundred should do nicely, Juarez. And you too, Gates. Ready to hit your inbox at 0700. Which means, at 0655, you're late."

Gates face blanched a moment. Then returned to his stare. "Yes, ma'am."

Wakefield turned to retrieve her coffee.

"Um. Ma'am?" It was Gates. "Did you mean we start tomorrow, ma'am?"

Wakefield rolled her eyes heavenward for help. In the reflection of glossy, mostly-black poster on the wall behind the coffee maker, she could see he had already moved back behind his desk. Juarez still stood at attention.

Judah did not bother turning around. "Yes. Gates." She spoke slowly. "We start tomorrow. Unless you want to start the next day with me at 0500."

She closed her door and leaned her back into it. "Where did these two jokers come from?" she mouthed.

CHAPTER EIGHTEEN

Little Creek Naval Base, VA
The Facility
March 18, 2003
2200 hours

Rivers had remained quiet, standing near the door as the other leaders spread out their maps and argued over the best primary approach and secondary approach. He observed the men. Assessing the human resources.

The noise escalated.

"We have to approach by air as the primary." LT (j.g.) Thompson was jabbing a thick finger at the blueprints of Saddam's Republican Palace superimposed over an enlarged photo of the palace grounds fixed to the white board up front in the utilitarian room. "We hit them with overwhelming force, waves of Blackhawks, with a drone or two sent in ahead, and with an AWASC circling at 50,000 feet for surveillance. We come in guns blazing and drop—"

"You know that's not how we operate," LCDR Chassey interrupted as he rubbed his fingers together in his "under-cover beard" as Rivers remembered that he liked to call it. Rivers could see frustration being held at bay in the stiff motion of the leader of SEAL Team 8.

"Silent and deadly." It was a confident dark-skinned man in his 30's on the left side of the room who spoke this time.

"I still agree with Wimple's strategy of the old-truck convoy where we dress up like volunteers from the back country. It is strong and will undermine morale for survivors while they are at Gitmo."

"How far into Baghdad do you actually think we'll get before we have to start fighting our way through to the palace grounds?" Rivers identified the voice as coming from a cluster of younger men also on the left side of the room closer to him in the back. Probably the kid with his lips sealed smugly.

"I think we could do it. With the right equipment and posturing…" Another man trailed off.

"Let's give everyone a chance to weigh in. Is there another approach?" LCDR Chassey spoke up again. Rivers felt the solid leadership and confidence emanating from the man even at a distance. "Let's hear from the back of the room."

Rivers turned to the men standing near him who had remained observational and raised an eyebrow at them. He could see an obvious third option that looked made for a stealthy SEAL approach.

A chief petty officer propped coolly against one of the blacked-out windows. His alert yet relaxed posture separated him from the group. "You there," Rivers called him out. He couldn't quite read his name from his uniform. "What do you see?"

"Seems to me we have neglected the approach most obvious for us, and most unobvious to them, at our fingertips." He shrugged, but remained perched on the windowsill.

The room stilled at his words. Several heads swiveled back to the whiteboard and then returned to rest on the chief.

"What's your name, Sailor?" Jonesy asked.

"Chief Petty Officer Luckhardt. Call me Lucky."

"All right, Lucky. What did we miss?"

"One if by land, two if by sea."

Several heads whipped back to the city map. Sure enough, the palace grounds sat tucked into a curve of the ancient Tigris River.

"Even if you come in via the river, you are still a solid quarter mile through neighborhoods and urban centers, away from the main palace structure." A nay-sayer shot back and then added, "Look at all those streets to cross by foot before the palace structure and that massive front lawn with virtually no cover."

"And who is to say that Saddam," a clean cut SEAL near the enlarged city map pronounced the man's name SAD-um, the same way President Bush Senior did, "is even at the Republican Palace?"

The room went silent until one man asked the obvious, "What was the intelligence report and where did it come from?"

Rivers began moving to the front of the room at that question. He had seen the briefing on a document, and he felt pretty sure it was in the lockable file box on the table next to the white board. Other team leaders and a couple of 2ICs who had been scattered throughout the room also converged on the table.

By the time Rivers had covered the 22 steps to the front of The Facility's main briefing room, dodging a few men who stood in the way, Chassey had opened the brief box and distributed the file folders to leaders as they approached. Rivers assumed these men had seen the same intelligence report and knew what they were looking for.

Papers shuffled and deep-throated whispers stirred in the room.

"Here it is!" Lieutenant Tad Marvel held up the sheet that looked exactly the way Rivers remembered it. He snapped shut his red-tape-lined top-secret folder and laid it back on the table. Rivers pictured the briefing as Marvel read it to the room.

"Coalesced March 17 at 2210 hours, Baghdad time. That's less than 24 hours ago." Marvel looked up. "Interrogations conducted on board the USS *Reprisal*, one of two carriers in the Strike Group, reveal a super-high-value target at the Baghdad Palace.

"Interrogators speaking directly in primary languages and translators who accompanied them are standing in agreement. Subjects showed extreme fear at the mention of the name *Hussein*, but refused to confirm this identity."

The SEAL continued to read, "One—name redacted—who worked in 1996-98 as a paper-goods delivery boy at the palace, described a vast underground labyrinth he viewed once when the storeroom manager was taken ill on his delivery day." LT Marvel looked up again and said, "There is a hand-written side note here that says the source was not captured but came out to a camp with a daughter seeking asylum as a Christian under religious persecution."

"Does that give the information more credence in anyone's estimation?" a deep voice asked from the crowd.

"I'd have to talk to him myself to make that judgment." Rivers spoke for the first time. "But we can't do that. We have to trust the judgment of our brothers on the ground."

"But this information is still unclear."

"I agree. Can we question the interrogators? The intel just says 'palace' and from the map I'm looking at…" LT Marvel trailed off. His finger moved around the map. "I count at least six palaces owned by the Husseins."

"Worse than that," Rivers frowned. "I heard the word *labyrinth*. If I were an evil dictator building palaces to protect my life and ego, I would install several layers of escape hatches and hide them among a myriad of underground tunnels."

Rivers could almost hear the men's heavy sighs.

"I think this job just got a whole lot harder than we first imagined." LT Chassey pursed his lips. "Every single one of us assumed that the intel pointed to Saddam being holed up in the main Republican Palace, the one we are avoiding bombing in the air raids. But now—"

"The only easy day was yesterday," a voice resounded from the middle of the room.

Lucky picked up where Chassey left off, "Now," he emphasized, "we do what we excel at: innovation and split-second timing across many fields of battle."

Rivers liked the way Lucky encouraged them. "We need every man functioning in his best field of expertise over the next few planning days," he said. "And then in executing orders in country."

One kid in the front punched a teammate's arm. "That puts Mathews here on rations." Rivers could see the room rallying back and the side chatter picked up again.

"Who here plays chess?" Rivers called through the din?

About eighteen hands went up in a room of 300-plus warriors.

"Who is any good?"

Six hands remained in the air. Rivers smiled to see Lucky among them.

"Good. You six remain here with me and the other Team leaders and 2ICs. The rest of you, go get some chow and rack time." Rivers gave the order. Technically he was not the most senior man in the room, Jackson was, but he was close. "We will regather on the lawn for PT at 0630. Your last sleep-in until you are back in your own beds."

The group stood still for a moment—there had been no clear leader or even a jockeying for that position to this point—the men waited for someone else to move first.

From the back of the room a solitary, "Aye, sir" was followed by a creaking hinge. The movement opened a floodgate as the room emptied of all but 23 men. Three of the six chess players were already Team leaders or 2ICs.

In the shuffle Rivers heard only a single identifiable, "Who put him in charge?" He pin-pointed its origin as LT Howard, the former SEAL Team Seven leader, now Rivers' 2IC. He leaned against the side wall with one foot crossed over the other and his arms folded just as tightly across his chest.

Jerusalem, Israel
Thursday, 19 March 2003
11:03 PM

Israeli Defense Force *Seren* Elisheva Dayan leaned forward to press stop on the film she had been watching all day. The room was overly warm even though the lights had been dimmed for the better part of the day of scanning security camera footage all around the holy city.

She and the other Israeli Defense Force (IDF) officers in the room had seen the bus blow up at King Solomon Street at least two hundred times in the days since the bus bombing. There were eight camera angles that had captured it in partial or full view. Ellie uncrossed her olive uniformed legs and stood up to shake the kinks out of her neck and back.

"If only the busses carried cameras with live links through the cell towers." David Silver said, not for the first time.

"But they don't. So drop it." Ellie snapped at the junior officer.

The loss of life on the street had been minimal, but every passenger on the over-stuffed Egged Route 30 bus had died. The surrounding vehicles full of people on their way to work or out for the day had been thrown in the explosion. They had crashed into other vehicles and several had burned. A full Christian tourist bus barely avoided the explosion, and was able to come to a safe stop on the sidewalk, but not before witnessing the entire episode.

Fortunately, in the surrounding roadway, all but three, including an eight-month-old infant buckled into her car seat, had been able to get out with only headaches, scratches, bruises, and nightmares. Those three unfortunates would join the bus passengers in the pages of history as casualties of the Second Intifada.

"We need to get out of here and get some food and sleep," Ellie called everyone's attention with her command voice. "I want to know your opinion as to whether this is an isolated incident or part of a bigger plan." She lowered her voice a little bit since all the other talking in the room had ceased. "I also want your best guess as to where the bomb was *supposed* to have detonated. Adom, we'll start with you."

The six of the seven other young men and women all agreed this was an isolated incident. The seventh, Shimshon, was a bit of a conspiracy theorist and saw connections that most of them never did. Sometimes they were real connections, sometimes they only existed in his mind.

Ellie toggled back to the live feed from the eight cameras to the large screen. Traffic had been back to normal after the *Chesed shel Emet* crew collected every bit of human remains and blood to bury within the 24-hour time prescribed by Orthodox Jewish law. They had become way too excellent in their job through experience in the few years since their founding.

"What was their target?" Ellie asked. There was no agreement on specific targets, but there was complete agreement on the general area: The attack was to have taken place in the Old City on Purim.

Something had stopped the attacker or attackers prematurely— *Baruch HaShem!*—but they would probably never know what.

"Let's allow the live watchers to reclaim their territory then." She gestured with a wave of her arm toward the cracked open door at the top of the stairway that hugged the wall. "Come on back in," she called. Her team cleared their accumulated garbage and notes. "I want a report from each of you by end of day tomorrow. And tomorrow is *Erev Shabbat*, so by no later than 3:00 p.m. I am flying out to join the Coalition Forces on the ground in Iraq for at least a fortnight on Sunday, and I need this case put to bed by then." She got seven affirmative nods. She had a good crew; they'd take care of it.

USS *Theodore Roosevelt*
Wednesday, March 18, 2003
1815 hours

Wakefield smiled when her computer dinged the incoming email. "Wow. He must have gotten right into my email this morning." It was from Commander Huntingdon.

She clicked to open it, and as it loaded her mind was still running a million directions with questions. The more she thought about the triad of the poison—the severe car crash— and MacSod, the stranger things seemed. Then his sudden show-ups and timing in her office, Wallace's abrupt departure without the usual handover to an incoming officer. The two dysfunctional sailors manning her outer office.

The email finally popped open, and Wakefield sighed as she skimmed it in her first read. Huntingdon's fine analysis of her questions actually added to her list of questions. Though he had not actually called the CIA, he was pretty sure MacSod was not an operative. Wakefield could hear his laughter in the tone of the paragraph. She smiled, maybe it *was* a little far-fetched.

She reached for the phone again, and this time connected with the coms office. "I need to use the secure line as soon as possible. Is the room available?" she inquired.

"Did you get a sign off from the captain and X.O.?" asked the operator.

"A what?" Wakefield focused on the dust in the keys of her keyboard. "This is naval intelligence. I need an HQ consult. Since when do I have to have permission?"

"Ever since I came aboard at the beginning of the cruise, ma'am. Is that not standard protocol?"

157

"No." Wakefield's eyes squinted in concentration. "I assume there is a form?" It was the Navy after all.

"Yes, ma'am. You can drop by the coms office at any time and pick one up." He sounded happy to help."

"Of course I can." She sighed. "Thank you."

Two decks up to the radio room and only a few hundred feet aft of the ladder. Wakefield opened the door less than three minutes later. "I need a secure room permission slip." She said when it was her turn in line, trying to keep the snarky to a minimum.

"It's just a form, ma'am." The desk clerk didn't pick up on her attitude and leaned down to the bottom shelf behind the counter and popped up with a half-sheet sized paper in duplicate. "Here you go."

"Thank you." She stood outside the door to read it before climbing all the ladders to access the captain and X.O. for their John Hancocks. The form seemed straightforward and had been updated for use about the same time the latest goings-on in the Middle East picked up. Maybe not such a mystery there.

CHAPTER NINETEEN

Rivers woke to the familiar mission-charge pulsing through his veins. The night had gone better than he expected. He scrubbed a hand over his stubbled chin and blinked to clear his vision and check his watch.

One other SEAL had been pulled off BUD/S instructor duty to join these teams, and CDR Jackson now led Team Five. The Jackson Five had become a thing within seconds of the announcement of him leading that team. Jackson would facilitate the morning's workout, and Rivers knew from watching the boys on the field during BUD/S training, that this morning's workout would be a heavy reminder of Rivers' age.

He slid out of bed, hit the head, and went to watch the sun come up while starting his hydration routine from a two-quart bottle.

Rivers sat on the concrete steps of the Bachelor Officers Quarters (BOQ) tying his second shoe when Jackson lowered himself heavily beside him.

"You're gonna want to watch Lieutenant Howard. I don't think he appreciated being bumped down to the number-two seat on his team in the distribution of Team Six."

Rivers grunted. "I probably wouldn't like it much myself. How are the other team leaders doing with the Desert Warfare experts taking over the lead roles?"

"Fine, far as I can tell." Jackson shrugged.

"How're you feeling about the raid so far, before the critique this morning?" Rivers asked.

"Wish they'd have brought in a joint team like this right after 9/11 two years ago. Bin Laden would already be in custody." Jackson tilted his head to look at Rivers from the slant of his eye. "Or whatever."

Rivers snorted. "I don't think Saddam will be lucky enough to make it to the hand-cuff stage, not with anger at its current level across the military right now. But maybe they'll surprise me."

Men had begun to trickle out various doors and move toward the parade field across the road from the BOQ's front door.

"You still have some 5-minute miles in you, old man?" Jackson rose and fairly skipped down the stairs, even though his sinewy body was on the far side of forty while Rivers still had closer to three years than two to approach the big "hill."

"You may have forgotten this is my home turf now." Rivers laughed. "Are we doing the loop?" The loop was an 8-mile track, some paved road, some small gravel, some grass—or mud depending on the weather—miles of unshaded path, and two stints that totaled 2.8 miles through the woods, complete with roots, around the perimeter of Little Creek Naval Base. It ran directly behind The Facility and the BOQ.

He nodded. "Last one back buys breakfast," Jackson challenged Rivers.

"You're on!" Rivers said and took off for the loop. He was pretty sure he would need the head start. Jackson was a beast when it came to physical training. "See you at the finish!" Rivers called over his shoulder.

Rivers heard Jackson laugh and begin shouting instructions to all the SEALs. It sounded strangely like, "Overtake Rivers and follow the loop," before he was out of earshot.

Rivers had been passed by three men by the beginning of mile 2, but only a handful more over the rest of the loop.

Heaving, he put on a burst of speed for the last half-mile of the course, Rivers did not slow until he had burst through his starting point and then pressed the stopwatch button on his watch. He gulped in four lungfuls of oxygen before he could even look at his time. 49.38.

"Not too shabby for an old guy," Jackson said. He didn't quite appear well-rested, but he certainly was not breathing very hard. Jackson had passed him before the first forest run just after mile 3 began—and Jackson had started at the back of the pack.

Rivers nodded. "Steak *and* bacon for you this morning. We'll slow you down one way or the other."

A wiry man from Detroit that Rivers had graduated in the BUD/S class before last, threw himself into the grass heaving for recovery. He snorted. "That'd do it, all right."

"Hey, PO Little." Rivers walked over still slightly bent at the waist. "How you doing, man?" he held out his hand. "Good to see you again."

Petty Officer Pete Little's eyes lit up as he reached up to shake hands with Rivers. "Thanks for remembering me, sir."

"Course." Rivers shrugged. Little rolled to his feet to shake hands properly. "You ever hear from the other guys in your class? I haven't seen any more of you since graduation."

"Stellar and I are partners now. A chunk of us from Team Eight were late to arrive since we shipped in from training exercises in Columbia. Just last night. He should be coming along any time now." Little glanced toward the men who streamed into the PT cool down area a few at a time from the track that ran behind the BOQ. "I'll tell him to come by and say hi." Little nodded.

"Do that." Rivers agreed and kept moving. So many men whose lives he had had a brief time to influence. He wanted to check on them, connect with them, give them encouragement, help them feel their worth and importance, re-instill any lost level of integrity that might have slipped away in the hard work required of SEALs' souls.

He saw Mass coming around the side of the barracks then, red faced and cheeks puffing with every quick breath. Yet he was encouraging the man he was practically dragging along next to him— in the berating, insulting way that battle-hardened men seem to find motivating.

Rivers grabbed two bottles of unrefrigerated water and went to meet them. "Lord," he prayed just under his still-slightly elevated breathing, "Help me pastor well these men you've given me."

USS *Theodore Roosevelt*
1920 hours

Judah Wakefield approached the bridge, and leaned a hand against the bulkhead to catch her breath before alerting the captain to her presence and asking permission to enter.

The sailor standing watch outside the door whispered to her, "Ma'am you may want to come back later. If you can, of course. Cap'n's been ripping the hide off some poor soul in there for nearly five minutes straight."

Judah turned to the young sailor. "What did he do? What happened?"

"No idea, ma'am. But his whole ancestral line has been called into question."

"Is that unusual?"

"Yes, ma'am." He paused and looked at the ceiling. "Well, now that you mention it, maybe not."

"How often to you stand watch out here?"

"Twice a day ma'am. And I have to say his temper is getting more severe. It's like the Cap'n has a black cloud around him all the time these days."

A particularly choice phrase from Captain MacSod seeped through the closed door at a volume that made Wakefield's chest pound. She frowned and made a face at the young sailor. "He does sound a bit thunderous."

Wakefield looked at the clock and wondered aloud, "Why is the captain on duty on the bridge at this hour?"

The young enlisted man seemed to be enjoying the easy conversation with a senior officer and perhaps the distraction from the yelling inside the room he was guarding. "Well, the cap'n would say, 'The cap'n of a vessel underway is always on duty, son. You alert me day or night if anything seems outta place.'"

Wakefield cracked an appreciative smile. The boy did a decent impression of the old man.

"Unfortunately," the sailor returned his voice to a whisper because the thunderstorm on the bridge cut off abruptly. "He did not say what to do if *he* is the thing that seems out of place."

Wakefield bobbed her head from side to side non-committedly. "Say, is the X.O. still on duty too?"

"Nah. I mean, no, ma'am. He's on nights. Though he did just visit. He left ten, fifteen minutes ago. Right before the fireworks began. Good timing if you ask me."

Judah took one step backward to go back to her cabin. Tomorrow would be good enough, right? But then the questions reignited. The call would have to wait 24 hours until Huntingdon was back on duty if she waited to get permission to use the secure line. This scene from Crazytown just increased the urgency she felt inside. She reached for the metal hatch handle.

A deep steeling breath to remind herself that where she went the Prince of Peace also went because He resided inside her. "I command peace in this room. Every evil and vile thing must shut its mouth right now, in the mighty name of Jesus."

Not that she needed to, but she always liked to give God a minute to work. Waiting a beat, she pushed open the hatch.

"Ma'am?" The sailor standing watch squeezed by her to announce her presence. "Captain, Lieutenant Commander Wakefield is here to see you."

"Permission to join you on the bridge, Captain?" She asked using her honey alto voice that sometimes smoothed the way ahead of her.

"What do you want, Commander." MacSod sounded tired instead of angry now.

"I need permission to use the secure phone." She fluttered her little permission slip and pen.

"First Wallace, now you, too. What is with the Intel Community? Always being so secretive."

"Well, you are welcome to review the topics I need to discuss, sir. I am sure you know the nature of the intelligence we deal with. We just want to keep that information secure." She maintained a small smile through their entire exchange, and she could actually watch his bunched shoulders relaxing.

A female Petty Officer behind him running the radar equipment pulled a tissue from her pocket and dabbed her eyes quickly and stuffed it back away. As far as Wakefield could tell, her eyes never left the giant green arm sweeping the seas around them. She must have been the one the captain was screaming at.

"How about over dinner, sir? Have you had your chow tonight? I hear its fish night with apple pie for dessert." *What the heck?* she asked herself. *How did that happen?*

"Thank you, Commander." He actually looked her in the eye, and seemed as genuine as Judah had ever seen him. "I am eating in my stateroom tonight. I need to think."

The end was so quietly voiced, Judah wasn't sure if he meant to say it aloud or not. Wakefield smiled, "Maybe a raincheck, then."

Thank you, God, I don't have to do that tonight, not with as many questions are spinning in my head. I'd never be able to make conversation without turning it into an interview. Probably a hostile one at that!

"Where's that form?" MacSod reached for his own pen to sign it. "Dismissed." He said crisply.

The door yawned open as she turned around and the sailor stood tight until she passed through and then closed it behind her. He whispered again, "How'd you do?"

"One down, one to go." She waggled the form. "Thanks for your help."

He twitched his left eye brow at her. "My pleasure, ma'am."

Wakefield stood back in the Coms Office twenty-five minutes later with her second signature intact. Apparently "just my biweekly check-in with the head office" was excuse enough for the X.O.

"You can go right in, Lieutenant Commander Wakefield." The same friendly petty officer she had spoken with earlier was still on duty. He spoke as if he'd given the speech a million times, "You'll have thirty minutes. If no one else is waiting by then, and you want to renew, you may extend for up to an additional thirty minutes for your call. I will knock twice when you have two minutes remaining at each interval. When you are finished just hang up, and let me know you are leaving so I can record the time." He handed back the duplicate copy of her form and it now carried an imprinted access code across the bottom space marked *for office use only*. "Any questions?"

Ahh, if only he knew how many, many questions she had. "Do you keep those time records on file?"

"Of course ma'am. The U.S. military keeps everything. We probably have a record of George Washington making a call to his chief of staff." He blushed a bit. "Well, if there had been phones then and all."

"I'd like to see a record of all my predecessor's calls, CDR Wallace, when I finish up my check in." She turned and walked down the short hall to the secured room door with an electronic keypad.

A simple, "Aye, ma'am." trailed behind her. She entered her hard-won code and the door unlocked with a metallic click.

Finally Huntingdon picked up the extension in his office. "Hello?"

"Hi there, sir. Lieutenant Commander Wakefield here."

"Judah! It is great to hear your voice. It was a beautiful ceremony. Congratulations."

"Thank you, sir. It was so nice to have you and Mrs. Huntingdon there to celebrate with us."

"We wouldn't have missed it. Maddie even made me take her out for cake and coffee after we left the White House. She said she gets cake if she goes to a wedding, so I said 'yes, ma'am'."

"Good answer, sir." Judah laughed. "I hope David and I can work on that one too. Sorry we had to move the reception time up."

"Speaking of David, you heard that the Teams are headed in your general direction?"

"I read a headline or two in the database, but of course, there would not be anything directly from David."

"But after all those questions I'm sure that's not why you called."

"No. I just needed someone to talk this weirdness through with.

"Why not bring in your team?"

"Sir, you wouldn't believe what I am trying to work with here. A couple of idiots that I wouldn't give access to my calendar to much less security clearance. Both men have zero experience, and less than zero, if that's possible, on the scale of reasoning skills. I don't know who has promoted them, but they should be forced to work with them as punishment." Judah grimaced, then modulated her rising tone back a notch. "I may have some unresolved office issues."

Huntingdon just chuckled from 8,000 miles away. "I've been there. You'll whip them into shape."

"That's going to take quite some whipping. But that is also not why I called." Wakefield wiped a hand across her tired features to clear the cobwebs of complaining and got down to business. "I can see from the records that MacSod didn't directly kill his wife. But things are so weird here on board, he is dealing with something that is eating him away." Wakefield described the encounter she had overheard outside the bridge. "That was just a few minutes ago, then he was all nice to me when he signed my permission slip to make this call. I don't know all of the ins and outs, but I don't think that's how bipolar disease or disorder or whatever works. It sounds more like a guilty conscience to me."

"Or it could be grief. As we've discussed in the emails. It has not been that long since his wife died, and she was sick while he was away at sea before that. So even though she died in a car accident, he could still be feeling some guilt over the fact that he couldn't save her from the poisoning."

"Or that he wasn't there for her while she was sick. I can see how that could be a factor." She drawled. "But—Lord, have mercy!—it is *not* fun to have to live under this unpredictable command. Even one of the sailors who stands watch on the bridge said it's like the captain and therefore the whole ship is under a black cloud."

"Maybe you should talk to Wallace."

"That's a great idea. Can you check his records for his current duty station, maybe a phone number or email? I don't have a computer down here in the secure room. Protocols are really tight on phone calls and internet access over here, sir."

"I'm glad to hear it. Apparently there is some serious chatter recently that hasn't even made it to the database yet, but Admiral Tamburillo was telling senior staff to expect some investigations to come down the wire in the next couple of days."

The connection was so clear, Wakefield could hear Captain Huntingdon's keyboard clacking as he looked Wallace up.

"I emailed you his email and home address. I assume you're going to want to piggy back that call on this one. You ready for the number?"

"Go ahead." Wakefield closed her eyes to picture the telephone number on her mind's eye, so she could recall it in a few minutes when she needed it. "Got it. I guess Wallace is from Texas."

"Yes?" Huntingdon confirmed slowly.

"Area code 940 is for Denton, Texas just outside Dallas. I read a list of area codes from a hotel Yellow Pages while I was waiting for someone to call me back." She explained.

"Of course you did, Wakefield." Huntingdon chuckled. "Was there anything else?"

"Yes. Now that I don't have any detainees to interview, what am I supposed to be doing out here?"

"You and all the other officers afloat are continuing data and calls analysis according to skill set and briefing senior level leaders aboard. You can offer to give security briefings to the pilots too, but usually the CAG likes to talk to his own flyers."

CHAPTER TWENTY

Wakefield scooped grounds into the coffee machine fully aware that after her little speech to her team yesterday she was almost fifteen minutes late herself this morning. She hated being late. It is a good thing it was so rare. Starting to replace the canister lid, she stopped and dipped one more scoop. It would definitely be appropriate this morning.

She had just closed her scratchy eyes for one second after turning off her alarm. And 44 minutes later she awoke with a jerk like she was trying to avoid a fall.

Judah hummed as the coffee began to drip. She stopped abruptly. "Wallace." She said aloud. Even though the name had kept her awake too many hours to keep track of last night, she had forgotten until just that second.

Lieutenant Commander Wallace was M.I.A. Well, she corrected herself, not M.I.A., technically. He had had 30 days leave owing at the time of his separation from the Carrier Strike Group. His next duty station was state-side and he was due at the end of those 30 days.

How had he gotten off sea duty to go home during a time when everybody was getting shipped out? Judah remembered the empty Suitland, Maryland Intelligence HQ office when she looked around

169

that last time before she shipped out; and that was head-quarters, which should have been more fully staffed than anywhere else in the Intel Community.

She scrolled through Wallace's service record on her secured uplink. He had started on track to becoming a pilot, a Navy Flyboy. Just as Wakefield had guessed from the pictures he had left behind in his office. Wallace had high marks on all evaluation testing that showed results in his record, and high reviews from C.O. assessments as an intelligent, aggressive go-getter, a self-starter. There was an interesting referral for psychological counseling from his C.O. at Naval Air Station Pensacola right before a request for a change of designator to Intelligence. Since the record was in chronological order, she scrolled back to read the referral more carefully.

A Commander Adams had written a bad-conduct review after Wallace had gotten in a fist fight. Then she got to the last paragraph

> This counseling referral request is not because of the fist fight. The officer apologized, even made unrequested restitution for a lamp that broke in the bar at the location of the disagreement. The officer got some bad news that morning about his eyesight deteriorating at age 28 and is now having to change his career path without any notice, and without any other interests.

Wakefield raised her eyebrows. "That must have been rough on a Type-A, high-D personality such as Wallace."

She kept scrolling to some more recent dates.

The date of his most recent transfer was "effective immediately." And was dated the day before the day she had gotten her assignment. Wakefield pursed her lips. She was only here because Wallace didn't want to be and had someone high enough on his side to make that happen.

Wait, she scrolled back. Where was his request for a transfer? How long did he wait? She wondered. It was not in his file. She scrolled past the transfer papers signed by Captain MacSod, and then Wallace's record stopped. Which made sense because he had not yet reported for duty in DC and been processed-in there. Wakefield opened a calendar on her computer.

Thirty days from the 5th of March, the day he officially transferred off the ship, was the 4th of April. Wallace still had 16 days to report for duty. That wasn't the problem.

The problem, as she remembered it from a flurry of phone calls to the States on her second thirty minutes of secure-line access, was that his wife of eight years, Lisa Wallace had not heard from him in a month. She had assured Judah that was not unusual. But when Lisa did not know about the transfer, they both found it disconcerting. When she called Wallace's parents, she found that both were still living, but neither had heard from him either. His daughter was four and not allowed to answer the telephone, or so said her mother.

No contact at home coupled with no record of requesting the transfer pushed Wakefield's feeling of disconcertion over into concern.

Wakefield remembered the records of Wallace's calls then. She pulled them up in her email. He had made one or two secure-room calls every day for his last week in her office.

The door in her outer office rattled and then shut. Wakefield X'd out of all of Wallace's records as her body heated like she might get caught looking at them. Why? She shook her head at herself. She had every right to look into any Naval personnel she deemed in the interest of national security.

"Oh!" her lips formed a little circle as the implication dawned on her even in the midst of feeling defensive about her actions. What if Wallace had been wrapped up in something he should not be and had run away, or had been caught doing something a higher up had not liked. What if he was actually missing and under duress, not of his own doing, but at someone else's will?

She had been thinking along the lines that the stress of leaving his sea duty so suddenly had sent him into a spiral similar to his change of designator ten or eleven years ago. But now, her eyes widened as she forced her face to relax. It could be so much more dangerous than that.

A Naval Intelligence officer with all kinds of password-limited and top-secret clearance access was nowhere to be found.

She needed some help, and Twiddle Dee and Twiddle Dumber out there were useless. They were too new to know anything, even if they had had the capacity.

Wakefield got lost in the shooting stars of her activated screen saver. What were the odds of an entirely new Intelligence Service office aboard an aircraft carrier that until yesterday had been providing interviews, translations, transcripts of detainees from a war zone?

Astronomical.

The Facility
Thursday 19 March 2003
0815 hours

A roomful of brown desert warfare BDUs shifted like a living sandstorm as the men re-gathered after a morning visit to the mess hall.

The team leaders had pushed Rivers forward as the overall commander of the supersized SEAL Team the night before. So he called the room to order.

"I hope you enjoyed a good night's sleep. I will go over the general plans we came to last night. Then we will break into smaller companies to work out the details, needs, and contingencies of each plan." The room stirred with whispers and nudges at that announcement. The bulk of the men had not heard that a three-pronged attack had quickly been decided until that moment.

"Then after a good lunch—I want you guys on high-protein and high-fat, low-carb diets with a lot of water for the next week to get us ready. Then after lunch," he started again, "we will stay in the same teams and critique another team's plan for weaknesses.

"Gus, why don't you give us the categories that will divide us up for planning time? We will be reforming our teams again, and your planning expertise choice today does not indicate which team you will join on the ground. We will need various field experts to spread among each new team in country."

Gus was on the slight side for a SEAL, but had a calm leadership about him that had promoted him to lead a SEAL Team for three years running. "We need bridge demolition, underwater demolition, underwater attack team—that's swimmers who will become the extraction team—drivers and gunners for the convoy, and you'll coordinate with the bridge demolition. We need a Blackhawk brigade and a riot team." Gus pointed to various parts of the room when calling out each need. The men dispersed with relative ease and little conversation. Rivers observed a smiling LT Thompson join the men standing around the city map where Gus had instructed the riot folks to go. Good, they would need his boisterous enthusiasm among rioters spread across strategic parts of the city.

USS *Theodore Roosevelt*
Thursday, March 19, 2003
0828 hours

After checking to be sure the outer office actually contained the usually tardy personnel, Judah Wakefield scrambled back to her desk. She dove deep into Wallace's background and personal life.

First things first. Email.

Judah looked around her closed office as if anyone could watch her and then shook her head at her actions. She slipped a memory

stick into her computer. It contained a code-breaking program
donated by Richmond Dietz on an assignment she had helped run
for the CIA almost two years ago. When she tried to return it, Dietz
had said, "You might need it someday." She had experienced
"someday" more than a dozen times since then. Sometimes it took
longer than others to break encryption, but the technology was still
better than anything standard email providers had come up with and
was much faster than a warrant request to force a company to turn
over their records. Anything learned, of course, could not be used in
court. But she wasn't a prosecutor, she was trying to figure out
where Wallace had disappeared and whether he was in trouble
himself, or just in trouble with his family for not getting in touch
with them about his transfer. Still, she frowned, she always felt
sneaky when she used the program.

Wakefield hit run and watched the little ball moving back and
forth along an arch as password decryption began. There was never
any sort of indicator of how long it would take, so she minimized the
program to a little one- by three-centimeter box on her home screen
and went out for more coffee.

MacSod was standing in the open doorway between the hall and
her outer office and Judah started so badly she nearly dropped her
cup and bolted back to her office.

She tightened her grip on the slipping mug handle. The captain
was saying something to a very nervous standing ensign and petty
officer, but the blood was rushing through Judah's ears so hard, she
couldn't even hear.

"Hello, sir," she said when his mouth stopped moving and he
glanced up at her. She forced herself to walk calmly away from her
office door toward the coffee pot, when all she really wanted to do
was stand in front of the door with her arms out blocking his
entrance to seeing her computer screen. "What brings you down to
the bowels of the ship so early this morning? Can we get you some

java?" She held up her empty mug with a grip that was sending her fingertips into a ghostly white.

"I just came down to check on the office. See how everybody is getting along down here." MacSod said with a smile that almost reached his eyes. "There's been a lot of turn-over in this office, and I thought I'd check on everyone. How are you settling in to your new station, Lieutenant Commander?"

Wakefield blinked. Hadn't he forced her into a couple of meals and conversations with him already? Now he was acting all concerned? And checking on her in front of her men?

"These guys giving you any problems?"

Wakefield broke eye contact to glance at Juarez and then Gates. They looked scared. "Nothing more than usual bumps in a new command, sir." Why had he offered up the information that everyone was new in the office, having never said anything before? Now, right after she discovered it on her own, he put it out there in front of all three of them. What did he have to gain?

Everything felt out of joint, and she couldn't quite pop it back into place. The timing sent shivers down her spine.

Judah stood in front of the coffee pot forcing herself to breathe at a normal pace, even as her throat and chest were compressing all the air out of her system. What was really going on here? Why did she feel so afraid?

Judah felt her spirit stir as she finally identified what she was feeling. She hated fear and weakness in others, and refused to let it operate in her. It was a horrible emotion to experience, and even worse to be held captive by it.

"Speaking of a new command and office turn over," Wakefield shuddered inside as courage welled up, "Why did Wallace transfer out so suddenly, sir?"

"You going to get some of that coffee or just stand in front of the pot blocking everyone else's access?"

Avoidance, she noted easily.

Wakefield reached for the pot, but focused her peripheral vision on MacSod's expression and body language. She poured her coffee. "Did you want some, sir?" She pulled another mug from the stand before he answered.

"Yes," he answered quickly. "To your office." He ordered and motioned toward the door, the one place she did not want him to go.

CHAPTER TWENTY ONE

J udah Wakefield straightened her uniform after setting her coffee cup on the front edge of her desk. She turned back to MacSod and tamped the urge to walk around behind her desk and exit out of the decryption program on her desktop. She prayed it would not ding with success while MacSod was lurking in her office.

The captain followed her into the cramped space and moved into a corner since she and the two chairs occupied the center of the room. He motioned with his eyes for her to close the door. She reached out and tapped it with enough force for it to swing closed and latch itself.

"Are those two behaving themselves?" MacSod spoke first. He held his coffee in both hands as if warming himself.

"Of course, sir. I'd rather know about Wallace." She managed a chuckle. "Sorry that sounded more forceful than I meant."

"Wallace wasn't getting the job done, commander. He had to be removed."

Removed? No, that wasn't ominous at all! Especially with the knowledge she had picked up last night. Wakefield reached for her cup again to take a moment to decide how to proceed. "Sir, you do know I have security clearance high enough to review his service record and psych evals, right?"

"Of course. What is your point?"

"I've already looked at his record, and you and I both know that his personality is one that cannot 'not get the job done,' sir. That's not why he left."

She could see anger begin to boil beneath the surface as his skin reddened and his nostrils flared. Or was it fear? She softened her voice. "It is just you and me in here, Captain. Can you tell me why Wallace is gone? It will go no further than me," *unless it is fishy*, she added in her mind.

"Never count on it being just you and me," he said cryptically. He flashed a glance around the room.

"What? What do you mean?" Wakefield whispered, feeling sucked into MacSod's odd display of paranoia.

"Never mind. Just be careful," he warned as he pressed himself as far away from her as he could go until he ran into the wall. "Wallace was into some extra-curricular activity, if you know what I mean. I'd drop it if I were you. We don't want anyone else getting hurt." He gave her a pointed look. She knew what he was implying, but did not know what he truly meant.

"That'll be all," he said and disappeared out her hatch, leaving it open behind himself.

Wakefield stared at his wake until he exited the outer office door too.

She closed her door and crossed one arm around her waist and held her chin with the other hand as her palm covered her mouth. She began to pace her office. That was the craziest conversation with a senior officer she'd ever had. He was warning her off. And that meant there was something to be warned away from. And there was that little word 'else.' Did MacSod even realize he had thrown her information in that one word? 'Someone else to get hurt' implied someone was already hurt. But who?

She stopped pacing. Why had he stood where he did? Was there something to it? He could have moved from the door to a couple of different spots in the small office, though not many. Why that corner? Wakefield returned in her mind to the strange feeling of paranoia she had felt when MacSod implied they were not alone. What was that about? She studied the wall across from her. A few filing cabinets. A bookshelf. She looked at the wall with the door, only a couple of posters. The wall she leaned against had nothing on it. And the other wall flanked her desk. Again posters and a few small framed pictures but that was it. The air-return duct had a little dust in its openings, but it was undisturbed dust.

The more she searched for a bug or hidden camera while trying not to appear to be looking, the deeper the feeling that she was being watched became.

Judah squared her shoulders and pushed off the wall. "Dude, you will not give me the heebie-jeebies." She said under her breath and moved toward her desk. Pulling up in her chair, she still could not shake the anxious feeling MacSod had left behind.

She put her forehead into her palm, with her elbow resting on her desk. "Lord, what is going on here? I need some wisdom and insight from you. You know all things, and I ask for some know-ledge on how to proceed here." Still speaking aloud, Wakefield focused on the fear. It did not belong to anything in her, it wasn't based on something she had done. "For the Lord has not given me a spirit of fear, but one of power, love, and a sound mind. Perfect love triumphs over fear."

The space of her office became less anxious as she spoke the Word of God's truth into her atmosphere.

Two things came to mind simultaneously: A flash picture of her office rearranged with her back toward the wall where MacSod had stood, and the emphasis on love. God's perfect love. It was not a concept, nor a feeling.

She felt like breathing was easier and easier as she focused on God's love for her, its perfection, its self-sacrificing quality that sent Jesus to the cross. *Perfect love gives itself away.*

"Yes, you do, Lord." She agreed aloud. "Thank you. It's so wonderf—"

Follow me in my ways. Wakefield heard the words cut her off.

She felt the walls of her heart start to rise in defense. "But I do follow your ways."

You love the lovely, those who get along with you, those who are healthy and normal.

"I hear a 'but' coming." Wakefield rolled forward to hook the heels of her shoes on the chair cross piece underneath her.

But will you love MacSod?

"But he—" She couldn't quite formulate what she suspected him of doing. "I think he hurt Wallace in some way. He threatened me just now."

He warned you, Judah. He did not threaten you.

"Oh." She said suddenly feeling very small.

Then all was quiet, but the peace remained.

Judah checked and saw that the decryption key was still at work. She minimized everything again and turned off the screen.

Opening the door, she said, "Juarez, Gates, I've got an assignment for you." They both stood.

"Yes ma'am?" Ensign Juarez asked.

"I need some furniture moved."

CHAPTER TWENTY TWO

Set up with her desk moved against the wall where MacSod had stood in the corner, Wakefield scanned the walls and ceiling again from her seat. The timing of the captain's visit was too suspicious. Her computer still sat in a chair across the room so the decryption key could continue working. She would move it to its new orientation after the ding of new information sounded when she could unplug it without disrupting its decryption.

Removing the posters would afford her a closer look. Ignoring the ringing of a phone in the outer office, Wakefield shot out of her chair and began removing all the framed pictures. Then starting at the far side of the room, one by one the posters of aircraft came down. The glossies she folded down to 8x10 size to match the photos. She reverently placed them all in a file, and into the cabinet they went. As she moved from left to right across the wall that had been the back wall of the office previously, Wakefield rubbed her fingers across every square inch feeling for divots in the paneling, raised places, anything that could hide a camera or mic.

There it was. Along the crease between the back wall and the ceiling, a small notch less than a centimeter across. The eye in the woodgrain pattern had been hollowed out. It was slightly off center with where the desk had sat in order to blend in.

Her fingers ran across the lens and she desperately wanted to yank the camera out of the wall and stomp on it. But she kept going, moving right past it, making sure her face did not give away her discovery. The camera was pointed directly toward where her computer screen had formerly stood. The angle of the camera created a little ditch of space on that far wall exactly where MacSod had stood an hour earlier. Unless it was a super wide-angle lens, the camera would not be privy to that one spot.

Judah continued to peel posters off the wall and look for any other hidden surveillance. Why? Who? Obviously MacSod had seen the video feed, because he knew exactly where to stand to avoid being filmed. That brought her back to why? If he knew about it, why did he avoid the camera? What did the camera operator want to see? Who was the camera operator? How long had it been there? And again, why? Was there a hidden mic?

Intuition told her no, at least not one MacSod knew about. He had ordered her into her office and had not even lowered his voice while inside.

Wakefield reached for her telephone, remembered the time difference, and tucked her hand back into an arms-crossed stance. She reached for the back of the chair with the computer monitor resting in it and turned it ninety degrees from the camera, then even if there was some sort of reflection, it could not be read.

Then, kneeling in front of her computer still in the chair, she pulled up Armed Services Registry database. Judah began to narrow the field of her inquiry by factors: Active, Deployed, Non-military. That brought the field of options very low. She ticked the box for sort by Aircraft Carriers. Then she began to scroll through the names of ships until she came to USS *Theodore Roosevelt*. Only a handful of names appeared there, and a Naval Criminal Investigative Service agent afloat was among them. She clicked on the name, Special Agent Grant Lawson, to view his service jacket.

Six years in NCIS and a former Navy MP. Eight years in the service in that designator. Commendations, great evaluations, not a ding on his record anywhere that she could see. No gaps either. It was unusual to be assigned agent afloat at that level of experience. Normally agents with his service record would be on a European or Asian assignment, or maybe even serving in a key headquarters position.

"I'm just thankful you assigned him here, Lord. For whatever reason." Wakefield smiled as she checked the decryption key still at work on Wallace's email password. She closed the screen down again.

Checking her hip pocket for the bulk of her keys, Wakefield locked her office door and walked through the office without sharing her plans. True to what she had come to expect, neither man asked her where she was going either.

Walking just eight frames aft, Judah Wakefield turned and opened a hatch labeled NCIS without knocking. "Oh! my apologies." She said pulling her mouth down in a grimace. She had walked in on a man working in his office. "There's no reception desk or anything?"

He did not look up but held up one finger asking her to wait. Wakefield stood with one hand on the hatch frame and the other on the metal handle in silence for close to fifteen seconds while he scanned a document. His eyes followed the path his middle finger traced through several rows of typed details.

"Thank you for your patience." He said as he organized several sheets of paper by tapping them twice on the desk top, laying them inside a manila one-third cut-out top file folder and closing the top. He still had not looked up, but Wakefield found that she did not mind the delay at all. His thick, coiffed hair was as black as night, with just a few silver threads at the temple. The slight wave was managed and smooth but not caked with product. The buzz-cut service photo she had seen on her screen did not do this man justice.

Finally he stood as he looked up for the first time. He bent at the hip to extend his hand across his tidy desk. "Lieutenant Commander Wakefield. Welcome. To what do I owe the pleasure?"

"You must be Special Agent Grant Lawson?" When he nodded while shaking her hand with just the right firmness, she wondered briefly if this former military policeman had gone to finishing school. His features and mannerisms reminded her of a 1940s and 1950s Cary Grant. "How did you know me?" She questioned.

"I've met everyone else on board, and I heard we were getting a replacement Naval Intel officer. Logical conclusion." He shrugged.

"Oh."

"Would you care for tea or coffee before you tell me what I can help you with?"

"Tea would be nice. Milk—"

"With one sugar?" he finished for her.

"There's no way that scuttlebutt that made its way around the ship." Judah raised a single eyebrow in questioning his source.

Lawson smiled, "Nope. That was a lucky guess." Grant Lawson asked polite questions about settling in to shipboard life while he set about boiling the electric kettle of water and readying a whole pot of proper tea with a tea leaf strainer and everything. Two tea cups. Two saucers, two delicate silver spoons that did not come from the ship's galley. He lifted a jug of milk from a mini fridge.

Judah's mouth watered, this was going to be so yummy. Her first sip of the steaming aromatic liquid sent a wave of comfort over her. She closed her eyes to soak it in. "Sometimes," she said still inhaling the sweet scent, "I feel God's love for me in a well-prepared cuppa tea."

"Well, I've heard that people like it, but that may be a little exaggerated."

Judah opened her eyes to find him smiling widely at the sincere compliment. Settling the cup into the saucer, Judah leaned forward in the visitor's chair in Lawson's office. Normally she would try to build a deeper rapport with someone first, but she trusted Lawson. Maybe it was basing his character on his looks and all the Cary-Grant movies she had seen, or even looking at his service record, but she prayed, *Jesus, I hope this knowing is from you*, and jumped right in. "Have you noticed anything strange going on aboard this ship?"

He chuckled. "I've got a paper tower of weird right there." He pointed to his in-box tray filled with about four inches of paper. "Was there something more specific?"

"I'm going to trust you." Wakefield said pointedly, "because I need your help. You are outside the chain of command since NCIS is a civilian agency, but I know you understand the dynamics at play here."

Special Agent Lawson set his tea on his desk, his brow furrowing deeper with her every phrase. "What is going on, Lieutenant Commander? You have my full attention."

Judah took a deep breath and dove off the high dive. "I just found a surveillance camera in my office, trained on my computer screen." Lawson's face lost a little of its color then. She could see his brain processing the kind of information that would pass over her screen and the implication of it getting into the hands of a person with the character to plant a camera.

"That's not all. I just had a visit from the captain this morning, before I discovered the camera. When he came into my office, he stood at the single place in the room that was outside the scope of the camera's range."

"Which captain? There are three men with the rank of captain on board."

He certainly knew his crew. With five thousand men and women on board that was impressive. "*The* captain," she emphasized. "MacSod."

Lawson's lips puckered out in thought. "So many implications and even more questions are running through my mind."

"I know. Mine too. 'How long has it been there?' is a new one that just came to me. I didn't smell any fresh-cut wood from the paneling, so I think it has been there a little while. Oh, and here is another dynamic. Wallace, my predecessor," she paused and Lawson nodded, "I think he is missing."

"What do you mean missing?"

"I was able to trace his movements from the ship to Germany, to base housing. For one night. He checked out, but never made any other reservations nor was his name listed on a manifest of any aircraft or ship heading back to the U.S. His wife and parents have not heard even that he was changing duty stations, much less coming home."

"That's the first thing you tell your wife when you're leaving a warzone or hazardous duty." Lawson's forehead rolls told her he was quickly coming up to her level of concern.

"The captain's signature is on Wallace's transfer orders. He is in this up to his neck."

"I notice you've been whispering." Lawson said, his voice matching hers. "Let me sweep this office so we will know—one way or the other—if we are bugged too."

Wakefield nodded her agreement and picked up her tea cup for a sip as she stood to help him examine the walls and furniture.

But Lawson leaned down to open his bottom drawer and pulled out a device about twice the size of her flip phone and turned it on before straightening up.

"What's that?" Judah asked.

"Bug sweeper." Lawson smiled tightly.

"That small?"

"It's a prototype my buddy is working on." Lawson explained. "Finds RF frequencies between 1 MHz and 6 GHz." He pointed it toward his computer, which like hers was equipped with an internal wireless Internet router. The bug sweeper beeped and vibrated. Lawson showed her the red lines on the indicator.

"Nice friend." Wakefield nodded and sat back in her chair to sip her tea and let Lawson continue to sweep his office.

"Go ahead and power down my computer if you don't mind. That way if something is in the housing, we can detect it, because I'm not getting anything else in the room."

Wakefield slid around his desk. No tabs or programs were open so she began the power down sequence and in seconds the computer sounded a little sigh and the screen crackled once with static and went black.

Lawson worked his way back around to his desk top silently. "We are in the clear!" he pronounced.

"Excellent, because here is as far back as I've been able to trace—" Wakefield interrupted herself to ask, "Did Wallace ever come to see you about anything like this?"

"I would have swept the office daily if he had."

"Ok." Wakefield nodded. "The thing is, well, you've seen the personnel changes in my office. Everyone is new."

"No. I only get copies of abbreviated service records of new hires, so to speak. But that is worrisome."

"There are only three of us, but both my admin assistants were brought in as Wallace was being transferred. The whole office is new, not a single carry over. Who were Wallace's assistants?"

"What happened to them?" Lawson added.

"Were they into something that got them in trouble?"

"I should have been brought in on any kind of investigation." Lawson was shaking his head. "Anything above board, anyway."

"MacSod alluded to a shipboard affair, but I think he was just trying to throw me off."

"I've heard nothing out of the office of intelligence at any time during this cruise. And frankly, nothing last cruise either. This is my second go round with MacSod and the senior leadership. Only the X.O. is new. Byers, the X.O. from the last cruise got his own command of a destroyer after our shakedown cruise for this deployment, and CDR Bradshaw got a promotion." Lawson sat back down and put the bug sweeper away. "Any charges or investigation should have come through my office. I get the missing food, even silverware, and alcohol smuggling problems, accusations of inappropriate conduct. Breaking up gambling card games is about as exciting as it gets."

"So if there had been a violation of the UCMJ it would have come to you to investigate?"

"Yes, ma'am. And it did not."

"Are you aware of Martha MacSod's death?"

Lawson cocked his head curiously. "Yes. I was interviewed during our shakedown cruise. And X.O. Byers, he was still on board then, took command of the ship for a week while Captain MacSod flew home to make arrangements. I, personally, think that is why he got his own ship. What does Mrs. MacSod's car accident have to do with this?"

"What if it wasn't an accident at all? What if Wallace was onto something that implicated the captain in his wife's death and the captain sent him away. Could he make him disappear from the base in Germany?"

Time looked like it slowed down for Lawson. "MacSod *has* been different since our early cruise. I put it off to grief."

"You read people for a living," Wakefield said. "Do you think it could be guilt that is eating at him?"

Lawson slowly wobbled his head from side to side. "They manifest in such similar ways. It's hard to say. Are you saying you think MacSod," his voice dropped even though they knew the place was bug-free, "killed his wife and then killed Wallace because he was onto him? Or had him killed, I suppose. Because I know for a fact MacSod has not left the ship since our deployment."

"How do you know?"

"I've seen him."

"It would take about 12-15 hours to fly from here to Germany and back. Can you say *definitively* that you have seen him at least *twice* every 24 hours for the last say, two weeks?"

"Well, maybe not that often. But it would be easy to verify. All I have to do is flash my badge to the Air Boss and check the manifests."

"What do you say you do that? Are you willing to help me investigate whatever is going on here?"

"I'd say it is my duty, Lieutenant Commander."

"Fantastic. I'm going to go see if I've been able to get into Wallace's email yet."

"You got a warrant already? Wow. That was fast."

"Um, not exactly. Technically he's not even missing yet. A warrant is impossible."

"Then how…"

"I could tell you my source, but then I'd have to kill you." Wakefield gave Lawson a little fake smile to tell him not to ask any questions.

"Ah, courtesy of one of the Washington Alphabet Soup guys."

"I used to moonlight a little bit." It was more than a little bit, but better to under-promise and over-deliver, she thought.

"I don't think we should be seen together. It will raise suspicions."

"Well, you can't come to my office. I left the camera operational so they didn't know I'd discovered it. They may suspect something because I've moved my desk, but they won't know for sure." Judah sighed. "I just couldn't knowingly allow access to classified material."

"You may want to install you own camera to see if anyone comes in to change the orientation or leave another camera. Especially keep an eye on your hard drive for mirroring equipment or keystroke software."

"Don't know where I'd get a camera without alerting the tech crew. I mean the captain could have people planted to keep an eye out for him in any department of the ship, and really they would believe they were helping him. And they would be, it just would be helping him get away with something. Watch your back with the Air Boss. Flag Officers talk amongst themselves."

"He is a friend of mine. And I can present it in a way that he would want to help me by putting the captain in Germany if he was there." Lawson nodded knowingly.

CHAPTER TWENTY THREE

LCDR Wakefield opened the hatch to the Navy Intelligence offices. The smell almost knocked her down. "Oh my!" she moved out to the hall choking. "Has one of you died in there?" she called out.

"I'm so sorry, ma'am." Gates charged out the door. "I've gotta hit the head. Right now." With one hand on each of her biceps, PO Gates physically moved her to the side of the passageway and practically jogged to the men's room.

"Juarez, you look a little green." Wakefield said from the doorway. "You feeling okay?" She heard his stomach gurgle from 15 feet away.

He sat bolt upright in his chair. "Excuse me, ma'am." He left his chair spinning behind him and dashed out the hatch. She stepped out of his way. Her hand went to cover her nose and mouth of its own volition. "Don't come back without air freshener!" She called after Ensign Juarez.

"I'm sorry ma'am. Don't drink the coffee!" Juarez warned her loudly before disappearing around the corridor corner. "Or the milk!"

Judah was trying to stifle a giggle. "That is horrible!" Her giggle turned into a chuckle, and then she couldn't stop it. She stood in the passage way guffawing like a schoolboy at the men's smelly misfortune, covering her mouth and nose so she wouldn't gag at the smell emanating from her office. "Oh my word! What did they eat? We're going to have to fumigate!" Wakefield was doubled over laughing even while wondering why it hit her so funny. But she couldn't stop laughing. Twice she though it was under control, but when she started into the room and caught another whiff, she was gone again.

A machinist's mate who wouldn't dream of initiating a conversation with an officer so senior under normal circumstances, approached her in the passageway.

Judah was still cackling. Literal tears in the corners of her eyes. She didn't even try to hold it together. "Take a whiff of that office." She challenged him. "I've got two guys with the runs and I can't even get back into my office."

The young man looked about eighteen or nineteen years old. Judah held her breath while he stuck his nose into the office and filled his lungs. He staggered backward making a choking sound deep in his throat. He swore colorfully. He shook his head as if he could shake off the smell.

Judah cracked up again.

"You ought to ask for double hazardous duty pay, ma'am. That is the rankest smell I've ever smelled and I've got four brothers!" The machinist's mate chuckled nasally. "I gotta go. Fast." He hurried up the passageway in the same direction Juarez and Gates had gone.

Judah saw his arm go back to his side about ten paces up. "Awe, man!" He gagged again, putting his hand over his nose again and turned around. "They came this way, didn't they?" When she nodded, he said, "Warn a guy next time."

It sent her into fresh giggles, and he kept a quick pace as far as she could see him.

Finally under control, she reached into her pocket, got her office key ready for the lock. Taking a deep breath from away from the hatch, Wakefield hurried through the outer office to her door. She fitted the key, felt the tumblers turn, opened the door, and slammed it behind her.

Slowly removing her hand she took a tentative sniff. No shared ductwork apparently. She was safe. She chuckled lightly, more at how hard she had laughed than at the circumstance itself. "I guess I was due for a good laugh."

Squatting down in front of the computer screen in the chair, she turned the boxy monitor on. Maximizing the window she saw the key had broken the password and she had been granted access to Wallace's email. Smiling, Wakefield opened another program on her computer and pressed half a dozen instruction keys. All of Wallace's correspondence, sent and received including saved drafts, since 1995 at this email address would be downloaded for her to be able to search with keywords, patterns of interaction, and special dates. This program would analyze whether it was probable that Wallace kept other accounts and possible email addresses of those accounts, especially if he had ever forwarded a note from one of those accounts to this one. She would have copies of every attachment, picture, file, and link.

He was a heavy corresponder. Just from the addresses she could see, Wallace used this account for work, play, and family. But it would probably take an hour before she would have searchable access to the download.

Wakefield felt on the front of the computer hard drive for the USB memory stick. She patted up and then down. Her heart rate stuttered. She scrambled around to look at it. Sure enough. There was an empty USB port. No little green drive.

All her laughter died as she collapsed flat to the floor in front of the computer, a hand over her lips.

USS *Theodore Roosevelt*
Intelligence Offices
1145 hours

"I need to report stolen property." Wakefield spoke into the phone.

"What is it worth?" Special Agent Lawson asked.

"To the right person a couple of million dollars, maybe." Wakefield shrugged.

Lawson gasped. "May I ask who is calling?"

"Lieutenant Commander Wakefield in Naval Intel." She said. Didn't he recognize her voice? She had only been gone a few minutes from his office.

"Hello, Wakefield. I apologize. I needed to know which form to fill out." Wakefield could hear rustling papers in the background. "What do you have on board that is worth that much?"

"You remember that little device I couldn't name for you?"

Lawson drew breath even more sharply. His voice dropped as it squeezed through a throat closing with fear. "It is not good having a little code breaker floating around a nuclear powered ship the size of a small city! What happened?"

"I came back in and it was gone. By the way, it worked before it walked off with some help. But it was locked in my office."

"Who had opportunity?"

"Just my two admin guys in the front office, Ensign Juarez and Petty Officer Gates." Then she groaned. "Actually anyone could have come in, picked the lock and absconded with my USB drive."

"With two people sitting right there?"

"I don't think they were sitting here the whole time." She explained the bathroom runs. The run she witnessed wasn't necessarily the first time for either of them. "Our favorite person was here just before all this happened messing with the coffee, and Gates attributed the food poisoning to the coffee or milk without prompting."

"Do you think McSod poisoned them?"

"Maybe we should check on him, to see if he is affected first, before I go accusing him. Come to think of it, I had coffee from the same pot, and I'm fine. So it happened after I poured my cup, leaving MacSod, Juarez, or Gates as the coffee spiker, unless someone else came in while I was gone." A long hissing noise in the outer office alerted her that they were back. "Hopefully that is air freshener," she told Lawson.

When it got quiet again, she muffled the phone receiver and bellowed, "Ensign, get in here."

The door opened and he stuck just his head inside.

"Quick. Shut the door." She ordered. When he complied she uncovered the phone receiver so Wallace could listen in, and asked, "Did anyone come by while I was away?"

"No, ma'am. Quiet as a mouse. Of course until the tummy rumbling began."

"Was the office ever left empty and unlocked?"

Juarez's eyes rolled heavenward and his black eyebrows stretched, "I don't think so. Either Gates or I were here the whole time."

"Who got sick first?"

"Well, I had to make the first dash to the head, if that's what you mean."

"Thank you, Ensign. Send in Gates. And when he gets back go get something from the infirmary."

Their stories matched.

When Gates closed the door behind himself, Wakefield put the phone back to her ear. "Did you get all that?"

"Yes. They are not in it together, because they would have said that the door was left unmanned to shift blame in a wider investigation."

"But I don't see how they could both be innocent either. If one was present at all times, he either broke in himself, or allowed someone else to break in, while the other was in the head."

"Do you think one of them poisoned himself? Or do you think they had a little present left from MacSod?"

"Depends on whether MacSod is sick or not."

"I'll look into that." Lawson stated.

"I'll begin going through the info from Wallace's email."

Wakefield hung up and moved back around to check the progress on the monitor. The analysis indicator line showed more than two-thirds complete.

Twenty minutes later, after sterilizing the coffee carafe and starting a new pot dripping, the Organiz-Analyz program trilled in her office. Wakefield smiled and walked back to her office to get the Wallace email investigation underway.

Since someone had been in her office, Judah did a careful hand sweep of the wall behind her for any additional implanted cameras before moving the monitor and computer to its new orientation on her desk. Closing her eyes, she invited the Holy Spirit into the process. "Come and point out the things I need to notice and give me discernment to see the connections."

Wakefield began compiling names of Wallace's military friends based on their email addresses, keeping charts listed by duty station. Each person's background and service record would have to be looked into. Another list compiled personal friends outside the military. Unless they had criminal records they would be harder to dig into. A third list of people included obvious family connections. A fourth list compiled companies to which Wallace had subscribed. It would give her a look into his personal interests. As soon as Judah came across his emailed bank statement she started a fifth list and typed "search checking account records for last 12-24 months" immediately under the heading *Further Research.*

The lists grew for an hour and a half and patterns began to develop. Wallace was a connected guy. He had not used this email address to send or draft a single email from the moment he stepped off the ship's deck. He had not made plans to disappear from this primary email account, nor had he arranged for anywhere to stay in Germany or researched restaurants.

Wakefield leaned back in her chair and exhaled heavily. "I am convinced," she whispered, "Wallace did not leave this ship by his own planning. Somebody helped him. Whether he requested that help or it was forced on him," she raised a single manicured brow, "that remains to be seen."

The main bothersome item sat unopened in his in-box: a letter from transport confirming his 1215 COD flight from the carrier to Germany on the day he was last seen.

USS *Theodore Roosevelt*
NCIS Office
1410 hours

"How much normal personnel turnover is there on a carrier?" Wakefield asked Lawson. She had stopped by his office after a lunch break to clear her head. She had knocked before entering this time.

"Depends." Lawson shrugged. "I assume the question you really want to ask is: how unusual is it for a complete changing of the guard in the Naval Intel office, especially underway."

Wakefield nodded. She hated being suspicious of her guys, but she had just seen with her own eyes MacSod finishing up his lunch with no ill effects from the coffee in the office.

"I've never heard of it happening before." Lawson grimaced. How was it that even the man's grimace looked debonair? Wakefield just shook her head.

"Then can you look into Juarez and Gates?" Wakefield asked, smoothing her hair back in thought. "And add anyone else who has shifted positions in the last month of this deployment? Whether a promotion, a demotion, anyone brought in via COD, whether military or civilian contractor or civilian agency such as yourself. I'd rather cast a wide net and narrow it effectively."

"Certainly." Lawson began to type himself notes. "I do have some official business to attend to as well. Not that this is not official, it is just that it can't go on the books yet, am I right?"

"I think that would probably be wise since we don't know who could be involved. I think we should tell someone trusted in both of our chains of command though."

Lawson's eyes widened. "Just in case we disappear too?"

Wakefield had not thought of it in those terms exactly, but she nodded. "I hope it doesn't come to that. There is one other place I want to check before we sound the silent alarm. My program, before it *also* disappeared, turned up a piece of lake property owned by Wallace's parents. Do you think you could call them on an unsecured line as a regular part of an investigation and ask them to check it out for us? Or do you think we should send someone from the nearest NCIS office?"

"Let's keep it unofficial for now." Lawson stroked his cheek moving the slight stubble back and forth with the back of his hand. If I ask a team to take a look around, I'll have to file paperwork. I think we can ask the parents. If you talked with them, they are already going to be a little on edge. It might make them feel useful. And they really would be."

Wakefield nodded. "Good call."

CHAPTER TWENTY FOUR

"Holy smokes." Judah Wakefield trilled. She threw herself back in her chair and then sprang back forward to touch the monitor screen in order to keep track of the count. "Twenty-three guys have been moved around in their duty stations since two weeks before I came aboard." Of course Wakefield's name was on Lawson's list as well, having arrived on board via COD within the timeframe she specified. "That seems like an awful lot of changes."

She scrolled up to read Lawson's email comments that she had skipped right over to get down to the good stuff.

LCDR Wakefield,
The following list is what I've been able to compile so far. There may be some pending that I've missed, because the paperwork has not caught up with them. As you will note, they are all over the ship. Of course you realize your office was gutted, but there are Operations Specialists personnel changes in the engineering dept., the electrical, steam propulsion and ventilation specialists, an engine mechanic too. In Navigation the night radar guy was reassigned, weapons, the galley has had 4 guys transfer out (my

source at NCIS HQ tells me that's not unusual though), flight maintenance crew, supply dept., safety dept., Ops, Ops maintenance, and communications, (that one gave me pause!). The highest ranking change-out was the Quartermaster (broken leg in a fall down a ladder; I confirmed in the infirmary) A few civilian contractors have come and gone. Two are still with us. One's a computer guy working on some training in CIC, I'm told.

There was also a group of 10 pilots not in the list who were flown out for the weekend to do Flight Quals. But all of them checked out and have returned to their duty stations.

Your Ensign Juarez was brought in fresh out of school at request of the captain. He received grades on the edge of par on his qualification exams, but passed his in-depth background check, you'll be happy to know.

PO Gates, has security clearance from clerking for a captain in the Department of Defense. He had only been there a week when his chronic lateness began to show up as notes in his record. About 4 months ago the captain at DOD had had enough and Gates got busted down to PO2 for missing a movement when he was late. He'd never had that problem noted along the way, but the captain warned him eight times, all in his record, before knocking him back a pay grade and shipping him off to the mail room, which is where he was assigned when we shipped out.

Another commonality to note is that for all of these crew who have moved their designator or position, this was their first cruise. I don't know if that is an explanation or suspect yet though.
Lawson

"Well, I certainly understand the DOD captain's frustration with Gates' lateness." Wakefield said under her breath. "I wonder what it would take to interview all of these men." She squinted at the screen and reviewed the new duty stations. "I'm not sure I could reasonably run into some of these guys 'on accident.' The engine room mechanics? Well, I suppose we all have to eat." She frowned. Even then, the officers and enlisted men were separated in different chow halls.

"I'll bet Lawson could get to the engine room and the electrical engineers with a petty crime investigation. We can make it up if we have to. I'm feeling creative."

Judah jumped at a knock on her door. "Chill," she told herself. "Enter," she called out.

"Package came for you in the afternoon mail COD." PO Gates, held up a box the size of a ream of paper like a loaded platter at a diner. "Were you expecting something?"

"Yes, thank you. Just set it on the chair there." she pointed.

Gates spun the box around as he set it down and touched the return address label as he straightened back up. It looked awkward in her estimation. Was he was trying to memorize it? Or was CAPT MacSod's paranoia striking again.

No time like the present to start interviews. "I heard you used to work in the mailroom."

"Yes, ma'am." Gates nodded and kept moving toward the door. "Hold up."

Gates spun toward her on his heel and kept hold of the door handle. "How did you come to serve in my office?"

"Before I got busted down to postman, I worked at the DOD. I assume my security clearance made me a natural choice for an empty post." He shrugged. A bit arrogantly. Wakefield didn't like it.

"Who was in your position before?"

"How should I know? My C.O. just said I was being transferred immediately, because they needed some admin help in Intel. Is that all?"

It most certainly was not all, but she asked calmly, "Your former C.O.'s name?"

"Petty Officer, First Class, John Parra."

She scribbled down the name and looked up. "Thank you, Gates. Welcome to the office."

He nodded and shut the door behind himself.

"Guy's so cagey." She rolled her eyes as she closed Lawson's email and slid out of her chair toward the box.

Wakefield groaned, "You couldn't be more discreet, Sheriff's Deputy K. Dougherty, of San Diego County?" She read off the return address label in black Sharpie.

Wakefield locked her office again on her way out, though she wasn't sure why she bothered now.

At the busy mail sorting room, she requested Petty Officer Parra from the first body she saw. The young woman dropped the plastic bin she had turned around with in her gloved hands to salute her. "Ma'am!" her eighteen year old voice creaked with stress.

"It's ok. At ease." Wakefield tried to keep a straight face. *Was I ever that green?* "No need to salute indoors. I'm looking for Parra."

The girl dropped one hand to her side and pointed toward a Plexi-glassed enclosure on the far side of the sorting stations. Machines hummed and humans sorted from clear bins and a conveyor belt. There was a lot more involved in getting mail to 5,000 sailors than she had imagined.

Wakefield rapped on the glass door to warn PO Parra, and leaned her torso inside. "Can I have a word?"

He popped up from his seat. His small eyes, buried beneath Navy regulation coke-bottle glasses, fixed on her immediately. "As you were, petty officer," she instructed. He relaxed immediately and

Wakefield noted that his back was beginning to hunch over even in his late twenties.

"Of course Commander Wakefield. Come on in. Lemme clear you a spot." He scurried around his desk to move two stacks of papers to the floor with about two dozen more stacks that to her looked identical.

"How do you keep it all straight?" She asked, perching on the edge of the chair he offered.

He tapped his temple. "It will all get filed over the next two days. What can I do for you? Was everything in order with your package? We had everything irradiated as per protocol after the anthrax scares last year, if that's what you wanted to know."

"With all this mail, you remembered that I got a package?" she asked incredulously. Maybe she should recruit him for her office.

"It just came in today, ma'am. And there's not too much call for packages at a 16.25 pound rate. Too expensive to mail. I had it delivered immediately. It seemed important. Was that right, ma'am? How is Gates doing down there in Intel? We couldn't have been more surprised when the orders came through."

On second thought, perhaps Parra was a little too talky for her office. Though she was certainly impressed with his memory. She held up her hand to slow him down. "The package is fine as far as I know." She nodded to put him at ease. "I have not opened it yet. Gates is why I'm here."

"How's he doing? Giving you as much lip as he did me? He had been one more warning away from me writing him up. And chronically late. Couldn't get it through that young man's head that the mail is so important to our boys, and ladies of course, ma'am. It brings 'em some happiness from home, and we need to get it out a-sap."

Parra took a breath to reload and Wakefield jumped in. "Who issued Gates' orders?"

"Well, Ensign Laslo brought it down and oversaw Gates' move to the new office. Right in the middle of the shift, mind you. And Gates didn't look none too surprised, neither." Parra's eyebrows drew together as if he was imparting some hidden message. "But it was issued by the captain's signature himself. Though he didn't write the orders himself. The X.O. wrote the orders. The captain signed them, and Laslo delivered and executed them. He even escorted him out of the mail room right then."

Parra actually paused of his own accord that time. But Wakefield thought it was probably part of his delivery, drop a bomb and emphasize it with quiet. So he thought it was important information. Ensign Laslo helped the captain with administrative duties that were not classified, so she didn't find it unusual.

"How do you know it was X.O. Bradshaw's handwriting?" She queried.

"The X.O. writes a letter home to his kids every week. Hand delivers it down here himself. That's unusual. It says even more about the man that he also comes to pick up letters from his kids every time a mail COD delivers. Within two, three hours, we can count on the X.O. being at that doorway." Parra tilted his head. "Hardly anyone makes the trip down this far—your visit being a great exception, ma'am—they just have us pick up letters on our delivery rounds. But the X.O. comes all the way down here, so we make sure we have his letters ready for him. A nice packet of letters from his kids in this shipment. They even draw nice little pictures on the envelope sometimes. That's nice. Real nice."

"Ok. Thank you very much, PO Parra. Have yourself a good rest of the day." Wakefield stood, and of course Parra stood with her. He was still talking, but she tuned him out as she began to massage and assimilate the information she had just absorbed. What did it all mean? Did it mean *any*thing?

CHAPTER TWENTY FIVE

S pecial Agent Lawson had appropriated to his office a free standing white board that could spin to a cork board on the backside since she had been there that morning. Wakefield dropped the box from the Sheriff's office the last three inches to Lawson's metal desk mostly for the boom its weight would make. "Well, here it is."

"I can't believe they let the evidence out of their hands, much less shipped it halfway around the world to the middle of an ocean."

Wakefield shrugged. "Apparently the deputy used to be in the service, and has a lot of autonomy in his county. But he does want it all shipped back when we are finished. Especially if we find something. My former C.O., CAPT Huntingdon, said the deputy sounded like he thought the situation was fishy, but could never find any evidence of foul play. Huntingdon passed on the deputy's 'good luck' to us."

Lawson flipped open a pocket knife. "Let's see what we can uncover." The honed blade sliced through the packing tape with a little crackle.

"Huntington also said I should give it a once-over and get back to work." Wakefield admitted, feeling a sheepish as she remembered his tone of voice. "The phone calls and documents needing translation are piling up."

"You're a translator? What language? And how did you end up on a ship?" Lawson straightened up holding the box top to look at her.

"I'm a profiler and analyst, actually. I just happen to be good at languages, and right now they need proficient Arabic-language translations and analysis." She shrugged again. "Oh, and Arabic interrogation. Which I also have a bit of experience with. Which is how I think I landed on this ship two days after my wedding." At his jaw drop she added with a wan smile, "I'm really trying not to be bitter at all."

Lawson's handsome dark features pinched together. "I would definitely be bitter."

"Some days are easier than others. I am finding myself sighing and shrugging a lot the last day or so." Judah walked over next to Lawson and began to take evidence bags out of the box. There was a thick folder of reports hemmed in place with the evidence. That report was what she wanted to take a first close look at.

"Why do you think the last couple of days have been more difficult?" Lawson asked his voice softer and full of compassion. He dipped his hand into the box and removed a clear plastic evidence bag.

Wakefield glanced up at him to judge his motives. His expression seemed genuine enough. "The last few off-book cases I've worked on, David and I worked together. I really miss him. He has such good insights about people. And he really is my best friend." They continued to unpack small and large items all wrapped in plastic evidence bags. It looked like there might be more paper in the bottom of the box.

"How'd you guys meet?" Lawson asked. "I'm always looking for new trolling ground."

Wakefield snorted in the back of her throat over the word *trolling.* "On a case," she said. Wakefield gave him the brief version of Filasek, the compound, the cave rescue, and Rivers. She left out the bit about the weapons cache and the nuclear weapons they had secured since that was still classified. "Rivers was the one who stitched up my cheek."

Lawson swore softly as he moved closer to take inspect her face. "He did a fine job." Lawson's hand came up to trace the scar. She took a half step back to put some room between them. "Did I mention my husband is a SEAL instructor at Little Creek?" She sweetly warned him off.

Lawson licked his lips as his eyebrows peaked in perfect twin arches. "No. No you didn't mention that." He turned back to the box and slid the file folder out. "An instructor, you say? He must be pretty good at his job."

Wakefield nodded and mm-hm'ed in her throat as she reached for the file before Lawson could even put it on the table. She opened the side and flipped half of the three-inch thick pile of paper to the left side. All the pages had been secured by a metal clasp built into the top of file folder and were free at the bottom. She fanned through the pages. All words. Both sides of the folder.

"Crime scene photos must be in the bottom," she stated as she began to read the top page. After six lines she recognized it as a transcript of an interview with the captain. "This is a transcript, are there interview tapes in there?"

He held up a baggie of several micro cassette tapes. "Yep. And photos of the *accident* scene," he emphasized.

"Of course." Wakefield shot him a single eye-brow raise. She went back to reading while out of the corner of her eye she saw Lawson begin to dig around in his desk drawers. She hoped he was looking for a cassette player.

Two hours later their connections board was beginning to come to a nice spider web of order. Color-coordinated post-it notes were connected by black threads crisscrossing the board. They had no twine, and the white thread from Wakefield's sewing kit didn't show up against the white board, so they had taped down black thread. Navy improvisation.

Wakefield set down the Scotch tape in a huff. "There just isn't that much new information." She sighed. "What do you see?" This was the first time Lawson had heard and assessed any other witness interviews. "Do you have anything that has come to mind since your interview that day?" She held up the closed three-inch folder where his transcript lay buried with nearly forty others.

"We cross referenced MacSod's official duty record, the plane manifests for his going and coming back and three weeks prior to his leaving. The dates line up with the record. So MacSod was at sea on the shakedown cruise testing the *Theodore Roosevelt*'s weapons systems and crew readiness for the deployment we are currently on."

Lawson stood at the board pointing to dates of a timeline that ran vertically along the left margin of the board as he went through the story as he saw it. Wakefield stood, her hip leaning into Lawson's desk putting her hand on each piece of evidence as he called it out. Or she would recall the piece of paper where she had read the corresponding information.

"The shakedown cruise departed August 7 and returned to port September 15 at Norfolk Naval Station. Captain MacSod would have had to report for duty at least two days prior to sailing, and we can add a day in transit from the west coast. So he left San Diego 4 August, 2002, at the latest, but maybe up to a week prior to that." Lawson moved his hand up the list to their hand written date range of JUL 28-AUG 4 DEPARTS SAN DIEGO.

"The captain said he began to notice tiredness in his wife when she cancelled their annual Independence Day barbeque." He touched

JUL 4-MRS. SYMPTOMS. He picked up the black dry-erase marker and said, "Let's squeeze in here Martha's doctor's appointment and diagnosis." He began to write in smaller all capital lettering:

AUG 17- DOC APPT

AUG 19- DIAGNOSIS OF POISONING; BEGIN TREATMENT

AUG 31- CAR CRASH—MARTHA DIES

"The flight manifest puts Captain MacSod leaving the ship the evening of September 1. With the time difference, he could have received notification within six to ten hours of her death." Wakefield pulled her lips tightly over her teeth. She scattered the photos across Lawson's desk while searching for the one she wanted. "Here it is. See how steep that angle is from the road to the car. Did someone witness the crash? Because drivers certainly couldn't see the car from the highway. Especially at night."

"A 9-1-1 call started this whole thing in motion. "We've got a copy of that tape in here somewhere too." Lawson fished into the bag of tapes turning each one so he could read the labeling inside the bag. "I don't recall reading a name anywhere."

A little clattering later, Lawson pressed play.

"9-1-1. What is your emergency?"

"A lady just drove off the side of the road. It's a real deep embankment over there."

"Can you see the vehicle, ma'am?"

"No. I'm driving. But they should probably hurry."

"Where are you located?"

"I'm on Torrey Pines Road. Um." There was a pause. "I am just passing Scripps Green Hospital. It was probably most of two miles back by the time I finally got through to you."

"Ok, ma'am, can you pull over and stay on the line with me?"

The engine noise in the background cut off abruptly two seconds later.

"Ma'am? Ma'am!? She hung up on me and didn't even stop to help at an accident." The dispatcher grumbled. The recording continued another few seconds as the dispatcher described the little information she had to relay to the San Diego County Sheriff's office responsible for patrolling the strip of road the woman had mentioned. Lawson clicked the player stop button.

"One things stands out to me," Wakefield said.

"Me too. You go first."

"Her voice was awfully calm for having just witnessed an accident. She sounds young and normally you'd expect to hear breathiness and jitteriness in the voice. You?"

"How did the caller know it was a woman in the vehicle? If she couldn't see it and was still driving?"

"Big hair?" Wakefield guessed. Do we have a photo of Martha in life, not on the autopsy table all washed and flat?

Lawson was already digging. "Yes!" He held up a photo triumphantly. "She did have big hair. Probably would have shown over the top or sides of the headrest so the caller might have been able to see it when driving behind her."

"Hand me that." Wakefield's eyes widened as she took in the family photo. The captain was wearing civilian clothes. His lavender tie coordinated with Martha's grey and lavender lace dress. Her hair was indeed left from fashion in the height of the 80s. A teenage girl sat between them, with long straight blond and black streaked hair. She carried a hard look on her face even though she was technically smiling. Her skirt and top also were in springy colors and she was frozen in time pulling her lacy t-shirt askew from her body.

"Who is this?" Judah asked. When she flipped the photo around, she saw "Easter 2002" handwritten in spidery female handwriting.

"Their daughter Elizabeth Ann. I think she is sixteen now. And she prefers 'Liz' these days."

"How in the world do you know that?" Wakefield stared at Lawson.

"She joined us on a Tiger Cruise about six months before that was taken, just before the *TR* went to dry dock for nine months of maintenance and repairs. That would have been just before 9/11 happened. I want to say August of 2001. Probably." Lawson hesitated trying to remember the last weekend when parents, children, and spouses of naval personnel were invited aboard the ship for a weekend to watch drills.

"So you met Martha?" Surprised, Wakefield turned to Lawson who was now standing at the board.

"No." Lawson looked into the middle distance to his left as he remembered. "The second day of the three-day cruise the captain's little cutie went missing for a few hours."

Wakefield caught her breath as she pictured everything that would have gone down on a ship at sea with a missing civilian, especially a captain's daughter.

"It was a madhouse around here for a little while. The noise, the constant announcement over the 1MC, the counting, the search. I came across little Liz right after the X.O. found her right here on this floor—of course Bradshaw wasn't the X.O. yet, he was working in the Nuke Plant then. I only saw the back of the young sailor with whom she had been playing kissy face. His heels were smoking on his way away from her. At the X.O.'s suggestion, I'm sure. Because I know Bradshaw saw him, but nothing was ever said or done, because it would have come through my office. But Bradshaw was reading the girl the riot act."

Wakefield's eyebrows shot up in surprise.

"That's what I thought too!" Lawson nodded looking directly at her. "You go after the sailor, not the captain's daughter."

Wakefield nodded.

"I didn't understand until the Mrs.'s funeral. Apparently the MacSods and the Bradshaws are old family friends."

"Bradshaw went to the funeral? The X.O. and the captain were both absent from the ship at the same time?" That did not jive with Navy regs.

"The Bradshaw had not been officially installed as the X.O. yet. Our original X.O., Byers, was still handing over the duties, so Byers took command of the ship for the seven days the captain was gone, and I think Bradshaw was only on leave three days, maybe. They returned on the same COD right after the funeral."

"Oh." Judah was puzzled. It sounded weird. She sighed. So many, many things on this ship were weird.

Little Creek Naval Base, VA
The Facility

Traipsing back down the steep front entry stairs of The Facility, Rivers heard an insistent high-pitched beep, beep, beeeep! Up the wide sidewalk to his left, a golf cart charged, dodging uniformed pedestrians, without regard to their rank or rating. Rivers' eyebrows shot up. It looked as if the duo in the cart were mid-getaway from a bank robbery. A black-sleeved arm leaned out to wave and nearly got taken off at the shoulder as the driver came close to sideswiping a pine.

"Rivers. Rivers, wait." He heard the driver call out.

Oh dear. That zany display was coming for him. He considered hiding or running, but by the time he had decided, he recognized Little Creek's Admiral and young yeoman, who apparently had given up a promising career in NASCAR to join the Navy.

Rivers stayed on the third-to-bottom step, where he hoped his toes would be protected. A man in the wake of Speedy Gonzalez bent to start picking up half a ream of paper scattered like snow across the green.

The pair rolled to a stop exactly even with the stairs to the BOQ. The admiral stepped out, looking a little green around the gills himself. He held onto the cart's rooftop and started to speak. He seemed to have been holding his breath because he was definitely breathing funny.

"What can I do for you, Admiral Burke?" Rivers smirked.

"I'm so glad we caught you." He pointed up the stairs. "Can I have a word?"

Rivers nodded and preceded the man up the stairs to open the door for him.

"Nobody in." Burke ordered the yeoman over his shoulder.

CHAPTER TWENTY SIX

"It's getting late, do you need some shut eye or are you comfortable?" Lawson said looking at his watch.

"I'm more comfortable here than running into my bunkmate," Judah admitted. Perhaps that was a bit too causal an info-drop to a new acquaintance, she thought after the words were already out of her mouth.

Lawson chuckled, "What does that mean?"

"Never mind." Wakefield wished she could take it back now. She hadn't even seen LT Melissa Garvey in about five days. Not since she gave her the ultimatum. "I'm fine for another hour or so. We need to go through Wallace's information too."

"Right. That's how all this started. Do you think the captain and Wallace are somehow connected?"

"I don't see any evidence but my gut says they are." Wakefield pulled her lips in between her teeth as she tried to assess why she connected the two bits of strangeness. She wished she could go crash into ADM Tamburillo's office and lay out the information for him as she had in the past. His mind was like a computer that could see correlations and connections and missing information in seconds.

Wakefield scattered the photos on Lawson's desk instead, and let her mind wander to try to pick up the missing threads she had not been able to see yet. "I never thanked you for sending over all those changes in designator earlier. You know what else might be helpful in establishing a connection, besides when we can start interviewing these guys' C.O.s? If you could get a print-out of the times and personnel using the secure line in coms. I got Wallace's but I'd like to see everyone."

"Shouldn't be a problem." Lawson shrugged. "You want me to pop up there now? I've got a friend who works 2300 to 0600."

"That'd be great." It would definitely be easier to acquire the information from a friend who might not think anything of it.

"Find out if any other former C.O.s of transferred personnel are on duty now." Lawson pointed at his computer and shut the hatch behind himself.

Wakefield began the research for 23 officers and enlisted servicemen and wrote a tidy list on a discarded envelope from Lawson's trashcan.

Not a single C.O. was on duty in the middle of the night Wakefield discovered within thirty minutes. But Lawson still had not returned. Coms was only three decks up. Wakefield leaned back to rest her tired back against the seatback. Her eyes fluttered closed, "What is taking so—" The creak of the hatch interrupted her and her eyes flew open.

Lawson stood in the doorway fanning his self-satisfied face with a thick pad of half-sheets of dot matrix printer paper. "Got it, he said. "And I almost got myself a date too."

Wakefield shook her head in mock frustration. "Ohhh! It was *that* kind of friend. Wasting my time so you could go a-flirting."

"My flirting got us the entire list from the moment the *Reprisal* put back in after dry-dock. Every call made from the secure room logged and in order. According to my *friend*." Lawson chucked the half-inch pile of records onto his desk. "She also allowed me exactly seven minutes, outside the log, but inside the room to look for clues."

"Look for clues?" Wakefield tensed. "What exactly did you tell her?"

"Don't worry. I made up a story which of course made me the dapper detective," he removed a pretense of a hat and placed a hand over his heart, "searching for evil to put it away and protect the innocent. Which would be her, of course."

Wakefield raised one eyebrow.

"Don't give me that. There was no one around and I thought I'd take a risk." Lawson shrugged. "I had to think fast."

"OK. So what did you find?" He wouldn't have gone to the trouble of mentioning the entry into the secure room, if he hadn't found something.

"Actually it wasn't something I found, but a person I called." He paused for effect, and it worked. Wakefield wanted to shake the information out of him, but she was too tired to move.

"So, who did you call?"

"Actually I talked to five people."

"In seven minutes? Come on, quit dragging this out."

"Don't you like a good story?"

"I like a good punchline." Wakefield said shortly.

"It was actually closer ten or twelve minutes by the time I actually got off the line. First I called information in San Diego and got the phone number for the public high school office for the MacSods' San Diego city residence. Information gave me a direct connect to the school because I had nothing to write down the number. Then I talked to one of the office clerks who put me on with the admittance counselor. She was able to recall the incident and even verified the dates for me while I was on the line."

"What did you ask her?"

"Liz has been bothering me ever since we talked about her."
Lawson ran a hand over his hair. "She was already having a hard
time. You could tell by her clothes and hair. Then her mother is
diagnosed with a poison toxicity, and then killed in a car crash. Her
dad sweeps in for a week and then heads back out to sea. Her
mother is gone; who is she living with? Who is taking care of that
girl? She is only 16 or 17 years old."

Wakefield was curious now too. A girl that age, already troubled,
would need extra loving care, not less. She would be desperate for a
father to show her how to grieve and to love. "So where is she?"

"The councilor said Elizabeth Ann never returned to school
after her mother's death. Her dad came in on her fourth day out and
requested to hand carry her transcript and school records to the
Navy base high school. He told the councilor Elizabeth Ann would
be switching schools when she went back to class."

"Hmm." Judah grunted. What was that all about? Seems like the
girl would need something consistent in her life—like friends at
school—in a life filled with so much upheaval already.

"After I thanked her for her help, I called San Diego Navy base
and asked to be connected with the high school admittance office.
And…" He drew it out.

Wakefield cleared her throat and rubbed her right contact in a
slow circle too unstick it from her over-tired eyes. "The punch line."

"Elizabeth Ann MacSod was never registered, not even an
application has been placed on file in the base high school. There is
no record of her."

USS *Theodore Roosevelt*
NCIS Office
0055 hours

"Where is she? She has to be somewhere." Wakefield fought
desperately to keep her mind from wandering toward the most

horrible explanation of MacSod's daughter's disappearance from the school record.

"Do you think he killed them both?" Lawson's whisper gave language to her wonderings.

"I was *really* trying not to go there." Judah said. Her heart rate accelerated as she considered it. "Surely not. Maybe her grandparents or an aunt took her in or something. And they live out of town."

"But the captain told the counselor she would be going to school on base."

"Maybe when he requested the records, she *was* going to go to the base high school, and then they had a change of plans. MacSod is an officer in the U.S. Navy; let's give him the benefit of the doubt as long as we can. There is nothing in his record that suggests him capable of a calculated murder of his own flesh and blood."

"Okay," Lawson drew out. "Give me another explanation."

"A hundred things could have happened." Wakefield threw up her hand and let it fall heavily in her lap.

"I'm with you, Wakefield." Lawson sounded reassuring. "Like what?"

Wakefield's head tilted to the side wearily and she sighed. "I can't think of a single thing right now besides the hope she went to live with a relative or family friend. But there's another thing."

"What's that?" Lawson's brow furrowed into three even rows.

"Well, I am questioning the veracity of the log book. If your *friend* allowed you into the room, who's to say she, or someone else, didn't let a senior officer or flag officer in without all the proper paperwork? I don't see your name as the last entry on this list. You talked to five people off book in less than a quarter of an hour. How many more secure calls were placed with no record being made?"

"Well, I suppose." Lawson wrinkled his nose, "But maybe it will help with the Wallace part of this mess. The record is a place to start. We have another piece of the puzzle. Or maybe another angle to a whole other puzzle." He shook his head as he changed his mind. "Did you have any luck with the C.O.s?"

Wakefield looked at the C.O. list she had compiled of all the men who had been transferred around the ship. "None of them are on the mid-watch. My eyes are beginning to cross. I'd better get some rack time. Do you mind if we divide this up and start interviewing tomorrow?"

"Not at all, I was beginning to wonder if you ever run out of energy." Lawson took a deep breath. "I'll store this in the safe. I will also look into family ties where Liz might be staying in the morning. We can make some calls tomorrow evening when they awake west coast time."

Wakefield nodded and sleepily trudged toward the door and her bunk. "See you tomorrow."

USS *Theodore Roosevelt*
Intel Office
1502 hours

The next afternoon Judah Wakefield pulled back abruptly as she walked from the passageway into her outer office. The hatch handle still under her hand. "Sir?"

What was MacSod doing in her office? The man's closed eyes told her he had been around for a little while. The stiff posture of Gates and Juarez confirmed it. She snuck a quick peak at her watch while the captain roused himself from his repose.

"Where have you been?" He growled coming slowly to his feet. He placed a hand to the small of his back and then pressed it into his side.

"I was conducting some interviews." Judah felt her face flush.

"I know." MacSod drew up to his full height. "Why's your office door locked?"

"Um," Wakefield stalled. Just make it seem normal, she coached herself even as her face heated further. "Don't you lock your office when you're not in it?"

"Yes. But LCDR Wallace never locked this office." The captain jutted his chin toward the hatch in a motion that ordered without the necessity of words that she unlock it and get her six inside on the double.

Wakefield opened her mouth to suggest that perhaps that was a reason that Wallace was no longer a presence on this ship, but then she remembered that the same power that just had Wallace removed could also have her removed, so she snapped her jaw shut and opened the door on the double. Then she reminded herself that she had a few questions for the captain herself.

Honey attracts more flies than vinegar, her mother's voice ran through her head.

She twisted her key in the knob and flung the door open for him to enter first. "Can I get you some coffee?"

"No, commander. The reputation of the joe from this office precedes itself."

Wakefield felt a little giggle start to rise from her belly. *Keep it together, girl!* She pressed the laugh down. When Juarez chuckled proudly behind her, she almost lost it. She shot him wide eyes and a tight seam of her lips as she pushed her fingers against her bunching cheeks, wishing she could tamp down her mirth as easily.

She snapped the door shut, flattened her features, and turned to MacSod completely composed. "What can I do for you, sir?"

MacSod stepped up nearly toe to toe with her. "I want to know what in the sam-hill you think you're doing running all over my ship stirring up a hornet's nest." His hot breath pushed over her face.

Wakefield held her ground, didn't breathe, and fixed her gaze a thousand yards away. "Sir?" she asked, still stalling while she discerned whether to make up a classified-above-his-clearance national emergency and give him small little lies or tell him she was investigating him.

"I've got people all over my ship reporting to me that you are asking questions and challenging my authority to move my people around to where they are better suited to serve the Navy."

Wakefield risked shifting her gaze to look him in the eye. She knew his words couldn't be accurate. She had had nothing but cooperation and smiles and wonderings from the C.O.s she had questioned all morning. Twelve short little interviews, on the spot and back-to-back, as she rushed around the ship to all the different duty stations. She had taken 14 of the 23 names from the list, the people she would have easier access to. Lawson took the other nine.

"Sir, I've done nothing of the sort," she blurted out. "I apologize. That came out more sharply than I meant it." She softened her voice. So much for killing him with kindness. She winced.

"How dare you." The captain worked himself up further, swearing up a blue streak. "Now you, a subordinate so far down the chain of command it is almost funny, are questioning me to my face?"

MacSod stomped over to her desk as Judah's ears burned. She felt her soul rise up in anger and offense; they were only separated by two ranks after all. The captain made it sound as if she were a private on her first day.

He continued yelling, even ordering her to put her office back in order, as he picked up a pen she'd left on her desk top. She had the briefest flash of fear that he would try to stab her with it, his anger was so boiling. She had only brought her arms up to her waist to defend herself physically when MacSod bent at the waist and began scrawling on a piece of note paper. "This is your final warning, Lieutenant Commander Wakefield. You have seen that I have the power to move people around. If you persist in this inquiry you seem so hell bent on conducting, like Wallace, I will send you somewhere you do not want to go for the remainder of your tour of duty!"

MacSod straightened up, "This is your official and final warning." He tapped the paper he had written on and left on her desk. He walked back to stand over her. "I mean it. You must stop this investigation immediately. Get back to your normal duties or you will be in grave danger."

With all Wakefield knew about this man, using the phrase "grave danger" did not seem trite. It functioned more like an exclamation point.

"I want you to follow my orders to a T. Or there will be consequences." He pointed back at her desk. His eyes' crinkles pushed deeper into his temple than the normal skipper appearance marked from years of squinting against the sun and its reflection on the waves. "Do we understand each other?"

Wakefield belted out the only answer she could give. "Sir, yes, sir!"

MacSod strode to the door in three powerful steps and slammed it behind himself with an echo that hurt her bones.

Wakefield waited a few beats until she heard the outer door repeat the crashing sound. Then her shoulders melted from her military bearing. She put a hand to her pounding heart. That was one of the worst dressing downs she'd ever experienced.

She moved to lean a hand against her desk for support. Her eyes widened as the scene replayed in her mind. The captain himself had connected Wallace to all the moving around of personnel she and Lawson were investigating. Did he ship him off to Siberia, or Thule Air Base in Greenland, Siberia's equal in the U.S. military? Where were Wallace's orders then?

Wakefield pounded her desk in frustration. This guy was in it up to his eyeballs! If only she knew what "it" was. She shook her head emphatically. She wanted to ball up his little written warning on stupid scratch paper and throw it at him.

Instead she stuck her head out her door. "I guess you guys heard that."

The two men looked up nervously. "Yes, ma'am." They spoke in unison.

"How long was he here before I arrived?" She softened her body language as she saw the young men felt uncomfortable.

"About fifteen minutes." Juarez said.

"Where were you? I really thought he might kill us." Gates added.

"I wasn't sure what he was going to do either, ma'am, but then he just kind of melted into that chair and drifted off to sleep for at least five minutes."

"Strangest thing." Gates commented.

Juarez smiled then, "Cap'n sure can put his words together."

Wakefield smiled wanly. "I feel like I need a Q-tip to clean out my ears. I'll try to do better about letting you guys know what I'm working on and where I will be, if I have to leave the office while you're on watch."

"That'd sure be nice." Juarez said.

"Thank you, ma'am." Gates mouth pulled into a small smile.

Wakefield closed the hatch and leaned her forehead against it to it support her weight. Two superior officers now had suggested she get back to her regular duties. Perhaps she was falling behind in production. She would follow orders. Well, to a point anyway. Her lips pursed, and she reached around the computer monitor to engage the on-button. Her translation and analysis would certainly be stepped up. But that didn't mean she wouldn't continue to unravel this thing with Captain MacSod in her mind while she worked and in her off-duty hours.

Dreading it all the way around her desk, Wakefield plopped down in her seat and spun the note around so she could read her official warning.

Her eyes moved across the paper. Then she started at the top again. What?

OFFICE BUGGED, VOICE/VIDEO
KEEP GOING!
BE <u>EXTREMELY</u> CAREFUL
PANTRY BY OFFICER'S GALLEY, 2345
COME ALONE. DESTROY NOTE ASAP.

Chapter Twenty Seven

USS *Theodore Roosevelt*
Intel Office
1510 hours

Judah read the cryptic note a third time. "Well, the 'come alone' is *never* gonna happen. I've seen that movie too many times," she whispered. Then she clapped a hand over her mouth. Her office was bugged for sound too. She had not seen a mic anywhere when she searched for the video surveillance camera.

She couldn't keep her eyes from searching the walls, the book shelves, the filing cabinet, the chairs. Ugh, it could be anywhere. What could they have picked up from her conversations and talking to herself?

Wakefield flopped her hand on the desk as she clutched the note. A bigger question: who is they?

If MacSod told her about the camera and mic, he obviously knew about them, and had seen the camera angle, but why give up his advantage by telling her? What did he have to gain? Could he know about it and not be behind it? How? Why?

Wakefield stood to go talk to Lawson. Then remembered the camera. Nothing could look fishy. She had to hold up a pretense of obeying the captain's verbal order for the surveillance. At least for longer than a minute and a half.

It felt creepy being watched, even though she knew that where she sat was probably out of camera range. She remembered MacSod

225

also ordering her to return the office to its original layout. That was not going to happen either. "It's my office, and I'll arrange my furniture however I want." That she spit out aloud for the obstinacy in her to breathe and for a little poke back toward whomever was on the other side of the microphone. It wasn't much, but it felt good to voice her say.

She folded the warning note in quarters and reached for the Velcro pocket on her thigh. Then thinking better of it, she undid her top blouse button and tucked it into her bra cup.

She would give at least an hour to translation and then go see Lawson. She still had two other C.O. interviews to conduct for the moved personnel too. This thing felt bigger and bigger.

The computer was booted up, so she entered her password. Then she thought of the camera that had been on her when she faced the other direction, and felt panic begin to rise. Had they accessed her Naval Intel account based on her hand movements on the keyboard? That could be bad. Very bad! Her clearance level accessed enough intelligence to throw a war to the other side if improperly shared.

She made a couple of clicks to go into the background account to check her log-in records. "Thank you, Jesus." She breathed out the words. Then got creeped out again because she knew someone was listening, if not live, then they would hear the recording.

Clicking back to her settings, Wakefield changed her password and hovered the curser over a small little clickable box that showed only if you knew you could scroll down on the password-change screen. It was labeled ARE YOU SURE? But as every intelligence officer with top secret or higher clearance knew, when disengaged, that little box brought expedited and extreme attention to an account in headquarters. It had nothing to do with being sure about changing a password. When sent, an alert would be brought to ADM

Tamburello's email account that stated that she felt her account access may have been compromised. That something was wrong.

Within minutes, a protocol she had helped devise would be enacted. A story would be concocted at HQ, and her "Uncle Louis" would begin to try to reach her. On that call they would set up a time to chat privately via the emergency SatFone buried in her locker. In the mean time, someone else would shut off much of her access to the Intel Site. But she would be able to access some intel, enough that if she was being held at gun point and forced to change her password, that she wouldn't be killed immediately. That part of the protocol had been Tamburello's suggestion when they served on the task force together in 1998. Tamburello would immediately assign someone to begin combing through her work product, system queries, and search threads for the last six months, working backward from the moment she unchecked that field. She used to be that person. She had twice in the six years she had worked at headquarters had to scramble for this protocol. It was a big deal.

She swallowed hard. You have to be able to admit when you're in over your head, she coached herself silently. LCDR Wakefield unchecked the box and hit enter.

USS *Theodore Roosevelt*
NCIS Office
1710 hours

"Where did you disappear? I was getting worried." Lawson stood up from his desk.

"Thanks for coming to check." Judah said. "I was in my office. Working. You know, a whole sixty feet up the corridor." She pointed.

"I said '*getting* worried'." He emphasized. "You look fine."

"Never mind all that." Wakefield shut the door behind her and quickly glanced around the small office to confirm that they were alone. "You've swept your office again?"

"Right after lunch. I finished all my interviews before—"

Judah cut him off with a hand gesture. "Hang on. We are way beyond our investigation now." She unbuttoned her top button and Lawson's eyebrows shot toward his hairline.

"Ma'am?" His voice staggered in pitch to create two syllables from the word.

Judah frowned at him. "No such luck," she said as she reached inside her uniform blouse to retrieve the captain's note.

"That would not be *luck*. That would be *dread* ... of your SEAL." Lawson was able to chuckle by the time the folder paper appeared in her hand.

"We have a big development on our hands." She handed the note over and righted her uniform while he read.

He gave a low whistle. "Do you know who it's from? Or—"

"MacSod."

Lawson's neck extended in disbelief. "Just when I thought it couldn't get any weirder."

"The skipper came into my office, put on a dressing-down show for the camera, and wrote me this note."

"I see you didn't destroy it." Lawson held up the note.

"Are you kidding? That's evidence."

"What do you want to do?"

"I've already started," Wakefield told him about setting up a call with Naval Intel HQ without giving away any protocol secrets. "That will be at 2105 hours."

"How are you going to explain the use of the secure line for permission from MacSod? Even if he is genuinely trying to warn you, he's never going to allow you a call."

"I have a SatFone. The thing is, I need better reception than I will be able to get in my cabin. I need guaranteed undisturbed space topside."

"How are you going to get that?" Lawson's handsome features rumpled in thought.

"You." She said flatly. "I need you to create a distraction."

"That sounds fun."

Wakefield took in Lawson's grin, and knew he wasn't being caustic. "Good. Because right after that, I need you to do a little something else for me." He was not going to like what she had in mind for this part.

Five minutes later he groaned but agreed when she had explained what she needed.

"What about your interviews? How'd they go?" He asked, handing the MacSod note back to her.

"Why don't you lock that in the safe?" She suggested. Lawson punched in a code as Wakefield sat down and began to describe her morning. "Everything was good. I had a few C.O.s that were glad their guys were transferred and a few that wondered about it."

"Same for me. Everyone was eager to talk. Two of them confided a concern for the captain's health and disposition recently. From what I surmised, the captain's yeoman delivered all orders by hand. No senior officer was present for any of the transfers."

"That's what I gathered too. Even though I still have two to go. Had that little interruption with the captain before I could finish."

"They are all new arrivals on ship, and in so many different areas. C.O.s did not request transfers, but some of the personnel did." Lawson was thinking out loud as he tried to work out a pattern.

"What if we were to assume there is some misdirection involved." Wakefield pursed her lips. "If we allow for 30-40 percent of our information to be thrown out, is there a discernable pattern?"

"Only problem is which 30-40 percent to toss out." Lawson sighed in frustration.

"What if we look at the areas people were transferred into?" Judah turned the list of 23 toward her as she allowed her mind wander into some dark possible plots.

"What are some worst case scenarios we could be dealing with here? Of course, there could be a cover up of murder." Lawson shrugged like it was nothing.

"Yes. But there has to be a reason bigger than that to warrant murdering an intelligence officer, or at least making him disappear."

"Maybe Wallace discovered that the captain was running drugs or something. We *are* headed to a region where poppies are more prevalent than corn."

"But we are *headed* that direction." Wakefield shook her head. "Wallace would not have been able to figure out a crime was being committed before the drugs were brought on board."

Lawson kept pushing. "What if he discovered the money MacSod was going to use to buy the drugs."

"Um," Wakefield winked one eye closed as she looked at Lawson. "I'm not sure people exchange big piles of cash in wholesale drug buys anymore."

"Well, I'm no DEA expert." Lawson shrugged. "What if there is a human trafficking ring and the captain is transporting people, or young women," His eyes widened further. "Or children."

"You think there is a cage of people hidden somewhere on this ship and not one of five thousand sailors has stumbled across it? Not possible."

"It's a big ship." Lawson pointed out. "And nothing is impossible. What have you got?" He challenged her back.

Wakefield folded her arms across her chest and tapped her first finger against her opposite bicep. "We've got to think bigger. And think of a crime either already committed, an infraction of the UMCJ by the top level, well, even that is not enough to tap my office. Yours, maybe." Wakefield frowned. "But not mine. Think. We are on a floating nuclear-powered city; what is the worst that could happen?"

"A melt down."

"A melt down used as a weapon." Judah added. Her heart beating a little faster.

"A weapon against the U.S. by first killing everyone on board. Second by a world media storm burning America at the stake for using a nuclear weapon against her enemies."

Further realization came to Wakefield. "And third, by the terror and confusion and wasted time it would infuse into the entire American military system as we started a witch hunt in every single branch of the service. If we have a captain that has gone rogue aboard a naval aircraft carrier…" She trailed off.

"But MacSod warned you." Lawson shook his head.

"You're still thinking like a good person, Lawson. What if MacSod also warned Wallace? And then sent him away. Had him killed. Or even had another officer impersonate him on the flight off the ship to change the timing and location of his disappearance. If this is a conspiracy with multiple players, nothing is impossible. And multi-players is credible because of all the transfers the captain set into motion at the same time Wallace disappeared."

"As you yourself said, we don't know for sure that Wallace has disappeared yet. He may have just needed some breathing room in Europe without telling his family." Lawson reminded her.

"Without his credit cards as well?"

"Maybe his wife does the finances, and he wanted to keep it secret."

"No. Every hour that passes with no word from Wallace, solidifies in my mind that he has been lost through foul play of some sort, whether on board this ship or in Europe."

"I have that feeling too," Lawson agreed. "I was just playing devil's advocate."

Wakefield nodded, deep in thought.

"Were you also issued a secret weapon when Intel issued you the satellite phone?"

"Unfortunately no." Wakefield tucked a stray hair behind her ear. "And with the personnel transfer into the armory, I don't think it would be wise to ask the master-at-arms to issue one either. The info would probably leak back to the captain."

Lawson pushed out all of his breath at once. "Just one more reason I think NCIS agents should be allowed to carry a weapon aboard ship. What if I needed to arrest the master-at-arms for something?" Lawson's eyes suddenly got big. He whispered breathily, "What if Wallace discovered that the captain is dealing arms, and is using this ship to transport American fire power for sale to the highest bidder, even to our enemies? That fits a crime where the evidence doesn't need to be fed like people, but that could be stored aboard without discovery. Perhaps even among the cabbages."

Wakefield could think of nothing to refute it. It did fit. "Thanks. The cabbages makes me feel extra comfortable meeting MacSod in the galley pantry at midnight."

They both sat in silence as the weight of what she was walking into pressed down in the room.

"It won't be any protection if he shoots you, but you should wear an inflatable life jacket under that uniform, in case he throws you overboard. And make sure you kick away from the side hard so there is something left of you for me to mount a rescue for."

"Yeah. I've practiced it. That's enough." Wakefield willed her heart to slow down and wished she was not as snippy with people when she felt ill-at-ease. "This may go down as one of the stupidest moves I've made."

"I'll do my best to back you up." Lawson promised. "But either way, you should probably write to your husband." Lawson gave a weak smile. "I don't want to die as collateral damage if he decides to hunt down your killers."

Wakefield snorted. "He's not that kind of man."

"No offense, but love is blind. He is a SEAL. Revenge is in the first inoculation they receive after their trident pin."

Wakefield just shook her head. David Rivers was not like other people. Not like other SEALs.

CHAPTER TWENTY EIGHT

Little Creek Naval Base, VA
The Facility

Lieutenant Commander David Rivers reached for the light switch and flicked the power off and on twice to halt the drill. "Bring it in guys." He bellowed and his voice carried across the almost-two-acre-sized underground bunker.

It took two minutes for the guys on the far end of The Facility's "basement" to secure their weapons and trot over to where Rivers waited, his mind still whirled with the new information ADM Burke had given him. It would certainly change things. The SEALs milled tiredly until the last man arrived.

They had spent five days setting in place a mock city of Baghdad. They'd used all of the pock-marked and many-times-used building materials available to develop the main palaces, represent bridges, and get height into the room. When they ran out of wood, they had borrowed scaffolding materials from Little Creek's maintenance building to represent the main avenues of approach toward the city they would be using. And it was pretty good. Fairly close to a very, very small scale. "We are still missing waypoints." Rivers held up the stopwatch he had been using to call out the time every three minutes on a three-hour planned assault.

Once everyone got still, Rivers called out, "Commander Jackson, where are you? Come on up here."

A bewildered Jackson threaded the hefty crowd toward Rivers.

"Congratulations," Rivers grimaced. "You are now in charge of this motley crew. I trust you'll whip them into shape." He handed over the clip board with the plan marked in three-minute waypoints on curling paper where he had bent it back over the top clip for Jackson to follow.

As Jackson took the clipboard with a nod, Rivers addressed the SEAL Team. "Men, there's been a development. Team Two ran a quick little interdiction at the border last night, and had a major run in with the drug cartel." Rivers shook his head. "I don't know much, but Admiral Burke delivered the news, and he assures me the only serious injury on our side was LT Chad Pickrell." A whisper moved through the crowd. "Chad took a couple rounds to the gut, a through and through to the thigh, and broke his arm. I know a lot of you guys have friends on Team Two. I do too. The Admiral's yeoman is going to keep you updated if any of the other injuries go sideways.

"Crazily enough, when they opened Chad up this morning to repair the damage, they found a mass in his upper GI tract. As you may know," Rivers inclined his head to emphasize the information, "Chad's family is no longer with us, through no fault of his own. He's had more than his share of tragedy." A few whispers swooshed through the open space. Rivers assumed some of the older men were informing the newer SEALs of Chad's parents' death, his brother's loss of his faculties and placement in a home several months later, and his wife's sudden disappearance and the police investigation, only to reappear with a new man and a handful of divorce papers three months later. "So we are his family." Rivers shifted his weight. What he was about to do he was pretty sure was unprecedented, but it was needed.

"LT Pickrell, Chad, and I were partners on Team Six for those years of chaos in his personal life, before he got promoted to lead Team Two. He never let the pain affect his work, as you can see, because I'm still alive." Rivers smiled as he looked as many men in the eye as he could. "He always had my six. Now I will have his."

"Never leave a man behind. Ooh-rah! Sir." It was Gus, standing to Rivers' left on the front row with his slight stature and calming presence, his arms were crossed loosely across his Kevlar vest. Every man Gus served with could count on his support.

"My sentiments exactly, Gus." Rivers stated with a quick nod. "The Team is recuperating at Corpus Christie Naval Air Station. Chad is at Fort Hood."

"The Army, sir? Say it isn't so."

It was said from the back of the room with such disappointment in the tone, implying the location had sealed Chad's fate for eternity. The room's solemnity cracked in laughter, but before more jokes could be tossed back and forth, Rivers cleared his throat.

"If the Army was able to recruit one the best oncologists in the U.S. to its humble reserve ranks, the least we can do is allow him to take care of our L.T. I am going to go and be with my partner when he hears the news. CNO Abbot has approved any changes we deem necessary here, to make that happen. I think it is high time you all get used to Jackson clamoring the time in your ears anyway, since he will be leading Alpha Company on coms during the event."

"How long will you be gone?" Jackson asked. The clip board hung at his side with a light grip as he stood shoulder to shoulder with Rivers facing the men.

"As long as it takes." Rivers looked at his replacement earnestly. "But I *will* be deploying with you all." Rivers promised.

Jackson nodded in his utilitarian way. "We're going to need to switch your Echo Company unit off the primary target then. If you're not here to rehearse with them." He shrugged.

It made complete sense, but Rivers felt disappointment scratch at his belly. He rubbed it away. "Of course, Commander. Do what you need to," he nodded.

Without even looking back at the notes on his clipboard, Jackson moved into his leadership role. "Rivers' unit with Howard in command as the 2IC will now move to the secondary target at the Al Faw Palace, while the Republican Palace will be stormed by the Echo Company Unit led by Ogden/Campbell. The third Echo Company led by Mendez/Chaffin, you will remain on your current assignment."

Rivers forced a smile. "Looks like you're all in capable hands." He lifted a fist in farewell.

"Give Chad our best." It was Gus again.

"Will do, buddy."

Rivers went out the door alone, and clambered up the metal grate stairs topside in the Facility. According to the admiral's yeoman there was a military transport to Fort Hood already scheduled. They would be held on the tarmac, until he could join them.

USS *Theodore Roosevelt*
Flight Deck
2101 hours

Wakefield leaned against the bulkhead looking out to sea one deck below the flight deck where a number of planes were due to land after drills. Her fingers felt itchy as she fidgeted with the SatFone behind her back. Her hair blew across her face in the stiff wind as she waited for Lawson's distraction.

Two more minutes. There were not too many outdoor spaces on the metal floating city where she had access to good reception for her SatFone. A second F-18 screamed to a stop above her head. The boys were definitely coming home.

One minute. Wakefield closed her eyes and pictured Lawson in anonymous white walking out to one of his buddies, a green-shirt operator on the deck. The friend worked on the deck in a frenzy during these flight patterns with such short breaks in between landings. He looked after the maintenance of the first of five arresting wires laid across the deck to stop the jets as they dropped their tail-hooks.

Chris had agreed to help them, no questions asked. Only Lawson wouldn't give Judah his last name. It was a nice gesture to try to protect his friend, but really, how many guys named Chris wore a green shirt, worked the one wire, and were friends with an NCIS officer? Wakefield breathed deeply rehearsing her information again in the order she wanted to present it in her coming call.

The klaxon sounded over her head and began to pulse its urgent warning. Wakefield knew that the LSO officer had engaged the lighting system and was physically waving the paddles over his head to wave off the jets lined up for the glide path. Lawson and Chris had accomplished their job. The deck was fouled. Everyone within the sound would be needed to clear the almost-full ream of paper from Lawson's office that he had strewn into the wind. They would have to work quickly so those planes could land after their evening sortie.

She would have to be quick too.

Judah Wakefield unfolded the antenna and dialed with her thumb the spongy numbers on the SatFone.

CAPT Huntingdon picked up as the second ring began. "Wakefield? You're on with Huntingdon and ADM Tamburello."

"Hello, sirs. I've only got a few minutes. We had to create a distraction to get some privacy out here."

"Is that the foul-deck alarm in the background?" Huntingdon asked.

"Yes."

"This had better be good."

"I think you know me well enough by now to know I don't ask for help lightly."

"No, you don't lieutenant commander. Now what is going on out there on the *Big Stick*?" the admiral broke in.

Judah quickly described the bugs and video surveillance in her office, the strange encounter with MacSod, all of the personnel changes aboard, connecting with NCIS Special Agent Lawson for help, and her concern about Wallace.

"When you initiated the protocol, Huntingdon got me service records of all the senior officers on board."

"Do either of you have any friends, especially friends who owe you favors, on board?" Wakefield asked.

"Just you," they answered together.

"I wish I did." Tamburello sighed so deeply she could hear it over the pulsing klaxon. Both sounds sent a shot of dread into her core. "Were you aware that MacSod was the one who requested his friend as his X.O.? Bradshaw has the background in place but no experience. The handoff occurred right around the time of MacSod's wife's death."

Huntingdon groaned. "The captain is in this up to his eyeballs!"

"That's exactly what I said, sir." Judah intoned.

"Could the X.O. be in on it too? That's too much of a coincidence." Huntingdon added.

"I have an uneasy feeling about this situation." Tamburello pronounced carefully. "You are so far from backup. Besides the Wallace situation you are dealing with MacSod over, it may be that the captain sees you personally as a threat to him. I looked into his denied promotion last summer. This is the second time he has been passed over. Once more and he's out. Not only do seadogs have trouble retiring when they no longer have anyone to command, but it

239

was Admiral Graham who got the appointment over him the first time he was passed over back in 2001."

"My dad?" Judah's jaw slackened and her eyes searched the smooth deep blue of the sea for an answer that was locked away only inside MacSod's brain. "So every interaction we've had has been like a torturous reminder that he is not good enough."

"How far is my dad's ship from us? Close enough to chopper him over? If MacSod was confronted by a flag officer who he probably thinks took his position, it might rattle him enough psychologically to make him reveal what is going on out here, where Wallace is."

"He also might shut down completely."

The air around Wakefield expanded as it became quiet again. The deck must have been cleared. "Here's the kicker though. He requested to see me—alone—tonight."

Huntingdon made a gasping noise as Tamburillo said, "Sounds like you're out of time, commander."

Wakefield felt her body relax in the quietness. She had not realized how tense every muscle had become with every pulse of the alarm.

"I've got a minute, and I'll start moving because the F-18's are going to be coming in hot, one right after the other now. I won't be able to hear." Wakefield glanced around for any eavesdroppers and began to walk a quick clip on the same deck where she had once raced Rivers on the *Reprisal*. She sure wished he was available for back up this time. "Something you said reminded me: MacSod's daughter. He has a teenager that was withdrawn from school after her mother's death. I can't find her on any school enrollment lists in the area. Can you see if the MacSods have any relatives or friends where she might be staying?"

"I'll get someone on that immediately." She could hear the deep frown in Huntingdon's voice and could picture him leaning over the speaker phone on Tamburello's desk, smoothing his comb-over flat in concern. "It sounds like you were right when we talked a few days ago, commander. I'm sorry I dismissed your concerns then. We might be much further along today. There are entirely too many people disappearing around this guy."

"Go ahead," Wakefield heard Tamburello release Huntingdon to start looking for Elizabeth Ann.

"If you find her, apparently she prefers to be called Liz." Wakefield called out to him over the speaker phone.

"Got it."

The first of the jets screamed to a stop one deck up.

Wakefield continued her trek up the starboard side of the *Theodore Roosevelt.*

"There is a bit of good news that just scuttlebutted its way across my path." Tamburillo stated. "Admiral Graham is being reassigned."

Wakefield chuckled. Her dad was running the show for Operation Enduring Freedom from the other aircraft carrier, the *Reprisal,* in the Carrier Strike Group making its way back to the Persian Gulf. "You know what you said about seadogs having trouble retiring, sir?"

"That'd be your dad to a T." Tamburello agreed. "With the morphing of the field from Afghanistan to Iraq, the Army is readying to run the ground war. Not a lot of beach-front property in Iraq for the Navy to park her ships. Graham impressed somebody well enough that he has been invited to join an advisory board to the Joint Chiefs in D.C."

Wakefield sucked in her breath and her chest expanded. That was a big deal!

"He will be stationed at the Pentagon for the next three years." Tamburello added.

He would be close to her in Maryland. Now to work on getting her mom to move from Minnesota. D.C. was practically the Deep

South compared to Minneapolis. It shouldn't be too hard this time of year when winter was over in D.C and still had a month or more when showers might still dump feet of snow over her hometown.

"Thanks for letting me know. That is a really nice promotion. I'm so proud of him."

"It will still be months in transition. The Navy Seabees will build the Forward Operating Bases in country, and the Army will follow a little at a time to fill them up.

"Wakefield, I'd feel better," Tamburello continued back to their previous topic without even a breath, "if you would take the master-at-arms aside and tell him what is going on. No. I will call him directly. Ask him to assign you a weapon for an arrest on board without giving him details. I'll ask him to enter it into the record *after* you return it."

"Can you do that?"

"Admiral stars hold a lot of sway. Give me about 30 minutes and then go down and collect a pistol from the armory. The master-at-arms will clear the space he needs."

"Thank you, sir. I'd feel much more comfortable in this meeting with a weapon too."

Chapter Twenty Nine

Wakefield pushed open the swinging doors into the darkened industrial galley where meals for 350-plus officers were cooked three times a day. She rolled the top of the paper bag containing the pistol the accommodating master-at-arms had issued her without question. He had actually seemed pleased to provide her the weapon; apparently the stories of her shooting matches aboard the USS *Reprisal* with CAPT Ellsworth had preceded her.

Unfortunately the U.S. Navy uniform did not offer a lot of hiding space for weapons; it was a general rule that guns were better on display, so they might be a deterrent. So she carried it concealed in a paper bag. The bag crinkled loudly in the quiet space as she unrolled it and looked for a space that would have ease of access and yet not be seen by MacSod when he showed up.

Cardboard boxes of dry goods, and open boxes of potatoes, sweet potatoes, and onions which didn't need refrigeration, densely packed the large, cool room. Or maybe it was nerves that caused a shiver to creep up her spine.

"Lawson?" she whispered? "Are you in here?"

"Yes," came his muffled reply. "You need something?"

"No. Stay put wherever you are." She looked toward where the voice was coming from in the back of the long room, but just shook her head. "We don't know when he'll walk in, and MacSod has a habit of just appearing around me."

The door in and out of the pantry was on the left short-end of the rectangular room. Wakefield preferred to be as close to the hatch as possible when MacSod walked in. But she also needed him to walk away from the hatch so she had an avenue of escape if things turned south in this little rendezvous.

Wakefield tucked the pistol into her belt at the small of her back. Certainly not the safest location, but the captain was not likely to give her a pat down either.

In the right hand front corner of the room exactly where she wanted to stand were stacked boxes of super-industrial sized cans of tomato sauce and alfredo sauce. She gripped the top one around the back, prepared to move the stack, and discovered right away why they had been stacked at the front of the pantry. No one wanted to move them any further than they had to.

"Well, that's going nowhere." She whispered under her breath and looked for something she could move forward to provide a barrier where she could take cover should the need arise.

On the shiny wire shelves she saw large 50-pound bags. She stepped closer, ever more aware of the approaching time. OATMEAL was stamped into the top of the brown bag near the stitching. From there, she could also see just further down the shelving, identical bags labeled DRY KIDNEY BEANS.

She would take them both. Oh, and the 50-pound bags of lentils just beyond the beans. Wakefield finished her sixteenth trip hauling the bags to the front right corner in front of the cans of sauce, right as the door rattled indicating her time was up. She had created a space to offer separation and absorb any slugs MacSod might send her direction in the close quarters, and hopefully give her time to draw her weapon.

Wakefield slipped into the turret made of food bags instead of sandbags. A bead of perspiration rolled down her stomach where the life preserver's plastic pressed against her skin. She had taken Lawson's advice.

The hatch opened hesitantly, but without a creak.

USS *Theodore Roosevelt*
Officer's Mess Pantry
2345 hours

MacSod's ramrod shoulders were hunched over and his eyes appeared puffy in the garish pantry light. The galley behind him was dark as Wakefield had left it. She had wanted to gain another moment of advantage as his pupils made the adjustment to the brightness in the pantry.

There was no weapon on his uniform nor in the hand he had used to open the hatch. The second hand swung forward into view as he stepped forward. Empty too. While there was still his back, Wakefield already felt more comfortable with the meet.

MacSod's eagle eyes found her quickly. His background in naval aviation that had allowed him to progress as far as he had to command a carrier, was not amiss. His eyes narrowed in recognition of her protection.

She knew he knew.

He managed a chuckle. "That's pretty creative." He acknowledged. "But totally unnecessary."

Wakefield did not let her guard down. "Thanks. But I think I'll be the judge of that. Sir." She tagged on the end.

"I realize this is rather unorthodox."

"You think? I meet contacts for interviews in the pantry just before midnight all the time." She cocked a single eyebrow at him, longing for the small talk to be finished.

"Oh, I didn't consider the time." MacSod waved his hand as if brushing an annoying mosquito away. "I just fixed it so that conniving little imp Bradshaw would be on watch and none of his lackeys are rostered in the mess anymore."

"Sir?" Wakefield nearly choked as she tried to swallow.

"I thought we could speak frankly here. I have a problem and after looking into your background, even with all of the classified line-items, I was able to pick through enough redacted reports to think you're just the one who can help me with it."

MacSod's features were broadcasting that he was sincere in his statements. He looked miserable. Judah refused to let her guard down though. Who knew how much lying this man was capable of? If he had been involved in perhaps three murders, two from his own family, and their cover-up, he was proficient at deceit.

But the quickest way to the heart of the information he was peddling was to play along. She softened her shoulders, and forced her face to relax. "What is wrong, Skipper?" She asked and tinged her voice with sympathy she did not feel.

"You mind if I sit?" he asked.

"You're the captain." She shrugged.

MacSod fairly melted onto the stack of oatmeal and bean sacks stacked to a height of three feet. His military bearing vanished. He stroked the greying ruddy stubble of his chin in a self-comforting gesture if Wakefield had ever seen one. He was either telling the truth about his concern or he was a good liar. Very good.

"I didn't want to believe it at first, but I think Bradshaw has lost his mind. I am convinced he is up to something big. Bigger than I can deal with on my own." MacSod's eyes were lost in a far-off stare at nothing.

"Why don't you start at the beginning?" Wakefield suggested. She would not fall into a trap of over-exaggeration tactics.

MacSod breathed deeply. "I think I've been a pawn for a very long time," he said softly. "Bradshaw was under my command and asked me to mentor him back in January, over a year ago now." MacSod shrugged. Wakefield didn't interrupt. "I was flattered.

"We became friends. Our wives became friends. He is really sharp, and though he can be really full of himself sometimes, I really liked him, her too." He sighed. "Right up to the time he asked me to promote him so that he could be my next X.O."

Wakefield's eyebrows rose. That was not done.

"I told Bradshaw he wasn't ready."

Wakefield chuckled deep in her throat. That's just what she would have said to a sailor was impertinent enough to ask for a promotion. "What did he say to that?"

"Well, let's just say the rest of the dinner was stiff. But he didn't beg, so he didn't have that against him. That happened in May last year, and he didn't say anything for a while, even though we continued having weekly meals with our wives at our house or theirs. But there were other little things that I didn't notice until later. He would occasionally flub standard military protocols, little courtesies he should offer to senior officers, even when offered to him from a junior. He was awkward around the ship-speak we use. I had not heard him initiate any ship-terminology on shore, but I thought he was just trying to include his wife in our conversations —so I guess I *did* notice it, even then. Bradshaw had suggested when we began career mentoring that he would like his wife to be present and for things to be very casual, off-base, maybe over dinners, so no one would feel jealous. I should have paid attention to the little weird feeling I got then.

"I remember thinking, when we were underway on the shakedown cruise to test our systems in August, 'has this sailor ever been on ship duty before?' There were interactions with others that did not make sense to me, and even before I promoted him, he had an attitude that made me want to smack him, as if he had heard nothing I said over all those dinners. To test it, I told him that the X.O. has to stand watch on the bridge overnight, every night. And then I asked if he was sure he wanted that. The man just shrugged, and went right along with me. I actually thought he smiled for a half-second, but then it was gone. The Officer of the Deck has the con (control) unless we are doing something particularly tedious. The X.O. doesn't actually have any watches where he is scheduled in the bridge." The captain shook his head as he explained the protocols of the bridge.

"Hmm," Wakefield interjected. She actually had not realized that. Every time she had gone looking for a captain or X.O., even that one time as an enlisted corpsman, she started on the bridge or in CIC. And she almost always found them there.

"There were other things too." MacSod continued. "So that is when I began to suspect he was up to something sinister. I mean normal people don't volunteer to work the night shift if you don't have to, right? But what could I do? It didn't make sense to me."

Wakefield had relaxed as the captain poured out his soul. There were too many corrective speech patterns, and admissions of him acting unaware, until later, for him to be making this up. Again, unless he was very, very good. Wakefield forced her listening to alert-status again.

"I had reviewed Bradshaw's service record back when he asked for mentoring, but I got it out again one evening on that shakedown cruise. According to his record, Bradshaw had two cruises under his belt, and had risen quickly through the ranks like some kind of a superstar. Every one of his previous commanding officers had high praise for him. What first drew my attention was Bradshaw's transfer date." MacSod paused.

He had been rambling for nearly twenty minutes. Now that she was on the edge of her seat, he chose to pause. Judah leaned toward him and wished there was a play or fast forward button she could press, like there was when she listed to taped interviews and phone calls for translation. "What was the date?" she asked breathlessly.

"The day before he walked into my office to ask me to mentor him. He said he had just gotten word that he would be stationed on my ship at the end of summer and since we were currently on the same base, he would come say hello." MacSod frowned. "I wish I had done some checking around then."

"For what?" Wakefield filled another pause. "What did you need to check for?"

"To see if anyone on base had ever meet Bradshaw in person before that date he and his wife arrived. There's always someone, after you've been in for thirteen years like Bradshaw."

Wakefield nodded. Even if you were not close, someone should recognize you from a previous posting. "But you didn't check?"

As MacSod shook his head, the very few reasons he might have wanted that information began to line up in Wakefield's mind.

"So you don't think Bradshaw is who he says he is?" She allowed her words to trail out long and thoughtful.

MacSod's lips disappeared into a firm white line. She could see the fight in him. "There is no way he could be. The psychological screening in recruitment and Basic are too thorough not to have caught a murderer."

Wakefield gasped. "I'm sorry, that was unprofessional of me." She moved a hand over her mouth as she realized what side of her belief and disbelief had won. MacSod was uncovering the secret that had held him captive.

The captain shrugged. "Believe me. I was just as surprised as I began putting things together when Martha was getting sick. My surprise came out more as a swearing streak." He huffed at himself.

"Unfortunately, I was on the phone with my wife when we put it together."

MacSod straightened his seat and pushed back on the bags of beans and oatmeal to lean against the wall. Airing his suspicions loaned him strength to continue.

"Martha?" Judah prompted.

"She had started feeling weak, missing her afternoon golf sessions with the ladies to take naps, and by July Fourth we knew something was wrong when she had to cancel our annual BBQ picnic for the lieutenants and their wives under my command. She always made such a big deal out of it, and they were delighted to come. The next day I made an appointment for her with the clinic. Earliest we could get in was two weeks, even with me throwing my rank around, which I hate to do.

"I was shipping out August 1 to prepare on the east coast for our shakedown cruise, and she was getting no better. Even declining. In fact, I was on board the *TR* before Martha got her blood work back. There was a toxic load of arsenic showing in her blood. They asked her for a hair sample that same day, and the doc, showed her that it had started three to three and a half months earlier." MacSod broke off to look at Wakefield. "Don't ask me how that works." He shrugged.

"Anyway I asked Martha if anything had changed at that point. We wondered if it was our water, but no one else on base was experiencing these symptoms and our water all comes from the same place. We checked her shampoo, cosmetics, protein powder. Then she remembered that although Maria—that's Bradshaw's wife—had given her a special blend of almond vanilla tea as a hostess gift, she had neglected to try it until Maria asked her if she needed more? Then Martha said she felt obligated. She was always more of a coffee drinker, but she tried it for Maria and actually liked it. So she began to drink a cup every morning, just over three months before the doctor took the hair sample.

"The tea was laced with arsenic," Wakefield pronounced. MacSod nodded. "The arsenic must have been hidden by the almond aroma and flavoring when it was wet with the hot water to make it into tea. The longer she steeped it, the stronger a dose she gave herself. Why would Maria want to poison your wife? They were friends!"

MacSod face hardened. "That is what I called him into my at-sea cabin to ask him as soon as I got off the phone with Martha."

"What did he say?"

"He asked me for the promotion again. The gall of that man!" MacSod practically spit. "He told me my wife and daughter were being watched, and not just by Maria." The captain's jaw muscle flexed in and out. "That if I did not recommend him for the X.O. position, Martha was dead."

"I dismissed him out of hand." His voice shook and softened. "A look of rage like I'd never seen except on TV came over him. I should not have just blown him off like that. But I thought they would be safe. I never dreamed—" MacSod's sigh came out in small uncontrolled spurts.

"I know what happened after that." Wakefield admitted. She didn't want him to have to repeat the story of his wife being rear-ended and pushed off the road into a copse of trees in a ravine, probably just days after he brushed off Bradshaw. "I assume Bradshaw was still aboard with you, so his wife must have been the one who forced Martha off the road and called 911. What did you do when you found out about her death?"

MacSod took a cleansing breath and it stuttered again as he released it. "I took him to the fantail by the scruff of the neck." Wakefield's eyes widened. That must have been a sight! "He didn't fight me at all. Until. When we were out of sight of the rest of the crew. I think I actually meant to throw the man overboard, and might have too. But Bradshaw shifted to the arrogant personality I had seen glimpses of over the months. Not arrogant like flyboys. I have some of that leftover myself." He tweaked his head sideways.

"He made just two moves and all of a sudden he had put me in a headlock, and I was bent backward over the railing. He said, 'you will recommend me for that promotion. You will take me back for the funeral, and we will continue aboard as if nothing has happened afterward because now you know we are serious.' The look in his eye scared me. He said, 'I'd hate for your poor daughter to get caught up in your mess. I have proof, receipts and such, that you were the one who purchased the tea and gave it to your wife.' I didn't believe him of course, because I hadn't. So I challenged him, even with my feet barely touching the ground and hanging off the back of my own ship. Not my best move.

"Bradshaw said, 'We opened a credit card in your name and purchased the tea, along with your preferred brands of household items.' They had actually been studying us for a year! He said the receipts were to establish a pattern, and he could show them to me. 'We have the proof.' he told me in this slimy voice. 'But we will hold onto it as long as you cooperate. If not, we will send it to the San Diego County Sheriff's Department.' Well, I was livid, but said, 'Ok. Prove it,' to him. I thought it would at least get me out of the dangerous position I had put myself in, and perhaps give me a moment to call and warn Elizabeth Ann to go stay with her Aunt Beth until I could get there.

"He let me up then and took me to his cabin. It was all there. It is probably *still* there." MacSod shuddered. "And it is bad."

"Can we go get it?" Wakefield asked animatedly. Finally something she could act on. "Even if it is in a safe, we could just deep-six the whole safe. We don't need access to the stuff, we need to break his power over you."

"You don't think I thought of that? That *he* thought of that?" MacSod sighed again. "He made sure to tell me that there is an electronic trail that is just as damning once the credit card number is released to Kevin Dougherty."

Something sparked. "Oh, where do I know that name from?"

"The deputy who investigated Martha's accident. He even interviewed some of my crew, I understand. Maybe you heard the scuttlebutt?"

Judah shook her blond head. "The return address label from the box of evidence he sent me."

MacSod's shoulders dropped silently. "I guess that means even if Dougherty cleared me, he still has questions."

"I'm sorry. But, yes I think he senses something is wrong but has hit a dead end. And the deputy is correct. We could give him Bradshaw. The truth will come out in the receipts. You could explain it just like you explained it to me. This guy cannot get away with extorting his way to power." Even as she said it, Wakefield knew that was not the point of all this. There were too many loose ends.

"Bradshaw is not after a promotion as power, at least not yet. There is still so much—" The skipper choked as his eyes filled to the brim with water that surface tension held in place.

CHAPTER THIRTY

USS *Theodore Roosevelt*
Officer's Mess Pantry
0045 hours

MacSod's sobs started as his left eye finally spilled a fat tear that rolled down his ruddy cheek and got lost in his stubbly beard. His chin quivered.

Wakefield reached out then stopped. This rendezvous had taken a turn she never expected. *Lord, what do I do for a bawling senior officer two grades up?* she asked silently as compassion stretched her heart wide. Just as quickly, a phrase from officer's candidacy school came into her mind. "The uniform is made to fit the man."

"I'm sorry." He snuffled. He was re-watering his cheeks as fast as he could push it away with his meaty fists. "I'm sorry." His neck was mottled red with embarrassment.

Wakefield moved closer and reached out and patted the back of his shoulder. When he bowed forward and began to shake, she rubbed her hand firmly across the top of both uniformed shoulders several times the way her mother had comforted her when she was small. "Do you mind if I pray for you?" she asked.

She could see a thinning space in the top of his hair as he just let the tears fall and shook his head back and forth in a tiny gesture.

"Father," Wakefield began, "I ask that you would send your Holy Spirit to comfort"—*ah quick, what do I call him?* she asked in her mind, glad she was speaking slow anyway, so hopefully it wouldn't show—"this one your heart loves so dearly. Would you heal his heart and remind him of whom you have made him to be, a leader who doesn't bend to opposition, who serves others with understanding and leading in such a way as to call the best out of others. Those ways that you showed him when his heart was steadfast on you in high school and he stood down a school bully and was voted class president. Lord, I thank you that your love for him has never faded and has remained the same."

Wakefield took a breath and slowed down further. She was just listening as her mouth formed the words and she didn't stop them. If MacSod's silently heaving shoulders were any indication, the Holy Spirit had indeed shown up. She found tears rolling down her own cheeks. This man of strength had kept a powder-keg of pain trapped inside under deep lock-down.

"Father, thank you for your ministering hand of kindness and wooing this dear one back to your love," she prayed when his shaking slowed. "Now Lord, I ask you for justice in this situation that he finds himself in, where he cannot control what is happening around him. I ask you to protect his daughter, and bring true freedom to them both. Would you untangle this web of deception that has surrounded him and his family? I ask for your mercy for them, Father. In Jesus' name I ask these things, thankful that you are faithful to provide all we need. Amen."

By the time the last word had slipped from her lips, MacSod was staring at her. Now her hand on his back was not as much comforting as awkward. Slowly, slowly, she withdrew and took a half step back to give him some space.

"How did you know all that stuff about Jimmy Maddox in high school? And I never even got to tell you about Elizabeth Ann. I was just about to."

"Well, the Lord knows all things. Sometimes when I pray, even if I don't know the details, certain things slip out of my mouth. It's because God loves you so much and knows what you need. And sometimes I think God does it just to get people's attention when they are far from him." *Oh Lord, boldness please!* "Could that be what he was doing with you?" she asked.

"Yeah. I was a strong believer as a child. We went to church every Sunday. I even preached in youth group on occasion, way back when." He looked sad. "In basic training I did not have time to maintain my relationship with God. Then flight school, then carrier quals. With the Navy life in my face pulling at me all the time, I just lost track of time." MacSod's head dropped again and he rubbed his arm with a work-scarred hand with neatly trimmed nails. "Oh how I have missed him."

His hand moved to his chest. "I feel so warm. I remember this feeling." His head came back up. "I didn't even realize how much I missed him. What does that say about this old sea dog?"

Wakefield smiled. The man was transforming before her eyes. His features were softened under the Holy Spirit's love. "Certainly nothing shameful," she said as she saw it glimmer in his features. "Perhaps it says that you are ready to return to him and make some changes."

The skipper gave a wide-eyed nod that seemed to say yes with his whole body.

Wakefield smiled. "I do have to say that I knew you have a daughter from the investigation we've, I've been conducting." She changed the pronoun quickly. It didn't seem important to keep Lawson out of it when it was quite obvious that the captain was innocent, but it would be a whole other conversation, and MacSod might feel betrayed.

"Oh, I forgot about Elizabeth Ann for perhaps the only moment of my life since she was born, just now. Do you know who took her? Where she is?"

Judah caught her breath. Worst case scenario manifested in her mind. It was the same kind of flash picture she sometimes got from the Lord. She hoped so deeply that that was not what had happened. She shook her head slowly. "No. I'm sorry. I wasn't sure what had happened until you just confirmed it. I just knew she had been withdrawn from school and had not shown up where you said she was going to be going. What happened?"

"Bradshaw happened." MacSod grimaced and his muscles tightened again. "He forced me to authorize leave for Martha's funeral. He showed up at my door two days after I arrived home, and he would not leave our house! He threatened to release the receipt trail to the deputy who was already sniffing around at that point, unless I withdrew Elizabeth Ann from school. He had the whole scheme worked out, what to tell the school, about hand delivering the school records because we were transferring her. He told me first that she would be safer at the base school. Then as soon as I got her paperwork in hand—literally I was still driving home after picking up the papers and then dinner a friend had made for us—she was taken while I was away. My baby, gone without a trace. Though someone packed her a bag because clothes were missing and her overnight bag that Martha and I bought her for ballet camp when she was eleven was gone too."

"How do you know she didn't run away and pack her own bag?" Wakefield was suddenly confused. Kidnappers did not normally stop to pack up their victims.

"She did not take her journal. She never goes anywhere without it." He huffed through his nose. "Afraid mom or dad will snoop and read it, I suppose."

"When was this?"

"Three days after the funeral. And I became sure when Bradshaw showed up around eleven that evening and made me call her Aunt Beth and cancel her coming to stay with her for the rest of my deployment. I did. But not before I got off a good punch in the face." The captain half smiled. "Then he brought out a Sig Sauer P210. Needless to say, I backed off."

"You haven't heard from her since?"

"Well, no." MacSod's expression asked 'how would I have?'

"Well, I think it is high time we changed all that." Wakefield pushed her weight away from the sacks of beans and oatmeal where she had been leaning. "Let's get out of here."

MacSod stood to his feet too. "I won't do anything that might jeopardize Elizabeth Ann's safety. I've already put her life at risk by talking to you. Probably your life too."

"I understand, sir. Don't worry about me. But we don't even know if she is still alive, but if she is, she's being held hostage by a terrorist for a reason. An end game. She's already not safe." Wakefield heaved the top reinforced bag of oatmeal to her shoulder, and carried it back to replace it on the heavy-gauge wire shelving.

"He's not a terrorist." MacSod shook his head.

Wakefield walked back for the next bag to look him in the eye. "If he has sway over the captain of 97,000 tons of naval warship, then he holds the lives of 5,000 men and women in his hands, whether they know it or not. He literally held a gun on you to force you to comply with his wishes. He has stirred up torment and terror in you. How is that not a terrorist? He has not gone to all this trouble, for the fun of it. There is more to come. I can feel it."

"I have some ideas about that." MacSod perked up.

"Let's start on it in the morning, if you don't mind, sir. I'd like to get this cleaned up before the breakfast crew arrives at 0400."

"Is it really that late?" He checked his watch. "Just leave this as a mystery for the early morning crew." He waved his hand and about faced neatly to head for the hatch. "A few hours of shut eye would probably do us both some good." Wakefield, now walking behind the skipper, saw his arms rise to his face. Probably checking for puffiness from his crying. "I hope I can count on your discretion, lieutenant commander."

"Of course, sir," she said as she latched the door behind her, but left the overhead light on for the hidden Lawson.

USS *Theodore Roosevelt*
Cabin 2-99-3-L
0418 hours

Wakefield had just pulled her sleep shirt on over her head when a knock sounded on her cabin door. She chuckled. She pushed her arms through the sleeves and pulled it down over her hips.

Special Agent Lawson stood rubbing his left hip leaning against the far bulkhead across from her hatch. "Just making sure you got back to female country before I retire. Flat. Completely flat." He pushed slowly off the wall and his hands moved around to massage his lower back.

"Where were you?" Wakefield squinted at him trying to picture where in the galley he would have been hiding that he felt stiff. His face looked a little puffier around the eyes than she remembered.

"You know that big box of Styrofoam take-out boxes toward the back wall?" Lawson winced. Wakefield nodded. "Well, it is smaller than it looked."

"You were squashed in that cardboard box the whole time? What did you do with the stuff in the box? So you heard everything?"

"Yes. That was not the way I expected things to go."

Wakefield couldn't interpret the look on the agent's face. "Why didn't you join us after we established that the captain was ok?"

"Um, well." Lawson waffled. "There never really seemed to be a good time to pop out of the box like a bachelor party cake and say, 'Surprise, sir! I've been listening to your very personal conversation for however many minutes and then hours now.' On the other hand, the content, mixed with my aching knees and hips from being folded up for hours kept me from falling asleep and snoring and giving myself away accidentally."

"Go on now and get some recovery. We'll figure out the way forward after our minds begin to unscramble this mess while we sleep."

"I'm really concerned about how elaborate and dangerous Bradshaw's plans are, now that we know for sure how much effort he has gone to and how many people are really involved." Lawson shook his head slowly.

"Well it is not likely to happen tonight. We are in the middle of the Adriatic Sea."

"True enough. And the rest of the carrier group is not too far away either."

"So get some sleep. I'll do the same and we'll reconnect after breakfast. Obviously not in my office." Wakefield saw movement out of the corner of her right eye. "Somebody is coming, better dash off before they can recognize you as not belonging in female country."

Lawson turned toward the approaching person, "Oops. See you." He quickly pivoted in the opposite direction and hurried off."

Wakefield hurried to close the door behind him. At that distance, with so many identical doors, no one would be able to ID which hatch had just had a middle of the night visitor. Feeling hurried, she slipped out of her uniform pants and was just stepping into her sleep shorts when Melissa Garvey opened the door.

Wakefield looked up. *You've got to be kidding me? Of all the women who lived on this corridor, Garvey is the one walking the hall as Lawson leaves? She should be on duty.* Judah felt her face color as Garvey smirked.

"Not a word!" Wakefield preempted Melissa's opening mouth. "This isn't what it may look like."

The lieutenant's face said everything she would have liked to voice. "Wouldn't dream of it, ma'am," she stated haughtily. She began to pull the bobby pins out of her hair.

"What are you doing here anyway? Aren't you on duty until 0600?" Wakefield asked as she climbed up to her rack and Garvey dug in her locker.

Melissa glanced over her shoulder, her red hair already coming untwisted from its regulation bun. "Actually, my C.O. sent me to bed. I have a fever. Didn't want me contaminating the rest of my watch, I guess."

Wakefield sat back up. "Oh, I'm sorry. Can I get you anything?"

"No thanks." She stood with a small bundle of clothing and tossed a bottle of water to her lower bunk and disappeared into the head.

The room was plunged into darkness as she shut the door.

The dark was plenty okay with Judah. She put her hands to her warm face even as her mind began to list the excuses to defend her behavior. Lawson being here had been perfectly innocent, their conversation had been one hundred percent work-related, even if it hadn't, he had never set foot inside, or even asked to come in. This could blow up so easily if Garvey decided to report her as some sort of retribution for being dressed down when Judah had first arrived.

Wakefield groaned and rolled over to face the bulkhead. "Lord, help. I need to sleep, not rehash this. 'You keep him in perfect peace whose mind is stayed on you, because he trusts in you.'" Wakefield whispered to the wall. "I trust you with my reputation and this situation."

261

She began to breathe deeply and recalled to her mind the details of a picture she had once seen that someone had painted of Jesus standing behind a sailor struggling at sea. She honed her attention toward those brown eyes behind her own closed eyelids while concentrating on relaxing each muscle group, starting with her feet and moving toward her head.

CHAPTER THIRTY ONE

"Is the captain on the bridge?" Wakefield asked the sailor standing watch just outside the hatch. She'd not met this one yet. Wakefield had already stopped by CIC on her way up top, and he wasn't there.

"No, ma'am."

"The X.O.?"

"No, ma'am. He went off duty at 0600. Officer of the Deck is Commander Kasich."

"Oh." Wakefield had never heard of him. Or her. "Never mind. Tell the skipper that LCDR Wakefield was asking after him, and I am in the NCIS office if he should need anything."

"Aye, ma'am." He bent his six-three tower at the waist and began to make a mark in the log.

Wakefield suddenly saw in her mind Bradshaw getting ahold of the messages log and putting together the investigative team. "Don't record the NCIS part." Better that there should be some sort of surprise if it should come to a showdown. "He can find me in my office."

"Is there a…" the tall you man trailed off.

Wakefield supposed the message was a bit unusual. "We had an appointment at an unspecified time this morning."

He nodded knowingly. "Captain and X.O. both favor those. People drop by at the oddest hours. But the captain doesn't stand a normal watch schedule. Actually the X.O. isn't supposed to have one either, but this one does." They young sailor shook his head. "He takes the 23 hundred hours to 06 nearly every night." His voice had dropped conspiratorially. "I can't tell if he is being punished or just likes the control of driving the ship."

Wakefield noted the information. It matched what the captain had stated the night before. "How does the captain feel about scuttlebutt, sailor?" she asked. Without giving him a chance to respond, Wakefield turned and traced her steps back toward her office, where she was sure Juarez and Gates were wondering about her absence.

Wakefield scurried along the corridors and attempted one quick-slide down the ladders, but thought better of it after landing hard on her heels on the deck below. Some sailors made it look so simple and fun. Instead she just moved her feet like pistons down ladder after ladder. She nodded good morning to her guys. "Any messages?" she asked on the way into her office.

Juarez lightning-fast hand held up a standard office yellow phone slip. "A Huntingdon called. Said you'd know."

"What'd he say?"

"That was it. He requested a call back. No message. No rank. Very cagey if you ask me. Sounded like a spook if you ask me."

Wakefield snorted and walked back to pluck the note from Juarez's fingers. "Well, I didn't ask you, but he's most definitely *not* a spook. And, he would probably think it very—" Wakefield paused as she remembered Huntingdon's strong objections to her being loaned out to Dietz and the CIA, "—distasteful that you think so."

She decided to forego using the secure line protocol when returning Huntingdon's call. It was too much effort, and she didn't know the location of either of the two signatories needed, but she had a strong suspicion that both were in their racks snoring away after the previous night's activities.

After cryptically warning Commander Huntingdon of the careful speech they needed to use, she updated the record from their previous call, requested an investigation concerning the dependents of the two highest-ranking senior officers on board, and received a stern warning to watch her six. "There is all kinds of craziness going on in the Navy right now, Wakefield." Huntingdon said before he broke the connection.

She caught her breath as the static of the dial tone rang in her ear. She decided then and there to skip her planned next stop at the armory to return the borrowed pistol. Instead, she scrounged through the desk drawers until she found another large manila envelope. Standing up, she ejected the magazine, and slid the unloaded pistol and then the full mag into the envelope and secured the gummy seal. Her eyes scoured the surfaces of her inbox, desk top, and shelves.

Then she spotted something that would work.

Keeping her body between the known surveillance camera and the shelf, Wakefield slid the heavy envelope onto a sturdy clipboard. There was nothing she could do about the sound ejection had made within the microphone's pick-up range, but she bet Bradshaw wasn't watching the tapes with sound unless there was a conversation he wanted to hear. He wouldn't have time to do anything but watch them in fast forward, and even then, it would be quite a bit behind real time, because he worked night shift. The man had to sleep sometime.

Stepping to her desk, and out of the camera's view, Wakefield picked up a sharp envelope opener, retracted the blade, and pushed it into her thigh pocket.

"I'll be in NCIS," she told Gates and Juarez, and closed the Intel Office door behind her.

Then she was off, eight frames down the corridor.

USS *Theodore Roosevelt*
NCIS Office
0905 hours

Wakefield tapped out a double rap on the metal hatch and pushed down the handle and leaned to step in the door. The handle stopped at three centimeters. Locked. Her shoulder collapsed into the hatch and she stepped back.

"Are you trying to break into my office, now, after all I've done for you?" came a cheery voice thirty feet away.

Wakefield turned toward the voice to see Lawson striding confidently toward her, stepping over knee-knockers and ducking under frames as he came.

"Good morning. Did your bones stretch back out from your jack-in-the-box hiding last night?" she asked as Lawson fitted his key and opened the door, motioning her inside first.

"Mostly. But it took forever to get to sleep. I am having a hard time wrapping my brain around this complete turn-around in our thinking. How did we miss it so badly?"

He pushed the door closed, and walked over to their board full of black threads taped between sticky notes and pictures and dry erase handwriting.

"Bradshaw, or whatever his name is really, wanted us to suspect MacSod of killing his wife, if we suspected anything at all."

"That is another thread we need to follow up on. If this Bradshaw is fake. Who is he and where is the real Bradshaw? Why hasn't his family made some noise about not seeing him?"

"That *is* awfully strange." Judah shook her head. "Bradshaw's record makes mention of Maria, his wife. MacSod is familiar with her. Obviously, that can't be the *same* Mrs. Bradshaw. So where is she? Or did someone mess with the official record?" An idea was taking shape in her mind. "If they changed the record, do you suppose they went as deep as changing the finger print and DNA samples kept on file?"

"We can access fingerprints digitally, but the DNA is stored in a physical form in a physical DNA bank. But you know we can't use it for identifying a criminal in a search. It is just to ID a body in case of death."

"I would wager a guess that a case like this one has not yet presented itself to the governing board that makes those sort of decisions." Wakefield dipped her head. "We *are* actually trying to identify a body. It is just still breathing at the moment." Wakefield pursed her lips. "Any idea who to make that appeal to?"

"Your admiral seems to know an awful lot of connected people."

"Admiral Graham? I hadn't thought of asking my dad."

"Whoa, wait!" Lawson whipped his head around from the board. "I actually meant Admiral Tam-something at Naval Intel. Your *dad* is the guy running this war on terror?"

Judah nodded and suppressed a smile. "I get that reaction a lot."

Lawson racked his fingers through his hair and its smooth waves fell right back into place. He gave a low whistle. "I had no idea. Heck, ask them both."

"If we do get approval, we will need to have captured this guy's DNA for a comparison sample." Wakefield felt her eyebrows peek. "I don't relish the idea of getting that close to him."

"I'll do it."

"Thanks. He should be asleep right now after last night's watch. Maybe you can nab his toothbrush or a hair from his comb after he leaves his berth."

Wakefield caught Lawson up on her earlier call with Huntingdon who would be initiating a search for Liz and Maria on the west coast. "We can look at property records for Bradshaw from here. But we don't have his real name to search there too. And what's to have kept him from purchasing property under any other aliases?" Wakefield's face turned further down, the longer she talked.

"Let's just look at what we can see right now." Lawson suggested, pushing the 'on' button to wake his computer from sleep mode.

Twenty-six minutes later Wakefield looked up from the monitor to stare at Lawson. "Could it possibly be that easy?" She stood up and pushed her chair back from the computer screen.

"It is never that easy." Lawson concurred. "A one-year lease on a mountain cabin off Alpine Boulevard initiated the same week that Martha MacSod met her Maker."

"In Maria Bradshaw's name. I wonder if they thought that because it was a rental instead of a purchase there would not be a record in their financial report."

"I'm guessing that's exactly what they thought, since you just scrolled past the place that mentions it was a cash payment in full upfront." Lawson pointed to his screen and then motioned to get her to move the mouse and pull the information back for them to study.

"I wonder what they planned to do after this year was up, because I don't get the feeling whatever is going on is going to last that long. I mean Liz has to be being held in that cabin right? And if not, maybe Maria is holed up, hiding out up there."

The gravity pull shifted slightly and Judah shuffled on her feet to accommodate it. "You feel that?" she asked. "We've begun our port turn from the Adriatic into the Gulf of Oman."

Lawson nodded. "If either of them are there, the San Diego NCIS agents will find them as easily as we found this property record."

**USS *Theodore Roosevelt*
Officers' Galley
1002 hours**

Bradshaw pushed open the swinging door to the officers' wardroom galley. One enlisted sailor was in the dining room wiping down tables, and the heads of two men and a woman shifted around the gleaming galley behind a pass-through window. Their quick jerky movements told him the surge of almost-end-of-shift energy had begun. "Is that coffee I ordered for the bridge ready?" he called out as he strode from the doorway toward the galley's swinging double doors.

"Just finishing the drip now, sir." The woman, a PO2 who seemed to be in charge of the galley, said, but she was not the person he had talked to on the phone. "We can send it up for you. It's real thoughtful of you to order it for them."

"Well, we are about to hit some of the heavy-lifting part of our deployment. Might as well celebrate the little things while we can." He shrugged, forcing the appearance of nonchalance. She had no idea what the coffee was really about. If all went according to plan, she never would. "I'll take it up myself. Everybody has their own mugs, we just needed something special to put in them."

"Well, now, sir, I didn't get the order for something 'special' in it." The lady smiled. "Perhaps after you're off duty, we can find you something special from the ship's stores."

Bradshaw allowed a grin to creep over his features. He would be on-duty from here on out, but said, "That's a nice thought, petty officer. I'll see to it."

She pulled the carafe out from under the industrial-sized coffee maker. One last drop hissed against the warm plate below. She popped the lid in place and made sure the lock was engaged and then lifted the carry handle for him. "If you're sure, sir." She offered again to get one of the guys to carry it up for him.

"No trouble at all." He grasped the handle and lifted it down from the countertop to hang at his side. He shifted to adjust for its weight. He could see now why she offered. The carafe must have held almost two gallons. "That size is deceptive." He snorted in his throat a bit to distract her.

"Yes, sir."

Bradshaw staggered out the door favoring his right side where the coffee hung in the insulated carafe almost to his ankle. He would make a short stop by his cabin for the real 'something special' and then head straight for the bridge.

Using tried-and-true measurements, Bradshaw converted in his head the 12-cup pot recipe for Montezuma's Revenge to two gallons. He kept the greyish arsenic in an ordinary Tums bottle. If anyone had ever gone through his belongings at the security check upon entering the ship, he had planned to say that his wife had crushed the tablets for him to make it easier to stir into Navy mess offerings, and thus save his gut. But no one had even gone through his sea bag. "Gotta love the Navy. Rank certainly has its privileges." He whispered in the silent room as he stopped spooning in the powder, and just dumped the last quarter of the bottle upside down. He wouldn't need it for the captain any more after tonight. This final dose should really do him in after the previous additions he had been making to his drinks throughout the entire cruise.

The arsenic dissolved like a little mountainous island being sucked under a dark sea. He used his little spoon to stir it all, and tapped it on the side of the carafe to displace the wetness. He very nearly licked the spoon as he usually did his coffee spoon before setting it on his desk top.

 The brown liquid settled into the bowl of the spoon like ordinary coffee as he fastened the lid back in place and latched it down tight. Just in case, he picked up the spoon again and went into his personal washroom and rinsed it in the sink. Then he tucked it next to his toothbrush in the glass he used as a holder.

At the bridge he offered the tall man standing watch the first cup.

"Thank you anyway. I don't touch the stuff." He replied.

"Your loss," Bradshaw shrugged and entered the bridge. He meant it too. If the man refused to go the easy way, he would relieve him the hard way, as soon as his man was set to come on duty.

"Congratulations!" He said by way of announcing himself to the bridge. His sharp eye caught MacSod leaning over the navigational screen first thing. "We have entered the Gulf of Oman. Everybody have some coffee. Captain, can I get yours first?"

CHAPTER THIRTY TWO

USS *Theodore Roosevelt*
NCIS Office

"I'm concerned I haven't heard from Captain MacSod yet." Wakefield rubbed her brow.

"Yeah. I got the impression he would be up at 0600 rearing to go." Lawson agreed. "Now that he is on board, do you think I can take down our string connection board?"

"Well, I'm still not sure what happened to Wallace or how he became involved. Or where the real Bradshaw is, but both seem connected to this mess. Go ahead and put it all away, but don't get rid of anything. I'm going back to the bridge via CIC, and if I still can't see him. I'm going to his cabin." Wakefield stood while she was talking and moved toward the hatch. "I want us to begin pressing Bradshaw for proof of life. That way, Maria will be forced to go to the girl and the agents can follow her, in case Liz is not at the cabin."

"Sounds good. I'll wait for the call here."

USS *Theodore Roosevelt*
Bridge
1023 hours

MacSod nodded his acquiescence to the X.O.'s coffee offer. Not only would it be the perfect opportunity to slip him the little note he had penned this morning before leaving his cabin, the coffee was a necessity after the short night before several maneuvers today. Strictly speaking, he had people to do everything, including overseeing the maneuvers, but being in the middle of the action was the best part of command. He wasn't about to skip this part. Certainly not with Bradshaw prowling around.

When Bradshaw placed his lidded mug with THE CAPTAIN'S. TOUCH AND BE FORCED TO WALK THE PLANK emblazoned on its side into his hand, MacSod was ready with his folded note.

They stood behind the radar operator whose eyes were glued to the screen with headphones on her ears. Not that there was any verbal conversation to overhear. Bradshaw's eyebrows went up in a question. MacSod fixed him with his best command stare. He could feel his sore jaw tense again with his anger. He stood there and moved his eyes from Bradshaw's face to the note in his hand. Then back to the junior officer's eyes, demanding that he read it.

Bradshaw shrugged. As he unfolded it, MacSod lifted the coffee mug to his lips and slurped the hot caffeine. "Is this flavored?" he asked aloud.

"You'd have to ask the galley." Bradshaw said. His eyes glued to the note.

MacSod rehearsed in his memory the wording he had scrawled before breakfast.

NOT ONE MORE MOVE WITHOUT GETTING TO TALK TO MY DAUGHTER, LIVE, ON THE PHONE.

Bradshaw shrugged. He didn't seem put off by it in the least. "It'll take at least two hours for someone to have the means. I'll make the call."

MacSod nodded precisely once. The nervous stomach was back. It was coming more and more often and more severely each time. He felt nauseated but with some shooting hunger pangs at the same time. Uncomfortable. He had to get his baby to safety before he gave himself an ulcer.

The other members of the bridge watch jostled around each other in a carousel of movement to and from the coffee carafe. MacSod took another long swig to settle the hunger pains. *Didn't I just eat breakfast?* He wondered, but then remembered he had only nibbled some bacon and push some eggs around his plate.

Bradshaw walked away after giving him a tight nod and tighter smile. But MacSod noted he did not make his way to the telephone on the bridge, nor to the hatch to go down to the coms office either.

MacSod's pains did not settle down as usual. So he drank some more, to try to hurry and fill up his stomach. He gripped the back of the swivel seat where the radar operator had slipped away from the screen to fill her coffee cup. A heat wave washed over him as he tried to control the pain. That ulcer must have well and truly burst through his stomach lining this time. Oh, it hurt!

He blew his breath out, fixing his lips so the air would blow against his forehead to try to cool himself and keep from crying out. "Are you okay, Captain?" the radar operator asked as she came to reclaim her seat.

"Fine." he hissed. Then swore aloud and doubled over as a stabbing pain ripped across his side.

"Call the infirmary and get someone up here immediately." MacSod heard Bradshaw order. MacSod tried to stand back up but the pain and nausea struck again. This time he could not hold it back and to his horror he threw up all over the floor. He could barely catch his breath between heaves.

He found himself on his knees, his hand pressed into his side to try to suppress the pain. It wasn't working. His mind began to wooze with flashes of his wife in a similar position when he finally took her to the emergency room.

He could feel people rushing around him like a school of spooked fish, and when he forced his eyes open, Bradshaw was kneeling over him. He saw the man's lips moving and heard a loud voice call out, "X.O.'s got the bridge." But it didn't seem to line up right, like a movie unsynced to its soundtrack.

Bradshaw smiled then and said. "I'll be sure to take care of your girl."

Fear redoubled the pain and flashes and sweats. He tried to threaten Bradshaw not to touch her, but all that came out of his mouth sounded like a moan, even in his own head. Then light became dark, and voices sounded like the buzzing of a beehive.

USS *Theodore Roosevelt*
Bridge

LCDR Judah Wakefield stepped over the kneeknocker and into the watchman's alcove in front of the main hatch to the bridge. Before she even looked up, she heard the sailor's heels click together as he came to attention. "Hi. I'm back." Wakefield stopped as she didn't recognize the petty officer on watch. "Where is the other petty officer? There has been no watch change since I was here last." The words tumbling through her mind were spilling out of her mouth, so she snapped her teeth together to prevent further speech and pulled the clipboard with the lumpy manila envelope on top of it close to her chest.

"I don't know, ma'am." He said it respectfully. "I was ordered to come relieve him."

Wakefield remained silent for a few beats and stared at the enlisted man as her brain worked feverishly to figure out what was not sitting right with her.

"Maybe a bathroom break?" he shrugged. "There's been an awful lot of coming and going from the bridge."

"Did the captain ever make it to the bridge?" She asked slowly.

"I don't know, ma'am." The young man shifted his weight from one foot to the other.

She stepped closer to him. "What do you mean you don't know? The officer of the watch is supposed to know exactly who is on the bridge at all times." She laid down the challenge in a slightly raised voice meant to intimidate.

"Like I said, ma'am," the younger enlisted man did not react to her authority the way he was supposed to. Did not react at all, in fact. "There's been a lot of coming and going." His voice had a cadence of boredom to it.

"Very well." Wakefield said and started to side step him and move for the hatch. "I'll just do your job for you and check to see if—"

The petty officer had lost all trace of boredom in his manner in a millisecond. He thrust his arm in front of her to bar her entry to the hatch as if he was a knight with a tall spear. Fortunately his fist was empty. "I'm afraid I can't let you do that."

"Stand down, sailor." She ordered.

"No, ma'am. You have not been cleared to enter the bridge."

She stepped up toe-to-toe with him and dropped her clipboard and package to her left side. She could feel each puff of her breath pushing through her nostrils circling off the man's face and hitting her skin still warm. "I am ordering you to get out of my way, sailor. I am going onto that bridge."

The young man's lips curled back like a junkyard dog guarding a prize bone. And he leaned in even closer to her. "You will enter that bridge over my dead body. Just turn around and walk away." His menacing face which had been so pleasant seconds before gave her chills. "Ma'am." He added as an afterthought.

"Last chance, sailor." She spoke modulating her voice to a pleasant pitch that she was not feeling on the inside and forcing a tight smile to light her lips. While at the same time she tried to discern the best course of action. She could always back down, go get the MPs, relieve the petty officer of duty, and have him dragged straight to the brig. Probably the wisest move, she determined as her mind raced right by the thought. She considered ripping open the manila envelope at her side and forcing him at gun point out of her way. Probably a little too extreme she assessed. But she did not discount it out of hand. Something was going down on the bridge, and that something was not good. This man standing watch had to be one of Bradshaw's replacement people, though she did not recognize his face from her files. Were there more that she and Lawson had missed?

The man moved the arm that had barred her entrance and place his hand on her shoulder.

Judah stiffened. So that's how it's going to be, she recognized. She softened her shoulder tension as if she was acquiescing and allowed him to turn her around. She felt the pressure in his hand pushing her forward. It was exactly what she wanted because she needed space to maneuver. Two steps back toward the hatch she had used coming in, Wakefield flipped her clipboard out in a twist that sent it sliding a few inches across the desk that was rarely used.

Wakefield could feel his surprise in his tightening finger tips. He had forgotten she was carrying anything. It was just the moment she was looking for.

Reaching up with her stronger right hand, she closed her fingers around the full width of his hand and squeezed, then yanked as hard as she could forward while bending at the waist to create space between their heads. She felt his wrist give and the carpel bones at the hand pulled away from his radius and ulna, then she twisted it with both hands.

While he was sucking in his breath in pain, she simultaneously jabbed her boney elbow into his liver, pushing it up into his lung, and snapping the back of her skull into his nose and teeth with the power coming from thousands and thousands reps of sit-ups and hanging double-knee-ups that had strengthened her core and lower back into a powerhouse.

The breath he had taken rushed out in a yelp followed by a gurgle. Still holding onto his wrist, Wakefield recommitted both hands to twisting it and raising it over her head. He was pulling against her hold. She assumed to try to grab his nose which was almost surely broken. She twisted out from under his bulk not releasing her grip on his wrist in the least, but continuing the twist as she pulled upward on his arm. His left arm flailed harmlessly out to his side as he tried to release her hold, but she used his forward-leaning momentum as he reached for her. She let her right hand continue the twist and pull, and she used the heel of her left hand to catch him under the protrusion of the occipital bone of his skull, forcing his head quickly to the desktop with a clunk of flesh-protected cheek bone.

She winced slightly. That had to hurt.

He donkey-kicked backward, but she was standing to his right side in order maintain the leverage she needed because they stood nearly the same height when they had been toe-to-toe moments earlier.

She let up pressure only one moment, and he started pulling his head off the desk. The moment gave her the glimpse she needed of a pair of handcuffs in his back pocket. She slammed the pressure back on his skull, twisting his face to the side to press his ear and cheek into the desk, and away from being able to see her. The desk made another hollow clunk as his head crashed.

He squirmed against her hold, and Wakefield could feel her muscles fatiguing quickly. She calculated how much time she would need to go for the envelope, tear it open and reestablish control over the situation. Her forearms, shoulders, and pectoral muscles screamed for relief. She wished she had not let her regular workouts wane since embarking on the ship. Using the dregs of her strength reserve, Wakefield jerked upward on his wrist and shoulder, with his arm still twisted behind his back. She felt the joint strain against her, but it did not dislocate.

His body relaxed and sort of deflated under her hold, and she had been in enough hand-to-hand combat training to recognize that he was about to make his move. She did not try to stop him. Her upper body strength was no match for a man's when endurance was factored in, even with her corpsman training in pressure points and bone structure.

So she released him with both hands just as he stared his upward trajectory. While he threw himself upward and to the left, she pulled out of his path and to the right, diving forward for the package she had brought in with her.

It slide further away as her fingers brushed the paper. But she closed her fingers on the reinforced corner and pinched down with all her remaining strength in her hands.

His momentum flung him back. But he was back on her within a second. Only now their roles were reversed. He stood over her left shoulder. Wakefield had time only to pull the manila envelope to her belly as he bent her over the desk and pressed her head into its metal writing surface. It felt cold against her cheek. Her ear's cartilage painfully collapsed flat against the surface.

As they struggled, rolling slightly back and forth, breath coming in little huffs, Wakefield managed to concentrate enough to rip the top of the envelope off. She dropped the small paper and attempted to reach in for the pistol. Missing the opening the first time, she stomped on his toe. In the steel-toed boots he wore, it didn't make much of an impact, and she heard him snort in derision. "Just give up." He suggested, reinforcing his words with pressure to her skull on the desk. His wide hand spread fingers like a vice against her forehead and the back of her skull.

The fingers of her right hand closed around the smooth nose of the cool-metal pistol. Underneath her belly Wakefield adjusted her grip, the pistol in one hand the mag in the other, and dropped the rest of the envelope on the deck. She stilled herself and quit struggling against him.

The room became quiet except their huffing breaths. Both her arms were hanging beneath her out of his sight as he pressed her head into the desk. Slowly, she brought her hands together. He didn't suspect a thing because her elbow was moving so slowly. Which was the point. As soon as she could reach she moved like lightening. By rote Wakefield shoved the magazine into the grip and she pulled back on the top of the barrel to chamber a round. It sounded like a quick pop followed by a shovel scraping metal in the quiet room.

Apparently the man was familiar with the sound. He immediately stepped back and released her. She straightened in time to see both his hands fly up in a surrender gesture. But his eyes were still hard, and she knew he was looking for an advantage, an angle to take back to upper hand.

"I feel it only prudent to warn you," Wakefield said, "my nickname on the last carrier I served on was One-Shot Wakefield." She gave a sweet tea-party smile. "I wouldn't try anything if I were you."

Anger boiled in his mottled red cheeks, but he stood still.

"Turn around," she gestured with her neck, the gun held steady. He turned, and she grasped the cuffs and plucked them from his pocket.

"Turn to face me. Slowly," she ordered and he complied. "Now down on the floor and cuff yourself to that pipe right there." Wakefield pointed with her left hand to the two-inch pipe fastened to the wall. She wasn't sure what was running through the pipe, probably electrical cables for the bridge since it was fastened to that particular wall.

"No," she corrected. "Both wrists in the cuffs. Slip the cuff behind the pipe so the chain goes behind it and comes back out the other side. And hurry up about it."

When he was sitting, awkwardly twisted on the floor, and attached to the pipe, she pulled on the pipe to test its strength. Not only would the many screws hold fast, they had been painted over, at least twice, so even if he had a way to loosen them, it would take a solvent to make the Philips-head shape a viable option anytime soon.

Laying the gun on the desk top, Wakefield began unlacing his boots in a hurry. She pulled them off of him, removed the laces, and tossed the boots by the tongue into the far corner. Crossing one of his one ankles over the other, she ran the lace around twice, double knotting it with each wrap. It was tight enough against the heel tendon that Wakefield could not even jamb her pinkie finger between the cotton laces and the little dip between his heel and his ankle bone. It might cut off the circulation enough to put his feet to sleep, but that would be an added bonus of time if he was able to free himself. She used the other bootlace to secure a handkerchief from her pocket into his mouth. She quadruple tied knots behind his head in a restraint that pulled his lips back at both sides.

She gestured once with her pistol. "How about if I just step over your *tied-up* body instead of your dead one?" Wakefield asked as she stepped over him toward the hatch. She was now nine minutes behind schedule. She pushed her pistol inside the crinkled manila envelope and was barely able to fold the top down. So she unfolded it and tucked it under the clip board's metal jaws.

Folding it up against her chest like a schoolgirl, Wakefield glanced one last time at the watchman on the deck with knees pulled into his chest, and she pulled open the hatch.

CHAPTER THIRTY THREE

L awson hung up the phone. "Good news, good news." He spoke to himself cracking a smile that pushed him out of his chair toward the printer in his office. He verified the document that the printer was spewing out was the one he had downloaded from his email and walked back to his chair to place the call to the bridge to authorize LCDR Wakefield to arrest Bradshaw in his bunk.

The hatch rattled and a tall petty officer stepped in and then froze. "Oh I didn't mean to barge right in. I thought you'd have an outer reception desk or something."

"Me too, petty officer, me too. Happens all the time. I am kind of in a hurry, can it wait?" he asked.

The young man tilted his head to the left. "I don't think so." He looked down at his hands. "I think something strange is happening on the bridge." He mumbled, sounding a bit embarrassed.

Lawson stilled his movements. "Shut the door, petty officer. You have my full attention. What makes you say that?" Lawson's pulse increased.

"Well, first the X.O. brought coffee in a great big carafe for everyone on watch. He offered me some, and looked disappointed when I didn't take any. I don't drink coffee." He explained. "Then twenty minutes later the radar operator made a mad dash out of there. One minute after that, a Petty Officer Sherer came and relieved me of my watch. I still have more than an hour left. He said he had orders. But I'd never met him before."

"But he out ranks you," Lawson guessed.

"Yes, sir. So I left. But as I was walking back to my rack for some unexpected down time, I remembered that that pretty lady officer in Intelligence was there earlier this morning. She left a message for the captain and it seemed urgent somehow."

Lawson just nodded.

"She had said she was coming here and then she changed her mind. That seemed odd, so I decided to come down and ask her. Now she's not here and you are. Is something going on, sir?"

"Probably." Lawson came around from behind his desk and clapped the guy on the shoulder. "You did the right thing by coming to me. I'll take care of it from here. Thank you. Dismissed."

Lawson couldn't technically dismiss anyone, but it seemed the fastest way to clear the office. He had picked up the phone before the hatch was sealed. This time he did not dial the extension for the bridge.

Cuyamaca Rancho State Park, CA
March 21, 2003
8:30 PM

Elizabeth Ann MacSod lay in bed fighting hopelessness, the same as she had every night for the past 196 days. "Why even bother? I'm going to die out here and maybe they'll discover my bones in a decade or two." She no longer chided herself for talking to herself. Her own voice and the wretched Maria Bradshaw's voice were the only sounds of humanity she had heard for six months.

The days she counted off in five-hash-mark groupings in the wall. Four down and one slanted across the four to hold them together. She had started it in defiance for the camera the day she had come to and found herself in a strange bed surrounded by strange and stark furnishings. Now it had become her closing ceremony of the day before bed. When she tried to get up that first morning to figure out what was happening, she found a shackle bolted around her ankle and fixed by a rattling and heavy chain to a central point in the one-room cabin.

After the terror had settled she remembered vague flashes of a bumpy ride in a trunk, but she couldn't say how long she'd been there. But it wasn't until her parents' friend Maria had walked through the door with a bag of groceries as the sun set that first day that she began to process her new life. By then she had seen the camera's eye on her and already realized she had only one hour a day when the sun hit the patch of pebbles in front of the doorway where her dog-chain allowed her to stand and experience normal. As the trees had begun to leaf for spring, the sun was more and more dappled cutting into her connection to normal.

"How did my life come to this horrible, horrible existence?" she whispered.

You're still alive, hope whispered back.

"I suppose I have gotten a lot of reading done." Liz rolled over to view her accomplishment; the chain rattled under the covers. The stacks of books were four across now and higher than her knee against one wall near the bathroom. She had hated reading and much preferred movies on the big screen or renting them with her friends from the base Blockbuster because it was so much cheaper. She had two books still unread next to her bed and had already opened her last cereal box. Maria would be coming day after tomorrow to replenish grocery supplies.

"Oh, I miss mom's hot dinners." She groaned as memories of the funeral rushed over her. She forced them back into the corner of her mind where they lived. "*Anything* hot would be so good. If I get out of here I'll never eat cold cereal again," Liz vowed.

USS *Theodore Roosevelt*
The Bridge

Wakefield could feel the tension as she crossed the threshold and stepped onto the bridge five floors above the absolutely quiet flight deck. The sun shone brightly casting rays through the surrounding glass onto the bridge flooring. The view was magnificent, save the empty leather chair that should have shown the back of MacSod's red-gray head.

"What can I do for you Lieutenant Commander? And make it snappy." It was X.O. Bradshaw's low growl coming at her from across the room. "How'd you get in here anyway? I asked the watch to keep everyone out in case we're contagious."

Her nose twitched involuntarily as the smell of sour sickness mixed with clean-up chemicals enveloped her. "Contagious?" There had been no indication that it was a biological attack. The word dropped from her mouth as she was trying to piece together all the little reasons something was wrong in her view. First, not one soul looked up from his or her duty station screen. There was no chatting, even work-related chatter. Maybe Bradshaw just ran a really tight ship, but she didn't think so. The attack had begun.

"Why don't you tell the officer what she's just walked into?" Bradshaw gestured to the lee helmsman sitting to his immediate right, but his question was a statement.

The woman started to rise, reminding Judah of a student about to recite. Bradshaw pushed her back into her seat with a hand to her shoulder.

Her head jerked away at the man's touch, and when she twisted in her seat to address Wakefield, the skin of her face was pulled tightly back from her features, except where her brows met in a puffy muscled bunch. "We've got a case of the runs on the loose," she said. "The captain is not doing too well, ma'am. He was taken to the infirmary."

It was the words *was taken* rather then *went* that chilled Judah's blood by several degrees.

"Oh, well, it was the captain I needed, so I'll just—" She started to take a step backward, but several things happened simultaneously to stop her.

The quartermaster of the watch cleared his throat, "Helmsman prepare to turn to a heading of 3-2-8."

"Belay that order, helmsman." Bradshaw said sharply enough for Wakefield to see the helmsman freeze with one hand in the air in her peripheral vision. Her main focus though was Bradshaw's face. He knew that she knew.

"But sir, we're going to miss our course turn window," the quartermaster said, his voice pitched two notes higher.

"Lieutenant Commander Wakefield," Bradshaw said without letting her gaze loose. "It looks like you are going to be with us for the duration. Come on in." He gestured in a come-here motion. Wakefield heard someone sigh.

"Nate," Bradshaw addressed a lookout by his first name, "Go check on Lee." Two first names. Yes. The attack had begun, Wakefield assessed, tightening her hold on the clipboard. The lookout immediately set down his binoculars on the shelf and left his watch to move toward Wakefield. "Wakefield, come on up here. You can sit in the big chair." Bradshaw tapped the top of the captain's leather seat with his fist but still had not let go of her eyes with his gaze. The man Bradshaw had called Nate slipped past her and was now moving out of the hatch. Things were going south fast.

The helmsman was still frozen, arm mid-air, in decision.

"Hey!" Wakefield heard Nate call out behind her as he discovered the man she had left cuffed and gagged at the hatch opening. "Boss." The one word contained so much.

Wakefield rushed at Bradshaw, but she had to dodge around the back-up navigational charts table to get to him. He saw her coming. And his right hand disappeared behind his back.

With as quick a draw as Wakefield had ever seen Rivers make, Bradshaw brought out a semi-automatic pistol. In the second it took for Bradshaw to pull it and bring it across his chest, pass Judah, and move on to level it at the lee helmsman's temple, Wakefield identified the weapon as the Austrian made Glock 17. Fourth generation. The enlarged magazine release catch, the checkered texture on the grip, and the roll mark on the slide. Glock 17, so named for the 17 bullets contained in the magazine tucked cleanly away in the grip.

When Bradshaw reached up with his left hand to pull the slide back, one round chambered. Wakefield raised her right hand, but gripped the clipboard with her left. There was a rustling behind her, but she calmly walked forward toward the chair Bradshaw had indicated.

"I am cooperating. No need to hurt anyone." She said softly, hoping to de-escalate the situation while she was closer to him and before the gaged watchman was ungagged and spilled the beans about her weapon.

"She's gotta gun!"

Too late. Wakefield recognized the watchman's voice, and Bradshaw responded in a flash. The gun in his hand whipped around toward her chest. "Hand it over," he demanded.

Judah looked down to see a little red dot dancing over her heart. "Laser guided. That's nice," she said, still using that honey sweet voice she used to pull an interviewee over to her side when interrogating family and underlings of terrorist suspects. "I'm just going to set it on the nav table here behind me." She turned slowly, but did not wait for approval. It was a psychological way of showing him she was not afraid and still in control of herself and the situation, even though he held the gun.

"Make sure that is all she's packing." Bradshaw looked at someone over her shoulder and seconds later rough hands patted her down thoroughly but professionally. That was interesting: A professional frisk from someone on a terrorist's team while they were taking over the ship. Wakefield wobbled her head a little as she corrected the verb tense in her mind. They had already taken over the ship, it was fully under Bradshaw's control.

The frisker took her letter opener she had been hoping he would just think was a pen. "She's clean," the frisker said.

And unfortunately it was true.

Bradshaw again motioned for her to sit in the captain's chair. As she took her first step she heard the letter opener drop onto the table with her borrowed pistol in the manila envelope. She risked a twist of her head to her left to check on the helmsman who was obviously not part of the team. The man's arm still hovered a few inches above his console, and his posture looked as stiff as a road-kill possum. She caught a glimpse of the quartermaster worriedly scratching his cheek as she swiveled her head back around.

Two would be with her, or at least not with Bradshaw. She kept moving to the chair. A commotion and a lot of swearing was coming from the hatch as Wakefield seated herself in the chair. The chair's arms were slightly wide for her frame, but the lumbar support and cushy seat were like a dream. If only this were just a nightmare.

CHAPTER THIRTY FOUR

A hum the size of an insect interrupted Liz's drowsy leanings into the night. It grew louder by the second. Maria had never visited at night and it was at least day, maybe even two, before she was due with more groceries. Hopefully she had brought the new shampoo Liz had requested by shaking the empty bottle of the cheap stuff upside down in front of the camera several times the day before.

The tires crackled and popped against the gravel road, until they rolled to a stop. The engine died. The parking break engaged.

Crunch, crunch. Shoes on the gravel. A car door slammed and more shoe crunching against the gravel coming toward the door. Then the door slammed again.

Wait. Maybe it was the trunk? Liz wondered. But the steps were getting closer and were now joined by a second set of feet on gravel.

Liz's heart began to pound in fear. There were two people. Maria had brought someone with her. And she was off schedule. Liz tugged thick air into her lungs in open-mouth panting as her throat began to constrict.

Hope was silent then.

You're going to die. You're going to die, was all she could hear, even drowning out the footsteps it was so loud.

The door knob turned and the familiar squeak of the hinges did nothing to soothe her heartrate. The scent that wafted through the room and the soft careful footsteps were not at all familiar.

A shaft of light pierced the darkness, and Liz squinted against it. A flashlight, she recognized. It had been months and months since she had experienced light after sunset in the powerless cabin. It made her want to cry. How odd, the connection she now felt between the light and her old friend hope.

She couldn't stop the cry now. Even if she was about to die, she remembered the warmth she associated with light in the dark. Comfort accompanied light for her.

Then the light shone in her eyes. "Over here, over here." A male voice called out. She heard the unmistakable metal sounds of a gun grip and leather.

"Get the light out of her eye, Keller."

The light went to the floor and the red brightness behind her eyelids lessened the pain stabbing her eyes. Cautiously she opened them.

Two men stood over her. One crouched down to her lying-down eye level. "Elizabeth Ann MacSod?" His voice went up at the end of her name like a question. When was the last time she had been asked a question?

"Liz." She corrected even as she nodded in agreement.

"We're with the US government and we're here to help."

Liz couldn't help a chuckle mixed with a snort that escaped through her tears. "My dad always said if I heard that statement I should run the other way. Unfortunately, I can't. What agency?" Liz sat up then as she studied the faces of the two men. They looked like rather ordinary California boys. Her chain rattled as it always did when she moved. The two men looked at each other over top of the light shining onto the floor boards.

"NCIS, San Diego." The older one said from the foot of her bed. He looked a lot like her friend Angelina Kim, so she assumed he must have a Korean heritage like her.

A second light joined the first. That shaft began exploring every part of the cabin. "We are alone. Maria won't be back until tomorrow sometime, or the day after." Liz informed them.

She swept her feet down to the floor and the chain made more noise as the links piled on the boards. Both shafts of light lit up her ankle and then followed the chain with the light back to the solid ring bolted in the center of the room.

"Oh boy," one of them said. She couldn't tell which one since their backs were to her.

They turned back to her with compassion and pity in their eyes. "Can you get me out?" She asked as she felt the tightness of tears pinch her nose.

"We have a tire iron in the back with the jack." The younger one walked over to test the strength of the iron ring and the bolts that held it fast to the floor. "We could probably shoot some holes into the wood to fray it some and then gouge the rest of it out." He suggested.

The one who looked like Mr. Kim said, "Or you could get the bolt cutters out of the kit."

"Oh yeah."

"Why don't you do that now, Agent Keller?" He looked back at her and rolled his eyes in the dimmer light. "They keep sending these green guys to me for training. I'm not sure if I am training them to be investigators or they are training me, in patience. I'm Special Agent Hardy." He reached out to shake her hand and Liz felt her cheeks bunch into a smile. "How you doing, kid? You need anything?"

"You have anything hot to eat?"

"Have they not been feeding you?" She felt Hardy's eyes measuring her face and the arms sticking out of her nightgown.

"A lot of cold cereal, raw vegetables, and a few other things that don't go bad without refrigeration or a stove."

Hardy stood from his crouched position and walked over to the door. He yelled out, "Hey Keller, bring this girl that hot coffee you picked up at the service station a few minutes ago."

Liz heard a mumbled reply.

"There is a store close?" she asked.

"Yeah. You are only four, five minutes from Highway 8." Hardy shrugged.

Liz felt her heart drop. All this time she was so close to civilization. And yet, she bowed her head as the tears welled up again, she couldn't have broken out of the chain, and which direction would she have gone? *I suppose I could have followed the road*, she judged herself. *Roads always lead somewhere.*

Hardy touched her shoulder and then sat down on the bed next to her. "Don't let guilt or regret take hold," he warned, practically reading her mind. "If you had gotten free and come home on your own, I wouldn't have a job. Thanks for doing what you could to help me feed my family."

Liz could tell he was trying to be funny, to cheer her up. She fixed him with a look and shook her head.

"Too soon? Yeah," he nodded and twisted his mouth which made his mustache wiggle like a mouse. "My teenagers tell me I tell dad-jokes. And I get the feeling they are actually telling me I'm not funny." He shrugged. "I don't know what happened. They used to laugh at my jokes all the time. Now they groan as if I'm killing them with embarrassment. Which between you and me," Hardy leaned in and whispered, "is the funniest part to me."

USS *Theodore Roosevelt*
Air Wing
Pilot Briefing Ready Room

Lieutenant Lenny Leibowitz hurried along the corridor between his small cabin shared with one other officer and the all-hands-on-deck briefing in the pilot ready room for the alpha strike tonight. He glanced at his watch. He was finally going to be on time. Today everything had been going right, the uniform was pressed and he didn't iron-in any wrinkles as usual when trying to get the razor-sharp crease in the leg of his trousers. The morning did not slip away as he read his Torah portion and recorded the events of the previous day on a little cassette player to send to his young son. He did not spill any breakfast on himself, or anyone else for that matter. He smiled to himself. It was going to be a great day.

He came around the corner and peaked into the hangar bay. He never tired of looking at the jets. He sighed with contentment. He may be a little clumsy in life on the ground, a little short, have a more-than-a-little early-receding hairline, he winced as he touched the top of his bare head, but he was living his boyhood dream, and when he was in the cockpit racing around the skies he felt, well, it just felt like what he was made for. And he held his head up while on the earth with the knowledge of who he was in the air.

Weren't they all going to be surprised to see him in his chair with his call sign, Le Le, stitched into the headrest of the fine leather when they all walked in on time? His C.O.s had little talks with him about punctuality and Navy standards nearly once a month, but in the end, because of his uncanny ability in the cockpit, he never received disciplinary action, just an awful lot of teasing over that and his accent. A fifth-generation New York Jew, Leibowitz couldn't hear any accent. He sounded perfectly normal, everybody else talked funny.

He pushed open one of the double doors with the small round windows. Only LTs Walker, Michaels, and Wheremachter were milling about yet. Eight minutes early, he looked at his watch as he walked in. He ignored the inevitable teasing from the three, and Ensign Andrews who walked in behind him and beat him over to the coffee table.

Leibowitz stirred the powdered creamer and sugar into his mug of coffee from the carafe. It was such a deep brown, that even the steam looked a little dingy to him. So he measured out three more shakes of creamer. If he hurriedly drank this one, he would have time to fix another before the briefing began.

Carefully he lifted the mug to his lips, leaned over slightly, and slurped to take the level down from the rim before trying to walk out of the way with it. He looked down, so far so good. No spills. He carried his coffee up toward the screen wall behind the Air Boss's lectern and leaned against the cool metal of the bulkhead while he slurped quickly, eager for a second cup to sip in his seat during the extended first of three briefings before 1900 hours when he would be in his flight suit instead of his uniform.

As he emptied his mug and the room began to fill, he realized that the two glasses of orange juice at breakfast and the cup of coffee might cause a problem mid-briefing. Still four minutes to go. So he set his empty mug back on the coffee table to refill after a visit to the head.

Turning from the urinal, Leibowitz began to wash his hands. In the mirror he saw a brown smudge under his left eye. What in the world was that? Grease? Oil? He leaned in for a closer look as he rubbed at it.

The porcelain sink's cold edge seeped through his uniform. That was too cold to just be the sink. He looked down. A dark wet line of wetness spread from one hip to the other about three inches in height. The exact width of the sink bowl's edge.

"No. No." He rubbed at it with his hands, which were wet and only made matters worse. Things had been going so well. He couldn't very well walk in the front door of the briefing with a wet uniform, especially not where this particular patch of wetness was located.

He bent awkwardly and tried pressing his sleeve into the wetness to absorb some of the water. "How did the sink get so wet to begin with?" He grumbled. "I mean who leaves water all over like that?"

He hit the button on the hand dryer and warm air blew across his hands. He pulled his trousers away from his body and stood as close as he could get to direct the airstream toward the line.

Eleven drying cycles later, the line looked enough like a shadow that he thought he could get away with it, walking in front of the whole flight squadron from those front doors to his seat.

Disappointed to be late once again when the whole morning had gone so well, Leibowitz took one more look in the mirror and forced a smile. "No second coffee for you." he told his reflection.

He traipsed back to the ready room and glanced in the window before pushing the door open. Something stopped him. He pulled back and glanced in to look for the Air Boss before stepping in.

The Air Boss was not standing at the lectern, nor was anyone at the coffee station. They were all at their seats, staring ahead, everyone's eyes tracking. Leibowitz changed his angle so he could view what they were looking at.

Adrenaline flash-pumped fire into his bloodstream.

He ducked down below the window. At least two men dressed in black from head to toe with large caliber rifles paced like sentries at the front of the room.

What in the world?

Leibowitz looked up and down the empty passageway and pressed himself against the bulkhead to sneak another peak.

The CAG and two younger officers who usually helped brief the squadron were sitting on their butts on the floor in a line against the far wall. The CAG did not sit on the floor unless he was under great duress. Especially this one, whom Leibowitz found a little prissy for a pilot. Where was the Air Boss? He scanned the room again. Every eye followed the men pacing at the front of the room, but there was the Air Boss, sitting in the chair Leibowitz knew was marked Le Le.

CHAPTER THIRTY FIVE

NCIS Agent Keller pushed open the door with his shoulder and kind of rolled sideways into the cabin. He carefully carried the bolt cutters in one hand with his flashlight. The beam bounced all over the walls. During the seconds the light was not searing the back of her eyeballs with a direct path to her face, Liz saw actual steam rising from the sip-hole in the cup lid he carried in the other hand.

He handed her the paper cup and Liz felt the warmth seeping through as she cupped both hands around it. She brought it to her nose first. It smelled milky and sweet. She sighed as she sucked in the first warm liquid and held it in her mouth to savor its warmth and sweetness. When she could delay no longer, Liz swallowed, glanced at Keller, and then she turned to look at Agent Hardy. "Just so you know, that is not coffee. It's hot chocolate." She looked back at Keller. "And it is perfect. Thank you."

Hardy let out a low laugh. "Keller, don't you ever complain to me again about getting a belly. It is not all the riding around. It's drinking hot chocolate with a grown man's metabolism."

"Hey," Keller blustered. "I don't *always* get hot chocolate." Liz thought it looked like his face pinked a little bit as he handed Agent Hardy the heavy bolt cutters. But it could have been the dim light.

Hardy squatted in front of her with a triple pop in his knees and fitted the open jaws around the first link holding onto the loop forged into the thick shackle on her ankle. She had pictured him cutting off the shackle, but the tool wasn't nearly big enough. One big huff later the smaller link snapped in two and fell away with a very nice sound indeed.

"They'll be able to get that shackle off in the hospital, easy as cutting pie. You ready to get out of here?" Hardy straightened back up. As Liz stood as well, Hardy began to pull the top blanket off the bed.

"Actually, I'd like to get dressed and gather my things, if you don't mind." Liz wasn't sure exactly what made her say it, because she wanted nothing more than to vacate this premises and never think about it again. She had lived here as long as some of the posts her father had had in all their moves back and forth across the country all her life. With two armed agents, it wasn't like Maria or anyone else was going to put her back in the chain.

She watched the two men glance at each other. She perceived that something was unusual in her request. "It is not like Maria is going to come busting in here. You'll hear her coming a mile away. And besides. She's seen you and your lights on the camera. She's probably booking a flight out of town as we speak."

The two men began to exchange information with each other, most of which was in jargon she didn't understand, so she took it as permission, and slipped into the bathroom, and for the first time could close the door all the way. No chain blocked the latch mechanism; she didn't have to throw a towel on the floor at the door jamb to keep the door from flapping open while she was on the toilet.

The buzz of their conversation rose and fell through the door. It was strangely comforting and unsettling at the same time when she had endured so many months of silence. When she came out she had put on her jeans for the first time since she woke up in a nightgown with the chain. They felt thick and confining after months of putting on a skirt over her head, if she bothered to get dressed at all.

Hardy leaned his head on his cell phone against his shoulder while looking out the open door. His stance said he had been there for a few minutes. "On hold?" she asked.

"They are trying to patch me through to your father so you can say hello and he will know you're all right."

Her heart tightened in her chest. She could not identify the emotion she felt rolling through her blood.

She did not see Keller so she assumed he was outside. She looked around the cabin. Picking up her ballet bag, she punched the few shirts from the dirty clothes pile into the main compartment with the folded clean clothes she had washed by hand and hung dry once a week for months. She wasn't sure why she was bringing these home, she knew she would never wear them again. She tightened her jaw. They belonged to her, and they were not going to be left behind. She let her finger trail over the spines of the book stacks. She picked some of her friends from the "best" pile. Those four got stuffed into a side pocket where she used to keep her pointe shoes. Then from her bedside, she picked up the one she had not finished and the two she had not started yet, and stuffed them into the pocket on the other end of the duffle bag.

"We can take them all if you want." Hardy offered.

Liz twisted around while still squatting at her bag. His face said he was serious so she gave a tight smile and nodded a quick up and down.

Hardy's mustache turned up at the corners and he covered the microphone on his phone and yelled at Keller from the door. "Come take this stuff to the car. We're ready to go."

Keller picked up an armload of books at once and disappeared back outside. Liz sat at the little card table by the window and the kitchen counter, savoring the hot chocolate and playing with her fingernails while her crossed leg swung a mile a minute. She pictured her dad in his uniform traversing all the long passageways and sliding down the ladders to get to the telephone and her.

Hardy began speaking into the cell phone at Keller's fourth trip with books, and Liz sat up straight in the metal folding chair. By the end of his first sentence, Liz had slumped back to her regular posture. People did not speak to a man in her father's position in the sounds Hardy was using.

Keller must have made some indication that Liz could not see, because even as Hardy was still talking away to someone on the other end of the phone, he turned and waved for her to follow him.

Liz picked up the long pink strap and stood. She slung the strap over her head and one shoulder, the same way she had carried it to ballet when she was eleven. She walked through the doorway in silence, carrying no chain behind her and shut the door a little more forcefully than necessary. She smiled as she pictured Maria's frantic packing to flee as her little plan fell apart.

Liz walked away. Strong and under her own power. In her own clothes. With some added life skills and a love for reading she had never known. The gravel crunched nicely under her shoes. Would she have ever chosen to gain those benefits in this way? No. But she would keep the good and throw away the bad.

"Seat belt." Hardy instructed as he snapped his phone closed and turned the key in the ignition.

The car roared to life. "The CSU people will be up in the morning to go over every inch of this place. Another team of agents is on their way to Maria Bradshaw's off-base house in case she missed our grand entrance on the camera and has not fled yet. Your dad has come down with a little stomach bug and is in the infirmary," Hardy rolled through the information and caught her eye in the rearview mirror. "Special Agent Lawson is the NCIS agent afloat and he is walking there to inform him of your release as we speak. We will try to get him on the horn again from the hospital."

Liz nodded. "I feel fine. I don't need to go to the hospital."

"Unfortunately, that is the protocol." Hardy would entertain no argument. "Your Aunt Beth is being contacted and a car is already en route to pick her up to meet you there. I'm sure you'll be able to go home as soon as they get your blood work back in good shape and that ankle bracelet off your leg."

"Anklet," she said absently. "An ankle bracelet is called an anklet."

"Hmm." Hardy nodded as the car began to roll forward. Liz watched the little cabin from the backseat window until it disappeared behind the trees when they turned left on the tiny gravel road.

USS *Theodore Roosevelt*
Hangar Bay

LT Lenny Leibowitz had backtracked in the corridor from the pilot's ready room to the hangar bay, which he knew was not under attack because he had just been there. *That's what that was, right?* He asked himself. Of course, he had just been in the ready room, too, drinking coffee and having a great day. But all that was different now. *Do you suppose they were just having me on for being late all the time?* a tiny doubt nagged.

He pushed down the handle to the hangar bay's regular sized door and cracked it open to look around before committing himself.

The place was dead silent and dim. There was always a watch on duty. Where was everyone? Plane captains and their crews should have been crawling all over the jets like ants attacking candy with all the last minute preparations and checks for tonight's alpha strike.

He let the door crack closed as he thought and wondered. That was when he saw it. A plain sheet of lined yellow paper torn from a legal pad and taped to the door that he had just been opening. In black magic marker in all caps it spelled out:

ELECTRICAL FAILURE. WATCHES DISMISSED UNTIL 1700 HOURS.

That explained why it was so quiet. But no one was wandering the decks either. It was like a ghost ship. The air squadron couldn't have pulled off a ruse that big, could they?

Leibowitz shoved the doubt out of his mind. This was a real attack. He pushed the door open, slipped inside the hangar bay, and made himself smaller than normal against the wall. What should he do about the men in the ready room? It sank in further and further over the next seconds, his friends and shipmates were being held at gunpoint on an American naval vessel.

Unprecedented! At least in his experience.

The electrical failure had to be a ruse. He looked around in the dim emergency lighting. "Now, where would I place a light switch if I were a sparky building an airplane hangar?" It took a precious ten minutes of fumbling around from hatch to hatch, while carefully keeping his back to the bulkhead, before he finally came across a panel of eight switches next to one of the hatches that was recessed into a small alcove.

He flipped each switch from down to up one at a time and listened for the buzz of the lightbulbs warming up. Three minutes later, there was still no buzz. "So maybe there is a grid problem after all," he decided. "But with the size of those rifles back there, someone probably flipped a breaker to this whole room. The passageway was ok," he reminded himself.

No time to speculate or play around, he decided when he saw the telephone on the hangar wall next to the dysfunctional light switches. He picked up the receiver before he had even figured out who he should call. The Air Boss and the CAG were out of commission, so the X.O., even the captain should be notified.

"Quicker to call the MPs," he mumbled into the receiver. All quiet. He reached up and tapped the hook three times. Still no dial tone.

"Tom T. Terrific." He slammed the receiver back on the hook. They cut the line. The airplane radio! Leibowitz looked down the tidy row of aircraft parked on perfect angles next to one another. Well, perhaps not *his* Super Hornet, but Jason Lennox's instead, since it already had a ladder staircase pushed up against its side. Speed was feeling like a priority now.

Leibowitz glanced left and right out of habit and dashed across the open middle driveway, scampered up the ladder, and dropped into the open bubble of Lennox's F/A-18 Super Hornet with one foot on each side of the joystick.

He reached for the Aux Power switch first and then punched the radio ON button.

Clicking the dial over to channel 16, Leibowitz began speaking his name and looking for vessels who monitored the emergency frequency. He just hoped the terrorists were not also monitoring that channel, so he did not give the name of his ship.

CHAPTER THIRTY SIX

USS *Mobile Bay* CG-53
Combat Information Center

"Sir?" Operations Specialist Allen looked up from his green radar screen to find his C.O. who liked to wander the room keeping an eye on all of his people.

"Yes, Allen?"

"The second carrier has not yet made her turn."

The lieutenant cut a quick step over to lean over his screen.

Allen pointed to the dot labeled CV-71 moving further and further away from the other dots clustered in a two inch radius toward the center of the sweeping circle.

"I've waited seven minutes past the window." Allen gave the timeframe.

"I'll get on the horn and give them a wake-up call to see what's going on." He did not sound worried, so Allen shrugged and went back to monitoring the rest of the carrier group's little blinking dots as they moved through the ever narrowing mouth of the Gulf of Oman.

Allen watched along the edges of the circle on his monitor for new dots, new threats. His C.O. stood only ten feet from his station, repeating his hail for a third time in a tone that suggested he was getting no response in the headset he had borrowed from the radio operator, PO Johnson.

Allen wiggled in his seat. A little nervous bubble made its way from his belly toward his throat. The Ticonderoga Class destroyer he served on did have some pretty big guns, but the real fire power and all the aircraft were on that carrier that was moving further and further away, right in the most dangerous squeeze of their cruise to this point. It may have been his first deployment, but Allen was pretty sure that was not normal.

USS *Theodore Roosevelt*
The Bridge

Wakefield turned her left wrist slightly toward her to read her watch. The lighting had changed since she walked in the door and the sun was coming more from the west than straight overhead now. Still, it was hard to keep track of time passing. The bridge was operating in silence. No radio. No chatter. Even Bradshaw walked away to coordinate on his walkie talkie with his men. Unfortunately he left Nate with the gun when he did that.

Still, there was no movement on the flight deck and she could see nearly the whole thing from the captain's chair. There had to be a threat to the Air Boss and on the flight deck. There was supposed to be an air campaign being fought to soften up Baghdad. Surely someone would notice that the *The Big Stick* was not contributing to the Carrier Strike Group's shared objective. And by someone, she meant someone who would bring it to Sea Duty VADM Graham's attention. He could send a helo or even a Zodiac over the few miles that separated the carriers as they were making their way through the narrow squeeze of the Strait of Hormuz, though either transport would show up on radar, and Bradshaw seemed to be keeping a close eye on that screen. Surely someone among the ten vessels of the group would notice that they were off course and question it.

She had spent the last nearly two hours making herself as still as possible in hopes that Bradshaw would forget that she was a threat. She definitely did not want to get herself tied to the chair, as comfy as it was. But a threat she wanted to remain.

USS *Reprisal*
VADM Graham's at sea cabin

Vice Admiral Graham leaned back in his small sofa, tiny actually, but it gave him a little place to think comfortably outside the din of carrier life, and a nice sized window to see the sea go by.

Isaac Graham closed the Bible in his lap. Over the years he had established a routine for evening alpha strikes, and he would see it through. Tonight would probably be the last initial air campaign that he directed in his life. He would be moving onward and upward to Washington as soon as the Navy could pave the way for the Army's boots on the ground in Baghdad.

But right now, he was exactly where he was supposed to be. He smiled as he began to pray for the wisdom and the safety of each leader of each ship and boat in the Carrier Strike Group.

His phone rang on the cabin bulkhead.

Graham turned to look at it, wishing caller ID was a thing on ships. Second ring. He finished praying for his senior leaders on each of the ten ships and one submarine by name. At the third ring, Graham set his Bible on the sofa and stood. It was two large steps, or three small ones, to his desk where the phone jangled a fourth time. Even admiral's privilege didn't get you more than a couple hundred square feet in the tower island, most of which was taken up by the bed. Of course his in-port cabin, much lower on the ship, was quite spacious with a large desk and several plush couches in the workspace. But he had always felt the need to keep it nice for meetings or dignitaries that visited, which was actually more often than he had thought as a young aviator during the Vietnam Era.

"Graham." He spoke succinctly into the receiver.

"Captain Ellsworth here. I hate to interrupt your pre-game warm up routine, Admiral. But I think we've got a situation with the *Theodore Roosevelt.* I'm in the CIC."

"I'll be there directly." Graham hung up the phone, and walked into CIC 27 seconds later. Twenty-seven seconds is a long time to hold your mind and heart in check when your daughter is on board the ship that "has a situation" dire enough to call in a vice admiral.

The whole CIC began to shuffle as the alarm, "Admiral on deck," went out by someone's loud voice.

"As you were." VADM Graham called out and the room resettled. "What is it, Ellsworth?"

"Put the radar on the big screen." Ellsworth bellowed. Then he began to explain.

Seconds later the room carried a greenish cast as the big briefing screen showed the *Reprisal* at the center of the radar and a sweeping green line that refreshed the view as it circled, moving the little blips of ships around the area.

Graham digested in a moment what had taken over an hour to develop. He recognized ALS numbers of all his ships in the strike group, and assumed the extra three were container merchant ships also traversing the shipping lanes based on their ID numbers.

"*TR* has not responded to a hail in over ten minutes." Ellsworth reiterated what his crew had told him. "Maybe their radio is just down. But it may be more than that."

"Zoom out at least twice." Graham called out. "I want to see what's in line with their heading."

The screen changed three times until a bit of land showed up outlining the Strait of Hormuz.

Graham stepped closer to the screen, then turned back. "Somebody get me physical charts of these waters, ports, channels from

India all the way through the gulf to Iraq's coast, both sides of the coast."

Then the little blip was gone. The sweeping arm cleared it as if it had brushed it off the table. Graham heard a gasp from someone in the middle of the room.

Collectively, the room stared at the screen and held their breath for the seconds it took for the arm to sweep around the radius again and refresh the view.

Nothing.

The *Theodore Roosevelt* had disappeared.

Graham didn't wait for a third sweep of confirmation. "Get me Captain Lucas of the *Mobile Bay* on the blower now. He is the nearest destroyer." He pointed to the woman nearest him, "Call the bridge on another line. I want to know if there is smoke on the horizon."

Seconds later a black phone was shoved into his hand with the statement, "Captain Lucas is on the line, sir."

"Lucas, Admiral Graham here. Deploy a pair of RIBs to check out the *Theodore Roosevelt*, now. I'll wait." He drummed his fingers and watched the sweeping radar arm while Lucas gave the order. He heard a voice at his elbow as his second order was carried out.

"No smoke plume, Admiral. Two lookouts are trained in the direction the *Theodore Roosevelt* was last seen. I will keep them on an open line."

Some lights came up quickly in the dim room, and Graham squinted against the intrusion. Ellsworth pointed to the area under the lights. Several people were unrolling scrolled maps and securing the curving edges on a portable table edge with clamps. "Maps are ready for you, Admiral."

CHAPTER THIRTY SEVEN

Coxswain Aaron Phelps maintained a strict military poker face at the announcement, but inside he was grinning like a madman. He had finally gotten tapped to drive the RIB.

The space around him swirled with activity as six Navy guys and eight Marines suited up in body armor, checked their helmets, weapons, ammo, and life vests. Half the boarding party would travel in each ridged inflatable boat from the *Mobile Bay* to the *Theodore Roosevelt*. The goal was not to board the floating city, according to his C.O., just to get within sight distance to make sure nothing was wrong besides the radio. A signalman loaded a large signal lamp into the RIB in addition to their normal equipment. He would be accompanying them, and the older sailor appeared a little green at the prospect as he turned back inside the ready room from the open hatch in the side of the ship where wind eddied inside.

"Load up." The order came from Phelps' C.O. The men of the boarding party streamed to form two lines and begin stepping into the boat. "Captain said Vice Admiral Graham is waiting for a report, so make it a fast run."

"Aye, sir." Phelps nodded, but inside he heard himself say, "Yes, please!" It was a phrase and cadence his younger sister always said when she was finally offered something she had been begging their parents for.

Phelps sat at the tiller and enjoyed the descent to the waves below. As soon as the men released the lowering cables and regained their seats, Phelps geared the powerful engine into action and began to run the crisscross pattern with the other RIB on approach to the coordinates he had been given. It was only minutes before the carrier came into view as a grey bump on the horizon.

USS *Mobile Bay* CG-53
Combat Information Center

Radioman second class Johnson received his radio-monitoring headset back from his C.O. who had practically shoved the earphones into his hands before heading for the wall phone to contact the bridge to call Captain Lucas. Johnson could see the man was on hold, so he returned to his pattern of channel-surfing. He switched from the chatter of channel 14 to channel 15 and let his ears settle into the frequency for a moment. Only static. No pattern to the static. Four seconds in, he twisted the knob to channel 16. This one was almost always quiet, as channel 16 was reserved for at-sea emergencies.

He had heard a few voices on this channel over his months of sea duty. Usually quite distant sounds. He had heard one mayday on his last cruise, but it had been 480 nautical miles away and several other ships, closer in proximity, had responded, so Johnson had never reported information gathered from channel 16 before. Johnson's heartrate picked up as he distinguished a clear, close voice, mid-sentence on the emergency channel. The voice was calm, he noted as he began to untangle the voice's message from the middle of the sentence.

Graham bent over the brightly lit maps. Without straightening his back, he lifted his head to view the radar streaming the green cast into the CIC from the big screen. He smoothed his fingers over the paper to touch the spot where the *Big Stick* had last been seen on the screen. Here, hovering over the maps, he felt like he could take in the information and process it. It felt real when he looked at paper charts. The screens still hit him first as war games. But this was no game. He could feel it, and Judah's life was at risk.

Drawing the course the *TR* had made with his finger onto the chart, he continued it past the scheduled turns, further until he reached a land mass. If she made no turns, the carrier would run aground just before she reached Iran.

Running his finger up and down the inlets of the bumpy coast, Graham looked for a target. A strategy. A port. An explanation.

Then it appeared under his finger. The Iranian port of Chabahar. It lay twelve degrees starboard to the *TR*'s previous heading. He didn't know why, but he knew that was where the ship was heading. He didn't know if it was under duress or malfunctioning equipment. But it was definitely a problem. As soon as the ship crossed the invisible line that lay 12 miles off the coast of every nation, the U.S. warship would no longer be in international waters, but would be violating Iran's sacred space. "And you'd better believe they already see her coming," Isaac Graham whispered aloud. "They've probably scrambled a welcoming party."

A U.S. nuclear-powered aircraft carrier with all its technology and human resources in Iranian waters? Nothing could go wrong there! Graham's blood pressure spiked.

Instinct alone spoke, "Scramble a pair of F-18s to escort that RIB that just left the *Mobile Bay*. Full bombing package available."

Mobile Bay RIB

The deep blue sea sprayed Phelps' face. Driving the boat over the open water was everything he dreamed it would be. A white ribbon of foam chased the grey carrier as the two RIBs continued their synchronized maneuvers on approach.

The signal man stood with loose knees, much less green now that he was doing his familiar job. He clung to a giant glorified spotlight with shutters that manually opened and closed by a lever on the side to send a message to anyone who could both see the light and read Morse code. The RIB pounded over the swells and the signalman hung on to steady the lamp, flashing messages as they approached.

Phelps didn't read Morse code himself, even though he had studied it in Basic. He remembered S-O-S, but that was about it. The signalman was getting after it though. His arm moved like he was shaking a toy rattle for a baby.

Phelps kept his eyes moving in rotation among the other RIB, the ever-growing length of grey hull ahead, the signalman's standing balance, his own wake, and the rest of the crew on his boat. When next he looked at the signalman, he was looking back and waving his arms like a traffic cop.

It looked like he was mouthing "stop." Then his finger began to make a circle in the air.

Phelps looked around quickly for the other RIB. They were a safe enough distance away for him to make a jag turn to port and circle back the way the signalman was emphatically suggesting.

Phelps didn't get all the way through his turn before a series of plunk, plunk, plunks of water displacement reached his ears over the roar of the engine. A line of stitches led from the *TR*'s deck-mounted .50 cal gun straight to the RIB's engine. Phelps didn't have time to digest what was happening, sound a signal, reach for his helmet's visor to cover his eyes, or detail a warning back to the *Mobile Bay*.

Fortunately, the boarding party he was driving saw the danger coming at the same time. Most of them bailed out over the side. The engine disintegrated under his hand; he was left holding the tiller handle. Phelps began calling out a warning over his radio mic to the *Mobile Bay* even as the bullets ripped holes into the inflatable sides of his boat.

They missed him altogether. But as soon as his radio got wet it would become inoperable. "They just shot us out of the water." He kept repeating in shock. His vision went from a slight pink haze to red to black as he stopped trying to blink it back and kept his eyes squeezed closed.

Cold water swished against his calf and then seeped into his boots from the top. When it hit his waist, he shivered. It was rushing fast and the momentum of the RIB was slowing with the weight of the water on board. Phelps realized then he could probably let go of the useless tiller.

His first boat sank out from under him.

As his head dunked under the water and he stopped his forward momentum, his head began to burn like someone was holding a lit cigarette lighter to his forehead. Bobbing up for air, Phelps swiped the seawater from his face with gloved hands. He kicked hard to maintain a surface position. The heavy Kevlar protection would have to go first. But he could see again.

Within sixty seconds a pair of jets roared low and loud overhead. He raised a hand to wave as if he was hailing a taxi. Stupid. It's not like they were here to perform a rescue. Jets attack. Helos rescue.

Jettisoning his boots and Kevlar, Phelps inflated his life vest with its blinking orange beacon already asking for a pick up, and began to swim back to his crew and boarding party, strung out in the water like a broken beaded necklace where they had bailed out.

He was kind of like a captain, he coached himself as he cut through the waves. And he had better gather his people together to await for a SAR helo. After sending a whistle signal and waving his arms to his guys, he huffed his disgust from deep in his chest. "I can't *believe* they shot my first boat out from under me!"

Chapter Thirty Eight

Graham watched the two signals of the RIBs from the *Mobile Bay* on the radar screen. They performed their crisscross maneuvers perfectly. Then one blinked and went out like a candle and then the other followed suit.

"Get me a SAR deployed. We've got men in the water." He bellowed before the room erupted in noise. A U.S. vessel had just fired on another U.S. vessel.

He detected no slowing in the *TR*'s speed toward the Iranian coast. The carrier had also not begun to turn toward the Chabahar Port. But that did not diminish it in Graham's mind as the destination.

His duty now was to disable the ship.

With Judah aboard and no word from her, he had to assume she was either unaware of the ship being off course and firing or she was under duress. Since it was hard to miss a .50 caliber weapon being fired un-suppressed, he leaned toward the crew somehow being held hostage.

"Come on MacSod! What is going on over there?" He had heard rumors of the captain's difficulties and the investigation after his wife's death. Had the man finally cracked?

The din of everything going on to carry out his orders behind him faded into the background as Graham pawed at the smooth paper charts and turned his eyes upward. "Oh Father," he groaned inwardly, "how am I supposed to order my men to fire on my own flag? And toward my daughter?"

I understand the pain. I sent my Son into the line of fire too.

Though it was not the words Graham expected—or wanted—to hear, somehow they were comforting in that radical-obedience kind of tone of voice God sometimes uses.

Give me strength to do what's right and wisdom to see it, Isaac Graham breathed prayer.

"We are taking fire." One of the pilot's voices had been piped into the room. "Permission to return fire?"

"Hold your fire. Make another visual pass and tell me what's going on!" Graham ordered.

He heard CAPT Ellsworth repeat his instructions word for word into the microphone.

"Aye aye."

Then the voice was quiet.

Graham wished he was topside as he stared at the blinking computer equipment and the dark walls inside the CIC. It might be more secure down here, but he felt blind. He liked to be able to see the contrails, the other ships, the sky and the sea. He was old school and he knew it. He never would have made it skippering a submarine.

CAPT Ellsworth was on the speaker for the whole room to hear again. "Go ahead Lieutenant Leibowitz, you are patched through and on with Admiral Graham in the CIC of the *Reprisal.*

A new voice broke in as Graham turned toward Ellsworth.

"Hi Admiral. Sorry to bother you like this, but I am pretty sure the *Theodore Roosevelt* has been taken over."

As those words were spoken, Graham's stomach sank and he jogged over to the mic. Leibowitz's voice continued echoing off the walls of the *Reprisal*'s CIC, "I'm in the *TR*'s hangar bay now, calling you from one of the aircrafts' radios. But I saw at least two heavily armed men who had taken over the pilot briefing room."

"Get him off the speaker phone. Now." Graham ordered as he took the mic Ellsworth held out to him.

The room fell to silence as every ear now strained to overhear the conversation between Graham and Leibowitz.

"What's your designator, Lieutenant?" Graham asked. Wondering what kind of sailor he would be working with.

"1-5-4-0. I fly F/A-18s, sir."

"Hmm," Graham grunted with satisfaction. "I prefer 14s myself. But you'll do." Naval aviators were a breed he understood. He could count on this one to follow orders, intuition, and make up the rules as he went along if needed. A plan was forming in Graham's mind.

USS *Theodore Roosevelt*
Hanger Bay

Leibowitz pressed the headset closer to his head to clear any radio fuzz. "You want me to do what?" A chill that ran through his soul at the admiral's words. "You've got it, sir. I'm sure it will be obvious if I made it or not. Le Le out." He signed off with Graham. Pretty cool to receive direct orders from a three-star to "do whatever it takes" to stop the ship. If he survived carrying out the orders, it would be a great story to record for his son tonight.

USS *Theodore Roosevelt*
Bridge

Judah Wakefield felt like she had been still for half a lifetime, but she knew it had been less than two hours. At least that is what her watch told her, and the Bermuda Triangle was in a different part of the water.

Bradshaw was doing a slow frazzle. He was holding it together for his men, but Judah's practiced eye could see it in his jerky eye movements, and his faster and faster fuse time with his guys. She watched him in the reflective glass, and she was pretty sure he had no idea he was being studied. He was checking in quarter-hourly with the rounds of at least three different spots where sailors were being confined, according to the number of different voices Judah had heard call him "boss" on the hand-held radio as he stepped out of the room to berate them, call them stupid, and threaten the consequences if he had to come down himself. His narcissism was on full display for his men and those he held at gunpoint.

Everything seemed to be going to his plan, as much as she knew of it anyway. He had full control of a nuclear-powered aircraft carrier. Judah squinted at the reflection of Bradshaw's tight shoulders as he again vacated the bridge to take a radio hail. So why was he so uptight?

There was some sort of shifting, whispering kerfuffle at the radar. Judah turned to her left from the comfy chair.

Unfortunately Bradshaw opened the hatch right at that moment and it caught his attention too. "What's going on?" He strode over with a hand on his now holstered weapon. His walkie talkie was fixed to his belt again. Wakefield watched as the radar operator fairly melted under Bradshaw's heavy hand on her shoulder.

"Um, sir, we have two unknown contacts that just appeared on the screen and they are heading in our direction." The woman stiffly pointed them out.

"How do they know where we are? I told you to extinguish that transponder thirty minutes ago."

"Yes, sir. I did, too."

"Prepare for evasive maneuvers." Bradshaw bellowed.

Wakefield couldn't stop a smile from becoming a small snort. Bradshaw might have played Navy for a while, but he still had a lot to learn. Submarines and small ships take evasive maneuvers. Aircraft carriers keep calm and plod on. And send a bevy of fighter jets after any threat.

For the sake of the pilots downstairs, she hoped he would not think of ordering them into the sky. She didn't know what would happen then.

The man Bradshaw had installed as the helmsman navigating the waters must have whispered something similar to Bradshaw.

"Look, just bring them on board." Helmsman's voice picked up in volume. "If we try to outrun them, the whole carrier group will come after us." Wakefield assumed Bradshaw was not listening to his argument.

Bradshaw studied the chart one last time. Then he unhooked his walkie and didn't bother to leave the room this time. "Chuck, get the gunner to take out those approaching boats to our port side. But give me as much time as you can before they get close."

Wakefield's heart sank.

Then he ordered up speed from the engine room, and a turn from the helmsman. "I think we can make it. I didn't want to advertise our destination just yet. But I think we can just make it before they catch up to us."

Bradshaw's reflected smile unnerved Judah.

If she was going to do something, now was the time. She touched her dry lips. She may have already waited too long. She could feel that the turbines were already picking up speed and thrusting the carrier forward at increasing speed, curving to starboard. And apparently their destination.

Then she heard the ack-ack-ack of the .50 cal on the deck.

Seconds later the results came through loud and clear on Bradshaw's walkie. "We got 'em boss."

Strafing the boarding party was her final straw. Judah Wakefield's indignation pushed her straight up in her chair. She no longer cared about who was with her or who was against her on the bridge. The fear and indecision over the best plan or whether she would be killed that had held her in place, she pushed right out those large front windows where she had been meekly watching the action take place. Bradshaw and his crew were not taking this ship with no opposition.

Tucking a stray blond hair behind her ear, Wakefield slid out of her chair with only a plan to subdue the first person who tried to stop her. Whether she had to hold that person hostage, or break that tender connection between the brainstem and the spinal cord with the quick twist at 32 pounds of pressure that Rivers had showed her, or go down fighting herself, she was on the move.

Bradshaw's back was turned, but the helmsman's was not. If Bradshaw looked up, he would have the same reflection in the windows that she had had. She caught helmsman's attention first as she figured she would, so she held her hands up. "I just need some water," she said calmly. She slowly pointed toward the water tank in the corner. The slow and small hand movements helped disguise that her feet were coming fast toward him.

Wakefield saw the letter opener on the table about half way between them. That would be nice. And easier to wield than trying to get the gun back out of that manila envelope before she could use it. The helmsman saw her glance at it; they both lunged simultaneously.

But Wakefield changed her target at the last second. She saw out of the corner of her eye behind the helmsman a pair of closely aligned contrails drawing a white line toward them in the blue sky.

As the helmsman reached his fingers out for the letter opener, Wakefield reached for his neck. Since he was focused on the table's

320

contents, he didn't see her coming. She grasped the fleshy pressure point between his neck and shoulder, and felt her nails dig into his skin as well. Bonus.

She pressed with all her adrenaline-empowered strength, and felt him writhe under her hand and begin to bow over. He gasped and his hands came after her to try to break her hold, dislodging the sharp letter opener and sending it clattering to the floor.

Bradshaw flung around at the sound of the struggle. He went for his weapon. Wakefield maneuvered herself behind the helmsman in Bradshaw's line of fire.

CHAPTER THIRTY NINE

Wakefield redoubled her pressure at the helmsman's pressure point and yet he struggled against her with his left arm. His right arm was completely immobilized hanging at his side.

Bradshaw's weapon was rising from his holster when a ruckus of shuffling just outside the hatch took his attention for the briefest millisecond.

It was exactly the break she needed. Wakefield twisted helmsman's neck at just the right angle and it cracked like the worst chiropractor visit ever. She dropped his body to the deck. His head smacked the table and then the floor.

Wakefield rushed Bradshaw, keeping her focus on his eyes as she reached for his gun. She did not need to take possession of it herself, just disarm him.

The jets arrived at precisely that moment. They split, one on each side of the conning tower, buzzing the tower. The jet wash shook everything in the tower: instruments, people, even the deck. Windows rattled with the supersonic blast of air and sound.

Wakefield had seen it coming behind Bradshaw as he had turned toward her because she had kept focused on his eyes rather than looking down to his weapon in fear. As his gun hand went wide with the sudden sound, she was arriving in his space and gave his wrist a chopping blow that increased the distance between her body and the muzzle.

The gun went off as Bradshaw's finger tightened on the trigger in surprise. The bang right next to her caused an involuntary tightening of her entire nervous system.

She could feel movement behind her but couldn't hear anything, deafened by the flyby followed by the gunshot next to her eardrum.

Wakefield felt Bradshaw's shooting hand swing back toward his center, now with more control. His height and position in front of her made it impossible to use the same pressure point as she had with the helmsman.

So she went for three soft spots at the same time. Bringing her knee up for momentum, Wakefield got Bradshaw in the groin and brought her foot down heel-first into the crown of his arch. She reached for the sensitive skin of his triceps, and pinched with all her might just inside his uniform sleeve hole. The uniform he was disgracing by wearing! He did not have time to flex the muscle to prevent her iron-tight pincher fingers from clamping down and twisting.

"Ahh!" She could tell he was yelping from his open mouth even though she couldn't distinguish the sound. He twisted like a sheet drying on the line in windy Texas. Still, she couldn't hear anything.

He head-butted like a bull and cracked her on the forehead. His other arm pawing at her. But still Wakefield did not release her vice grip on his skin. She dug in deeper and felt his warm blood flow over her finger tip. The wetness would soon loosen her grip, she knew. Bradshaw was slightly bent at the waist from her first strike, and she could now reach the pressure point between his neck and shoulder, but she decided to maintain her first pinch and redouble her twist.

Shifting her weight, Wakefield brought her body into a crouch and shooting from her hip, brought her right leg around into the side of Bradshaw's left knee. She sensed it giving away as his body crumpled to the right. While he was adjusting his balance she dug deep and shoved him backward and to the right to use his own momentum against him. Of course she had to drop the underarm pinch or start falling after him. "Just drop it." She heard herself growl at him. But the words only made noise inside the bubble of her head. She still couldn't hear anything outside.

There was lots of air movement going on behind her. She could feel vibrations in the deck under her boots as well. But she did not dare take her eyes off the broadcasting channel of Bradshaw's eyes and body language.

He seemed to bounce right off the sailor in the chair behind him and catch his balance again. Back on two feet, Bradshaw twisted back to deliver what Wakefield thought could be a knockout punch to the side of her head because of his superior upper-body strength. While ducking down in what she knew would not be enough time to dodge the blow completely, she also delivered an uppercut, not to his jaw, but to the wrist of his gun hand, still gripping the pistol whipping toward her temple.

It was enough power to throw off his aim so that the heel of his hand grazed her hair rather than the metal of the pistol knocking her out. He was yelling something that still couldn't penetrate her hearing loss. While his breath was out, Wakefield used her left fist to punch him in his already deflated lungs. It wasn't as powerful as her right, but it was enough for him to stagger backward into the chair again. He reached for his chest, his mouth gaping like a guppy starved for oxygen.

Wakefield rushed after him, justice forefront in her mind. As Bradshaw was bent trying to reflate his lungs, she slid her left arm around his neck and tightened her hold with her right hand pulling against her own wrist. She would cut off the blood supply though his carotid artery in a head lock until he collapsed. No air and no blood would make it very hard to fire a weapon. But as he wind-milled his arms trying to reach back to break her hold, he managed to squeeze off another shot. Some glass shattered. The change in the air pressure must have loosened the ear bubble sound protection mechanism in her ear, because she heard the tinkling of the glass on the metal sheeting of the bridge deck.

She also heard her name. She jumped forward. The sound was coming from right behind her ear. Wind sluiced like a storm into the room from the shattered window. Whirling around and bringing Bradshaw around in front of her, she knocked Bradshaw into Special Agent Lawson who came away with the weapon that Bradshaw had been waving around for hours.

Lawson took a settling step, and said her name again. Softer this time.

He held up a pair of metal cuffs. "You want to do the honors?" He raised a single finely shaped eye brow. Not a hair was out of place. How did he do that when she felt like she had just clawed her way out of a hole to hell?

"You go ahead." Wakefield released her chokehold and shoved Bradshaw toward the floor. In his weakened state he fell hard to his knees. "I was starting to get a muscle cramp anyway."

She stepped back and straightened both arms against the tension she had just forced on the muscles. Raising her hand to her temple, she felt for damage. Blood pounded in a steady fast rhythm against her skull. Pain screaming with each pulse. But there was no damp stickiness to her fingers as she ran them over her hair.

As Lawson knelt to snap the cuffs around Bradshaw's wrists Judah saw the helmsman lying on the deck. His eyes bulged and his neck lay at an insurmountable angle.

Judah's stomach heaved at what she'd done. Sourness filled her mouth and tickled under her tongue. Her hours-old breakfast came spilling out of her mouth and splashed on her boots.

The ship gave a mighty rattle and heave just then. Everyone standing on the bridge shifted in a stutter step to regain balance. A terrible screeching sound filled the air, and Wakefield almost wished back the bubble of sound protection in her ears. Had they been torpedoed? She glanced warily at the unflappable Lawson, but even his eyes were wide. It took a lot of power to shake a 97,000-ton ship.

USS *Theodore Roosevelt*
The Engine Room

LT Leonard Leibowitz stood with a grin that he couldn't contain. The man who had three minutes earlier held a gun trained on the engine room crew now lay crumpled on the deck courtesy of the iron rod he had wielded against the man.

Leibowitz sliced through the zip ties of the closest man with a box cutter, avoiding the man's skin. Then he tossed the box cutter into the man's lap and pointed to his shipmates. "Admiral said do whatever it takes to stop the ship!" Leibowitz yelled as he ran toward one of the great pistons with the rod. The metal sheeting of the walkways vibrated under his clomping feet. He could hear a din of orders being shouted behind him, but with the noise of the engines the words were unclear.

The heat coming off the engines made his head tingle as sweat began to generate.

He reared back and fixed his grip on the iron rod to take a jab against the main propulsion system. At least he was pretty sure it was the main engine. Starting forward a vice grabbed his bicep and he could not move his arm.

"Don't even think about it." A growl overcame the engine noise.

A wide-nosed master chief who looked as if his veins were filled with oil instead of blood removed the rod from his grip like taking an empty sucker stick from a baby.

"We've got this." The growl came from inside the hardened sailor, Leibowitz saw his lips moving. "But not like this."

"Sorry. Better ideas?" Leibowitz dropped his empty hand to his side. "Admiral needs this ship stopped. Now." He yelled.

The old sailor's muddy green eyes blinked once and he turned and headed back up the metal walkway. His pace increased as his large body built momentum. Leibowitz followed the bobbing body in front of him.

The master chief called out "Hard left rudder!" and a young sailor began twisting a huge dial counterclockwise nearly as quickly as the piston was working on the other side of the engine room. "Emergency stop engines." The heel of the master chief's left hand smashed into a red plastic button on the wall.

Leibowitz cupped his hands over his ears. A metal screech began small but grew to unbearable levels.

"Brace, brace, brace!" someone yelled.

The crunching metal of the main propulsion system turbines' motion disruption caused a shudder like he'd never experienced. How was he supposed to protect his hearing and brace himself against the bulkhead simultaneously?

Wide-eyed he looked at the others as the huge engine seized and shook the room like a ragdoll and then ceased. Leibowitz felt that the spinning of the propeller had stopped.

There was still motion at the controls. Seamen were engaging the reverse thrusters in order to stop the great ship's forward momentum as fast as possible. At least that is what it sounded like to his pilot ears. He didn't know what it actually looked like from the top deck, but Leibowitz pictured a car skidding to a stop with smoking tires and the back side spinning out to the right.

Only a hum of smaller engines remained.

A long whistle broke through the relief of noise first and then applause and cheers.

The man who had held the engine room crew captive lay motionless on the floor, but he wasn't bleeding.

"Doesn't look like I was too late this time." Leibowitz rubbed the chest of his uniform with self-satisfaction. "We should probably get him to sick bay. Can somebody help me get him up?" Leibowitz smiled as he thought of calling VADM Graham back from sick bay.

CHAPTER FORTY

"Who did this?" one of the uniformed and Kevlar'ed-up MPs flooding the room asked Judah as she stood over the helmsman's body. Batons held at the ready upon entry were quickly retracted and cuffs brought out as the line of MPs entered the bridge.

"I did." She swallowed hard.

The noise and confusion on the bridge swirled dizzily around her head; she just wanted everyone to settle down. Everyone was being taken into custody. Even as she herself was being flipped around and her stiff and pulsing right hand was being pulled behind her back, she halted and jerked her arm out of the MP's grasp.

She loosed a whistle that pierced all the bedlam. "Hold on everybody. Where's the captain? Somebody needs to get a loyal helmsman back up here pronto. We've got a carrier that needs steering immediately."

"I'll get on that." A voice said from the hatchway. Judah looked up to see the master-at-arms watching the proceedings with his arms folded tightly across his chest like a pair of ham hocks straining his uniform at the bicep and shoulder. He reached for the phone on the wall next to him, just inside the hatch. "Johnson, you may release her, but, take everybody else. We'll sort them out downstairs."

Wakefield's heart had begun to assume its normal rhythm again, even with the ship still offering an occasional shudder from deep in its bowels. She walked up to Bradshaw and unclipped the walkie talkie from his uniform belt. "I'll take that." she said. "And you guys get him out of this uniform a-sap." She ordered the pair of MPs who flanked the man. "He's not earned the right to wear it!"

She looked at the master-at-arms who had checked out her pistol earlier the day before. "Make preparation for more men in the cells. We are putting an end to this right now."

"I'm going to need a little trip to the doc first." A voice squeaked out through gritted teeth. Wakefield saw a young officer holding his left shoulder with his right hand, blood seeped through his fingers. One of Bradshaw's stray bullets had found a target, and it was one of his own men.

"He is one of them." Her initial surge of compassion at the sight of his pain and blood dissolved quickly as Wakefield identified him to the master-at-arms. "Make sure he is secured by whomever takes him to the infirmary." Based on location in the fleshy part of his shoulder muscle, the shot was probably a through and through. "Don't worry," she addressed the man. "You'll live to stand trial for all this."

"Ma'am?" it was the radar operator's thin voice. "Can you press that button just to the left forward of my station?" Wakefield had to interpret her shoulder gesture since the woman was cuffed. "It will turn our transponder back on. I've been sending out an S.O.S. on it, but it was off when this went down."

"Well done, petty officer. They'll sort you out downstairs. After you give your testimony get some rest."

"The captain was taken down to sick bay. Some of the others too. Several hours ago." One of the men in cuffs sounded worried. "The captain was a whole lot worse off than the others, ma'am."

"Thank you. I'll check on him shortly." Wakefield said as she walked to the radar station and depressed the button. It held at the IN position and lit up a happy green color. "We are back on the radar!" She announced with a smile as she turned back to the crowd, but the MPs were already marching them out the hatch. "Lieutenant commander has the con." She shrugged at the almost deserted bridge and added, "Apparently. Lawson, do you know how to turn our radio back on?"

"I probably shouldn't," he shrugged. "But I know how it works on a frigate. It is probably similar enough to figure out." He was already moving toward a station.

"Thanks for bringing in the cavalry. I think we have some explanations to make. And some warnings to give." Wakefield ran her hands through her hair again as she caught her own reflection in the glass. A halo of blond hair surrounded her face. It looked less than angelic though; she grimaced and smoothed it down as best she could.

Wakefield breathed deeply as an announcement formulated in her mind while reaching for the 1MC mic. "All hands." She paused picturing the sailors who would look up at the ceiling as the announcement went all over the ship simultaneously. "There is no piping call for this time. This is Lieutenant Commander Wakefield of Naval Intelligence. The X.O. and a crew have attempted to take over the ship, as I'm sure most of you are aware. Bradshaw has been detained and will only be presiding over a cell in the brig. We have retaken the bridge and are in command of the vessel.

"For those of you on Bradshaw's crew, I give you fair warning. Your names have already been given up." So it was a little fudge. But it was for a good cause. "You have sixty seconds to turn yourself in to the highest ranking officer near you. In sixty seconds we will go to general quarters, and I cannot guarantee that you will survive the encounter with a top notch *Theodore Roosevelt* crew that feels less than hospitable after being held at gun point. But I *can* guarantee that the experience will not be a pleasant one for you, even if you manage to get off a shot or two before you are taken out." Wakefield heard Lawson chuckle at the radio. "Sailors of the U.S. Navy," she continued speaking slowly and clearly into the microphone. "Please secure anyone who turns himself over to your custody and escort him to the brig. Then you may return to your duty station.

"Should any member of Bradshaw's group, known by their involvement in this attempted take-over remain armed at the end of sixty seconds, you are hereby ordered to disarm them as you see fit when I pipe general quarters. Gentlemen, your sixty seconds begins now. First shift, bridge operations, report to your duty station as you are and on the double." She pursed her lips. "Unless you are in custody." She needed help on the bridge.

"Lawson," she held out the walkie talkie to him and swapped over to the radio chair where he held out the radio mic. "Can you cycle through these channels? A couple of seconds per channel while you count down from sixty over the channels. I want to throw the fear of God into them."

"Fear of God and a few good Navy men." Lawson smiled, as Wakefield saw him press the talk button with his first finger and began, "Fifty-eight, fifty-seven."

Wakefield turned to the radio.

USS *Reprisal*
CIC

Graham stood surveying his kingdom on the sea. He never thought he would have to fire on one of his own Strike Group ships, especially MacSod's domain. He had met the man, for Pete's sake.

"The USS *Buffalo* reports that they have their submarine in position to fire. Torpedo doors on two silos are open and flooded. Four tubes are loaded with Harpoon missiles." The information struck the air like lead in the *Reprisal* CIC. Every man in the room knew the weight of these circumstances in which they had found themselves.

"I want those Harpoons trained on the rudder." Graham ordered. He heard the radio operator repeat his order to the sub's skipper who Graham knew would be on the horn personally in a situation as dire as this one. To Ellsworth, Graham leaned and said, "I don't relish getting an invoice for refitting an air craft carrier in dry dock if I breech her hull, or God forbid, sink her."

"No, admiral, I don't suppose you do."

"SAR reports men in the water. Survivors. They see hands waving." A radio woman monitoring their frequency for updates reported to the room.

A cheer erupted. It was short lived.

"That's enough." Graham growled. "We have a long way to go people. Keep focused."

"Sub reports gunshots heard over the sonar."

"Confirm, gun shot heard."

Graham assumed it was their own sonar operator. Ellsworth would know these men by name, but Graham had been focused on big picture for his months at sea. "Copy." Graham stated. He would give it some time to see what developed.

"No change in the *TR*'s new heading or speed."

"Get those 18s to do another flyby." Graham ordered. "Then line up to strafe the deck, and await my order."

"Aye, sir." Graham's words were repeated into a mic.

"Still no response to our hails on the radio."

"Come on, flyboy, get down to that engine room," Graham urged Leibowitz on in his mission just under his breath. "I don't want to disable one of our own."

Graham turned to Ellsworth, "Would you order your crew to slow our speed so we are not getting further and further away? We may have to get over there in a hurry."

Ellsworth nodded and said, "Make your speed 16 knots. Continue heading and plan through the Strait."

Moments later the sonar operator spoke up again, "Cavitation from the *Big Stick* has changed. Sounds like a turn to port. Whew! is it loud."

"Cannot confirm," spoke another. "Not the slightest change of course from her. Yet."

"Copy." Graham let a smile play at his mouth. The lieutenant had gotten through. He knew it.

"The 18s are in place."

"Send the 18s around again. Repeat, no strafe at this time."

One of the four backlit clocks on the wall showed ship's time. He watched as the second hand swept around. Time stretched long, and Graham thought he could feel himself aging in those moments as they crept toward the deadline moment he had appointed in his mind.

Would he really order a torpedo toward his own daughter and a U.S. ship? He had to. The outcome of not stopping the carrier toward its destination would be disastrous.

"Slight change of course detected by radar. Sir. Confirm that she is coming to port."

Graham let out his breath.

"Transponder reacquired, sir."

"Excellent." Graham shoved a hand into his pocket and found that he had crossed his fingers, a left-over boyhood trait. Hope inflated his lungs.

"The 18's confirm knowledge of transponder acquired."

"Radio contact!" The shout rang out. This time when the *Reprisal*'s CIC crew shouted in relief he did not stop them.

"Put them on the speaker." Graham ordered and pointed at the radio operator who had gotten them. The man was pressing the earphones to the side of his head as he concentrated on the words coming over his headset.

"Lieutenant Commander, you are on loud speaker with Vice Admiral Graham of the USS *Reprisal*.

"Lieutenant Commander, have you effected a mutiny and taken the crew on a pleasure cruise? Where is MacSod?" Graham asked gruffly.

"Hi, Dad," were the next words he heard. And though Judah's words certainly must have continued, he heard only the sound of pressure steaming off his soul. She was alive.

When he tuned back in Judah was saying, "…under my control until a crew who knows what they are doing arrive and can relieve me. Then I'll go down and check on MacSod with my own eyes. "It was the X.O., Bradshaw who attempted the mutiny, and he is now in custody of the master-at-arms."

"LCDR Wakefield you need to go ahead to general quarters and have the entire ship swept for any stragglers."

"Yes, sir. We just hit my deadline for turning themselves in. Just a second." The entire CIC heard Judah's muffled orders, "Lawson, sound general quarters." And the alarm rang out over the speaker as a male voice called "General quarters, general quarters. All hands, man your battled stations. This is not a drill."

"I'm back." Wakefield's voice was no longer muffled.

"We heard gunshots fired. Are you all right?"

"Yes, sir. One of Bradshaw's coup crew got what he deserved with a through and through in his arm. He'll live. Bradshaw just popped off a couple of accidental shots as I was subduing him."

A low-pitch wave of whispers undulated through the CIC at that statement. Graham began walking toward the radio operator who had patched Judah into the system. "With me, Ellsworth." He commanded. "Get her off the speaker. I'll take the headset. The 18s are to continue as escort until refueling or I order otherwise." Graham said as he adjusted the headphones from the woman's small head to actually cover each of his ears at the same time.

"Judah, listen." He spoke succinctly. "I need you to get the Air Boss up to the bridge to reestablish a chain of command aboard that carrier, and he needs to make the announcement that he has the con over the 1 MC. He needs to relinquish control over flight ops to his second before he comes. I'm sending Ellsworth over." He made eye contact with Ellsworth over the radio operator's head. "He will take command of the carrier as soon as he reports to the bridge. But, you understand that the helo will need permission to land on the carrier, so the Air Boss has to give over responsibility of his tower to his second."

"I've got it. I'll send the master-at-arms upstairs to him directly."

"No. Send that Lawson you're working with. He's the NCIS officer aboard right?" He was remembering from his leaders' prayer list. "Keep the master-at-arms on the bridge at the hatch with you. Every person he allows in must be searched. I wish you had someone trustworthy who could recognize the shift as they arrive and ID them for you."

"Did you disable the ship?" Wakefield asked.

"I sent a pilot who had gotten out of the ready room where all the airdales were being held to the engine room. We'll talk about all that later. Leave this channel open," he instructed. "I'll stay on the line with you. I want you interviewing each person after the master-at-arms pats him down. Ask their name, duty station—"

"I have conducted interviews looking for deceit before. It is kind of my job." Wakefield chuckled in stereo even as she interrupted him.

"I suppose you have." He paused. "But I'll still be listening in. Two are better than one."

Graham looked back up to Ellsworth. "I am transferring you immediately, to command the *Theodore Roosevelt* and bring her back up to our scheduled course." He paused only a quarter beat and added, "After the day they've had, why don't you authorize a beer day tonight."

Ellsworth cracked a smile, "That'll help ease the transition. I already let my X.O. know that he will be getting some extra leadership practice, sir. But don't hesitate to look over his shoulder. This is only his second cruise at this level." Ellsworth nodded. "I'm looking forward to reacquainting myself with One Shot Wakefield."

"Give her my love." Graham said quietly. "And Ellsworth, I'll get you back in command of your own ship as soon as I can get two qualified officers out here to relieve MacSod and Bradshaw. We are going to be in this for the long haul. Report to the flight deck now and I'll have your yeoman put together your uniforms and personal articles and send another helo when chain of command has been firmly re-established, or before dinner, whichever happens first." Graham nodded as he put out his hand to shake Ellsworth's. "Thank you," he nodded deeply. "Dismissed."

CHAPTER FORTY ONE

L CDR Judah Wakefield swallowed hard as she pushed open the door into the infirmary receiving area twenty minutes after the Air Boss appeared on the bridge.

Quiet, cold, and brightly lit, at least this area of the ship was more white than gray. Judah felt a shiver as a medic swathed in white surgical gear pushed open a hatch from the backroom. "Hello there, ma'am. I'll be right back," he said as he brushed past her. He held at chest-height an orange medical waste disposal bag the size of the ones she used in her kitchen at home.

She had heard the low buzz of voices when the hatch was open as he had come through, so, Wakefield plowed back the way the medic had come.

"Hello?" she said a moment after stepping through the hatch to an equally empty surgery space. The tables for instruments were empty. The bed had been stripped down to its plastic cover, and still had a swath of wetness reflecting the overhead lights where it had been wiped down with the strong antiseptic that permeated the air.

The scene did not bode well for MacSod's prognosis. "And what about the gunshot victim?" she whispered aloud.

"You a friend of his?" asked a pleasant female-pitched voice from a doorway slightly behind her peripheral vision. "You shouldn't be back here."

Wakefield turned around. The woman wore all white scrubs so Wakefield could not identify her rank. Her charcoal-black hair was tied back from her face, and her expression of authority along with the way she held her hands away from her body told Wakefield that she was the surgeon.

"Definitely *not* a friend of his." Wakefield emphasized. "Did you know he helped try to take over this ship?"

"I did not know the details." The surgeon smiled wanly. "I find it's easier to treat them if I don't know. But he was admitted with cuffs and a security officer, so I had a pretty good idea he was not of the finest character."

"So where is everybody?" Wakefield tried to peer through the doorway and into the space behind where the surgeon stood. The woman put one hand on the doorframe, so Wakefield knew that was the doorway she wanted.

"Well, we treated the gunshot wound. It was a through and through, so no surgery. I just cleaned him up, and put a dressing on both sides of his shoulder." The woman continued talking about the gunshot wound which Wakefield cared nothing about. She wanted to hear about MacSod. To see him. Was he even still alive? Wakefield stepped closer to the woman who kept jabbering on, but also adjusted her body position more firmly in Wakefield's path.

"Please!" Wakefield finally interrupted her. "I don't care about the gunshot!" She held up both hands with splayed and stiff fingers to stop the surgeon. "I'm here about the captain."

"How do you know about the captain?"

"Never mind. Is he alive? I need to report back to Admiral Graham a.s.a.p." Wakefield was standing only a foot and a half in front of her white scrubs by the time she flipped her trump card of using her dad's name.

Fear flashed through the woman's eyes, and Wakefield's stomach got butterflies. She started to push the woman aside and charge past her, when the doctor turned sideways. "He is still in recovery," she said.

"Where is he?" Wakefield pursued.

"You shouldn't be back here."

The surgeon was behind Wakefield now as she assessed the layout of the recovery room. There was a curtain partitioning off part of the room in the back, and a murmur wafted out from behind it. She charged toward it. As much as she had disliked MacSod in her first days aboard, Judah had turned around completely now. His daughter though was foremost in her mind. She had survived so much only to be faced with the prospect of losing her father now? No. It wasn't going to happen on her watch. She remembered what that felt like. No way!

The surgeon caught up to her just as she was ruffling the curtain to find the opening. She placed a gentle hand on Wakefield's arm. "Over here." She said. "But brace yourself."

The surgeon guided Judah to the edge of the curtain where it met the wall, and pulled it back about two feet for her to slip in.

The hope she had felt combatting the butterflies inside was squashed when she saw MacSod. The voices Wakefield had heard, she now attributed to the two medical people standing on either side of his recovery bed.

"Why does he look like that?" Wakefield racked her brain for something in her corpsman training years ago to explain his blackened lips. Even her photographic memory couldn't help her if she had never read about that symptom. She couldn't tear her eyes away. Machines with tubes and hoses beeped in a familiar rhythm. His heartrate sounded just slow of normal. The IV bag hanging above his head was clear liquid, so there was no transfusion going on. The cannula under his nose and his sunken-in cheeks that normally had appeared so full, gave him the look of someone who had been ill a long time. He looked so much smaller out of uniform. He had not looked like that last night. Was it just last night?

"We gave him a heroic dose of charcoal after pumping his stomach." The surgeon explained. Her voice was back to that gentle surgeon voice that some physicians find in medical school.

"What was wrong?"

MacSod lay there still as death itself as they spoke over him.

"He was poisoned. Arsenic." The surgeon explained.

"But the others? You obviously didn't have a rush." She gestured back to the empty recovery room behind the curtain. "They were okay."

At the surgeon's questioning double eyebrow raise, Wakefield explained the coffee situation as she had understood it.

"Just a situation like the coffee, would not have put MacSod in this state of deterioration." She shook her head. "I could see from his hair sample with a naked eye that he has been being dosed with arsenic for some time. The coffee probably just sent him into critical toxicity levels."

"Why didn't he say something?" Wakefield sighed.

"He probably did not notice. Just had a queasy belly, some fatigue. Symptoms that could have been attributed to any number of things. I wouldn't have even known to check his hair sample for a confirmation of poisoning except that he reminded me of those little almond windmill cookies when I leaned over him on the gurney."

"What are his chances, doc?" Wakefield asked.

"We are hopeful that he will make a full recovery. Though he will be spitting and pooping black from the charcoal for days. It will absorb all the toxins in his system and carry them right out of his body."

"Thank God!" Wakefield patted the captain on the bulge of his blanket-encased foot. "I'll be back to see you, but rest easy, Captain, your ship is back in good hands. The Air Boss has the con. Ellsworth is on his way over to run her for you. And your daughter is safely in NCIS custody. I'll have Lawson let her know you'll call as soon as you're up to it."

Wakefield backed toward the crack in the curtain at the bulkhead. "Thanks, Doc." She ignored the questioning stares of the three medical personnel and slipped behind the curtain.

Next stop, the brig or NCIS?

Little Creek Naval Base, VA
The Facility
23 March 2003
0220 hours

"Welcome back, Rivers." CDR Jackson greeted him with a firm hand shake. "How's Chad doing?"

Weariness had seeped into David Rivers' bones in the last five days and nights, but he had come directly to The Facility's underground bunker from the airlift from Texas back to Virginia. The men were streaming back to their starting cues.

"He is gone already." He spoke sparingly. David didn't trust his own emotional barriers not to let down on him again. He didn't want that in front of the Team. Not at this critical time.

"Oh, I'm sorry." Jackson placed a hand on Rivers' shoulder. "He was one of the best. And he will be missed."

David nodded silently. He dropped near the door his small plastic grocery bag of items he had collected at the hospital at Fort Hood and decided to bring back with him. Jackson must have sensed his need for physical space around him, because without a word, he directed the men of the combined SEAL teams away from the doorway where Rivers felt glued.

"One more vocal run through. I want Rivers to see where we are. Full packs and in the full timeline," CDR Jackson commanded from the corner. "This time I want it in quarter-light. Everyone reset." He walked back toward the middle doorway and Rivers and then flipped three of the four overhead lighting switches to off. He set aside the clipboard of notes as pairs of men made their way to their start point. Rivers knew from experience that Jackson had memorized each portion of their drill by now, and he couldn't read it anymore in the dim light anyway.

"We've made a couple of updates to the plan." Jackson said lowly. "But I still want you leading your Echo Unit. That LT Howard's attitude—" Jackson shook his head and left it unsaid.

Even after two in the morning Rivers did not detect one sigh among these warriors who were likely in their twentieth hour of drilling for the day. The mock-up of Baghdad and the suburb villages built in small scale only provided room for about half the men assigned to each company to walk through the plan that had been developed, refined, and then tweaked more than twelve hundred times in the days since it was first hatched.

The mission still ran on a three-hour timeframe, meticulously laid out in three-minute waypoints. Jackson told him, "Most of the other drills we conducted at triple-time speed. We will see how they do endurance-wise tonight." The smaller setting of the mock-up city was nowhere near a 1:3 ratio of the actual city of Baghdad. But based on their mapping early in the planning sessions, the waypoints had been set realistically. As long as everyone kept a hustle on. Which was not unrealistic in the midst of an adrenaline-pumping mission. Unless they ran into firefights on the ground and had to slow it down. Had Jackson thrown any of those into the mix yet? Rivers wondered. The room was stilling as everyone re-set. The men who had been in the preceding walk-through drill efficiently traded places with those critiquing every move around the perimeter of the small airplane-hanger-sized room in The Facility's basement.

"You want to call time?" Jackson asked him, passing the stop watch over to him.

Rivers shrugged. He would still be able to view mission changes as his 2IC, Howard, ran the "dress rehearsal" for Echo Company. The room became thick with tension as each team stood at their start position. "Go." Rivers called out as he pressed the start knob on the old fashioned stopwatch that someone had added on the first day of collecting all the needed procurements. He liked the ticking sound and it made him want to move faster.

Delta Company, demolitions, led by LCDR Chassey started moving first from the "outskirts" of the city toward the "city center." Their objective, designed primarily by Luckhardt, though Lucky did not end up serving in Delta Company, was to set charges to bring down all bridges surrounding the three main presidential palaces in Baghdad, except one entry/exit point for each palace, where the demolitions crew would stand guard and allow entry to their brothers in arms only. Their plan included civilian dress, small dirty pickup trucks with .50 cals mounted in their truck beds, erratic driving, and boisterous threats shouted into the air to dissuade any interference with their route. And avoiding the airport in case any American troops should mistake them for actual enemies, since that is how they were masquerading.

Echo Company, extractions, was the largest of all the groups, and had dispersed among Delta Company to catch rides into town. As Delta set the charges, Echo would make their way across those bridges or through the water in certain cases, and enter each presidential palace to sweep for known leaders. Their priority of remanding each man for trial was second to safety. If fired upon, the SEALs were under rules of engagement to shoot to kill.

Charlie Company, chaos and riots, departed from their start mark next. Rivers had not been surprised when Thomas had volunteered for that team. Most of Charlie Company drove or rode in civilian dress. Open-air lorry trucks full of men deposited their live cargo along their painstakingly chosen routes. Every 60 seconds pairs of agitators jumped out of the trucks. Some ran, some walked. But all were making noise all the way. Their objective was to start fires, pick fights with Republican Guardsmen, and encourage freedom lovers to join them in it or hunker down with their children behind locked doors. By the appointed time, they would converge at the many city squares to which each pair had been assigned.

Bravo Company, Blackhawk helicopter crews, were the last to leave their post. They were divided into three groups of four helos each, full of men. They were dressed in black from head to toe and carried enough ammunition to sink a ship. Their objective was to fast rope down to palace roof tops and grassy lawns and appear to be the main fighting force, drawing the trained soldiers to engage in a battle of bullets while the real objective would be taking place inside by Echo Company, the extraction team, who had snuck inside the secured palace walls—hopefully undetected.

Alpha Company, the smallest crew, was in charge of monitoring communication and big picture movements. They would stay outside the city in one of the Forward Operating Bases. Camp Liberty, to the north of the city, if Rivers got his first choice. If men needed to be redirected, CDR Jackson, would give the orders, and his Alpha Company members would put out the word via coms headsets with each unit of each company. Rivers hated to lose Jackson's physical longevity in the on-the-ground battle, but his vast experience and the men's trust of that experience was more valuable back at base giving direction and oversite. Rivers felt himself sinking back into the familiar cadence of ops rehearsals, his load from Texas lightening significantly.

Seated next to Jackson in the coms center would be CPO Luckhardt and LT Lincoln the two most strategic chess players among the entire squadron. Their team would be equipped with maps and computers and coms gear.

For this drill, each of the three palaces that Echo Company infiltrated had a bean bag hidden inside it to represent Sadaam. Echo Units were to find him and carry out him to the extraction point. Dropping "Saddam" on his head several times seemed to be a favorite pastime if a team was not behind scheduled waypoints.

Running the drill in real time was a lot of hurry-up-and-wait, Rivers noted, as they gained each waypoint. Action-itchy SEALs in the drill fidgeted with no opposition as they would have in the real thing. After calling the one-hour mark, Rivers leaned over to Jackson. "I'm sending in opposition." Jackson nodded.

Rivers sent a whisper message like a telephone-tree-game through the SEALs critiquing from the shadowed sidelines, first to his left, then to those on his right. "At the 1:21 mark we move in as insurgents. No holds barred. Spread around the entire perimeter."

Rivers saw the first two transfers of information from SEAL to SEAL before he lost visual in the darkness.

"One-fifteen." He bellowed out the waypoint time. Everyone in the game was on mark and began to move to their next waypoint.

Howard's smaller group of extractors, whom Rivers would be leading on Event Day, went belly-down under the water of their fake Tigris River again, to torch their way into the underground labyrinth at the most iconic and newest of the three palaces, Al-Faw.

The Republican Palace was the one where Rivers, after studying all the blueprints and reinforcements made in their Intel reports, was pretty sure they would find the Hussein family. Which was why he had earlier assigned himself to lead that group in the actual assault. But with his unexpected little trip over to Fort Hood, Echo Company leaders Ogden and Campbell got that plum assignment. So leading the Al-Faw Palace breech would have to do for Rivers. After experiencing the gravity of Chad's quick succumbing to the cancer as soon as his gut had been exposed to the air, Rivers was fine with taking the second-string assignment now. He had learned to expect death on the battle field at his age; not from cancer. Still, he kept a closer eye on the Republican Palace Echo Team than on any of the other teams during the drills, because he still felt most drawn to that palace's breech.

"One-eighteen." He called again over the loud speaker since the rioters and agitators were definitely accomplishing their task.

He felt the men on the perimeter spread out. Rivers squinted into the darkness as he saw some of the SEALs remove their packs and take up their customized rifles and begin to move forward into position to rush an attack at the next waypoint.

He smile. This was going to go well.

"One-twenty-one." He marked, trying to use the same tone as usual. He heard a little bit of excitement tinge the echo back to his ears though.

Soundlessly the dispersed "insurgents" scurried to sneak up behind the SEALs in the drill. They went through buildings to move ahead of where they knew the Companies would be arriving. Rivers had been about to hustle in himself, but stepped back. "One-twenty-four," he called time again.

From his position he could watch the action and instruct later. At the first surprised "Hey!" from one of the SEALs on the riot team in Charley Company who was toward the outskirts, Rivers knew the action was underway. While he couldn't see it, he heard a metal burn barrel rolling over the seams in the concrete floor. He hoped a fire had not been set when the insurgents sent it rolling. Then he shrugged. "I did say 'no holds barred'." While he was pretty sure the brass at Little Creek Naval Base would not appreciate smoke-scented classrooms of The Facility, the SEALs all had fire suppression training and wouldn't let the building burn down even if their mock city did catch on fire.

The insurgents were lighter on their feet without their packs, and without exception, when they were "shot" and left for dead, they "came to life again" after the SEAL walked away.

"One-twenty-seven," Rivers called. He grinned from his vantage point as he watched hand-to-hand combat and rifle barrels used like bayonets. Grunts and punching sounds joined the rioters' boisterous stirring up of trouble singeing the air. The sound of "*Allau Akbar*" was used like calling "Geronimo" before a particularly big surge, when someone jumped from a first floor rooftop onto a previously-unsuspecting SEAL below. After the first call, it seemed to catch on and was repeated in several American accents as Rivers called out the waypoint times.

At the 2:39 mark all teams were to have begun their individual exfiltration strategy. The helos were to break gravity at the 2:48 mark.

Howard's team had had to abandon their primary entry strategy when met with a pair of insurgents who had thrown buckets of sand on their underwater torches until they had run out of fuel and then the SEALS had to leave the metal grid fastened over the hole in the labyrinth floor where they were trying to gain entrance before they ran out of air in their SCUBA tanks. They did finally gain entry into the palace walls, but they had yet to find the bean-bag Sadaam. A trio of "insurgents" kept moving the Saddam-effigy.

CDR Jackson ordered over the com system the pilots of two of the four Blackhawks on that palace roof to remain on their mark while the others departed. "Howard, exfil! Exfil immediately. To the rooftop waypoint with or without your prisoner." Jackson ordered him.

Rivers nodded at Jackson's decision. It was going to be a nasty debrief though. He could feel Howard's resentment from the other side of the room.

The pair of leaders watched Howard jump aboard the platform they designated as a Blackhawk before the rest of his team had arrived. Rivers was prepared to ignore it. But then a team member tripped. He sprawled face first on the rooftop.

Whether it was disappointment, actual injury, or accident that caused the tripper to delay getting up immediately, Rivers now couldn't ignore the break in protocol. Leaders always exfilled last.

"Three hours." Rivers hit the stopwatch button and buried it in his hip pocket before the tripper was able to scramble aboard the closest helo.

"Put out the barrel fires and meet in the debrief room. Breakfast will be brought in." Jackson's flat voice announced.

CHAPTER FORTY TWO

USS *Theodore Roosevelt*
NCIS

Wakefield could feel the adrenaline beginning to work its way out of her system. She rapped once on the door to Lawson's NCIS door, and turned the handle. It stopped under her hand as a familiar voice accompanied quick steps in the passage way.

"I'm coming." Lawson called out.

"Hey there!" Wakefield brightened a little at his wide grin. "Where are you coming from?"

"I was giving the master-at-arms the highlights of our investigation. He has a very full brig." Lawson tossed her a carefree smile, "And a que to the interrogation room eighteen people long. He said about half of them asked for a deal on their way in." Lawson unlocked the door and held it open for her.

"That sounds good. He's probably going to need some help processing that many people." Wakefield smoothed back her hair which felt like a rat's nest under her hand, and she began to call up more reserve energy. "I can be down there as soon as I get a shower and change of uniform."

"Actually, he kicked me out. Said I was too close. But my statement would do. I am guessing you would be just as unwelcome."

"Well, of all the—" Wakefield huffed.

"Just be grateful and let them finish the job. You've done enough. In fact, those were the very words Master Chief Lourdes said to pass on to you."

"Hmm." Wakefield crossed her arms in the room she had spent more time in than her own office in the last 48 hours.

"I saw your Petty Officer Gates down there in holding." Lawson twisted his mouth to the side. "I guess he turned himself in. Sorry. But now we know how information was being passed to Bradshaw." Lawson looked apologetic as he took his seat behind his desk and offered her the one on the guest side of his desk.

"Hey, maybe he still has my codebreaker USB drive in his desk." Wakefield said wistfully. "You don't need to apologize."

"Yeah, but I know what it is like to find that you've had a mole right under your nose."

"I suppose it is a betrayal. But right now, I don't even care. I didn't like him all that much from the beginning. He didn't belong in Intelligence. And I kept as much from both of them as I could. So," she shrugged. Getting offended at someone who was only acting out of his own sin nature that was just a bit more fully developed in his heart than in others, even her own, wasn't worth the effort of walking through forgiveness, so she just decided to cut it off from the pass, and let it go.

"I stopped by the sparky on my way just now. Signed a work order for them to dismantle the camera in your office."

"We'll probably need to get a computer tech to trace the signal and see where Bradshaw was watching the video feed. That will need to be cleaned up too. I wonder if that tech who came in with me on the COD a few weeks ago is still aboard. I know the captain had a list a mile long for him."

"Pretty soon those computer geeks will be standard issue on ships, the way technology is advancing."

Wakefield nodded, but her head was starting to feel heavy. "Let's place that call to Liz." She looked at Lawson's desk phone. "I've got to get some rest."

"Excellent idea." Lawson smiled and reached for the phone. "I talked to her briefly and said I'd get her dad on the line as soon as he was able. And it sounds like that might be a little while."

Wakefield nodded. Just as she slid forward in her chair and Lawson had begun to dial, the 1 MC piped up.

"Captain Ellsworth here," came a slightly tinny but still recognizable voice through the speaker in Lawson's office. Lawson replaced the receiver in the cradle while Ellsworth explained what had happened that day to the best of his knowledge. He finished up the briefing in about three minutes with, "We have some heroes among us today. Tonight with chow, we will hoist a can, or two, and salute the fine men and women who made them possible. It's Beer Day, by order of Admiral Graham in appreciation for your bravery. Now, I told him you were just doing your duty. But he insisted. Mess line is open at 1830 hours tonight. That is all."

Wakefield glanced wistfully at Lawson. "Too bad they're not offering bottles of wine."

"If you don't want your beer, I'd be happy to make it disappear for you. You know, just helping out a fellow sailor." He added as she shook her head.

"Why don't you just place that call, and leave my celebrating to me." She smiled.

BOQ Little Creek, VA
23 March 2003
1720 hours

Rivers stood stock still in the blind ante-room of the bunk-house where SEAL Team Six was assigned to sleeping quarters. He had been pushing the door to open it into the main room, but quickly drew back as he heard his name coming through the crack.

"Rivers doesn't deserve to lead this team." Rivers easily identified the venom as LT Howard's deep bass voice. "He hasn't even been here for *days* of rehearsals. I've heard about some of the things he has done in the field. That's probably why he picked up Mass as his buddy. I guess they deserve each other. But I wouldn't go back for either one of them."

"I suppose I've heard a couple of the guys telling stories." Rivers recognized the second voice as one of the younger SEALs but couldn't put a face clearly to it. "But most of the guys who've trained under him recently have only good things to say. Well, except his stupid no cussing rule."

Rivers cracked a smile then.

Howard guffawed and swore colorfully. "Obviously he wasn't my BUD/S instructor."

"Doesn't sound like it, sir."

"One of the instructors he works with told me that he—" Howard's voice dropped in volume, but the derogatory tone still carried through the crack in the doorjamb even though Rivers couldn't distinguish every word.

As the conversation deteriorated, and the younger SEAL's responses sounded less and less sure of his former good opinion, Rivers pushed open the bunkroom door fully and called out, "Hello, gentlemen." He hoped his tone conveyed that he was unconvinced of the gentlemanliness of either of them. "This conversation has run its course through the gutter, and I suggest you double time it over to the chow line before all the good dessert is gone. We are going to be running shy of dessert for perhaps a very long time in a very short time."

The younger man Rivers now ID'd as Peter Morrison stood there stone faced at being caught. But Howard went on the offensive, as if he had not been offensive enough already. "It's not polite to eavesdrop in doorways," he accused. "You might hear something you don't want to hear."

"No *might* about it." Rivers shrugged. "Now why don't you two move along! And from now on Lieutenant, if you have a problem with the way I've handled a mission or a story you've heard on the grapevine, why don't you try manning up and asking me about it face to face?"

Howard's hard jawline told Rivers how likely that was to happen. But the two men did steam out of the room. Rivers wasn't sure which of them wanted out of the room more. Though Morrison did glance back over his shoulder and Rivers glimpsed what he thought might have been an expression of regret in the young SEAL's eyes.

Rivers held his posture until the door swung closed and then hurried to his lower bunk and footlocker to throw his belongings in his bag. What he had said about dessert was true, and he really wanted to snag another slice of that chocolate silk freezer pie with the whipped cream in Russian-steeple swirls on top before they shipped out.

USS *Theodore Roosevelt*
Cabin 2-99-3-L
1340 hours

Wakefield woke with the taste of sour cotton on her tongue. She rolled to her side and clicked the button on the side of her watch to illuminate the time. Forcing her eyes open against the brightness, she sighed.

It was Sunday, March 28, according to her watch. She had missed the Protestant service. And oh, she was stiff and sore all over. She had slept from just before 8 PM all the way through past noon.

She squeezed the fingers of her right hand into a fist. She could feel the swelling there and it brought back the events of the previous day in a rush of little flash pictures.

She heard the shower stop. The sounds in the bathroom must have been what awakened her. She tried to call up moisture to her mouth, but was so parched, there was nothing. She patted her upper bunk mattress looking for her water bottle she always climbed up with.

Her fingers closed around it and she scooted up to a sitting position and leaned against her pillow to block the chill from the metal bulkhead. Judah sucked the bottle dry until it crackled under the pressure.

LT Melissa Garvey cracked the hatch to the head and light spilled out. She quickly stole a glance toward the top bunk. "You're awake." Garvey sounded strangely cheerful. "I was going to give you until I had to leave at 1500 hours and then wake you."

"Oh?" Wakefield rubbed her eyes and tried to process this new sound coming from Garvey. They had not spoken civilly even once. Now she sounded downright friendly.

"The captain summoned you for 1900 hours." Garvey passed a note to her on the bunk.

"Which one?" Wakefield asked, remembering that Captain Ellsworth had sat with her at dinner the night before, and Captain MacSod was laid out in the infirmary. "Never mind," she said when she saw MacSod's signature across the bottom of his personal stationary. "Looks like MacSod is out of the woods."

"Yes, ma'am. Scuttlebutt is that he was released at 10 hundred hours."

That was an extreme turn around. "Excellent news." Wakefield pushed the covers off of her legs and crawled to the end of her bunk to descend. When she was at eye level with Melissa Garvey again, she said, "You sound different today. What changed?"

Melissa shrugged but a smiled tugged at her lips. "I had a pretty good scare yesterday." She admitted then looked at the floor. "And

I've decided to make some changes in my life. Told that guy to get lost."

"And will he?" Judah prompted.

Garvey sighed. "After a few choice names, and a threat or two if I ever squealed to his wife, he said that I'd never see him again. I feel like life is going to be so much better now."

Wakefield nodded. Grateful for the dim lighting from the direction of the bathroom and Garvey's shadow over her face, as she stood between the light and Wakefield. She knew unless Garvey replaced her loneliness with Jesus, the hope she felt would not last long.

"That's hope," Wakefield said and hugged the younger woman. As she released her, Wakefield moved toward her locker for fresh clothes. She knew in her knower she should say something to Garvey. She should tell her the secret to retaining hope and comfort.

Judah blinked long. She was tired. *Later, Lord. Next time. See, I can ask her how it is going, and she is heading out shortly anyway.* "You done in the head?" Judah asked turning around with a crispy new uniform laid across her left arm and a wad of under clothes in her hand.

"Sure. Go ahead." Melissa smiled and waved her in.

CHAPTER FORTY THREE

L ieutenant Commander David Rivers stopped with his hand on the doorknob, listening to the pre-mission buzz and bravado in The Facility room they had lived in together mission planning for nearly 11 days—give or take, with his absence. The base cleaning crew would probably be happy to have them out. The coffee cups they had gone through could have supplied a small nation for a month.

"Lord, it is not too late to stop me," David sent up a breath prayer.

He pushed open the door.

"Attention on deck!" the call went out as quickly as he was noticed.

He could hear breath being sucked in and shoes snapping on the industrial tile floor. Then silence.

He let the silence settle over them all.

"This is our last moment together state-side," he stated formally. "I will release the team leaders for our various transports to the arranged bases in a moment. But in this moment, I want to give you my word, brother to brother, that we, that I," David corrected, "I will leave no man behind. We all come out of this, and we all come home."

The room did not even stir as usual when he got to this part of the speech he always made before a mission.

"None of us have been in the position into which we are about to walk. We have seen our share of bad guys succumb to our will. But today, this mission, it is a fight of good against evil. I don't have to remind you of the atrocities Saddam Hussein has committed against his own people, those entrusted to his care and leadership. Over the years, many of us have seen the aftermath with our own eyes.

"You have trained mentally for this mission. You have trained physically for this mission. And in those areas I have every confidence in you. You have been hand-picked and qualified yourselves as the best of the best."

Rivers watched a few nervous faces along the sides of the room start to brighten. "Because this mission is so important, I would like to do something a little different as we set out to fulfill our roles. Those of you who have served with me before will attest, I've never done this before."

He saw his most recent former buddy from right before he went into training, Roger Klingler, standing at attention only about eight feet from where Rivers addressed the room from the back door. Klingler threw up a curious eyebrow.

"At ease." Rivers instructed.

As one, the men dropped to a shoulder width stance, clasping their hands behind their backs. Rivers smiled as the whump of 282 boots hitting the tile floor reinforced his words.

"This mission's underlying goal is to free the Iraqi people from the evil and fear that are holding them captive. And mark my words this is also a spiritual battle."

Rivers paused. This is where he was embarking onto the Lord's script that had downloaded into his spirit as he was eating that final dessert with the Russian-swirly peaks of whipped cream.

"I want us to pray together before we separate into our respective teams. Some of you say you don't believe in God. And that is your choice. I just hope you don't meet Him before you come to understand that He is real after all. Until then, I ask that you stand respectfully with your brothers who *do* believe as we dedicate our efforts to God's use over these next few weeks.

"Let's pray." Rivers said and bowed his head, but not before witnessing every other head start forward too.

"God, we come to you tonight, in a humble posture asking for your blessing of strength and wisdom to lead us in this fight ahead. We dedicate ourselves and the strength you've given us to you, that you would use us and guide us. If it is our time to go to our eternal rest with you, we ask that you would continue to watch over our families and help them to heal. If any of us should become captured by the enemy, we ask that you would give us endurance to not betray ourselves or our country."

A holy silence fell over them. Rivers recognized the Lord's abiding presence resting in the room, and so he completed the prayer the Lord had given him. He had not been sure he could go through with it until that moment.

"And Father, I ask, that you would make yourself known to each man in this room. Bring each into your Kingdom. That they would be warriors on earth and in the heavenlies.

"Father, we ask for success in this mission, and we leave the definition of *success* up to you." Uniforms rustled in the room. "We ask you to execute your divine justice upon the leadership in Iraq. If there is mercy destined for Saddam and he humbles his heart, we thank you for that. But either way, Lord, it seems like we have been appointed, like Queen Esther, for such a time as this: to arrange a meeting between you and Saddam, whether on this side of eternity or yours. Again, we dedicate our bodies and minds and hearts to your service. In Jesus' mighty name. Amen."

Rivers took another moment, alone with the King, in the midst of the crowded room which had begun to stir in earnest now. *Forgive me, Father, for hesitating to pray before my men. And for almost looking up for their approval before looking to you, for your approval and pleasure.*

Rivers gave a final nod and opened his eyes.

Many pairs of eyes glistened in the room.

He made eye contact with each man in his field of vision, hoping they felt his personal promise to them and their families. He tried not to dwell on the certainty, based on statistics, that some of these men would not be returning alive.

"Fall out!" Rivers called.

MacSod's at-sea cabin
Sunday 27 March 2003
1900 hours

Wakefield tugged her crisp khaki uniform blouse down once more and smoothed each sleeve. She raised her left hand to knock on the captain's door. Precisely on time.

"Enter." She heard the growl from within.

Wakefield licked her lips and turned the knob. She had never been called to a captain's cabin while underway and certainly not while in the middle of an air campaign. It felt a bit like being called to the dean's office, but on a much larger scale. "Reporting as ordered, sir." Wakefield stiffened reflexively.

MacSod faced the bulkhead on the right side of the room as he sat at his desk, piled high with bound reports and loose papers. What a mess, she couldn't help thinking.

The sound of the desk drawer nearest her sliding open drew her eyes back to the foreground. MacSod reached in and grasped the single sheet of 8x6 paper. "This came in for you this morning. But I thought you could use the sleep."

"Oh, yes, sir. I slept like a log. How are you feeling?" Wakefield assessed him as she reached for the paper. He seemed to be all business. The black tint on his lips was gone and his color and fullness of cheek had returned, mostly.

"I'm feeling claustrophobic, Lieutenant Commander. They won't let me leave my own cabin on my own ship for 24 hours. But then I guess it's not my ship anymore is it?" He grumbled cryptically.

MacSod separated the carbon copy of the form from the back and handed it to her while reading the original for himself. Wakefield watched him and knew from the set of his head and relaxed shoulders that it was not the first time he had read the missive. Only when the captain reached for one of the thick black binders and began to pull the rings apart to file the transmission away did Wakefield stop staring and let her eyes take in the information on the smudgy copy in her fingers.

"A transfer, sir?" She sputtered and her wrist bounced off her thigh as she dropped her hand. "I just got here." She didn't know what she had been expecting but this wasn't even close to it.

"Nothing to do with me, Commander. As you can see, this came from the top. I personally appreciate what you've been able to accomplish in the few days you've been aboard. More than I can say." He quickly averted his eyes as he spoke softly.

"It's been thirteen days, sir." Wakefield continued reading. She was being moved in-country. A task force was being assembled. New rules of engagement had been set forth. The detainees who had previously been brought aboard ship for interrogations would be questioned in the camps in country.

"That's it?" She flipped the meager paper over to check the back for more information. Just the usual pre-printed disclaimer was there. "Do you know why procedures have changed?" Wakefield looked up to see MacSod's nostrils flare slightly.

"Probably has something to do with the petty officer who lost a detainee into the drink day before yesterday. Or the detainee rioting that attempted a ship takeover the day before that."

Wakefield felt her eyes grow wide. "What? Why haven't I heard about any of this? What happened?"

"The riot was quelled quickly. And Captain Lockerby ran over the guy who went overboard, and he became chum for the sharks. Guess he forgot to account for the propeller when he jumped." MacSod passed on the information like he was talking about a tea party goer who had dripped tea in a saucer.

"Was he high value?"

"The officer who had interviewed him at length wasn't able to get much out of him—"

"That suggests training," Wakefield interrupted. Training suggested value, at least to her.

"According to Lockerby, the kid was about to be transferred."

Wakefield took a step back. "The interrogator or the detainee?"

"Hmmph." MacSod frowned. "Probably both now."

Wakefield shook her head. So many lives were at risk every day. No one in her line of work could afford even one mistake. "I wonder why the incident didn't show up in my newsfeed stories from HQ." She spoke even as she realized it might have been there. She had been a little busy for the last few days. Had she even signed in since the midnight rendezvous in the galley?

"Probably trying to keep it quiet until the brass figured out what to do about it. They are always in CYA mode."

Wakefield allowed a slight smile to curve the left side of her mouth. MacSod must not identify himself as part of the CYA-brass.

"Stop in to see the master-at-arms before you leave on the morning COD. He will set you up with a side arm and anything else you need as the base of operations is being set in place by the Seabees over the next 48 hours."

"Master Chief Lourdes did a lot to set us up for success over the last few days. He has a full load in his brig right now." Wakefield tried to bring the conversation around to the giant elephant that the captain seemed to be doing his best to ignore.

"Actually Ellsworth already sent a flight off the deck this morning for over half of the men involved in the incident. For once, Bradshaw was not exaggerating when he told me had men planted in every department of my ship. Ellsworth told me Lourdes didn't have enough beds in the brig. Beds? I don't think any of them should ever sleep on the Navy's dime again. But they'll probably live out their days at Leavenworth."

"Maybe not. Lawson and I uncovered that there might have been quite a few non-Navy personnel among Bradshaw's insurrection crew. They would get shipped off to Gitmo."

That news brightened Captain MacSod's dour features for a moment. Then the smile crashed. "So I allowed non-Navy infiltrators on my ship." His head shook. "I suppose that reinforces the Navy's decision then."

"What decision?" Wakefield asked.

"I requested leave this morning as soon as the doc released me. I need to go home and check on my daughter after her ordeal."

Wakefield nodded. Of course.

"They decided a transfer with a promotion was more their style. A permanent transfer and promotion to *civilian*." He spat the word out like a six-year-old gagging on Brussels sprouts.

Wakefield let the angry words hang because she didn't quite know how to tell this old sea dog that life back on land was the best course for everyone involved, including himself. He would not be able to lead an effective command after being extorted and controlled for six months. His trust-er needed repair.

"The ol' chicken dinner?" Wakefield asked neutrally.

MacSod shook his head and closed the records book with a metallic snap. "It's not a dishonorable discharge. They're calling it *retirement*. They said I needed to rest. I told 'em I'd rest when I was dead. Apparently, I'll rest day after tomorrow, when I'm retired."

Wakefield could feel his pain, his shame and disappointment. She wanted to turn his perspective. This really was the best way forward. "Permission to speak freely, sir?" she asked.

"I suppose you've earned it, Wakefield."

"You've earned full benefits for the rest of your life. You have nothing to be ashamed of. You'll only have Liz around maybe as little as two more years before she goes off to college."

"She tells me she wants to be called Elizabeth Ann again." MacSod's teeth peeked through his smile then. "I always hatted that *Liz* business."

Wakefield nodded. "You told me you were ready to make some changes. What if this is the Lord's way of putting you in the right place at the right time where you can be most effective?"

MacSod's forehead wrinkled as he listened. "Elizabeth Ann is probably very behind in her classes. I could get her caught up pretty quickly." As he began to nod, liking the sound of a new objective.

Wakefield went on, "*If* that is what she needs. Of course, you'll ask her what she wants to do and let her assess her own readiness, right?"

"She sounded ok on the phone."

"Of course she did. She's your daughter. Navy daughters know what their fathers need to hear. But now *you* need to figure out what *she* needs to hear."

MacSod's eyes cut like lightening from the hole he had been glaring into the bulkhead above his desk to her face.

Wakefield couldn't stifle a chuckle. "It's nothing to be afraid of." She promised.

"Her mother always took care of this kind of stuff."

"Well, then it is definitely your turn." Wakefield said pointedly. There was only an aunt as an alternative. "It is mostly about talking. And options." Wakefield smiled. "Girls Elizabeth Ann's age like options." She shrugged and rephrased, "All girls like options."

MacSod smoothed his hands over his face as he inhaled deeply. "Maybe I need that recovery time after all. I think I just got the sweats. We're on the same COD to Germany as a layover tomorrow. Maybe you could give me some more tips?"

He looked so hopeful Wakefield couldn't help but give a real laugh then. From the gruff and slightly creepy captain she had meet less than two weeks earlier to this. She never expected it. "Of course, sir."

"Very good. Now I've got more packing to do and so do you. Dismissed."

"Thank you, sir." Wakefield about faced as her head spun. She reached for the door.

"You'll need to shred that, Commander," came from MacSod.

She had forgotten. Maybe she needed a rest too. With a new assignment, she wouldn't be seeing that anytime soon. Judah glanced at the paper again, to fix it in her mind. She noticed for the first time it was VADM Graham's signature at the bottom of the page. She smiled as the door-side shredder buzzed through the thin paper. If her step father was sending her in, it would be okay. Even with the late, late notice.

CHAPTER FORTY FOUR

Wakefield was feeling the pressure of her coming 0500 departure. She still had so much to do to be ready for this new assignment. Her head had barely recovered from this one. Who was she kidding? That was exactly why she was headed in to see Master Chief Lourdes. Getting her pistol swapped out had very little to do with her standing—lurking, if she was honest—in front of the big blue hatch in the passageway outside the area that housed the brig, and all the men who had joined Bradshaw's mutiny and had not yet been transferred off the ship.

Wakefield couldn't wrap her head around the psychology of it. Why had Bradshaw gone to this elaborate plan? What was his end game? She had to know or it would plague the rest of her life with that circling why question.

The heavy iron bar clicked down to open under her hand. Wakefield quickly shuffled backward a few steps so as not to get run over. Lawson stepped over the kneeknocker.

"Lawson. I was coming to find you as soon as I finished here." She narrowed her eyes. "How do you look fresh as a daisy after the last few days we've had?"

Lawson just shrugged and tossed her a Big Band-era flirty grin and struck a pose with one foot still on either side of the kneeknocker. "Aw, it's just my natural self."

Wakefield offered him an exaggerate sigh that asked 'why do I put up with you?' while he came through the hatch. "What are you doing down here?" she asked.

"I could ask you the same," he pointed out.

"Fair enough. I just can't wrap my head around why Bradshaw did it. My profiler-mind is trying to make sense of it all, and I just need to interview him and," Judah shrugged, "I don't know…figure out why."

Lawson's grin fell and took Judah's expectation with it. "I'm afraid that's impossible." He said. "Ellsworth ordered him off the ship with the first group of detainees this morning. He is probably halfway across the Atlantic by this time of night."

"What?" Wakefield pushed her breath through her teeth in frustration. "How did you know that and I didn't?"

"I stuck around and observed his interview while you went back down to MacSod last night."

"He had an interview?" a spark of interest ignited. "Can I watch the tape?"

"The tape went with him."

Wakefield shook her head. "Ugh. They must still be on analog instead of digital down here. Come on, Navy, catch up!"

"I'm sensing a bit of frustration here." Lawson reached for her arm as he leaned back and unlatched the brig hatch again. "Come on, let's grab Master Chief Lourdes and buy him a coffee. Between the two of us," Lawson was already tracing his steps, and since he had Wakefield in tow, she followed him, "we can recount most of what Bradshaw said. But I can tell you right off the bat, the DNA sample we sent off to my friend a few days ago, will not match the record on deposit in DC. He is not Bradshaw."

"Oh boy." Wakefield sighed as they approached the weapons check counter. "I need to wrap this up. I'm being transferred in the morning."

"What?" It was Lawson's turn for a surprise.

"Heading into Baghdad with the Seabees. FOB Beta." She explained simply. "MacSod and I are flying out together to Germany and then I backtrack all the way back to Iraq. Maybe I'll have a chance for a meal on the ground, but I'm not counting on it."

"What can I do for you?" it was a young enlisted man that Wakefield did not recognize behind the counter.

"Well, that's too bad, I was hoping to get to know you in calmer seas without all the twists and turns." Lawson said. He waited a beat before turning to the counter. "I need. We need," he corrected, "to see the master chief again."

"Oh right. You we're just here," he addressed Agent Lawson. "One moment, ma'am," he said to Wakefield. "You guys can come right through." He buzzed the lock and Lawson pushed the door inward with one hand while gesturing for Wakefield to pass through first.

They had barely taken a seat in the same Interview Room A which Wakefield had used to conduct her detainee interrogations just days earlier when everything was so much simpler, when Master Chief Lourdes entered soundlessly. His heft not making a sound.

"Back so soon, NCIS?"

"Yeah. Lieutenant Commander Wakefield wanted to go over some questions, so I thought two minds might recall better than one."

"Certainly." Lourdes stuck his head out the hatch. "Whitby! Coffee!" he thundered.

"Thank you." Wakefield said as Lourdes took a seat nearer the door. "As a profiler in Intel," she jumped straight in, not having any packing time to waste, "my biggest disappointment is not being able to figure out the why. Did he let on? Did he give any indication?"

Lourdes and Lawson exchanged looks. "Oh you'd have never figured this one out, ma'am." Lourdes raspberried his lips. "Don't give yourself a bad time. After we paraded Bradshaw in front of all the men involved in the mutiny, he growled at them like a wounded animal, but then it was like a switch went off. Bradshaw got all cocky and spilled ev-ry-thing. Like he needed someone to admire his skills and plan. Craziest thing I ever saw!"

"Well?" she prompted.

"In 1990, Ashkan al Khadem, an Iranian national whose features looked more Italian than Persian, entered the U.S. on a student visa." Lourdes leaned back in his cold metal chair and crossed his beefy arms over his body. "When his visa expired the school did not double check with the State Department when he said he had renewed it. He had not."

"Who in the world is al Khadem?" Wakefield interrupted.

"Bradshaw," Lawson dropped. "But I think it starts even before that," Lawson said. "Before he came to the U.S. for graduate school, al Khadem had a former professor in Iran by the name of Mahmoud Ahmadinejad. They had some sort of teacher-student hero worship going on from what I could gather." Lawson looked at Lourdes who nodded in agreed assessment.

"Ashkan al Khadem wants—yes, *still* wants, if you can believe it—to be hailed as a hero by this former college professor who has just been appointed Mayor of Tehran! Well, Ahmadinejad's theology is at odds with the current president of Iran, Seyyed Mohammad Khatami, as you may know." Judah just shook her head. She'd never heard of Ahmadinejad. "President Khatami is also an Iranian scholar like Ahmadinejad, but Khatami is a Shia theologian, and reformist politician. Ahmadinejad does not like the reforms that have been in place since 1997 and wants to take his city, Tehran, back to Taliban extremist rule before he makes a run for president himself. Course that's not the language al Khadem used. I think he said something about—

"Pure and undefiled religion," the two men quoted together.

Whitby knocked once and walked in with a coffee tray. "Engine sludge, just like you like it, Master Chief," Whitby said and disappeared just as quickly.

"Oh my." Wakefield felt her jaw loosening at this story. They were right, she never would have uncovered this. Bradshaw or al Khadem had not even seemed religious to her, much less an extremist Muslim.

"So in 1999, al Khadem was still in the U.S., no visa, no nothing." Lawson brought the story around while Lourdes poured blackest-black coffee into three sparkling white mugs. "He moved near Norfolk Naval Base and struck up a friendship with a Lieutenant Commander named Bradshaw."

"He told you all this?" Wakefield was incredulous. She stirred the coffee Lourdes set in front of her and decided she might not sleep until next Friday if she consumed even one drop of that thick liquid.

Both men nodded. "Like the master chief said, he seemed to need to brag about it to someone." Lawson said. "That narcissistic disorder of his was raging last night!"

Lourdes smirked. "We are providing you the toned down version. It's a wonder Whitby is not still wiping arrogance off the walls in here along with Bradshaw's spit. I never saw with my own eyes a man who was 'spitting mad' until yesterday."

Lourdes slurped his coffee and picked up the story. "After just a few months at Norfolk, Bradshaw was due to be transferred out to California for a brush up course before being assigned as the Chief of Engineering on the TR. That was when al Khadem decided to make his move. He had learned that Bradshaw only had a mother left from his family, and they were estranged. Had been, since he left for college. She didn't even know he had joined the Navy. So al Khadem murdered Bradshaw and assumed his identity. He showed up at San Diego Naval Air Station and started the leadership course on day 1. No one knew him, so no one noticed. It is not like Bradshaw is a terribly uncommon name, and the two men looked similar enough that apparently no one noticed."

"What about his fingerprints on IDs?" Wakefield could hardly believe this tale.

"Said it wasn't that hard to woo a lady who had access and dump her body later after the files were changed." Lawson said. "I asked him about that after Lourdes had finished his interview and they were taking him back to the brig. It had me curious too. NCIS San Diego is following up on that cold case as we speak."

"So, al Khadem just showed up as Bradshaw, learning military protocols on the fly? That couldn't have been easy." Wakefield said.

"Oh, despite his arrogance, he's highly intelligent, ma'am. And he had been friends with the real Bradshaw for a while. I assume he had been learning some along the way as his plan began to take shape." Lourdes rested his mug on one forearm still crossed across his chest, and he leaned back.

"What swung this particular plan into action was bin Laden's attack on 9/11." Lawson picked up the story. "Al Khadem had not been notified of the attack coming through any of his Middle Eastern contacts, and though he did not actually say it, I think he was a little jealous of the notoriety the attackers received. When he arrived on the west coast, al Khadem, masquerading as Bradshaw, immediately began to worm his way into MacSod's life. He contacted an Iranian national who was part of a sleeper cell in Seattle to pose as his wife. Her alias was Maria, because her features, like his, didn't look distinctly Middle Eastern. I saw a photo," Lawson quipped, "and if I didn't know better, I probably couldn't tell that she was

Iranian instead of Central American. With the name Maria, you just want to think south, not east.

"So Bradshaw and Maria gave the arsenic-laced tea bags to Martha MacSod, who as we know, started getting very sick."

"Al Khadem said—and one of my MPs already confirmed—a call to Maria by 'Bradshaw' on the shakedown cruise when al Khadem said he ordered her to run Martha MacSod off the road and then call 911 so that her body would be found and the captain relieved of duty to grieve. Bradshaw had assumed MacSod would resign his commission in order to raise his daughter. When MacSod did not, Bradshaw and Maria kidnapped the Elizabeth Ann, and held it over MacSod's head on a daily basis, forcing him to move al Khadem's people that he had snuck on board in place of other people he had murdered and stripped of their identities so that their security clearance and base IDs would not be terminated. There's going to be a lot of cases to follow up on." Lawson's mouth tugged to the side. "Bradshaw promised to release MacSod's daughter if MacSod would just recommend him for captain and retire, leaving the ship to him.

"When he refused over and over, al Khadem began to administer small doses of arsenic to MacSod too. MacSod plodded on through the symptoms, never even visiting the infirmary."

"That goes with what the surgeon told me last night." Wakefield confirmed.

"Al Khadem was not getting anywhere with MacSod no matter how much he threatened him. Then he became suspicious at all the time MacSod was spending with your predecessor," Lourdes nodded at her, "Commander Wallace. After installing a surveillance camera in the Intel office al Khadem caught them investigating him. Bradshaw said he lured Wallace out to the fantail one night slugged him and pushed him overboard. He told MacSod he would do the same to him if anyone else started asking questions."

"That would have been around the weekend of March eighth." Wakefield stated.

"Yes. The fifth." Lourdes confirmed. "How'd you know that?"

"I got my orders on March sixth, and was approved to delay my departure for my wedding on March eighth." She slid her coffee cup on the interview table as it was cool to the touch now.

"Oh boy." Lourdes said with wide eyes. "So MacSod had to help cover up Wallace's disappearance by sending him stateside. But there was no Wallace to send, so one of al Khadem's crew stepped in and pretended to be Wallace on the COD to Germany and then caught the very next COD back to the ship."

"Then I came." Wakefield said.

"And you began spending time with MacSod too. Even though he had planted a man in the Intel offices, it made al Khadem nervous because he was coming down to the wire in this plan that he had been building toward for over a year." Lawson added. "And Gates wasn't providing much intel."

"What was the plan?"

Al Khadem was planning to hijack the ship—which he did—and then as the Carrier Strike Group maneuvered through the Strait of Hormuz he would be the last ship through and break away and steam for the Iranian deep-water port, Chabahar. He was going to arrange it to look as if the U.S. was leading an unprovoked nuclear attack on Iran. Since President Khatami would not be able to handle it with no build up and no notice of a change in a relationship that had been pretty quiet during his presidency, al Khadem was providing his old college prof with detailed instructions, and a massive set of underground holding cells were already prepared in Chabahar to receive 5200 U.S. sailors as hostages, or as many as survived the nuclear attack. A contingent of Iranian sailors would brave the nuclear fallout to take control of the aircraft carrier as soon as it hit Iranian waters. They would drive it right into the port, and set it up as a war trophy in Ahmadneijad's name. Al Khadem said it might have been open for tourism as early as 2004, once it was stripped of all our proprietary technologies."

"They were going to nuke themselves? That doesn't even make sense." Wakefield shook her head.

"It seems they were going to aim the nuke at the uninhabited region of Iraq near the Pakistan border. The wind would carry the fallout toward their enemies. Iran would have a win-win-win. Ahmadinejad would be pulled into power because of his prowess against the dirty Americans. Iran would gain world sympathy for being bombed mercilessly. And Iran's border problems would literally melt away in the nuclear fallout."

Wakefield's mind was spinning. "The world would have been pushed into chaos. Probably World War Three."

"But it's over now. You guys thwarted it." Lourdes said. "I don't expect you've heard the end of it once the story gets back to the big brass in DC or if the story breaks in the news."

"It had better not. We don't need our enemies knowing how easy it was to hijack a nuclear aircraft carrier." Wakefield threw herself back in her chair. "It's getting late," she said as she stretched her long legs under the table and then drew them back in. "How am I supposed to sleep after a bedtime story like this? It's like 'and the wolf ate all the little kiddies up, good night, Sweetheart. Sweet dreams'." Wakefield raspberried her lips in an echo of Lourdes earlier.

"You asked." Lawson reminded her. "At least you won't be wondering now, and you won't be surprised if a bronze or silver star ceremony is in your future."

Wakefield stood. "I imagine that this whole incident will be classified and locked down as soon as that tape hits the Pentagon. We won't hear another word about it for decades, until we are too old to remember the details." She held out her hand to Lourdes and then Lawson. "It's been a pleasure working with you both." She was ready to hit her rack for a few hours before her next assignment. "Oh," she turned back to Lourdes, "Master Chief, I'm going to need a side arm and ammunition for FOB Beta in Iraq tomorrow. MacSod said you would set me up."

Lourdes smiled then. "Only the best for you, One Shot Wakefield."

Judah just shook her head. "I bet that juicy piece of scuttlebutt follows Captain Ellsworth everywhere he goes. Poor man. I should have let him win."

"No, ma'am," Lourdes grinned. "Much better this way."

CHAPTER FORTY FIVE

Wakefield sat in the plane, strapped into the window seat. Her sea bag stretched its seams again so soon. Her six-month deployment on sea duty condensed to just fourteen days. "But those days certainly did not lack for adventure." She shook her head.

Judah leaned forward in her seat as far as the tight harness would allow. The flight deck and all the balconies including vulture's row were packed with white summer uniforms. MacSod didn't know it, but Captain Ellsworth had been busy making the morning's arrangements since she had been to see him immediately after receiving her orders from MacSod the evening before. After her explanation of MacSod's grief and shame, Ellsworth had simply said, "I'll take care of it." Then she had received an email marked secret and extremely urgent. Over a thousand sailors on the ship had received the same order to appear on deck in Summer Dress Whites by 0430.

The band struck their first note then. And the music worked its way into the open COD door.

MacSod exited a hatch onto the open deck and halted mid stride. Clearly he had not been expecting the fanfare. He followed the dignitary carpet unrolled between the hatchway and the plane's unfolded three-stair entry. Wakefield felt her cheeks rise in a mirror of MacSod's smile.

With military bearing and dignity that would remain with him through retirement, and probably the grave, he marched up the carpet inspecting his sailors' presentation for the final time in his career. The band played a jaunty little tune that Wakefield recognized, but couldn't quite name.

"Oh shoot." Regret quickened her. "I never saw Melissa Garvey again." Wakefield sighed. "I sure missed that one. Sorry, Lord. Maybe I can email her?"

All the senior officers lined up next to one another, with the CAG, then the Air Boss, and finally Ellsworth in the spot closest to the COD.

Wakefield watched as the sky threw its own spectacular fireworks display. The sun was rising to cracks of neon orange and hot pink that streaked the sky to eight inches off the horizon from her measurement. What a last morning at sea for MacSod.

"Thank you, Lord, for a beautiful send off for him." she whispered. "You know how much he needed it."

The last notes from the band died out as Ellsworth returned MacSod's salute and then shook his hand and leaned in to whisper something next to his head. MacSod laughed.

Wakefield leaned hard against the glass as MacSod mounted the lowest stair. She was able to see him turn and take one final glance around the kingdom that had been his domain for more than two years.

A whistle pierced the wind.

The entire ship's company standing for inspection saluted. Hands rose over their brows at matching angles perfected in boot camps from the oldest officer to the newest seaman. Navy tradition at its finest, Wakefield smiled. "Oh" she remembered again. "Rivers! I didn't even tell him I was changing duty stations to go in country."

She shook her head. "I'm not very good at this marriage thing yet, Lord. Help me please."

The honor guard of five sailors, aimed for the clouds and fired. The first crack of the fifteen gun salute, allowed for flag officers departing or arriving, seemed to break open the sky even further. Five seconds later, Wakefield flinched again. She flashed back briefly to Arlington Cemetery where her biological father was buried to this same soundtrack. Today, it wasn't so hard to remember. Hmm, between her Father God and Isaac Graham, they really did fill the gap of his absence in her heart now. When had that happened? The final shot rang out and dissipated over the waves.

Captain MacSod lowered his arm while the rest of the company held theirs. The whistle piped its signal. It sounded lonely and distant in its shrill pierce after the low register of the gun salute.

"Captain departiING!" bellowed a voice outside the aircraft.

Wakefield saw MacSod turn, but he disappeared from view for a moment as he climbed aboard.

Then she could see him again as he ducked to enter the hatch. His hand brushed across his face, and Wakefield wouldn't swear to it, but she thought she saw the reflection of a tear in that moment.

The engine roared to life, and MacSod donned the anonymous white flight helmet and buckled himself in for the four hour transition to his new life's commencement.

Inside three minutes the entire flight deck had been cleared of officers, bands, instruments, and carpets. The engine spooled up. The co-pilot slammed the pressure door in place, locked it down, and took his seat.

"Here we go," the pilot warned in her helmet headset.

Glad for the ear protection against the catapult, gravity slammed Judah against the seatback, compressing the light cushion until she was sure she could feel her flesh forming around the screws holding her chair together. "Here we go indeed!" For once she had a case that was mostly tied in a neat little bow with 'why' answered.

She left everything done, and undone, there on the deck and moved her mind forward toward next.

Beth MacSod Allen's House
San Diego, CA
2:15 PM

MacSod waited until the petty officer driver opened the back seat door and the hefted himself from the confines of the fairly new Crown Victoria Navy Yard pool car, and slung his laptop bag over his shoulder much more casually than his gut felt.

As he admired the nice lines of his sister's shaded new house with a windy path from the street, he gave his last order. "Petty officer, just leave those bags on the porch there, and you're dismissed."

Dismissed, that is a perfect last order, he smiled in a little bit of sadness. It was a good run. A great run. But now, he had a Savior to get to know again, a little girl who was not so little any more to get to know, and a wife to grieve. His Navy pension would hold them just fine until he got restless enough to get a job or start some new project.

He had talked often enough to officers under his command about transitioning to their new life after the Navy or even deployment, he nodded, as even right then, he gave himself grace to take whatever time was needed to learn to do civilian life well.

The trunk slammed behind him back at the street. The door opened in front of him before his feet even hit the first porch stair. A young woman came flying out the door and launched herself into his arms. "Elizabeth Ann," he breathed out the name he and his wife had agonized and argued over for months after her first sonogram photo.

379

"Daddy. I'm so glad you're home," she whispered after at least a full minute of the tightest hug MacSod remembered since her third birthday.

His grin widened until he thought his cheek bones might burst right through his skin. "That is a good thing," he said, "because I'm going to be home a whole lot more from now on."

She released him, and he set her back on her feet on the porch step, which brought them very nearly eye to eye. "I've resigned my commission."

"For real?" He read confusion in her eyes.

"We will figure this civilian life out together." He said with confidence. "What did you do to your hair? Did they do that to you?" he asked.

She touched the short red curls self-consciously, and he felt an old wall beginning to rise. "You complained when I dyed it, now you complain when I leave it natural."

"Not complaining. I think it is beautiful." He reached out and ruffled it the way he might have if he'd had a boy. "The length was just a little shocking." Her hair had been long all her life, even in the jet black Goth era, which he desperately hoped was behind them.

"Yeah," Elizabeth Ann jerked a thumb over her shoulder toward the doorway. "Aunt Beth suggested it. The seven months of red roots growing out from a fading black-to-green color job was not my best look, she said. First day out of the hospital, we went to get our hair done."

MacSod looked up to see his sister fidgeting nervously in the doorway and sporting the exact same cut. "Well, I think you both look terrific."

She broke into a grin. "Ron was a little shocked too at first," she admitted of her husband. "Come on in." She stepped back. "I've got coffee brewing and Elizabeth Ann made some cookies from Martha's recipe from memory. They're still hot."

He put his arm around his daughter's shoulder, and they climbed the steps side by side.

After his fifth or sixth cookie Beth rose to start dinner, leaving them alone at the dining room table. "How are you doing? Can you talk about your time?" He did not even know what to call it.

"I'm okay, dad." She reached across the table to pat his hand. "The first few days I was scared. And I cried for mom a lot. But then, Maria pretty much left me alone. She brought food and books—Dad you'd never believe how many books I've been reading!—I love reading. And there in the cabin it kind of gave me an escape into other little worlds."

MacSod shook his head. "Where is my little TV-watcher who wouldn't touch a book? I feel like I should take your temperature in case you're sick. I am so sorry I wasn't there to protect you."

"It's ok. I'm ok."

"I can't tell you what a relief that is to me." MacSod pulled himself together and locked down the tears of relief that threatened to spill over. She really did seem no worse for the experience. Really, she seemed better than ok. "So how is your schoolwork faring? I'm guessing you must be pretty far behind."

Elizabeth Ann leaned against the chair back and crossed her arms. "Aunt Beth said it would be best to wait until you got home to go back."

MacSod had no delusions about how that conversation had come around with some convincing and begging from his daughter. His sister was a former high school teacher, and she highly valued education and structure.

"Well, I've been thinking about that," he said. "And I think you have a couple of options. I know I could get you caught up with your classmates by the end of summer. Perhaps we could do the schoolwork while we do some traveling here in the U.S. Or maybe you'd want to just start the year over and be a year behind your age group. What do you think?"

"I get to decide?"

"You can't learn to make decisions if I make them all."

"I think I am going to like this new dad." Elizabeth Ann grinned.

To be continued...

See how all the threads come together.
Join Judah Wakefield and David Rivers
in their next adventure
on the ground in Baghdad.
Who will survive an encounter
between Saddam Hussein's Special Republican Guard
and the U.S. Navy SEALs?
Catch up with Takita and IDF *Seren* Ellie Dayan too.

Book 5 of the Desert Sailors series.
BAGHDAD GREEN ZONE
Available September 2018.

www.ingramcontent.com/pod-product-compliance
Lightning Source LLC
Chambersburg PA
CBHW060151260626
47160CB00001B/220